BETRAYAL

ALSO BY VANESSA KIER

<u>The Surgical Strike Unit (SSU) Series</u>

Vengeance

Betrayal

Retribution

Payback

Aftermath

Undercover (Prequel Novella)

<u>The WAR Series</u>

WAR: Disruption

WAR: Intrusion

WAR: Opposition

BETRAYAL

THE SURGICAL STRIKE UNIT
BOOK TWO

VANESSA KIER

CHAPTER ONE

Thursday, Night
Branco River, Amazon River Basin
Upriver from Caracaraí, Brazil

KAI PATERSON PAUSED at the edge of the warehouse. A wide, exposed strip of dirt stretched between him and the safety of the trees along the riverbank. He checked behind him for signs of pursuit, then quieted his breath and listened.

The night contained only the sound of the river softly slapping against the hull of the boat waiting for him in the shallows and the occasional cry of a nocturnal animal. Reassured that it was safe to proceed, Kai sprinted across the dirt and into the protective darkness of the stand of trees. Then he flashed a signal with the red LED light on his flashlight and waited for the proper response from the pilot.

The answering flash completed the correct pattern. All was safe.

Kai picked his way carefully along the slippery surface of a thick root jutting into the river. Then he leapt lightly onto the deck of the boat.

"Any trouble?" he asked the pilot, Giovanni, in Portuguese.

"No. Did you get it?"

Kai nodded and handed the package over. The man grunted in thanks, then handed Kai a pair of night vision binoculars.

As the boat pulled away from shore, Kai scanned the land with the glasses. No sign of human activity. Good.

He might actually pull this off.

Moonlight rippled across the river. The boat stank of fish and diesel fumes. Then the wind shifted, carrying the jungle's stench of rotten vegetation and sweet flowers. Trees loomed on either side of the river, forming an impenetrable wall of darkness that called to him.

Blood dripping onto the jungle floor. A primitive cry of triumph that scared birds into flight and scattered a colony of monkeys.

His heart pounded.

Shit, shit, *shit.*

Nausea churned in his belly. His fingers tightened on the wooden railing.

A fish broke the surface of the river, then quickly disappeared into the murky depths. Yeah, wasn't that a metaphor for his life these days? Barely able to take a clean breath before he waded back into the muck.

I shouldn't have come. It's too dangerous for me here.

But who else could they have sent? No one else had worked under Nevsky. No one else would be able to tell if the data on the microchip was actually Nevsky's backup data.

Snap out of it. You have a mission.

He couldn't fail. Wouldn't fail.

Shoving the memories deep, Kai slipped off the backpack that contained his personal supplies and stowed it in the cabin next to his weapons and ammunition. He hesitated. It was tempting to stay here, out of sight of the jungle.

But he wasn't a coward. A scientist turned spy, yes. A ruthless killer, when necessary.

Coward? No. And he wasn't a quitter, either.

This was almost over. All he had to do was get Susana Dias to safety. The SSU doctors would extract the microchip from her. Then, no matter what his boss wanted, Kai would destroy the chip.

And at last, this entire nightmare would be over.

Clinging to that hope, Kai stepped outside. A noise caught his attention. He tilted his head. "Do you hear that?" he asked Giovanni.

"Yeah. Someone's coming up behind us."

Kai nodded. His hands trembled slightly. He couldn't be captured. Not again.

Relax. Everyone thinks the chip is with Susana Dias. They don't care about you any more.

Repeating that like a mantra, he grabbed his M-4 assault rifle and got in position.

The pilot cut the engine and steered them closer to shore. They took refuge behind some branches extending over the river and Giovanni cut the lights.

Kai watched through the rifle's scope as a powerboat came into sight, going too fast for this section of river at night. Kai barely breathed, but the boat passed without slowing.

The wake rocked their boat. Kai automatically adjusted his balance, keeping his attention on the other boat until it was lost to sight.

"I didn't see anyone but the pilot, did you?"

Giovanni shook his head. "Could have been a couple, maybe three inside, though. You still want to head downriver first?"

"No. We need to get to the dig fast." He'd originally planned to travel away from their destination in case someone followed them. But if that other boat was after Susana Dias, Kai needed to get there before everyone disappeared.

An image of the supermodel turned archaeologist flashed into his mind. The half-American, half-Brazilian beauty had graced the cover of every fashion and gossip magazine during Kai's high school and college years. He still remembered how the hint of laughter in her large brown eyes made her seem approachable. As if she saw the world as a giant party and had been inviting him to join her.

The irony of the cruel, amoral Dr. Nevsky fathering sexy, vibrant Susana Dias didn't escape him. No one had known he even had a daughter.

Fortunately, nothing indicated Susana had any involvement in her father's work. If the report was true, she'd never knowingly had contact with the man. The media coverage about Susana claimed her father was dead. Kai suspected she didn't even know Nevsky's name.

Which made Kai's assignment all the more delicate. He wasn't looking forward to explaining it to her.

Oh, by the way, your father developed a program for turning men into super soldiers. He backed up his data on a microchip that he implanted in you during your appendectomy.

Yeah, that would go over well. The source of the intel was reliable, yet he still had trouble believing it.

But the word was out. Meaning it wasn't just Kai after Susana Dias. Whoever was on that other boat, plus a whole roster of government and criminal agents, were all about to converge on Ms. Dias's archaeological dig.

He checked to make sure no other boats were approaching, then stowed his rifle. He felt bad for the danger bearing down on her. Since leaving modeling to enter the world of archaeology, she'd made a number of significant discoveries and published several articles in prestigious academic journals, proving she was intelligent and insightful as well as beautiful.

Hopefully, she was smart enough to stay alive until Kai found her.

He'd do his best to keep her alive and unharmed. But he had

to retrieve the microchip. Too many lives had already been lost. Too many lives would be destroyed if it fell into the wrong hands.

This time, he could not fail.

CHAPTER TWO

Friday, Afternoon
Amazon Jungle
Upriver from Caracaraí, Brazil

"SUSE, THE SUPPLY BOAT'S HERE." Susana Dias's assistant, Jacie Black, unzipped the screen door and stepped inside the tent. "The captain says the food and fuel crates have been damaged," she continued, "but he doesn't know how seriously."

"Son of a bitch," Susana snarled, slapping her hands down on the table and surging to her feet, the map she'd been studying rolling closed with a snap. "May fire ants crawl down the throat of whoever's doing this."

At Jacie's smirk, Susana tried to calm down. But dammit, between the vandalism and not finding any evidence yet that Amerinis had indeed been built here, she had reason to let loose her volatile temper.

Her team had been under attack since the second day on site. At first the incidents had been annoying, but harmless. Dirt shoveled back into a pit that had taken hours to uncover. Bags of artifacts disappearing. A few threatening notes that she hadn't taken seriously because they'd been so B movie—*leave now before the spirits seek revenge*—and her fame inevitably attracted a crackpot or two. But then the attacks had escalated. Several days' worth of food supplies had been ruined, leaving the camp on reduced rations for the past week. The boat used for fishing had been damaged beyond their limited ability to repair.

When news came in yesterday that the supply boat was going to be late because of engine malfunction, the mood around camp had turned downright grim. Most of the crew had just come off another long project with her, with only one precious week of downtime behind them. They'd agreed to the tight turn-around only because they knew Susana had been obsessed with finding the fabled city of Amerinis since she'd been a girl.

Yet the lack of adequate rest meant her crew had started this assignment more on edge than usual. Like prisoners awaiting release, they'd been counting the days until the next food delivery, tired of filling out their meals with fruit scrounged from the jungle. If rationing continued much longer, she feared she'd face a full-blown mutiny. Some superstitious crew members were already talking about leaving, afraid of further angering the local spirits.

She needed to find the temple of Amerinis to take their mind off such nonsense. Unfortunately, she suspected they were digging in the wrong spot.

"I'll be down in a minute to take a look," she told Jacie. "Don't say anything to the others until I see what the damage is."

Jacie raised one perfectly plucked eyebrow. "All right," she said in the tone that indicated she was just humoring Suse. "At least there's one piece of good news." She tossed a small bundle on Susana's worktable. "The mail came."

"Hallelujah." The last two mail deliveries had never arrived. After meals, mail distribution was the highlight of the crew's day.

As Jacie backed out of the tent, Susana quickly flipped through the stack of new mail. It was mostly personal letters she'd read tonight before she went to bed, but at the very bottom sat a pretentious cream envelope with gold embossing. The return address was a law firm in Moscow.

Hmm.

She slit the envelope open, pulled out the top sheet, and quickly scanned it.

We apologize for not contacting you sooner, but due to the circumstances surrounding your father's death, the American authorities did not notify us until recently that he was deceased. Per the instructions in your father's will, we are forwarding to you the enclosed envelope.

Susana sank onto her chair, staring blindly into space. Her heart pounded in a slow, ominous rhythm.

No. This couldn't be true. Her father had died in a car crash in the States when she was ten. Her normally unemotional mother had wept with relief, having lived in daily fear that the man she'd run from when Susana was just a baby would find them, even hidden away on a series of ranches deep in the heart of the Amazon.

According to this, her father, one Dr. Mikhail Nevsky, had been alive until two years ago.

She shook her head. Was this letter an attempt by the saboteur to mess with her mind? No, the thick cotton paper and embossed letterhead appeared legit.

More importantly, did she want to know what the letter said? Her mother had refused to talk about her father except to say he was an evil man who'd fooled her into thinking he was one of the good guys.

What could he possibly have to say that Susana would want to hear? But even as she moved to toss the letter aside, her curiosity got the better of her. Part of what drew her to archaeology was the thrill of solving puzzles from the past. Much as her gut told her to ignore the letter, she just couldn't let this mystery go unsolved.

Taking a deep breath, she slowly unfolded the two remaining sheets of paper.

Dear Daughter, she read. Her lips pursed on a flare of anger. How dare he claim her as daughter when—

Crack! The ground shook under the impact of something heavy crashing to the ground.

Susana leapt to her feet. "What now?" She threw the letter toward her bed and bolted from the tent.

"Damn." One of the thick wooden supports holding the canopy over yesterday's excavation had collapsed. "Was anyone hurt?" she demanded as she slid to a stop next to Jim Delano, the man in charge of the dig's interns.

"No. Everyone's either in their tents or taking siesta in the jungle." He gestured to the two kapok trees where some of the crew members had settled against the buttressing roots.

"Suse, you'd better take a look at this," Erika Rhodes called, pointing to a broken section of two-by-four.

Susana's heart sank. *Please let it be rot.*

But no. The piece had been sawed through. "Maggoty son of a putrefied goat!" The collapse of the heavy canopy was the first act of sabotage that could have seriously hurt someone.

"Jim," she pushed out between lips stiff with anger. "Where are Celio and Mateus?" The two guards didn't seem to be having any luck at deterring or catching the guilty party.

Jim looked around and shrugged. "Probably down at the dock guarding the supplies as they're unloaded."

"I want you to work up a schedule for all of us to take turns patrolling the site. I'm not going to give our enemy another chance to hurt someone." She stared off into the trees. "But I'm damn sure not going to run, either." She'd dreamed of finding Amerinis since she'd first heard the stories of the city built by warrior women. Even if the television crew from the Adventure Channel wasn't expected the day after tomorrow she still wouldn't give in to the demands to leave. This dig was too important for her to tuck tail and run.

"Make certain those posts are bagged as evidence, then put them in my tent. And send two of the interns down to the supply boat. The captain should have that new load of timber we requested for shoring up the next phase of excavation. I want this canopy back up before dinner." She glanced around the dig, wondering if the culprit was among her crew. Hoping her growing suspicions were wrong.

"I'll tell the cook to prepare something special tonight in celebration. In the meantime, I'm going down to inventory the supply crates." Turning away, Susana grabbed her sunglasses and hat from her tent, then strode down the path toward the river.

As she pushed through the thick jungle humidity, she jammed a wayward lock of long dark hair back under her hat and wiped her brow with her bandana. Even though her long-sleeved shirt and khaki pants were the latest in breathable material, they'd long since given up the fight against the water-logged air and clung to her sweaty skin like plastic wrap. The clothing designers wouldn't be happy with her report, but she certainly wouldn't be giving these new fabrics her endorsement.

As she rounded the bend, the camp's temporary pier came into view. From this angle, it appeared the squat, heavy supply boat tied up at the dock was so crammed with crates it would take on water and sink at any moment. But that situation wouldn't last long. The captain stood on deck, feet planted shoulder-width apart, arms crossed over his thick chest, scowling as he supervised two interns unloading a stack of two-by-fours.

Susana glanced around, then frowned. Where were the damn guards?

"Got some damage on a crate," the captain grumbled in Portuguese as she approached.

"Where?" she asked, walking up the warped piece of plywood that served as a gangplank.

He jabbed his thumb toward the back of the boat.

Following his direction, she moved past the cabin to a stack of crates draped with a canvas sheet. Lifting up the heavy covering, she gave the crates a quick once-over.

Huh. The six wooden crates appeared undamaged from the front. Maybe the damage was on the other side. She sidled between two crates, leaned slightly over the railing and turned her head to check the rear of the crates.

That was strange. The backs were also undamaged. Maybe these were the wrong crates. She straightened up.

Something hard slammed into the back of her head, knocking her stomach-first into the railing and driving the breath from her body. Another blow caused her vision to dim. Then a shove between her shoulder blades pushed her over the side.

She blacked out as the murky water closed over her head.

Susana woke to a pounding headache. The fetid stench of unwashed clothes and rotten food assaulted her nose. Her lips curled, pulling against a tight cotton gag.

She tried opening her eyes, but her right lid was held closed by something sticky that extended down from her forehead. Blood?

She peered out of her left eye. Oh, man, this wasn't good. Everything she saw was double.

She blinked several times, trying to align her vision. The floor tilted and Susana rolled several inches to her left. The motion set her stomach churning and sharpened the pain in her head.

Oh, God. She was going to be sick and her mouth was gagged. If she threw up now, she'd choke.

I won't be sick. I won't be sick. I WON'T. Breathing shallowly through her nose, she tightened her throat against the bile that wanted to rise. Slowly, her stomach settled down, leaving her sweating. Dots danced across her vision in time to the percussion jamming inside her skull. A second later, she passed out again.

When she regained consciousness, she was alert enough to notice the hum of a motor. The sound of waves hitting wood. The low sound of male voices. She was on a boat.

What had happened? She remembered checking out the supply crates. Being hit. Falling into the river. Had the captain shoved her in then scooped her back out and locked her in his cabin?

Sweat had loosened the dried blood on her right lid enough to allow her to cautiously open both eyes. This time, her vision wasn't so blurry.

She tried to sit up and discovered that her hands and feet were trussed with thin, bright yellow nylon cord. Twisting her wrists only drove the rope deeper into her skin, cutting her until she bled.

Bastard sons of piranhas, tying her up like an animal! Once she got free she'd see that whoever had done this rotted in jail.

Taking a deep breath to cool her temper, she looked around.

Light snuck between paper thin cracks in rough plank walls and shone in a pale yellow rectangle through a small window propped open with a stick. Clothes lay scattered over every horizontal surface. Discarded plates of food sat rotting on a small table made of heavy wood. Six hammocks hung from the ceiling. A ladder-back chair lay upended under one hammock with a pair of muddy pants hanging off one leg.

Several iron gun hooks sat in a neat line above the door. Two hooks cradled a rifle. The other hooks were empty.

The room was too big to be the cabin on the supply boat. Which meant...what? Had she been kidnapped by the mystery person trying to shut down her dig? Had the captain or the interns been involved?

Betrayal formed a hard lump in her throat. She blinked back

tears. *Buck up, girl. Worry about who did this to you and why after you get yourself free.*

Using her elbows, she pushed to a sitting position. A section of damp hair fell across her face and she automatically tossed her head to clear it from her eyes. Then realization hit and she froze mid-motion.

Someone took out my braid.

Susana shook her head, confirming that her thick mass of hair was loose. She sank back on her heels, each possibility running through her head more frightening than the one before.

Had letting down her hair been part of some sick male fantasy? Had she been raped while she was unconscious?

She glanced down. Her shirt was buttoned and her pants zipped. Her waterlogged boots were still on her feet.

Most importantly, there was no ache between her legs or on her breasts.

Her breath whooshed out and her spine sagged in relief.

So. Her kidnappers had unbraided her hair, no easy task when wet. Why? Were they sex traffic slavers? Had someone sold her out? She'd heard that women with long, thick hair were more likely to be targets, although she couldn't imagine anyone finding her hair attractive in its tangled, wet state.

To hell with that. She was not going to be sold as someone's sex slave.

She struggled to her knees. By twisting her bound arms like a contortionist, she was able to search her pants pockets. Lip balm. Soggy tissues.

No pocket knife. No satellite phone.

Her eyes scanned the cabin for something sharp to cut through her bindings.

But although the men were undeniable slobs, they apparently weren't stupid enough to leave a knife lying around.

Okay then. Maybe one of the walls or a piece of furniture had a loose nail.

She inched over the filthy floor, stopping to feel her surroundings for a sharp edge. Eventually she found the broken leg of a chair with a bent nail sticking out of it. She set to work sawing on her bindings, praying with each breath for the men to stay away just a little longer.

Just as the rope began to give, she heard a crash outside the cabin, followed by the sound of glass breaking. A man shouted, "Fire!" in Portuguese. The floorboards shook under the impact of running feet and smoke floated in through the open window.

This was her chance. Susana jerked her arms apart, breaking the last strands of rope joining her wrists. Bracelets of yellow cord still circled each wrist, but at least now she could move her hands freely. She yanked the gag out of her mouth, then tested the ropes at her feet. Damn. The tight knots would require too much time to work free, so she just hobbled over to the door.

Locked. But the window looked just wide enough to clear her hips.

She pushed one of the chairs into place, crawled onto it, then boosted herself up. A quick hop landed her stomach-down across the window sill. The pressure almost made her vomit, but she clamped her teeth onto her tongue and used the pain to focus her attention.

Up front, the men yelled at one another.

Using their voices as cover, Susana dropped to the deck.

CHAPTER THREE

"Amigo, come look."

Kai put down the rope he was coiling and walked to the front of the boat. The pilot Giovanni handed him binoculars and pointed at the stern of a retreating boat. Kai raised the glasses.

The boat was configured much as Kai's was. Low hull. Central cabin. Pilot station in the bow. Not the same one that had passed them last night.

The other pilot glanced frantically from the river in front of him to where a heavyset man in mismatched fatigues used a jacket to beat at pile of burning rags. The fire shifted sideways and engulfed a nearby crate. Another man grabbed the AK-47 propped against the cabin wall and pulled it out of the danger zone.

Mercenaries. Kai recognized one of them from town. As long as they were distracted by the fire, they wouldn't be a problem.

Still, Kai quickly scanned the rest of the boat to see how many more men were on board. Two. Four. Six, counting the pilot.

"What the hell?" A female figure dangled half-way out the window at the back of the cabin. Long, dark hair cascaded to the deck, hiding her face.

She squirmed and fell, landing hard on her right shoulder. Kai winced in sympathy, then grinned as her hair slipped away to reveal her face.

Susana Dias. Well, hell. Looked like someone had beaten him to the scene. But Kai would be damned if he let them steal the lady away from him.

"Closer," Kai ordered Giovanni as he shifted the binoculars to the activity at the other boat's bow. A second man had joined the first and together they almost had the fire contained. Their focus remained forward, so they hadn't yet noticed Susana's actions.

"Come up behind them so the men won't notice us."

Giovanni grunted acknowledgment and kicked up the boat's speed.

THE PAIN from hitting the deck radiated from Susana's shoulder into her neck and back. Her vision wavered. Her headache screamed. She closed her eyes and sucked air through her nose in rapid pants. It didn't take long for fear to overwhelm the pain.

She had to get away.

Opening her eyes, she lifted her head to look around her. The low side of the boat was perhaps three feet to her left. Frantic curses still colored the air at the front of the boat, but she didn't know how long her captors would stay distracted. She needed to get over the side and into the river before they spotted her. The current would move her far from the boat and hopefully spit her out at some safe distance.

A trip on the river couldn't be worse than whatever her kidnappers had in store for her.

Not daring to stand up in case she drew the men's attention, she turned onto her back, put her weight on her elbows and used her bound feet to propel her in a push, pull movement across the deck. Every few seconds she checked over her shoulder to judge her progress. Two feet to go.

Ignore the splinters tearing into her palms like hot needles.

One foot.

Pause for just a second so her burning muscles could rest.

Inches.

Made it!

The men were still yelling at each other. She grabbed the gunwale, bent over at the waist and let the weight of her upper body topple her into the water.

An instant before her head went underwater, she thought she heard a man shout.

Kai watched Susana inch across the deck. From the awkward way she used her legs, he figured her feet were bound, and he felt a flare of anger over the idea of her being mishandled.

One of the mercenaries left the smoldering fire and rounded the corner of the cabin just as Susana's feet disappeared over the side of the boat. Breaking into a run, the man shouted an alarm. When he reached the side of the boat his head moved back and forth as he searched for Susana in the water.

Crazy woman, Kai thought. How long did she think she'd survive in the river with her feet bound?

The mercenary pulled a pistol from a hip holster.

"Shit." Kai trained the binoculars at the fast-moving current, trying to see where Susana had gone.

"Do you see her?" Giovanni shouted, giving up any pretense of stealth and increasing their boat's speed.

"No." Kai continued to sweep the binoculars over the water surrounding the other boat. "Where are you, Susana?" he muttered. Until she surfaced, she was in danger of being swept under the mercenaries' boat. But the moment her head broke water, the mercenaries would be on her.

"There!" Giovanni said, pointing to starboard.

Unfortunately, the mercenaries had also spotted Susana. The

one with the pistol fired into the water, barely missing her. A second man charged across the deck and knocked the shooter's hand down before he let off another shot. The men got into a shoving match, accompanied by angry shouts.

Kai lowered his binoculars and raced for his cabin. The glasses bounced against his chest with enough force to bruise, but he didn't care. He needed his weapon.

When he returned to his position, M-4 in hand, one of the men had Susana in a headlock and was slowly dragging her across the gunwale.

Kai set his M-4 on manual. His first shot went into the shoulder of the man holding Susana. As she dropped into the water, Kai's second and third shots hit the hull right beneath the water line.

He might be a scientist working mainly as a spy, but the SSU made sure all its operators were excellent shots.

Susana heard a grunt of pain, then her captor let go of her neck. She dropped back into the river and promptly inhaled water. When her head broke the surface, she snorted to clear her nose, then pulled in as much air as she could hold before letting herself sink beneath the current.

A second later she bumped against something hard. Her head breached the surface and she realized the current had pushed her right back against the hull. She shot a terrified glance above her, but didn't see her kidnappers. What she did see was a man, silhouetted by the sun, standing on the deck of a second boat.

He aimed a menacing machine gun right at her. Her heart stuttered.

Get away! She pushed her shoulder against the hull, trying to drive herself underwater.

Then she heard another cry of pain from above her. "Do

something," one of her captors snarled. "Before the cock-sucker shoots me again."

She turned her head. Oh. The man on the other boat wasn't aiming at her. He was aiming above her head. At her kidnappers.

Her relief was so great, she forgot to tread water and sank.

Come on, girl. You're being rescued. Don't drown now.

She pushed to the surface and a life preserver splashed down next to her.

"*Senhorita,*" her would-be rescuer shouted over the pulse of the boat engines. "Grab the line and we'll bring you aboard."

Her heart soared. Even though his words were Portuguese, his accent was American.

Remembering something she'd heard a long time ago about water rescues, she grabbed hold of the life preserver and turned her back to the boat. The line tightened and began to slowly pull her against the current.

As her rescuer's boat picked up speed, her head bounced against the surface of the river making her headache flare, and she had trouble holding her head up high enough to stop water from getting up her nose. It seemed like forever before the boat slowed, then stopped so she could be dragged aboard.

For several long, agonizing moments Susana huddled on the deck, coughing up river water and shivering despite the midday heat. She was dimly aware of male voices talking above her and of the engine throbbing underneath her as the boat started moving again.

A warm male hand lightly patted her back. "Here, take my coat."

Susana opened her eyes and sat up. A man knelt next to her, holding out a heavy rain jacket. Even though her teeth were chattering, she didn't grab for the coat. Instead, she stared at her rescuer.

Oh. My. God.

He had the most beautiful eyes she'd ever seen. A rich, clear amber. Wild and fierce, reminding her of the jaguar she'd seen last week at the river's edge. The man's eyes combined with lean, stubbled cheeks, a square chin and a sensual lower lip to create a picture of male strength and vitality. The lithe muscles of his arms and thighs strained against his sweat-stained clothes. Suddenly Susana felt way too warm.

Susana had known more handsome men, but none had knocked her speechless or caused this hot, aching longing.

"Ma'am? Are you okay?" Oh, God, he even had a husky, sexy voice.

Get a grip, girl. Susana shook her head, realized she was still staring, and lowered her eyes as she reached for his coat. "I'm um...just...um...glad to be out of the river and safe. Thanks."

"You're welcome."

She wriggled into the jacket. For a second she caught him eyeing her chest and her nipples tightened. Then he quickly glanced away and she thought she heard him mutter, "Sorry."

His embarrassment over being caught ogling her boobs restored her equilibrium. At least she wasn't alone on this admiration train.

But he recovered quickly. His long, almost elegant fingers pushed up the sleeves of the jacket to reveal the swollen, red and purple skin at her wrists.

He sucked in a breath. For a moment something dark and fierce passed over his expression. His fingers tightened on hers almost painfully, then released.

"Let me cut your bindings away," he said.

It was a sign of how overwhelmed she was that Susana didn't so much as blink in alarm when he pulled a large hunting knife from a sheath on his leg.

"Brace yourself," her rescuer said. "The rope's embedded in your skin. This is going to hurt." He worked with surprising gentleness, but there was little play in the rope and the blade nicked her skin despite his caution.

Susana hissed in pain. Hell yes, that hurt. Tears stung her eyes and she quickly turned her face away from him.

Then immediately turned back as she felt the feather light stroke of his finger next to her damaged skin. Without meeting her startled gaze, he repeated the process with her ankles.

Next, displaying more of that surprising gentleness, the man rubbed circulation back into her hands and feet. At first the increased blood flow felt warm and soothing. It didn't take long for the piercing, hot-pins-and-needles pain to take over.

"Ouch!" The protest came out as a harsh croak.

"Sorry," he said. "It'll get better in a minute. I think there's some salve in the cabin we can use on your cuts. I—"

Behind them, the boat's cabin exploded in a flash of light.

THE SHOCK WAVE knocked Kai on top of Susana. He crossed his arms protectively over his head and ignored the sting from burning wood pelting his back and legs. In the silence that followed, Kai heard frantic cursing from Giovanni.

How in hell had the other boat gotten close enough to launch an RPG? They'd been sinking.

Kai levered himself off Susana while telling himself not to notice how soft her breasts felt or how if he moved his head just a few inches, he'd be able to kiss that lush mouth.

"Was that a *missile*?" Susana squeaked, effectively bringing Kai's attention back to business.

"Rocket-propelled grenade," Kai corrected, turning to assess the damage. The cabin's roof and front wall were on fire, but that wasn't crippling. "Keep your head down in case they have another one."

"Who the hell are you and why are those men firing rockets at us?"

"Kai Paterson. I'm with a private special operations group from the U.S." He grabbed Susana's hand and started crawling toward the front of the boat. He needed to see what was going on.

"You okay, Giovanni?" he shouted to the pilot.

"No. Those fucking pirates tried to blow up my boat!"

Kai's mouth twisted with a wry smile. Yeah, Giovanni was fine.

Susana slipped on the wet deck and Kai reached out to steady her.

"My name's Susana Dias," she said as they started crawling again. "I'm an archaeologist. So...special operations? That's like a covert soldier, right?"

Great. Susana was one of those women who chattered when scared. "Yeah."

"Watch out!" Giovanni shouted. His warning was accompanied by the sound of incoming automatic weapon fire. "There's a second goddamn boat."

The deck tilted sharply left, then right, throwing Kai and Susana sideways. Susana's head cracked against the side of the boat and she slumped unconscious.

Kai checked Susana's pulse and moved her into a more comfortable position. Poor woman, she'd been through a lot. The memory of her swollen, torn skin where she'd been bound threatened to send a flood of rage through him.

From the front of the boat Giovanni cried out in pain. The deck continued to tilt to the right and the pilot's body slid into view before jamming against a spool of rope. With an ominous stutter, the engine died. Then the deck slammed horizontal again.

Kai grabbed his weapon and peered around the burning remains of the cabin. An armored gunboat was heading toward them from upriver. A man stood on the deck behind a mounted machine gun. He noticed Kai and let loose a volley of gunfire.

Kai fired back, then ducked out of sight. Shit. The cabin provided him some protection, but Giovanni lay in the open.

Kai fired another burst at the gunboat, then raced across the deck and pulled Giovanni to safety behind a stack of crates. He put his fingers to the man's neck.

No pulse.

He turned the man over. Bullet holes perforated Giovanni's chest. The package Kai had retrieved tumbled out of the man's pocket.

The treats for Giovanni's young daughter rolled across the deck.

Dammit. Kai hadn't known the man well, but he'd been honest and as quick with a joke as he was to anger. Kai bowed his head a moment, then closed the man's eyes. A brief glance showed the gunner on the other boat had turned his head and was talking over his shoulder to someone behind him. The gunboat blocked Kai's view of the mercenaries' sinking boat, but when the gunboat's deck tilted away from Kai, he figured the newcomers were taking the mercenaries on board.

Knowing he didn't have long before the gunboat either used another RPG or sent men to board them, Kai crawled into the remains of the cabin. He searched the debris until his fingers closed around the nylon straps of two large backpacks. Giovanni, God rest his soul, had looked at Kai like he was crazy the first morning he'd repacked his bag. *Why you taking down your hammock, 'migo? You pack it away, you only got to put it back up tonight.*

But after two years on the run he'd learned to have everything packed and ready to move at a moment's notice, including bedding. Four months free from the hunt and the habit still hadn't faded.

He hoisted one pack onto his back. He located several extra boxes of ammunition and shoved those into the second pack, then looked out what was left the door.

The other boat's gunner stood behind his weapon with arms crossed. He faced a second man, who nodded in the direction of

Kai's boat. Cradled in the second man's arms was an RPG launcher. Both men wore olive green uniforms without any insignia.

Special forces or private soldiers?

On the deck behind the men, the three sodden mercenaries eyed the soldiers with varying degrees of wariness. While they were distracted, Kai slid down the canted deck to the side of the boat. Susana lay in several inches of water, conscious now and blinking against the sun's glare.

"We've got to get off the boat before it sinks or is blown out of the water," Kai said as he landed beside her.

He placed his arms through the straps of the second backpack so it rested against his chest. It was going to be a bitch to navigate the river laden down with the packs, but they were going to need these supplies and she wasn't in any condition to carry a pack in the water. He took off his baseball cap and shoved it into his pocket.

The rope he'd been coiling earlier lay in a tangled heap a foot away from him. He pulled free a length and cut it with his pocketknife. He tied one end of the rope around his waist, underneath the backpacks. Then he knelt awkwardly beside Susana and held out the rope. "I'm going to tie this around your waist so that when we go into the river we won't get separated."

Her eyes widened, but she nodded. Damn it, he wanted to kiss her and tell her everything was going to be okay. That she just had to hold on a little longer.

Instead, he quickly tied the rope and tugged to make sure the knot was secure. Heading into the river like this was dangerous. But he wasn't losing Susana under any circumstances.

He heard a shout. The other boat's engine revved.

Shit. Out of time.

He had to time this just right. He didn't want to go overboard too early. The attackers needed to think they were dead, blown up with the boat.

He grabbed Susana's arm. "Get ready," he whispered in her ear. Unable to help himself, he brushed a quick kiss against her temple.

"On the count of three, we're going into the river."

He waited for the hiss of the rocket being released. "One... two...three!" Kai pulled air deep into his lungs, then threw himself overboard, pulling Susana with him.

CHAPTER FOUR

Susana considered herself to be in good shape, but after being kidnapped, rescued, hurled from an exploding boat, swimming through the river while being shot at, then climbing up a riverbank and running into the jungle while her damn kidnappers got out of their boat and friggin' *followed* them, she had almost zero energy left.

"C'mon, we've got to keep moving," Kai said.

Grumbling under her breath, Susana let Kai pull her into a run. Once her body got moving, she could keep her momentum going. But she didn't know what would happen if he let go of her hand. Besides, she liked the warm, calloused feel of his skin against hers. It reminded her that she wasn't alone.

Some sixth sense had her turning her head to check behind her in time to see the ground torn up by bullets not three feet away. Kai cursed and veered left, dragging her into an area of thick undergrowth.

It forced them down to a jog, but she hoped it also slowed their pursuers. Although, really, all they had to do was keep shooting. Eventually she or Kai would be hit.

As if summoned by her thoughts, she heard gunfire again. It sounded closer.

Kai moved faster, dodging around trees, ducking under branches, and leaping over logs. Hauling her with him every step of the way. Did the damn man never tire?

Finally, he slowed to a walk.

Kai reached his hand up to move a vine out of his path.

"Don't!" She smacked his arm away. "That's dangerous. Like poison ivy."

"Thanks."

She nodded and looked up at him. Then nearly drowned in the look of heated tenderness in Kai's eyes. Ignoring the fluttering in her belly, she broke from his gaze and cleared her throat. "This way," she announced, taking the lead and heading right. If only the men chasing them didn't have guns. She could booby-trap their path. She could...

The ground turned spongy under her boots. She planted her feet and spread her arms wide so Kai couldn't get by. "Stop!"

"What's wrong?"

"Quicksand."

"Damn. That's twice I owe you."

Oh, she liked that. "And don't you forget it," she tossed back over her shoulder with a wink. Of course, she owed him her life, so they still weren't even.

She backed up carefully, checked the color of the ground, and led them around the dangerous territory.

Gunfire ripped through the trees somewhere close by.

"Damn," Kai said. "How do they keep finding us?"

He grabbed her hand and they broke into a run.

Oh, no, here we go again.

Kai glanced back to the bend in the thickly overgrown path. *Come on, let us get away this time.*

He felt like a little kid, praying to be invisible during a game of hide-and-seek. Only this time a hell of a lot more was at stake than his pride.

The butt of an automatic weapon poked into view between two heart-shaped leaves.

Shit.

Kai tugged Susana deeper into the bush.

Who the hell were these guys? Some sort of mystic ninja soldiers? Because for the past hour he'd used every trick he'd learned in escape and evasion training. Susana had even created some quick but nasty jungle booby-traps, and their pursuers *still* never lost their trail for more than a few minutes.

At least the booby-traps had taken two of the men out of the chase. Susana was proving to be a valuable partner. Smart, creative and resourceful.

He helped Susana over a fallen log. She stumbled on the other side and almost pulled him down, but he quickly took hold of her arms and steadied her.

"I'm okay," she murmured. She reached up to brush a sweaty hank of hair out of her eyes and he saw that her hand was shaking. As soon as she saw his eyes narrow, she dropped her hand and stuck it in her pocket. Her expression dared him to say anything about her show of weakness.

Kai felt an unfamiliar wave of protectiveness and tenderness wash over him. He wanted to kiss her for being so strong, but he heard men crashing through the brush, coming toward them.

This time she broke into a run. "Let's go!"

He followed, amazed at her endurance and at the way she didn't complain about the relentless pace, yet knowing they couldn't keep it up much longer. They both needed to rest.

At least Joe trigger-happy back there had stopped spraying the trees with bullets every time he caught sight of them.

The idiot had probably used up all his ammunition and that of his friends.

After several minutes of running, Kai slowed to a walk. They trod carefully at an angle to their original path, then walked for a good ten minutes more trying not to leave an obvious pattern of crushed vegetation behind them. Finally, Kai pulled them to a stop behind a tall clump of bushes.

If the mercenaries didn't lose their trail this time, it could only mean one thing. Susana had a tracking device on her. But until they lost their pursuers, he wouldn't have a chance to find and destroy the device. And while he and Susana had managed to stay out of kill range so far, once the sun went down they'd have to stop running.

He was damn sure the mercenaries and their soldier allies would have flashlights or night vision equipment. So all they had to do was follow the tracking signal right to Susana.

He wasn't going to let that happen.

Susana muttered to herself and swatted at a mosquito.

Kai hid a smile. Susana no longer resembled the polished woman in her modeling photos. Sweat had cleaned little runnels through the thick dirt and blood covering her face, giving her the appearance of a fierce tribal warrior. Her hair hung in tangled ropes down her back and stuck to her face. Her clothes were as filthy as his.

But somehow she still managed to instill every movement with heated sensuality.

Or maybe he just saw it that way because it had been much too long since he'd been in the company of a woman both sexy and strong.

And this former supermodel had unexpected grit. She'd kept up with his furious pace. He'd noticed her steps weaving a few times, but she hadn't asked him to stop or slow down. Instead, she'd muttered to herself. He hadn't been able make out all the words, but the tone suggested she was egging herself on. Or maybe cursing the mercenaries.

He found himself almost smiling, despite the whole being-

pursued-by-untiring-gun-toting-mercenaries thing. And felt glad
that he'd been the one given this assignment.

"Hey," he whispered to her. "See if you can find some quicksand. We need to trap these guys once and for all."

Despite her exhaustion, Susana's eyes brightened. Once again
he felt the urge to gather her into his arms and kiss her. Tell her
everything was going to be okay.

Even though she was too smart to believe him.

So he kept his hands to himself and followed her through the
jungle, listening to the sounds of their pursuers drawing closer.
Just when he was about to say to hell with it and start running
again, Susana motioned him to a stop.

She picked up a piece of deadwood and poked it into the
ground in front of her. The stick started sinking with a slurp.

Kai sank to a crouch beside her. The quicksand appeared to
be about ten feet by twelve. Perfect.

"Okay," he said quietly. "Here's the plan."

Belém, Brazil

"This problem wouldn't exist if you'd completed your mission
at the fundraiser," CIA Director of In-House Projects Wayne
Jamieson pointed out across the satellite phone connection.

"I explained what happened, sir," Mark Tonelli replied,
keeping his voice even. "Susana Dias was never alone. I was
unable to get close to her. She left in a hurry immediately after
the presentation of the check to fund her expedition. The crowd
was too thick for me to follow her closely. By the time I got
outside, she was gone." Mark was glad his new boss was thousands of miles away, across a thin, static-filled phone connection,
so the man's infamous bullshit sensitive nose couldn't scent
his lie.

The truth wasn't something he was eager to share. Or even admit to himself.

"And she never returned to her apartment?" Jamieson queried.

"Correct, sir. I had a man watching it." He'd later learned that Susana had left on a dawn flight to Boa Vista, returning to her dig earlier than expected.

Susana's disappearance gave Mark time to catch his breath and regain his equilibrium after meeting her in person.

It was a weak excuse for letting his prey get away. But she'd taken him by surprise.

He'd known Susana had modeled from the time she was thirteen until she entered graduate school for archaeology. The most recent pictures had shown a stunning woman with long, slightly wavy black hair, wide dark eyes and a huge smile that managed to be joyous and sensual at the same time. Mark had dated women equally as beautiful, so he certainly hadn't expected to be struck dumb with adolescent admiration when introduced to her. But it had happened. His famous suave manners had deserted him and he'd barely stammered his greeting. Later, his voice had returned enough to ask her to dance, but he'd been unable to make small talk with her.

Holding her had been like holding the sun. All vibrant life. He'd never wanted to let her go. He'd forgotten the syringe in his pocket. Forgotten the fake ambulance waiting a few blocks over for the call that Susana was "ill." Forgotten that she had Nevsky's microchip inside her and that the chip was Jamieson's price for the information Mark needed to complete his revenge.

It was the first time during his career at the CIA that Mark had lost his focus. For at least an hour after he'd danced with Susana, he'd remained in a daze. By the time he came back to awareness of his mission, she'd left.

But his informant at Susana's dig had come through. Susana should now be in the hands of the mercenaries Mark had hired to retrieve Susana. Under no circumstances would he ever personally set foot in the filthy, bug-infested jungle.

"You're certain you can trust your men to bring Dias back?" Jamieson demanded.

"Yes, sir. I've paid them well. We should have the microchip by the end of tomorrow."

"Good. I need the data on that chip. And I know you're anxious to receive that name."

Mark clenched his teeth. It wasn't a new threat. Jamieson held the name of the man who'd ordered the hit on Mark's father. Even today he still felt the mix of rage and helplessness as his five-year-old self cradled his dying father's head. Thugs in a black town car had shoved his father's tortured body onto the family's front lawn, then sped off. Mark had vowed then to track down and kill the men responsible.

Until two years ago, Mark thought he'd succeeded. Now Jamieson claimed Mark had only killed the ones who'd carried out the hit. He insisted that the man who'd planned the death of Mark's father still lived.

But without the chip, Jamieson wasn't talking. And Mark hadn't been able to discover the man's name on his own.

There followed one of the heavy silences Mark dreaded. Jamieson might be powerful, and Mark might consider it an honor to work for the man and his secret CIA division of In-House Projects, but Jamieson was a difficult bastard to deal with. He always made Mark feel as inept as a schoolboy being chastised by the principal.

"Our informant at the SSU notified me that Paterson is on his way to the dig," Jamieson finally said.

Shit. Mark had worked with Kai Paterson years ago, before Paterson left the CIA to join the SSU, one of those upstart private special operations groups. The man was brilliant. And ruthless.

But for once Mark's luck put him ahead of the SSU. Paterson was too late.

"Tonelli, are you listening to me?"

"Yes, sir. I'll warn the mercenaries of potential interference from Paterson."

"That's right. The next time I call, if you don't have Dias, I'm sending down a cleanup squad. And you're one of the items they're going to clean up."

Amazon Jungle

"I THINK you have a tracking device on you," Kai said, making Susana's blood run cold.

"A tracking device?" she sputtered. "Like they use to monitor cattle?" Her mother had used rudimentary microchips to follow the cattle she'd studied on ranches in the Amazon basin, searching for a way to make a breed that was both drought and disease resistant.

Kai nodded. "That's the only explanation for why the mercenaries keep finding us. Create three more booby traps and set them in a half-circle out from the far edge of the quicksand, there." He pointed to an area that had several large bushes.

"You hide in the bushes," Kai said. "You'll be safe. If anyone tries to circle behind you, they'll hit the booby-traps. I'll take care of the men at the quicksand."

Susana narrowed her eyes. "Take care of? You mean kill?"

Kai shrugged. "Whatever's necessary."

He said it so calmly. Yet despite the way he'd handled his weapon as he fired back at their pursuers, she saw the hint of a shadow cross his eyes. As if he wasn't entirely comfortable with killing, but would do what was necessary to survive.

With a nod, Kai brushed off his hands and got to work helping her set up the trap, then vanished into the jungle.

Leaving her alone. Sitting in this tangled bush guarding the backpacks. Wondering how her life had gotten so out of control so quickly.

Damn Kai. She felt like she had a giant X painted on her forehead.

Remembering the lessons the tribal kids had taught her about staying still enough to lure prey in close, Susana tried to still her mind and slow her heartbeat so she'd hear any mercenary sneaking closer.

But her life had never been in danger like this before. Her mind just wouldn't settle and her heart continued its frantic beat.

Hard fingers clamped onto the back of her collar and yanked. "Wha—?" she yelped.

She was pulled out of her hidey-hole and into the midst of four men with hard jaws and cold eyes.

Susana screamed.

One of the men backhanded her. The force split her lip and caused her to bump into the man holding her. With a grunt of annoyance, he shoved her to her knees.

Where was Kai? How come these men hadn't tripped any of her booby traps? How did they avoid the quicksand?

"Let's kill her now," the man behind her said in Portuguese.

He kicked her between her shoulder blades. She managed to turn her head at the last second, so her cheek slammed into the ground, not her nose. Then the man stomped his foot on her back, driving all the air out of her lungs. She felt something cold, round and hard press against the base of her skull.

Oh, God. His gun. Her pulse spiked.

She was going to die. Where the *hell* was Kai?

"No!" The rough male voice sounded vaguely familiar. Susana's face was scrunched into the ground by the pressure of her captor's weapon, but she rolled her eyes until she could see the protester.

Yes, it was one of her kidnappers from the boat. But he wasn't dressed like the other men. His fatigues were old and plain. A faded olive color rather than the deep evergreen with jungle print like the men surrounding her. Maybe her kidnapper wasn't part of this group. Maybe he could stop them from killing her.

"The man said he wouldn't pay my cousins and me the rest of our money if the woman was hurt," her kidnapper protested.

Yes!

"What the fuck do we care what your client told you?" The speaker was a thin man with a tiny button of a nose and lips that put Angelina Jolie's to shame. "Our orders were to bring the woman back dead. Hell, we don't even need her whole body, just her abdomen."

What? Her...her torso? What did that—?

Bright red exploded out of Thick Lips's chest and neck. Susana screamed. She wanted to look away, but her eyes refused to close, leaving her staring at the ruined mess that had been the man's chest. A second later, her kidnapper fell beside her, eyes staring at the sky through a blood-covered face.

Then something heavy fell on top of her, knocking her breath away and obscuring her vision. From the strong body odor, it was the man who'd been holding the gun to her neck. Susana tried to buck him off, but he was too heavy.

Oh, no. She wasn't going to stay trapped here underneath a corpse. She worked her hands up underneath her shoulders, took a deep breath...

And the body was lifted away.

Susana scrambled to her feet. Cold, hard amber eyes met hers. The eyes of a killer. Seeing only death, she backed away and bolted toward the jungle.

"Shit," she heard behind her. "Susana, wait! I'm not going to hurt you."

But fear and panic pulsed through her veins, urging her to get away before she was killed.

One minute she was running, the next she was falling, strong male arms capturing her around her waist. But Kai shifted his body mid-fall and twisted so she landed on top of him.

"Dammit, Susana, what's wrong with you?" Kai growled. "It's me. Kai. You're safe."

Unable to think past the image of Thick Lips's exploding chest, Susana slapped at Kai's face and tried to stab her knee into his balls, but he simply captured her hands in his much larger ones and rolled over so that she ended up on her stomach with him lying on top of her.

"Susana, I'm not going to hurt you. I swear. Just calm down. Okay?"

He had her hands pinned to either side of her face and her legs tightly pressed together between his. His hold, while firm, wasn't rough or bruising. But it was the soothing words he murmured that finally broke through the wall of horror and fear.

She stilled.

Oh, God. She felt foolish. He'd just saved her life. Yet she'd panicked and run from him, afraid he'd kill her next.

"You okay?"

No, dammit. She wasn't. She'd just seen...just seen...

Gaah, she didn't know whether to be sick or be mad. But after a few seconds, mad won out, destroying the last of her fear.

"What the *hell* were you thinking?" she snarled. She wanted to hurt him for putting her through the worst scare of her life. But he had her restrained so tightly she couldn't hit or kick him.

So she bit the part of his forearm that was closest to her.

"Hey!" he protested, although her teeth had made only a faint indent in his shirt. "What the hell was that for?"

"Where were you? What took you so long to show up, you bastard? You said I'd be safe!" Susana heaved, trying to dislodge him, but Kai's weight was evenly distributed along her body, pinning her completely.

Kai pressed harder against her. "Settle down. I'm sorry. When I realized they were skirting around the quicksand I started to follow, but then another two men showed up. I had to disable them before I could come for you."

"Yeah? Well they almost put a bullet through my brain." She tried to slam the back of her head into Kai's nose, but he moved out of the way. That just stoked her anger higher.

"I've been knocked over the head, pushed into a river, kidnapped, shot at, now this. Those men said they don't need me alive because all they need is my torso! For the last time. What the *hell* is going on?"

Kai cursed under his breath.

"Kai?"

He sighed. "You've got a microchip implanted in your abdomen, Susana. A microchip containing scientific research men will kill to get."

CHAPTER FIVE

"THAT'S NOT FUNNY." Susana's body jerked in another attempt to free herself and Kai shifted his hips just in time to avoid having her hit his growing hard-on.

"I'm not joking, Susana. There's—"

A radio squawked. Shit. When the dead men didn't check in, their buddies would come looking for them.

"I've got to go shut that radio off. Promise me you won't run and I'll let you up," he said.

She actually thought about running, he could sense it in the way her muscles tightened. She gave a sexy little hmmm of indecision, then exhaled heavily. "Okay. I...promise," she said.

Gee. She sounded *so* sincere.

Still, if he didn't trust her they'd be stuck here all day. And after a while she'd realize his body was experiencing a typical male reaction to being pressed so tightly to her perfect ass. He didn't want to give her another reason to be wary of him.

So he'd have to take her promise seriously. For now at least. "Thank you," he said. He rolled off her and stood.

She refused his offer of a hand up and crawled a good five feet away before she stood.

O-kay. So she didn't want to be anywhere near him. He supposed he couldn't blame her for being freaked out. She'd probably never had a dead person fall on her before.

Well, maybe she had. But any corpses she'd encountered as an archaeologist would have lacked the...gore...of what she'd just witnessed. Yeah, probably not a lot of spraying blood from those bodies.

Susana finished brushing the leaves off the front of her shirt, then crossed her arms over her chest and glared at him.

With her dark hair escaping its braid in wildly curling tendrils, her full lips pursed and her dirty, sweat-stained clothes, she looked ferocious. Sexy as hell.

And exhausted.

Ignoring another surge of protectiveness, he turned his back on her and knelt beside the bodies. "Uh...you might want to go into the jungle a bit."

"Why?" She sounded suspicious.

"Because in order to search the bodies for the radio and the tracking device monitor I'm going to have to turn this guy over. You don't need to see what's on the other side. Why don't you see if the tracking device is somewhere on your clothes?"

He heard Susana stomp away, muttering under her breath.

"Hey," he called after her, removing the man's pistol and holding it up. "Can you shoot?"

"Yes, I can. Will I?" She glanced quickly at the bodies and bit her lip. "I don't know."

"Take this anyway. Just in case." He tossed her the weapon.

She caught it. The way she checked the safety reassured him she knew enough not to accidentally shoot herself. Despite the look of revulsion on her face as she tucked the gun in her pocket, he figured her temper would kick in and have her firing at anyone who threatened her.

Including him. He'd have to be careful. But somehow, that thought brought a tiny smile to his face. He liked her temper.

Hell, he liked everything about her. Didn't it just figure she'd ended up witnessing his violent side in action.

Kai watched her move through the brush until he was satisfied she wasn't going to see anything, then turned over the first body. It was the man who'd held his weapon to Susana's head.

Before he could stop it, the rage came back. When he'd seen Susana on the ground with the butt of the automatic weapon digging into her neck, he'd lost it. He hadn't consciously decided to shoot. He'd acted on instinct. Given in to that savage part of himself that he still didn't fully understand. Or trust.

But let's hear it for being aggressive. Susana was alive and untouched by any stray bullets. And he had six less opponents to worry about. Still, the back of his neck itched, telling him they'd better leave as soon as possible.

Kai quickly searched the bodies. The radios were short-range only, no good to him, so he turned them off. He took the weapons and extra ammo.

The third man had the tracking device monitor in his pocket. It looked like a Blackberry, only this screen showed a rough map instead of a menu of features. There was a dot for the person holding the monitor and another dot roughly where Susana was standing.

Okay. That was both good and bad. Good, because he now knew how the mercenaries had stayed on their trail.

Bad, because the tracking device had to be found and removed. And if Susana didn't find it in her clothes, then it was inside her. Like the tracking device he'd recently allowed the SSU to implant under his skin to make sure they could rescue him if he ever disappeared.

Or find him if he went rogue.

He had to hope the device inside Susana could be easily removed.

Otherwise, they'd never escape the mercenaries.

"WHAT ABOUT HERE?" Twenty minutes later Susana indicated a fallen log hemmed in on one side by trees and on the other by a sluggish stream. A drape of vines and branches hid the spot from view until you were almost past it.

She hadn't located the tracking device during her self-pat-down, so Kai had told her to keep an eye out for a sheltered spot where he could perform a more thorough search.

Kai nodded. "Yeah, this'll do."

Susana let her backpack slide to the ground as she sank onto the fallen tree. Every muscle in her body wanted to go slack in relief, but she forced her back muscles to straighten. She would not collapse into an exhausted puddle at Kai's feet.

But God, it felt wonderful to sit.

She let her mind drift, thinking of nothing. Her eyes must have closed, because the feel of Kai's hand shaking her shoulder made her jump.

"Have a drink," he said.

"Mmm, I'll take a piña colada," she murmured.

"Er...Sorry. Today's special is Amazon river water. Filtered, of course." Kai spoke in the haughty tones of a four-star maître-d'.

Her cheeks flushed and her eyelids flew open. Kai was holding out a canteen, his lips curled in amusement.

"Thanks." She took the canteen, but carefully avoided looking in his eyes. What an idiotic thing to say. She must be more tired than she thought.

The warm, slightly brackish water spread smooth as quicksilver across her tongue. She forced herself to drink slowly and stop before she was satisfied. It took a long time to filter and purify water. She couldn't take the chance that this was Kai's only canteen.

But when she handed it back to him, he took a long swallow.

She got distracted by the muscles of Kai's throat working as he drank. By the angle of his jaw and...

What was she doing? Kai was just *drinking*. Yet she was getting turned on.

She quickly turned her head away. At least he'd been looking up while he drank so he hadn't seen her watching him.

She waited until she heard the snick of the cap being replaced before she turned around.

"Stand up and hold your arms out."

"What?"

Kai held up a device that resembled a Blackberry. "Tracking—"

"—monitor. Yeah, I know. The ranchers carried a similar device to find lost cattle."

"Ranchers?"

"My mother was a scientist. I spent most of my childhood on ranches here in the Amazon while she tried to develop a drought and famine resistant breed of cattle."

"Just for the record," Kai said. "I'm not comparing you to cattle."

The male appreciation in his eyes triggered an honest-to-goodness blush. Dammit, she never blushed. Susana quickly looked away before he saw how deeply he'd affected her.

"I'm hoping this device has a sensor that will let me know where on your body the tracker is," Kai said.

"I didn't feel anything on me or my clothes. What size are we talking about?"

"Small as an eraser head, and flat as a piece of paper. Now, arms out."

She obediently raised her arms out to her sides as Kai swept the monitor along the line of her body, several inches above her skin.

Dear...Lord. It felt as if he was caressing her.

Susana closed her eyes. She'd heard that the downside of an adrenaline rush was a sudden need for intimacy, but this was ridiculous. Kai wasn't even touching her, yet her tired body sparked with tiny jolts of electricity as he swept the device above her skin.

Under other circumstances she would have embraced her reaction. Answered it by touching Kai in a way that would leave no doubt what she needed. Because God, if he could arouse her this much without making contact with her skin, what would he be able to do if he decided to seduce her?

But she didn't know him. He'd *shot* those men. Without remorse. Without, as far as she could tell, feeling *anything*. While she was going to relive the moment in her nightmares.

Despite the fact that he'd saved her life, she wasn't ready yet to fully trust him. So she ignored her inner sex goddess and didn't pull him closer.

"Your front is clear. Turn around."

She presented her back to him.

The device chirped.

"Found it."

She felt his fingers probing along her left shoulder blade. "Ouch."

"Sorry." He ran his fingers gently over the sore spot again. "There's a small tear in the fabric here." His finger wiggled until it touched her bare skin.

She arched her back at the sharp pain that followed.

"Damn. I didn't mean to hurt you." He pulled back and she could have sworn she felt his lips press a butterfly kiss to her shoulder. "You're going to have to take off your shirt. It feels like the device is under your skin."

"What?" She craned her neck around, but she wasn't flexible enough to see where he was pointing.

"The tracking device is between your shoulder blade and your spine." He lightly traced a large circle on her back, but didn't actually touch the sore spot.

She slipped out of her shirt and clutched it to her chest like a shield. Dammit, her cheeks were heating with another blush. Her friends would howl with laughter if they could see her.

They loved to tease her about her lack of modesty. But honestly, she didn't see what the big deal was. So some guy got a glimpse of her breasts? So what.

She wasn't ashamed of her body. Far from it. She'd posed nude on more than one occasion.

Yet for some reason, with this man, she felt the need for propriety. So here she stood, modest as a vapor-prone maiden, hiding the bare skin of her torso even though her sports bra covered her better than most of the bikinis she owned.

It was enough to make her roll her eyes.

But not enough to make her drop the shirt.

The soft touch of Kai's finger against her bare skin shocked her with a flash of sexual heat that singed all the way to her core. The sound of his breathing so close to her ear as he leaned in to get a better look sent tingles of pleasure down her spine.

She gritted her teeth and prayed that he finished soon, before this stupid arousal deepened to the point she had to act on it. Turning around and kissing him would be a bad mistake.

"Is it there?" she demanded in a voice just a tad too hoarse.

"Yeah, I see it." He paused. "The skin here is puffy." He touched her again. "And hot." Another prod. "There's pus as well. You've got an infection."

Susana's blood froze, all thoughts of arousal gone. In the jungle, infection was one of the deadliest threats. Bacteria flourished in the heat and damp. A healthy person could die within days of an untreated infection.

"How bad?" Her voice cracked on the last syllable.

"No red streaks."

Okay. That was good. She took a deep breath.

His finger explored the sore area and Susana tightened her back muscles so she wouldn't flinch.

"Whoever inserted the device was lucky," Kai said.

"Lucky? He's a guano-brained, hairy-tongued rock-dweller," she muttered. Who would do this to her?

"I can't see the device itself but I can feel it. I think there's a tiny dart in here. Probably shot from a blowgun."

Oh, how very Indiana Jones.

"Since it tore through your shirt, you probably have fibers embedded in the wound."

"This shirt is supposed to be rip-proof," Susana said. "The fabric is an experimental weave I'm testing for the manufacturer. This will definitely be in my report."

"Yeah." She thought she heard the hint of a smile in his voice. "You tell them that they haven't dart-proofed the shirt."

She tried to summon up a smile of her own, but couldn't manage it. Dart guns. Tracking devices.

When had her life spun so far out of control?

"You've got an open sore the size of an MP3 audio jack. The wound hasn't started to heal yet and there's pus oozing out. To get this amount of pus buildup, the device must have been inserted several days ago."

"But—" She was very conscientious about investigating any open wounds on her body, no matter how small. A friend of hers had lost a hand's width of muscle on her thigh because she'd ignored a tiny, bleeding bug bite. Infection had set in, and by the time her friend noticed and got herself back to civilization, some of the tissue had died. "I don't remember feeling any irritation or pain. Wouldn't I have noticed if they shot a dart into me?"

"Not if they dipped it in anesthetic first. It would numb the skin as it entered. Hold on while I get the first aid kit. I'm going to have to cut the device out."

Susana spun around. "You can't be serious!"

"Susana," he said gently, "if I don't remove the tracker, the rest of the mercenaries will find us." There was too much sympathy in his eyes for her comfort. She preferred being mad at him.

She backed up until she felt the bark of a tree digging into her bare skin. "You...are...not...cutting into me!"

All she could think about was the mercenary's blood-drenched face. And the hard expression in Kai's eyes when he'd found her.

He'd just killed four men in front of her and she was supposed to trust him to cut open her skin? How she wished she were fully clothed, instead of still hiding behind the crumpled fabric of her shirt. It severely limited her options.

"Susana." Kai didn't move toward her. He just watched her with steady, compassionate eyes, all trace of the killer gone. "I'm trained in field medicine. I'll make this as easy on you as possible, but we don't have much time." He held the tracking monitor toward her.

"See that third dot in the lower left corner? More mercenaries are on the move, Susana. I have no idea how many men were inside the gunboat's cabin. Or if reinforcements have arrived. The bottom line is that as long as the tracking device is inside you, they're going to find us. And next time I might not be able to save you."

She stared at the tiny dot as it slowly moved toward them. Inevitability pressed against her as relentlessly as the approaching men. She wet her lips with her tongue. Swallowed. And tried to stop the tremors that wanted to shake her entire body. "By cutting into me, you're opening me up to another infection."

"I have some alcohol in my medical kit," Kai reassured her. "This will be as sterile as I can make it."

She closed her eyes in defeat. "Fine. Just do it."

She heard him move away. He hadn't promised her this wasn't going to hurt and she tried to prepare herself.

"When you're ready, please come over here and sit on the log."

At least he had the good sense not to gloat.

She took a deep breath and walked over to where Kai was rummaging in his backpack.

"Shit." Kai held a satellite phone in one hand and a shattered pair of night vision goggles in the other. He turned the phone over so she could see the hole where a bullet had shattered the LCD screen and exited through the back.

"I guess there's no calling for help, huh?" she asked, wondering why Kai hadn't mentioned he had a phone. Or why he hadn't called for backup.

Oh. Wait. They'd been too busy running.

He shook his head. "It's possible the GPS locator still works. You should keep this on you." He set the phone aside and shot her a wry glance. "You're not the only one with a microchip inside them. Only mine is meant to help headquarters find me in situations like this."

"About that microchip," she began.

He reached into his pack again and his hand reemerged holding a blue-and-white first aid box. Her stomach sank and all thoughts of the microchip fled.

Please give me strength.

She sat down on the log and fought not to whimper as Kai moved behind her. She heard the sound of paper tearing, then felt the cool swab of an alcohol wipe against her skin. It only stung slightly when it hit the entry wound.

"Okay. I've sterilized my knife. Brace yourself."

WITH A QUICK DOWNWARD SLICE, Kai cut to the right of the infected area. Susana hissed and her muscles flinched, but other than that, she held it together.

Jesus, she was amazing. That she trusted him to freaking operate on her, even after watching him kill the mercenaries, was...terrifying. Because if she knew just how big a mess he was inside, she'd surely run away screaming.

"I'm making three incisions," he said. "Forming three sides of a small square. Then I'll peel back the skin, scrape the pus away, and lift the dart out with tweezers."

Nice, clinical words. Only, as Susana's blood flowed out of the wound, his hand began to shake.

A shaft of light caught a crimson drop, rimming it with gold. He stared at it, transfixed.

Sunlight had filtered through the canopy that day, too, glistening on the assassin's blood as it dripped onto the jungle floor. Turning Kai's blood-stained hands into sparkling crimson gloves.

God, he could remember the hot, tangy smell of the blood. The—

"Kai?" Susana's voice was tight with pain.

He shook his head and looked down. The tip of the knife was digging into her skin. Blood ran in a thin trickle down her skin.

Kai jerked the knife away. "God...sorry." Shit. He had to stay in the present.

"Are you done yet?"

"Ah...no. I...uh..." *I don't know if I can cut you again.*

He raised the knife. For a god-awful moment his hand remained suspended while his mind fought images of another day when his knife had brought death.

He swallowed heavily, forcing back the memories.

What had she said? Just do it. He could do this. He *had* to.

He made one more quick cut, then peeled back the half inch by half inch flap of skin.

Christ, there was a lot of pus. He used the tip of his knife to scrape it away, then poured some of the filtered water over it.

Susana whimpered, but immediately bit the sound off.

"It's okay. You can scream if you want to. I know this hurts."

But she only shook her head.

The water carried the last of the pus away and there it was. A black metal dart with smooth flanges, embedded in Susana's muscle.

Jesus Christ. She was innocent in all this, yet someone had shot the dart into her as casually as a hunter tagged a deer.

He took a deep breath and pushed aside his anger. To minimize the damage along its exit route, he needed to stay calm and steady while he removed the dart.

He picked up the tweezers, swabbed them with alcohol, and clamped them around the end of the dart.

"Hang on."

Susana felt the prod of the tweezers, then white-hot pain as Kai yanked the dart out. She couldn't stop herself. She screamed. *Ouch. Ouch. OUCH.* That *hurt*.

Little silver dots danced across her vision. The metallic taste of blood flooded her mouth. Dammit, she'd bit her tongue.

"I've got to get some debris out now."

The knife pricked deep and Susana swayed under a new wave of pain. Darkness crept along the edges of her vision and she closed her eyes so she wouldn't pass out. But the swirls of color dancing across her lids made her light-headed and nauseous, so she opened her eyes.

"Bend forward."

She tilted her torso until her chest rested on her thighs.

"Good. Right there. This is going to hurt."

As if nothing yet had hurt? Was he nuts? She had just enough time to wrap her arms around her knees and tighten her muscles when liquid fire poured into the wound.

This time she released a low, animal keen of agony.

"Done. Next a little antibiotic ointment...a gauze pad...and you're all set. You can sit up now."

Susana was too busy gulping air, fighting against the pain that hadn't yet receded, to answer.

"Hey, you okay?"

"Just...give me...a minute. What...the hell...was that?"

"Vodka. From the mini-bar at the hotel. I wanted to make sure the wound was flushed."

To her surprise, she felt Kai's fingers gently pushing her hair off her forehead. His hand skimmed over her head and stopped at the back of her skull.

"Shit." His fingers parted her hair as they explored the bump he'd found. "You've got a cut here. And quite a lump."

She winced. "No kidding. Remember how I said I was pushed into the river? Someone whacked me in the back of the head while I was checking boxes on our supply boat, then shoved me over the railing."

"Do you have any headache? Double vision? Nausea?"

"Of course I feel nauseous! Someone just poured vodka over a hole in my back."

"Susana," he chided.

"Okay, fine. I had a moment of double vision when I first woke up in the kidnapper's cabin, but it's gone now. No serious concussion here."

Kai gave a noncommittal grunt, dabbed at the wound with another alcohol wipe, then patted her shoulder.

The gesture made her want to cry.

"Do you need help sitting up?"

"No." The pain was slowly fading, so she gingerly sat up, shirt still clutched protectively in front of her. When the world didn't tilt, she gave a deep sigh.

"Let me see your wrists."

She glanced down in surprise, having forgotten about the cuts from her bindings.

Dried blood circled her wrists, making it appear she was bound by dark crimson rope. The skin around the cuts was puffy and bruised.

It looked awful, but her pain receptors must be on overload, because the wounds didn't hurt much.

She watched in amazement as Kai's lips thinned. He cradled

her hand gently in his while he washed the blood away, then poured another mini-bottle of alcohol—gin this time—over the broken skin.

Susana clamped her molars together and pressed her tongue to the roof of her mouth.

She'd already done the screaming thing. She'd stay silent this time if it killed her.

"Next wrist, please."

Her stomach sank. She had to go through that *again*?

She held out her other hand and closed her eyes. Maybe if she couldn't see what he was doing, it wouldn't hurt so much.

"Ga-aah," she gasped. Dammit, that stung!

"You can open your eyes now."

She blinked. She'd been so lost, she hadn't noticed he'd already covered the wounds with antibiotic ointment and gauze.

She looked up.

Oh. Wow.

Kai's eyes weren't cold or angry. Instead, they held warmth and...a hint of approval? Before she could be sure, the look was gone.

Kai picked up his canteen and shook it. "The water's gone. Can you take a couple of aspirin dry?" he asked.

She nodded and swallowed the pills he handed her.

She'd been holding her back erect, trying not to move and jar Kai's hand while he worked. Now she let her head hang and her back soften in a grateful slump.

Behind her, she heard the rattling of bandage wrappers and the crinkle of a plastic bag as Kai collected the waste.

"You held up well."

Okay. That was definitely a note of approval in his voice.

It made her feel slightly warmer toward him. Plus, he'd handled the whole operation with unexpected tact and gentleness. It was still scary to think how easily he'd killed those men, but that didn't make Kai a monster.

The men who were following them, however, were a different story. She straightened her spine.

"I want to see this tracking device," she said.

"Let me clean it off first." A moment later his hand appeared in front of her. In the center of his palm lay a tiny dart no longer than a pencil eraser. Next to it was a speck of black, roughly the size of a pin head. Kai pointed to the dot. "That's the actual transmitter."

Seeing it made the whole thing terrifyingly real. Someone had...*shot*...this thing into her. So the mercenaries could find her.

No. Find her body. Kai hadn't said as much, but she knew it was the truth. They'd intended her to drown.

She reached out to touch the menacing speck, then withdrew her finger before she made contact. She didn't want to risk some of its evil rubbing off on her.

Kai's fingers closed over his palm, hiding the transmitter. He turned away and she heard more rustling, as if he'd placed both dart and transmitter into a baggie.

"Tell me about this microchip. What's so important that those men want me dead?"

Kai sighed. A moment later, he came to sit beside her on the log. "Your father was working on a top-secret government research project. He encoded his notes onto a microchip and had it implanted in your abdomen during that appendectomy you had two years ago."

"No." Susana pushed to her feet. "That's not possible. My father didn't know where I was. My mother was very careful to hide us from him. Besides, he died when I was ten." Then she remembered the letter from the lawyers. "Or maybe not. The letter said he was alive until..." Oh, hell. "...two years ago."

"What letter? When?" Kai's voice was sharp. He stood up so quickly, she stepped back in alarm.

"From some lawyers in Russia. It arrived the day I was pushed into the river. They said my father was dead. There was a letter from him enclosed, but I didn't have a chance to read it. We had another incident at camp and I ran out to help."

"What—" Kai shook his head. "Never mind." He pushed his sleeve back, revealing a watch with several dials. "What are the coordinates of your dig?"

"What? Why?"

"I need to call for a helicopter to get you out of here. I want you safely back at headquarters. Your dig is the closest habitation. You do have a working radio, right?"

"Yeah." She gave him the coordinates and he punched them into his watch. "My father really had his microchip put inside me? Like I'm some kind of human filing cabinet?"

"More like a safe deposit box," Kai muttered.

Susana snorted in amusement. Then her hand crept to her abdomen, touching her appendectomy scar. For two years she'd been carrying an alien object in her body.

Her stomach turned over. Her knees wobbled and she sank onto the log. "How did he find me? I didn't even know his name until the letter arrived." She'd never wanted to know the man her mother only spoke of in frightened whispers. "My mother ran from that tarantula spawn..." She turned her head and spat to the side. "...when I was only a few months old."

"His name is on your birth certificate. Anyone with strong research skills could find you. And your father was very smart."

She shuddered, unable to comprehend why her father would even think to use her in such a way.

"Are you cold? Here, let me help you with your shirt."

The last thing she wanted was for Kai to touch her again and raise that pointless desire, but all her strength had vanished with her anger. She barely found the energy to push her arms through the sleeves as lethargy slammed into her. Fastening the front was beyond her abilities, her fingers too stiff and clumsy to work the buttons.

Kai moved in front of her and pushed her fumbling hands away.

She watched, oddly fascinated by the ease with which his fingers placed the buttons in their holes. He had very nicely shaped fingers, despite the scarred and calloused skin. His fingers were larger than hers, of course. Long. Yet almost graceful.

Beautiful.

Her vision blurred as if she were looking at his hands through a rain-fogged window. Her eyelids drooped and she slid off the log onto the ground, wincing only slightly when the movement jarred her wound. "Got to rest a moment," she murmured. A second later, she was out cold.

CHAPTER SIX

Saturday, Afternoon
Washington, D.C.

"I HAVE A TEAM FOR YOU." Dr. Kaufmann announced when he called.

"Finally." Jamieson refused to let any of his fierce satisfaction show in his voice. Being thought emotionless carried great power.

"Do you have an assignment for them?" Kaufmann asked.

"I want your team to retrieve the microchip from Susana Dias," he told Kaufmann. "And eliminate anyone who gets in the way, particularly the SSU's Kai Paterson."

The silence from the scientist wasn't what Jamieson had expected. "Is that a problem?" he demanded.

"My men lack finesse," Kaufmann reminded him. "The chip is too sensitive to risk in such clumsy hands. They're as likely to destroy it as bring it back safely."

"I thought the conditioning held up well at the beginning, giving them more subtlety."

"If you call it subtle to differentiate between shooting a man once in the head and pummeling him to a bloody pulp, then yes, they're more subtle in the early stages. We've never tested them successfully on such a delicate, sensitive mission."

"You will this time." Jamieson had to work hard to stop any hint of anger from leaching into his tone. "The man I currently have searching for the chip may no longer be trustworthy."

Tonelli had been a useful tool to date. His thirst for revenge had made him easy to manipulate. But Tonelli couldn't be allowed to tell anyone about Jamieson's interest in the chip. No one knew that his secret black-ops group, Kerberos, was depending on the chip to create mind-controlled superhumans. He'd already decided to send one of his special assassination teams after Tonelli once the man had turned over the chip. But now that Tonelli had missed his last check-in and left his hotel, Jamieson had to wonder what Tonelli was up to.

Jamieson well knew Tonelli's finicky nature. The man wouldn't have risked getting dirty and sweaty by going into the jungle after Dias. Which meant he was in hiding. If Tonelli was simply hiding because Kai Paterson had shown up, he wouldn't have missed his check-in. Which meant he was hiding from Jamieson.

He ran his thumb down the sleek leather border of his desktop blotter. Tonelli's death would have to wait. Assassination teams didn't come out of Kaufmann's lab. That skill set was too specialized yet for the scientist's program. Unfortunately, Kerberos's team of assassins was currently on assignment elsewhere.

Soon Kaufmann's lab would create subjects to specification. Mind controlled soldiers with enhanced strength and endurance. Spies with superior speed and intelligence. In the meantime, it wouldn't hurt to put this newest group of Kaufmann's men to work.

"I need your team as backup."

"Very well," Kaufmann replied. "Give me the details."

Saturday, Afternoon
Amazon Jungle

UNDERNEATH THE LEAN-TO he'd quickly constructed out of leafy branches, Kai checked Susana's pulse. Assured she was just sleeping, he indulged himself and just watched her for a few moments.

She'd been through hell the past twenty-four hours and she looked it. Her hair, which was a shiny, flowing mass in her modeling photos, was now a dull, tangled mess, sticking to her face and shoulders in sweaty clumps. She was filthy. Her skin was covered with scratches and bruises. And she stank of river water, mud and sweat.

Yet she still managed to be incredibly sexy. And it had nothing to do with her clothes or her appearance.

It was the vibrant, utterly female energy she gave off that pulled his eyes toward her. The angry flash of her eyes. Her muttered self-pep talks. And it was her unpredictability that kept him watching her, fascinated to see what she'd do next.

Despite knowing that as an archaeologist she'd worked in some of the roughest, end-of-the-earth places, he'd still expected more silk and fashion from the ex-model, instead of practical, high-tech working clothes.

He bit back a smile. There were hundreds of men who'd be disappointed to learn that the woman once voted one of the top ten sexiest women alive wore a plain black sports bra. And was so modest, she kept her shirt in front of her the entire time he'd worked on her.

Or maybe it was just a sign of how uneasy she was around Kai.

He rubbed the back of his neck, annoyed to discover that he didn't like the idea. His mission didn't depend upon her liking him. With the jungle and the mercenaries bringing out the violence in him, it was probably safer if she didn't fully trust him.

Yet he wanted not just her trust. He wanted her to like him.

Hell.

A bee flew toward Susana's face and Kai waved it away. He didn't want her waking up. She needed sleep.

And he needed to get the tracking device the hell away from her, so the other mercenaries couldn't find her. He grabbed the baggie with the device in it and crawled out of their hiding place. In the distance he heard men shouting. Shit. The second group of mercenaries had found their comrades sooner than he'd expected.

Memorizing landmarks so he could find Susana again, Kai headed toward the river. He wanted the mercenaries to think he and Susana had been flushed out of hiding and were making a break for it.

But Kai didn't make it more than several hundred feet before he broke into a sweat, the world tilted, and his stomach heaved.

Not now, dammit!

His body ignored him. Kai fell to his knees and vomited into the bushes. From experience, he knew the sickness would be gone in less than five minutes. Until then, he shook and heaved as his body tried to clear itself of the memory of death.

Murderer.

God, how did field operators like Rafe and his brother Niko handle the death that was part of their jobs? Every time Kai killed, he got sick. Yet he could never predict how long it would take for the vomiting to hit.

It was a damn good thing Rafe wasn't here to watch, because his friend would laugh his ass off. Then tease him about it for the rest of Kai's life.

His stomach gave one more lurch, then settled down. He could almost hear the damn thing saying, okay, all done now. Carry on.

Right.

And a guy whose body parts started talking to him was one hair shy of a straightjacket.

He wiped his mouth on his sleeve and pushed to his feet.

From the sound of muted conversation and snapping branches, the mercenaries were somewhere to his right, approaching fast. Just great. He was still feeling wobbly from his little episode. Not up to running through the jungle.

Kai put his hand out to steady himself on the branch of a tree. His skin met something warm and furry instead of cold bark.

The screech of an enraged monkey shattered the air.

Uh-oh. He'd somehow grabbed its tail.

The monkey met his eyes and leaped. Kai raised his arm to protect his head and the miniature creature latched onto his forearm, still screaming madly. Its claws dug into Kai's arm and its black, furry tail whipped Kai in the face.

Before it could escape, Kai grabbed the creature by the scruff of its neck. This was the answer to his dilemma. "Sorry, fella," he said. Holding the squirming monkey with his left hand, he pulled the baggie containing the tracking device out of his pocket with his right. Then, using his thumb, he forced the monkey's jaws apart and shook the tiny transmitter out of the baggie and into the monkey's open mouth.

The monkey glared at him and struggled to turn his head, but Kai held the creature's jaw shut and waited until it swallowed. Kai then opened its mouth to check that the tracker was indeed gone. Yep.

"Okay, you're free." He released the critter up a tree.

It scampered up the closest branch, then turned and hurled monkey curses at him, before disappearing further into the canopy.

The monkey was moving in the direction of the river. Leading their pursuers away from them.

Perfect.

Kai smiled and faded into the trees. He made one stop at a sluggish creek to fill the canteens, set the ultraviolet purifiers to work, then returned to Susana.

Saturday, Afternoon
Santarém, Brazil

"WHAT DO YOU MEAN, you've lost the woman?" Mark Tonelli demanded into the phone. "You said she was secure." Which was the only reason he'd left Belém and traveled further up the river to Santarém. He was supposed to be taking over control of Susana. Not learning she was gone.

"Yeah, well, see...she escaped. Went out the window and into the water, even though she was tied up." The lead mercenary didn't sound so much apologetic, as admiring of Susana's courage. "Some guy on a boat pulled her out of the river. They both survived the rocket attack."

"Rocket attack? I told you I need her alive."

"Yeah, but the other men said it didn't matter. Dead or alive, it's all the same."

Mark barely restrained himself from yelling. But the walls were thin in this cheap hotel and he couldn't afford to draw attention to himself. "Other men? I thought you said there was one man and he was with Dias." It had to be Paterson. The bastard.

"Well, yeah. But the guy who rescued her shot up our boat. We were sinking. Then this gunboat comes up, with a dozen men onboard. Mercenaries, but outfitted real well, like soldiers. They fired an RPG at the guy's boat. After, they pulled us aboard. Said they were hired to bring back the woman's body. They had a monitor for this tracking device their boss had shot into the woman." The man paused, and Mark could hear the sound of voices arguing on the other end of the line.

"But...uh...the guy and the woman made it to land. Now, the group that followed them are dead. And the tracking signal is out of range."

Shit. Mark rubbed between his eyes, but it didn't lessen the growing headache. The only person with close enough access to Susana to shoot a tracking device into her was his contact at the dig. He should never have partnered with someone holding such a grudge against her, but at the time he'd been desperate for information.

Unless he found Susana, he'd just lost his one chance at getting the name he needed from Jamieson. He winced at another stab of pain behind his eyes. He just wanted his revenge over with. He needed that damn chip.

And these imbeciles had managed to lose her.

"Where are you now?" he asked the mercenary.

"On the gunboat. They've got a team searching for the woman."

"And when it gets dark?"

"Don't know. Let me ask...uh...we're anchoring here tonight."

"Good. Tomorrow, you and your men head upriver to the archaeological dig and wait for Dias to arrive. There's a good chance she'll head back there. Don't let anyone see you. I'll warn my contact that Dias is alive and to notify you if she arrives."

"We...uh...don't have a boat."

Mark cursed. "Then you need to convince the other mercenaries that the best way to find Dias is to head to her dig. I don't care if you have to take over the gunboat, just get to her camp before she does! Notify me when you've arrived."

Mark pressed the off button and tossed the phone on the bed. He paced rapidly from door to window and back again. He was due to check in shortly, but he couldn't talk to Jamieson when he was this angry.

The next time I call, if you don't have the chip, I'm sending down a cleanup squad. And you're one of the items they're going to clean up.

Mark stopped pacing. He'd heard rumors about Jamieson's cleanup crews. Assassination crews, to be honest. Still, the odds of being found in this low-rent hotel were slim. Jamieson couldn't yet know he'd left Belém.

Could he?

To hell with it. Jamieson probably had someone watching

him. If not, there was always the possibility that the mercenaries he'd hired would talk to the wrong person.

Mark grabbed his suitcase out of the closet, added his toiletry kit, and was out the door within five minutes.

Amazon Jungle

"Uh...do you have any more aspirin?" Susana asked. "I think I might be running a fever."

Kai choked back an involuntary sound of dismay. Fever in the jungle was as potentially lethal as infection. He stepped toward her, hand raising to check her forehead. Then he shook his head. "The air is too hot, you're going to be warm to the touch either way."

He turned so his rear backpack faced her. "The first aid kit is in the front pouch. Right...no, your left side." He felt her rummaging around. Heard the rattle as she shook some pills out.

Then she moved next to him. With a tired smile, she said, "Okay, I'm ready."

Damn, she looked exhausted. No wonder, he'd been pushing them hard, knowing the mercenaries would eventually lose the signal from the monkey. And keep searching regardless.

Susana, bless her, hadn't complained once.

He frowned a little. She hadn't muttered, either. For a woman who talked to herself, a lot, her silence was disturbing.

She really must not be feeling well.

And why not? She'd nearly drowned, been kidnapped, seen violent death, had minor surgery performed on her, and raced through the jungle. She had to be both in pain and exhausted.

Yet she kept going, regardless.

Kai wanted to kiss her.

Out of respect. Comfort. A show of strength. Who the hell knew.

Just because.

And if he stood here being sappy all evening, they'd never find a place to make camp before the lowering sun disappeared completely. "Hang in there just a little longer. I promise we'll make camp soon."

Susana hummed slightly in acknowledgement. Or maybe it was disbelief.

He walked past her and started along the faint animal track they'd been following.

Fifteen minutes later he heard the murmur of running water ahead and noticed that the trees thinned to his right. He changed course and discovered a patch of uncluttered ground perhaps fifteen feet by twenty. More importantly, two sturdy trees at the far edge had just the right distance between them for the hammock.

Susana stumbled to a halt next to him. Her skin was stretched tight at her eyes and mouth, showing her exhaustion. He felt a twinge of guilt, then immediately directed it at her father.

If Nevsky hadn't implanted the chip in her, none of this would have happened.

"We'll set up camp here," he told her.

She nodded and just stood there as if now that they'd stopped, her body didn't know what to do with itself. He put his hands on her shoulders and guided her over to a fallen tree. "Sit," he said gently. He took off the backpacks and set them at her feet, then pulled out the foldable water jug, purification tablets, and the small purifying system.

"Guard the packs while I fetch water." He was also going to scout around to make sure there was no sign of wildlife, but she didn't need to hear that.

"Okay." Her voice was thick and slurred. He figured she'd be asleep when he returned ten minutes later, but she was awake.

Sort of.

Her eyes were open and looking across the clearing, but he couldn't say if she recognized what she saw.

He placed the gallon jug full of water on the ground. The purification tablets would have it drinkable by morning. A smaller amount of water was running through the UV purifying system in the canteens. Satisfied that they'd soon have enough water to drink, he set about quietly unpacking the supplies. He pulled out the hammock and strung it up, then draped the mosquito net across the top.

There were facial wipes in the pack and he used one to clean himself up. Then he dug out the insect repellent and sprayed himself. The light was about to go and the insects swarmed, searching for food.

He repeated the cleaning routine on Susana. She blinked up at him when he touched her, but otherwise was non-responsive. He checked her pupil response, which was normal, and her temperature, which was only slightly elevated at one hundred.

So her near-catatonic state was just exhaustion. And shock.

Kai checked to make sure her bandages were still secure and not bleeding through, but left them alone.

"Hold out your arms. I need to spray you with bug repellent."

Susana obeyed, but her arms quivered and she couldn't quite get them all the way up to shoulder level. Feeling an odd tug in his chest at this sign of how deeply depleted her energy was, he sprayed her quickly so she didn't have to hold her arms up for long. Then he got his hands wet with the stuff and carefully applied it to her face, trying his best to avoid the cuts and scrapes.

When he was done, he stuck a straw into a packet of energy drink and made sure she swallowed the whole thing. She needed the electrolytes.

Once she was finished, he lifted Susana into his arms.

She was asleep before he took two steps, not even stirring when he placed her in the hammock and tucked in the mosquito net.

For a few moments he allowed himself the luxury of watching her, taking an inordinate amount of pride in having her safe and under his protection.

"I won't let anyone hurt you again." The quiet promise slipped out of his mouth with a conviction that shocked him.

What the hell was he doing? He knew better. Protection wasn't something that could be guaranteed. He'd thought by working to keep biochemical weapons out of the hands of terrorists, he'd make the world safe for his family.

Instead, his work had led to their deaths.

Yet his promise to Susana rang through him, firming his muscles with resolve. Practical or not, he knew this was a promise he'd die trying to keep.

CHAPTER SEVEN

Sunday, Morning
Rocky Mountains, Montana

"Niko."

Every hair on Niko Andros's neck jumped to attention. His younger brother's voice was barely recognizable, little more than an animalistic growl across the phone line.

"Rafe. What's wrong? Where are you?" Niko's worried voice caused his wife, Jenna, to glance at him in alarm. His brother had been missing for two months, ever since Ryker, their boss at the SSU, had sent Rafe and his team to take out a lab run by Nevsky's former second in command, Dr. Kaufmann.

"God, Rafe," Niko said. "We've been searching frantically for you."

On the other end of the line, Rafe gave what might be called a harsh laugh, but sounded more like an engine choking. "In trouble, bro. Ouch...Shit..."

"Rafe!" Niko's fingers tightened on his cell phone as if he could force the pain away from his brother.

"Ah...sorry...headaches..." His brother cut off with a gasp of pain.

"Stay with me, Rafe. What happened?"

Niko heard Rafe take several shuddering breaths. He was afraid his brother wouldn't answer, but finally, Rafe continued.

"Security...waiting for us...others dead..."

Ah, fuck.

"Gave me...drugs."

"Jesus Christ!"

An icy fist squeezed Niko's heart. *Dios, por favor*, not his brother. Kaufmann had been continuing Nevsky's work and there was currently no way to reverse the mental and physical changes caused by Kaufmann's drugs. Subjects only lived a few months. By the time the drugs caused an internal hemorrhaging that killed the host, the men had deteriorated to being little more than enraged animals.

"New...treatment...accelerated results...aagh!"

Niko stared helplessly down at his wife, surprised to find her hand tightly gripping his own.

"Rafe, where are you?"

Another frightening laugh. "New York City. Heading...to Brazil...They...ordered me...find Kai...kill him...Kill anyone... tries to...stop me...Ordered...get chip...get Susana Dias."

"Rafe, what has the drug done to you?" When they'd first learned that Rafe was going after the lab, Niko had insisted on learning everything the SSU knew about the drugs. He'd needed to understand what his brother was up against.

According to the doctor who'd once worked at Kaufmann's lab, his treatment program increased muscle strength and mass, turned off pain receptors, reduced the body's need for sleep, and opened up the mind, making the subject highly suggestible. It also dimmed intelligence and destroyed the ability to tell right from wrong. Subjects did exactly what their handlers told them to do, and were as unwavering and unstoppable in their mission as robots.

"Body," Rafe panted. "Small changes...mind...shit, I'm losing it again...mind only sometimes my own...headaches when can think inde-pend-dent-ly...otherwise, only think of mission... shit...I'm losing control again...will try to...slow myself...down... Please, Niko, you gotta...stop me...do whatever you have to do... don't let me succeed...They tell me...hate you...hate everyone... can't do it...can't kill you all..."

"Rafe!" Niko tried to draw his brother back via his voice.

But on a harsh groan, the line went dead.

Niko squeezed his eyes closed. Holy Christ, his fear all but suffocated him. They'd recently lost their father. He couldn't lose Rafe, too.

Jenna's arms encircled him from behind and she pressed her cheek between his shoulder blades.

"What's wrong with Rafe?"

Niko spun around and crushed her in a desperate hug, needing her warmth and vitality to chase away the chill of fear. He didn't know how long he held her, absorbing her strength and soaking up the comforting words she offered. Then, in a shaking voice, he began to explain. "Rafe has been sent to kill your brother..."

Sunday, Morning
Amazon Jungle

"Let's head toward the river," Kai told Susana as they prepared to leave the campsite the next morning.

She was feeling much better today. Kai had let her sleep late, then fed her a meal in a pouch that was passably close to being eggs, and some energy drink. He must have been a Boy Scout as a kid, because the depth of his supplies was mind-boggling.

He'd had the hammock and mosquito net stowed by the time she'd finished eating. He strapped on both backpacks, ignoring her protests that she could carry one. But he'd agreed that because she was more familiar with the jungle, she should lead today.

His suggestion to get closer to the river made sense. Not only would they be able to use the river as a navigation aid, letting them know which way was upstream toward her camp, but if a search party from her dig was out on the water, she needed to be able to signal them.

She knew Jacie and the others would organize a search party. Yet even if someone had witnessed her being pushed into the river and convinced the supply boat captain to follow immediately, the current would have quickly carried her out of sight.

"Susana?" Kai prodded, making her realize he'd been speaking to her. "You okay?"

She shrugged. "Just thinking about my crew. They've got to be worried sick. When they don't find me, they're going to think I'm dead. Or that I've been kidnapped by the person who's been trying to shut the dig down."

"You mentioned something about that before. Tell me what's been going on."

She shoved aside a hanging vine before it slapped her in the eye. As concisely as possible, she told him about the property damage and the threatening notes.

"It has to be the same person who knocked me into the river," she concluded.

"No," Kai said. "The person behind the threats targeted the entire dig, not just you. Having you disappear into the river won't make the others go home, will it?"

Susana hesitated. "Not right away. They'll stay and search for me. Then most of them will probably stick around and work until the first scheduled break. But after that?" She shrugged. "The funding comes through my contract with the Adventure Channel.

I don't know if the producers care enough about the site itself to finish excavation."

"Right. So if someone wanted the site closed, he or she had to force all of your staff to leave. But the mercenaries only needed your abdomen in order to retrieve the chip, and the tracking device gave them an easy way to locate you."

Susana flinched. God, it made her sound like a thing instead of a person. "But...that means there's one person in camp in league with the mercenaries. Plus a second person vandalizing the site?"

"Most likely."

"Damn. I can't believe one of my crew is involved. It makes no sense."

"How well do you know them?"

"Most of them have been with me for years. I trust them absolutely. I like to have consistency. And that's particularly important after my deal with the Adventure Channel. Viewers want to see the same people on each show. It gives them a better chance to identify with us." She'd much rather think of a stranger hiding in the jungle, coming out only to wreak havoc, than to think one of her crew hated her enough to conspire to have her killed.

She glanced back in time to see Kai raise his eyebrows in disbelief.

"It's not one of them," she insisted. "I trust them with my life. Out in the jungle, you have to know and trust your crew. They're all the support you have."

"Just like you trusted Elena Dominguez?"

Susana planted her feet and spun around. "How do you know about that?"

"Background report."

Susana narrowed her eyes, hating that she couldn't get beyond her past. "That was five years ago. And Elena and I only worked together on that one dig. Yes, she betrayed me. But I didn't have the level of trust in her that I do with my crew."

Kai just shrugged. The cynical, almost pitying look in his eyes made her want to shake him. Instead, she muttered a string of curses and turned her attention to the path she was clearing.

Elena had been an average archaeologist. Not as smart or lucky as some, but she'd had some minor successes. Unfortunately, she'd resented Susana's assignment to spearhead a large dig. When valuable artifacts went missing from the site, Elena had accused Susana of selling them on the black market. Even after Susana was proven innocent, it took years to restore her reputation. Her contract with the Adventure Channel had restored her credibility with the public, but plenty of her colleagues still saw her either as a brainless bimbo who'd been falsely credited with successes that rightly belonged to the men she'd worked with, or considered her a fortune hunter.

Susana knew she was lucky to have a crew that believed in her one hundred percent. She didn't care what Kai suggested. He wasn't going to seed her mind with suspicion. Maybe Kai didn't understand the idea of trust and loyalty, but she did. Her crew was her family far more than her mother had ever been.

She trusted them.

SEVERAL HOURS later they stopped for a break by a small stream.

"Let me check your bandages," Kai said. He dumped the packs on the ground and turned to face Susana.

She nodded and started to unbutton her shirt. Her finger slipped the first button out of its hole. Then some change in the air made her pause and look up.

Kai stood in front of her. His head was lowered, eyes trans-fixed on her hands where they hovered above the next button.

Her heart stuttered. The thick, humid air grew even heavier, sexual tension clinging to every damp molecule.

And suddenly it felt like she was performing a striptease.

Slowly, hands unsteady, she undid the second button. God,

she felt as nervous as she had the first time she'd posed for the camera, back when she was thirteen. The photographer had asked her to undo the very top button on her blouse, the one holding the fabric together under her chin. Unused to having a roomful of strangers watching her, she'd been unable to work the button free because her hands were shaking so badly.

Much as they were now.

No more than two inches of skin showed, but she felt exposed. It was ridiculous. She'd modeled for over ten years, changing clothes countless times in front of total strangers. Posing nude a time or two.

And she'd stripped for lovers.

But somehow, with Kai still standing a good three feet away and him not even meeting her eyes, she felt the power of her own sexuality like never before. She was filthy, sweaty and bloody, and she'd have sworn her body was too exhausted to feel desire. Yet every nerve was deliriously awake.

She needed to undo one more button in order to expose the bandage on her back. Watching Kai's head, she slipped the button free one millimeter at a time.

With a delicate shrug of her shoulders the fabric fell back, exposing her collarbones.

Kai sucked in a breath and finally looked up.

Oh, God. She'd never seen such a look before. Here was desire at its most elemental...wild and pure. Turning his eyes into pools of molten gold that sucked her under.

An answering heat flared to life in her veins.

She stared, feeling both trapped and free. Vulnerable and strong. A shiver skittered across her skin, raising goose bumps. Anticipation? Or fear?

The breath in her lungs evaporated.

She waited for Kai to do something. Step forward. Touch her. Kiss her.

Not sure if she would welcome him or flee into the safety of the woods, but knowing that she needed him to act. Needed him to break this delicious, maddening tension.

Instead, Kai flinched. The fire in his eyes disappeared as if doused by ice water, switching him from an aroused male ready to pounce, to a cool stranger. His eyes swept over her once, impersonally, then he spun away from her, like he couldn't bear looking at her another moment.

Susana glared at his back. What was that all about? She'd never seen a man change expressions so quickly, and she'd known quite a few excellent actors.

"I'll check your bandages later," Kai threw back over his shoulder. His voice was so hard, if she hadn't witnessed it herself, she'd never have believed that a moment ago he'd wanted to jump her.

He grabbed a canteen and headed upstream. "When I get back, we're moving out."

"To hell with you," she called after his retreating back. She was childishly pleased to note his hands clenched and unclenched at his sides as he walked away.

She shivered and hitched up her shirt.

What on earth had he seen in her eyes to make him flee? Okay, she'd been stunned, and a little frightened by his look, but also turned on. Had he somehow missed that last bit? Had he run away because he thought she didn't want him?

Stupid man.

But no...the look he'd shot her before he turned his back on her had been unfriendly. Maybe he didn't *want* to want her.

Maybe he couldn't wait to get out of the jungle and away from her and the trouble that was after her. "Cowardly bastard," she muttered.

Truth was, it didn't matter why. Kai didn't want her. Fine.

She would just forget the whole thing. Pretend that the heat had been her imagination.

She jammed a button through its hole.

Really. He hadn't even kissed her. How hard could this be?

CHAPTER EIGHT

Sunday, Afternoon
Santarém, Brazil

"Your man Tonelli was in Santarém, not Belém." The agent's voice crackled over the satellite connection. "Knew we were coming, too. Bastard snuck out of his hotel. Our point man saw him take a taxi toward the docks, so we gave chase. The taxi driver was good, though. We knocked the vehicle off the road, but he got it back under control and got away from us."

Jamieson let his silence communicate his rage. Cursing was so uncouth. "Find him," he ordered after a sufficient amount of time had passed.

There was only one reason Tonelli would run. He'd lost Dias.

Jamieson wasn't giving the man any more chances. "The job has changed. Don't just scare Tonelli. Eliminate him."

"You need proof?"

"Yes. Full body. Don't bother me again until it's done." Jamieson replaced the receiver in its cradle. Had Tonelli run to Paterson and the SSU for help? Or was he going after Dias and the chip on his own?

Jamieson sighed. He'd had big hopes for the man. No matter. Kaufmann's team was ready. They'd take care of finding the chip.

Amazon Jungle

THANK GOD, Susana wasn't speaking to him. Because Kai didn't want to talk about that supercharged look they'd shared. Hell, he still hadn't recovered. He'd been walking around half hard for the past two hours.

Susana had no idea how close he'd come to pouncing on her. She'd met his eyes almost shyly, and his primitive instincts had exploded, ready to devour her. To claim her as his mate.

He'd wanted his mouth against hers. His tongue on her skin. Her body flush against his.

The need hit him so fast, with such animal ferocity, he'd almost lost control. But then he'd realized she was frozen, in what appeared to be fear, and his desire vanished. He'd been terrified that Susana had seen some of the violence swirling inside him and hadn't felt safe.

Hell he'd scared himself with the surge of uncharacteristic possessiveness he'd felt. Even now his instincts screamed *mine* when he thought of Susana.

Damn jungle. He had to get out of here. He rolled his shoulders, ignoring the familiar throb of tissues damaged when the bone had been dislocated during torture intended to get him to reveal the location of the chip.

Kai placed his hand on the branch Susana had held back for him, but made sure he didn't meet her eyes or touch her. Until he knew that this gut-wrenching, got-to-have-this-particular-woman-now-or-I'll-die feeling toward Susana wasn't part of the aftermath of killing the mercenaries, he didn't dare touch her. She deserved better than that.

He bit his tongue, forcing back the urge to apologize for

scaring her with his raw need. For having to cut into her to remove the tracking device. For killing the mercenaries in front of her.

Useless words.

Up ahead, Susana stomped down the path she was forging, leaving a thick wake of anger behind her. Good. Let her stay mad. That was better than the flash of hurt he'd seen on her face just before he'd turned his back on her.

Silence was better than questions he couldn't answer.

As he lengthened his steps to catch up with her, he caught a whiff of her scent. Need twisted through his belly. He swallowed heavily and focused on placing one foot rapidly in front of the other. Just a few more days of ignoring his attraction to her and they'd be at her camp.

A few more days of keeping his hands to himself. Of doing everything in his power to make sure Susana kept her emotional distance so he wouldn't be tempted to give in to this mess of need swirling inside him.

Once they reached her camp he'd get on the radio and call for an extraction.

And the temptation of Susana would be taken out of his hands.

Sunday, Evening
Washington, D.C.

THE DIRECTOR of the SSU snatched up his personal cell phone on the fifth ring. "Ryker."

"Rafe's been compromised," Niko Andros said, his voice crackling with fear.

"Details?" Ryker fired his damp gym towel at the nearest flat surface and watched it land on his scarred cherry credenza, narrowly missing a classified government file.

"I don't know much. Kaufmann's security was waiting for his team. Some of them are dead. Rafe—" Niko's voice choked off.

Ryker waited for Niko to get control.

"Rafe was injected with Kaufmann's drugs. Put through the mind control program..." Niko took a deep breath. "His mission is to kill Kai and Susana Dias, then retrieve the chip. He called me from New York City. He—"

Another crack in Niko's usually steady voice, but Ryker couldn't blame him. So far, no one had survived these drugs.

"Rafe...doesn't have many moments of clarity," Niko continued. "He's already experiencing headaches."

Ryker strode over to the battered nineteenth century globe resting in the corner of his office. According to Dr. Gabrielle Montague, the woman who'd fled from Kaufmann's lab, Kaufmann's subjects experienced headaches only after approaching Level 3, which typically occurred at week eleven. It usually took three to four weeks for a subject to achieve Level 1 status, the most optimal stage of the progression. One month after reaching Level 1 the subjects would start deteriorating into Level 2. When they reached Level 5, their internal organs failed and the subjects died. Since Rafe had only disappeared slightly over seven weeks ago, something must have changed in Kaufmann's formula to accelerate Rafe toward Level 3 so quickly.

And it meant Rafe likely didn't have the full three months before his mind and body self-destructed.

Ryker had sent a recovery team in after Rafe's first missed report, but the lab had burned to the ground. There'd been no trail to follow and the subdermal tracking devices in Rafe and his men had gone dark, suggesting they were either alive and underground. Or dead.

Ryker allowed himself a moment of relief that Rafe was alive, before demanding, "He specifically mentioned Dias?"

"Yes."

Ryker swore softly, turned away from the globe, and started

pacing back and forth across the office. He hadn't given Dias's name to Rafe for precisely this reason. If captured, he wouldn't be able to tip the enemy off about Nevsky's daughter.

Which meant the spy within the SSU was more dangerous than Ryker thought. Or maybe there was more than one spy. He could name several government and private security organizations that wanted the SSU to fail.

On his next pass in front of the credenza, Ryker snatched up his towel and finished drying the remaining sweat from his neck and back. The loose, energetic feeling he'd gotten from sparring with his sensei faded.

Ryker snapped the towel against his leg. The spy had discovered not only the name of Nevsky's daughter, but also learned about Rafe's mission to investigate Kaufmann's lab.

Since Mark Tonelli had been present when Niko learned that Nevsky had a daughter, then unnamed, it was possible Tonelli or his CIA colleagues had done their own research, discovered Dias's name, and let it slip to someone who was associated with Kaufmann's lab.

But only a select few within the SSU had been aware of Rafe's mission. That made the search for the spy a little easier.

"We've tried to raise Kai on his sat phone," Niko said. "No answer. When's the last time he checked in?"

"Ah…" Kai was on a forty-eight hour cycle for reporting in by text message. Ryker counted back. "Two days ago. He was on the river on his way to Dias's camp. His next scheduled report is in three hours."

Ryker spun the globe, watching the continents fly past. Two years ago, Kai had failed to check in while undercover at Nevsky's lab. When Ryker learned that an explosion had destroyed the lab and killed Nevsky, he hadn't wanted to believe Kai was responsible. Or that Kai had stolen the microchip. But the security video showed Kai fleeing the fire. That, plus additional evidence, had eventually forced Ryker to consider Kai a traitor.

He'd sent SSU agents after Kai, but they'd never been able to catch him.

Six months ago Kai had resurfaced and the truth had come out. Kai had been framed. He'd been searching for the microchip the entire time, trying to prove his innocence while staying alive.

Ryker was not going to doubt Kai now. If he didn't check in on schedule, Ryker would assume Kai was in trouble, locate him via the subdermal tracker, and send backup.

"It's possible he's out of range," Niko offered.

"Possible. Or Rafe got to him."

"I don't think he's had time. He was in New York this morning."

"That's assuming he was telling the truth."

Niko's silence was painful. "Yeah, but...even though they may be controlling Rafe, I'm going with my gut on this. I believe him."

"I assume you're on your way to Brazil?"

"Right. Uh...Jenna's going with me."

Ryker smiled. Niko's wife had trained to be an SSU agent for the wrong reasons and was now pursuing a career in wildlife rehabilitation, but she still had good instincts. Top that with a fierce protectiveness for her brother, and...

Hell. Niko's brother versus Jenna's brother. Wasn't that a lose-lose situation?

"Tell me when and where your flight's landing and I'll have a team at your disposal," Ryker told Niko.

The silence on the other end was potent. Ryker's muscles tensed and he forced them to relax.

Finally Niko said, "I'll need some sort of...tranquilizer gun."

Ryker's fingers dug into the towel he was still holding. Dammit, he hated the unspoken message in Niko's words. If he couldn't stop Rafe with a tranq, he'd be forced to kill his brother.

Rafe wasn't just a good agent. He was a brilliant strategist with a personality that was equally comfortable teasing playfully or going for the jugular. Over the past nine months, Ryker had started training Rafe to be his successor, exposing Rafe to the political and fundraising side of the SSU. The machinations Ryker used to keep the SSU running with access to the best technology, yet without being beholden to men with selfish goals, were sometimes Machiavellian. Rafe had a rare gift for navigating that path, yet had only reluctantly agreed to eventually take over the job.

Ryker would find someone else to replace him as SSU director, but no one could replace Rafe as a friend.

Ryker thought about his schedule for the day and mentally juggled commitments.

The faster Kai retrieved the chip, the better. Lacking access to Kaufmann's lab and the details of what had been done to Rafe, the SSU would have to hope Nevsky's notes provided enough data to allow their scientists to develop an antidote.

Ryker eyed the door to his office bathroom with regret. He no longer had time to shower. He needed to meet with Dr. Montague. She'd run from Kaufmann's lab when she realized the drug she'd formulated to combat the rages suffered by veterans exposed to certain chemical and biological agents was being used by Kaufmann to strengthen control over his subjects.

Dr. Montague would be a pivotal part of the team to save Rafe. He'd get her started on locating an appropriately secluded lab and assembling a team of scientists.

God, they'd better be able to save Rafe. "I'll make sure the team has the tranquilizer you need, properly calibrated for Rafe's body weight," he told Niko.

"Appreciate it."

Ryker paused, deliberating what to say next. To hell with it. Words wouldn't ease Niko's pain. "Good luck."

"Thanks." Niko's voice was thick and he cleared his throat.

Ryker couldn't leave it on such a grim note. Rafe would have lightened it with humor. "Say, Andros?"

"Yeah?"

"Keep your wife in line."

Niko's faint chuckle made Ryker's mouth curl up in a fragmented smile.

Godspeed, my friend. You'll need it.

Sunday, Afternoon
Amazon Jungle

"ARE YOU CRAZY?" Susana demanded, gesturing toward the pale slice of river that glimmered through the trees. "Do you have any idea how wide the river is? How strong the current? I don't care if you have an inflatable raft in that bottomless backpack of yours. There's no way we can safely cross."

Kai just shrugged. Actually, his plan was to build a raft. Which admittedly sounded even crazier. And yeah, he'd already considered all of Susana's arguments. Plus the fact that the current would invariably carry them downriver, only adding to their hiking time once they were back on land.

Not to mention the possibility that the mercenaries and their boat would be searching for them.

"Listen," he said, trying to sound reasonable and confident, even though Susana was definitely the expert on all things Amazon. "Your dig is on the other side of the river. We have to cross sometime. The mercenaries won't expect us to try it this far downriver. Would you rather risk the current or automatic gunfire?"

Susana made a sound of disgust. "You're crazy."

"Come on, where's your sense of adventure?"

"Hmm...let me think. I must have left it behind when I was kidnapped. Or when I nearly drowned in the river. Or...maybe when I saw you kill four men with a single sweep of your gun."

Ouch. Well, he'd wanted Susana pissed at him, hadn't he?

They pushed through a strand of skinny saplings and there it was, the raging Amazon. Yeah, it was damn far to the opposite bank, but he thought they could make it. Especially if he acted as a rudder and swam behind the raft to steer it.

Leaving Susana on the raft so her wounds wouldn't be exposed to more of the bacteria-laden water. Or piranha. Which he would *not* allow himself to think about.

Unfortunately, the current here was too strong. Plus, there were tiny rapids. He shook his head.

"Told you so," Susana grumbled.

He raised his eyebrows and gestured for her to lead the way. "So find us a calmer crossing, Jane of the Jungle."

Muttering under her breath in Portuguese, Susana pushed past him, heading upriver.

CHAPTER NINE

Something was wrong with Kai. They'd continued to follow the river, but still hadn't located a place where the current was calm enough to consider crossing.

On a raft.

They had, however, been forced to lay low a few times. Once when they heard a gunshot deeper in the forest. Another time they'd heard the tramp of multiple feet moving fast with no attempt to be quiet. Kai had pulled her to the ground behind a thick clump of vegetation. She'd waited with her heart lodged next to her tonsils as the noise grew closer, certain they were going to be found and killed.

And then a herd of wild pigs had burst through the undergrowth.

She'd bitten down hard on her swollen lip to stop herself from breaking into hysterical laughter.

Now, she watched as Kai shrugged his jacket collar further up his neck as if he was cold. Today's temperature had to be in the nineties, with matching humidity and Susana was sweltering inside her breathable, long-sleeved shirt. Just looking at Kai wearing that jacket threatened to give her heat stroke. Yet he'd just run his hands up and down his arms, as if trying to warm himself up.

What was going on?

And he wasn't walking right. She'd spent hours hiking behind him yesterday, memorizing the graceful, jaguar-powerful way he walked that said he owned the forest and every other creature had better get the hell out of his way.

Yet at the same time, he managed to walk quietly.

Not now, though. He crashed through the vegetation. Instead of rolling his weight from his toes to his heels as he walked, he now plopped each foot straight down, as if he wore concrete shoes and lacked the strength to lift his leg.

He also held his arms stiffly at his sides instead of letting them swing free.

Something was definitely wrong. She stopped and started to walk back to him just as Kai ducked under a low-hanging branch. He stumbled and went down on one knee.

"Kai?" She reached out to help him up, but he slapped her hand away. He tried to brace himself against a tree trunk, but his whole arm shook so hard he missed his target.

She knelt down beside him. Dear God, his teeth were chattering. "Kai, what's wrong?"

"C—c—cold. M—ma—la—ria." He pressed his lips together as a particularly violent spasm shook him.

"No," Susana said soothingly. "You haven't been in the jungle long enough for malaria to incubate."

Kai shook his head and met her eyes for the first time since that heated glance. The fear and vulnerability she saw there shocked her.

"H—hel—p, m—me."

Malaria or not, he was sick. "Okay," she said brusquely. "You lie down. I'll find a safe place for us to rest."

"N-no." His jaw was clenched so tightly, she could see the

muscles bulging. But he managed to fight back the stuttering. "Stay with you."

She knew enough about stubbornness not to argue. "Okay, but I'll take the backpacks."

Kai glared at her and stepped away, holding fast to the straps.

"Idiot, stubborn, macho, male," Susana grumbled. "See if I catch you when that extra weight makes you fall on your face."

She thought she saw him roll his eyes before she started searching for a place to make camp.

It took them twice as long as it should have to move forward because Kai was unsteady on his feet. But after twenty minutes, she finally found what they needed.

A tangle of vines had grown over the exposed roots of a toppled tree until the vines formed a sort of blanket. Susana stuck her head inside and found a space wide enough to allow both of them to lay down, and tall enough to sit without bumping her head.

Best of all, the spot was only a hundred yards from a stream.

"We'll make camp here. Why don't you settle yourself inside? I'll collect wood for a fire."

"W—wait. You h—help. M—medi—cine."

"Kai, we don't—"

He shook his head. "In...p—pack."

"You have medicine in your backpack?"

He nodded.

It figured. The man really was prepared for everything. "Okay." She followed him into the shelter.

Kai shrugged out of his pack and rummaged inside. A moment later he held up a rolled-up black canvas pouch. He unrolled it and lifted the flap. Held inside by sturdy leather ties were a glass vial, a syringe and a metallic strip of plastic-protected pills. A piece of rubber tubing peeked out of a pocket.

Whoa. This wasn't your typical first aid kit. When he'd said he needed medicine, she'd thought aspirin, not...whatever this was.

She glanced up at him, then back down at the syringe. Was he an addict of some sort? Was he undergoing withdrawal?

But then Kai pointed to the foil-covered pills. "N—need one. P—please."

There was a familiar name on the package. One of the more powerful drugs used to treat malaria. Oh, God, he'd been telling the truth.

She released one of the pills and handed it to him. "You really do have malaria?"

Kai nodded and popped the pill into his mouth. His shaking had subsided enough to allow him to drink from his canteen without too much spillage.

"But...how?"

"I...uh...picked up a mutant strain of malaria a while back. During an...assignment...in Indonesia." His teeth stopped chattering enough for him to speak normally. "There's no incubation period. The doctors haven't been able to cure me completely, only to get me into longer hibernation periods."

"So, if a mosquito bites you and the mosquito carries the malaria parasite, could that influx of new parasites tip you over into an attack?" Thank God he'd been using insect repellent. She'd seen him spray himself. Plus, there was the mosquito net. She frowned over a sudden hunch.

He shrugged and glanced away, which increased her suspicion.

"You only have one hammock and one mosquito net," she said, not liking where this train of thought was leading. "Dammit, look at me. Is that right? You've been sleeping without a mosquito net?"

Kai met her eyes, but he was good. His expression gave nothing away. Yet his very lack of response made her certain she was right. How could he be so stupid? Did he think she would be glad he put himself at risk for her?

She moved closer to him, letting anger darken her voice,

while keeping the volume down in case the remaining mercenaries were still out there somewhere close by. "Are you *nuts*? You come into the jungle knowing that all you need is a single mosquito bite and you'll be back in the middle of a full-blown malaria attack and you give *me* the mosquito net?" She shoved him, but since he was sitting down, all that did was make his upper body sway.

"Talk about suicidal!"

Kai just shrugged. The casual way he brushed off her concern made Susana growl in frustration. "Stop acting like it's no big deal. I've had friends die from malaria, dammit!"

He gave her one of those placating smiles doctors used with crazy people. "I'm not going to die. The attacks last a day or two, max, then I'm f—fine. Sh—shit." He started shaking again.

Susana lunged forward and caught the canteen before it spilled.

Kai wrapped his arms around himself and closed his eyes while the tremors became more violent.

Watching him fight the shakes, Susana lost her anger. Feeling helpless, she dug through the backpacks while she waited for this latest attack to finish. Damn, he really was prepared for anything. She found enough ready-to-eat meals and nutrition bars to last them at least three more days. She also counted five energy-drink packets, three add-water-to-reconstitute soup packets, and maybe a quarter cup of instant coffee granules. He had plenty of water purification tablets, an extensive first aid kit, more ammunition than she hoped they'd ever need, a map, matches, binoculars, a survival blanket, a folding, solar powered lantern, and a Biel tool.

The combination pike, claw and axe would come in handy for cutting down branches to make her a bed, so she set the Biel within easy reach.

By the time Kai's shaking subsided, she'd made him a bed by laying out the hammock on the ground and putting the survival blanket on top. She tried to get him to lie down immediately, but he shook his head.

"I need the other drug." He nodded at his medicine kit.

While she retrieved the canvas pouch, he removed his jacket and rolled up the left sleeve of his shirt. "Tie the tubing just below my elbow."

His arm trembled slightly as she complied. "Kai, what's in the vial?"

"An experimental new malaria treatment for mutant parasites. Supposed to be fast-acting. First the pill, then the intravenous solution." He removed the syringe and vial from the pouch. "Should stop the symptoms within twenty-four hours." As if he'd done it a hundred times before, Kai inserted the syringe into the top of the vial.

"Have you ever taken this drug before?"

"No." He pulled the syringe out and pumped it to remove any air bubbles. "The doctors had me on something different before. Not as powerful. This is an emergency drug only."

She shot him a look. "And you're willing to just take it on faith that it'll work?"

He shrugged. "Don't have much choice. Nothing else has proven effective." He made a fist with his left hand, then stuck the needle into his vein.

He nodded at the rubber tubing and she released it.

"Am I going to have to do this for you?" she asked.

"Yeah, probably. I'll need another dose of two cc's in twenty-four hours."

Susana bit her lip. She didn't think this was the time to tell Kai that she'd never given an intravenous injection before. Somehow she'd manage.

He withdrew the needle, cleaned it with an alcohol wipe, and replaced it and the three-quarters filled vial in the pouch. As he rolled up the pouch and replaced it in the backpack, she noticed how his hands vibrated with tiny tremors.

Her eyes scanned his face, cataloguing the lines of strain around his eyes and mouth. She touched his cheek gently, and found it cool beneath her skin.

Too cool for this hot weather.

Don't freak. Kai needs you to stay strong. She swallowed back panic and tried to convince herself he'd be fine. After all, she'd grown up with malaria. There hadn't been a month when someone on the ranches didn't come down with chills and fever. Susana had suffered through it a time or two herself.

But Kai wasn't from a malaria-prone area. He didn't have the resistance she did. Plus, he had a mutant strain of the parasite. For all she knew, the attacks were totally different for him.

"I...uh...may say some things while I'm out of it. Just...ah... ignore me, okay?" Kai kept his eyes on his hands as he spoke.

Was he blushing? "Okay," she told him. What on earth was he afraid of telling her?

"If you need to leave, to, you know, attend to personal...ah... business, that's okay. There's a primitive alarm system in the front pouch of my pack. I'll show you how to set it up."

She opened the pocket and pulled out a wooden rod as long as her hand. A thin green and brown wire was wrapped around it. At the bottom, hanging from a tiny peg, was a camouflage-colored blob.

He explained how to string the wire at calf-level around their camp. The blob, which turned out to be a tiny sound box, would be positioned to the right of the entrance to their shelter. "To arm it, you attach the end of the wire to this node here." He pointed to a silver nub on the underside of the blob. "The battery is supposed to last a month on one charge, so you don't need to worry about it dying. When you need to leave, just unhook the wire and re-hook it behind you."

"You set this up around last night's camp?"

He nodded. "It's simple, but it does the job. I doubt the mercenaries would be expecting it. Even if they knew what to look for, it's hard to spot in the dark."

He told her to hook it up, then had her push the wire down.

The box emitted a series of sharp, steady chirps, like a mechanical cricket.

"In the middle of the night the sound will carry clearly. It's close enough to an insect's call that it will take a hunter a moment to realize it's not a natural sound, giving us time to get away."

"Clever."

"In case something goes wrong with the alarm system, take this." Kai thrust his gun at her.

Susana tried to hide her revulsion as he showed her how to operate it. She remembered all too well how easily this weapon had killed the mercenaries. It was far more sophisticated than the shotgun she used at camp to protect against wild animals and thieves.

Kai lay down and Susana helped him roll up in the survival blanket. Then he turned his back to her.

Trying not to feel shut out, Susana picked up the Biel, the lantern, and the mosquito net and moved outside.

An hour later she had the mosquito net strung over their shelter to provide more protection against insects, had cut enough branches to form a bed for herself and to camouflage the top of their shelter, and had strung the security system. She'd also created a small fire pit in an area she'd cleared several feet away. She couldn't keep a fire going for long, because it would give away their position, but she wanted to get some hot liquids into Kai.

With the solar lantern charging in a patch of fading sunlight, Susana filled up their canteens at the stream, then heated some water using, wonder of wonders, a telescoping pot she'd found in Kai's pack. The man had a serious Boy Scout thing going, but given the situation, she couldn't complain. When she carried the hot soup to him, she was smiling.

KAI HAD HIS EYES CLOSED, but roused when she shook his shoulder. He was shivering again and need her help to sit up. She'd found a straw in his pack and that helped get the hot soup into him, although it was slow going and some of it ended up dribbling down his chin.

"Man, that feels good inside," he mumbled as Susana set the pot aside.

She blotted the soup from his chin, then put her arm around him. "Here, let's get you lying down again."

Once he was prone, she tugged the blanket around him. With just his face showing, he looked like a dirty mummy.

"Mmm...warm."

She thought he'd drift off to sleep again, so she turned away and picked up the pot.

"Hate...this," he said. His voice was soft, almost dreamy.

She halted and turned back to him. His eyes were closed. "How many times have you had these attacks?"

"Don't know. Too many." He paused and frowned petulantly. "No treatment in warlord's prison. Very sick."

Oh, Kai. She bit her lip so she wouldn't ask all the questions racing through her mind. "Shhh...you're safe now. Try to sleep." Her voice was choked with emotion.

"Mmm...sleep."

Susana hurried outside, fighting back a sudden surge of protectiveness.

She rinsed out the pot, then went searching for two fist-sized rocks. She set the rocks in the glowing embers of her fire, then removed her boots. She took off her socks, then put her boots back on over her bare feet.

When the rocks were hot, she used sticks to roll them inside her socks. She tied off the ends and, voila, instant foot warmers.

Which, thanks to several days' worth of foot odor, stank to high heaven. "Phew," she muttered. "Be thankful you're sleeping, Kai."

Holding the socks by the knots she'd just created, she returned to Kai and tucked the sock-wrapped rocks next to his feet. "Mmm," he murmured. His lips curved in a slight smile, although his eyes stayed shut.

Susana went back outside. The light was starting to fade, so she quickly prepared her dinner—a heated mash of under-ripe fruit and edible leaves—and washed it down with water.

Fire extinguished, she set the trip wire and crawled into the shelter.

There was nothing to do now but watch Kai sleep. Even with his eyes closed and his cheeks fuzzed with several days' growth of beard, there was still an aura of danger to him. It lay in the steep, clean line of his nose, and a jaw that tapered to a square chin.

She judged him to be about her own age, late twenties, but after the violence of the past two days, she felt years younger than Kai in experience.

The proof was in the not-yet-vanished scar a few inches off his forehead. The slightly puckered two-inch gash of pink skin was frightening. Had someone tried to bash his brains in?

Although she knew she shouldn't, she reached out and smoothed her finger over the scar, as if she could erase any lingering pain. Scratches from hiking through the jungle covered his cheeks and forehead and she found herself tracing them, too, with her finger.

Then Kai stirred, mumbling something unintelligible before settling back into sleep. She jerked her hand away from him and crossed her arms across her chest to make sure she didn't reach for him again.

God, he lived in a world where being shot at was ordinary.

Correction, not just ordinary, but part of his job description. That's what special operations was about, wasn't it?

And this ultra-capable man trusted her to care for him while he was unconscious. To stay and give him another dose of his anti-malaria treatment instead of abandoning him and heading for her dig.

His life was in her hands. It was humbling, and more than a little scary. Because while she was quite confident she could nurse him through the malaria attack, she had no such confidence that she'd be able to protect him if the mercenaries found them.

CHAPTER TEN

Sunday, Evening
Manaus, Brazil

MARK TONELLI JABBED his finger against the off button on the prepaid cell phone he'd bought before leaving Santarém. He hurled the phone onto the thin comforter on the lumpy hotel bed, all too aware that his normally sedate temper was dangerously close to exploding.

He stalked across the worn carpet to the bathroom, limping slightly from the fall he'd taken out the taxi door. Not that he was complaining.

After all, he'd made it out of Santarém alive.

Even now, he felt a cold trickle of sweat down his spine. It had been pure luck that he'd been in the lobby of his hotel, already on his way out of town when he'd seen the men walking down the street.

They'd worn jeans with windbreakers, even though in the midday heat anyone with sense wore short sleeves. And they'd walked with the arrogance of men who expected the world to get out of their way.

Mark had known they were from Jamieson.

He'd spun around and fled out the back door, yet somehow they'd managed to find him, chase his taxi, and run the taxi off the road. Before the driver got the vehicle back on track, Mark had taken advantage of the cover of the surrounding bushes, grabbed his overnight bag and bailed into the shallow ditch.

Luckily, Jamieson's men hadn't spotted him and he'd made it to the airport without further incident.

Now he rifled through his shaving kit until he found a bottle of ibuprofen. He chased the pills down with some bottled water, then headed back into the bedroom without looking in the mirror. His reflection was not something he could face right now.

The black eye, puffy lips and scraped cheeks were vivid proof that his life was spiraling out of control.

His revenge was in jeopardy all because the damn mercenaries had lost Susana Dias. She was a woman, for pity's sake. How hard could it be to keep her contained?

And he knew, he just *knew* that the man with Susana was Kai Paterson. Damn the bastard, Mark wished he could kill the SSU agent himself. But he had to stay hidden. Jamieson's men would still be searching for him.

He wouldn't be safe again until he had the chip.

Only then would he be able to bargain for his life, and Susana's. Plus, he'd finally get the name he needed from Jamieson.

But on the off chance that Jamieson wouldn't bargain, Mark figured Ryker and the SSU would be willing to strike a deal. Amnesty for the chip.

If the SSU wasn't interested, he could name a dozen criminal organizations who'd pay top dollar to get their hands on a formula that created superhuman soldiers.

No matter which scenario came to pass, he'd make sure he ended up with Susana.

Mark flipped open the local map he'd bought at the airport.

He'd instructed the mercenaries to bring Susana to him, promising to give them an exact delivery location once they had her back in their possession.

He scanned the map, looking for a suitable rendezvous spot. It had to be someplace with multiple exit routes. Jamieson's assassins would eventually find him, so he had to be prepared to bolt at any time.

Mark pulled off the wig of curly, gray, chin-length hair. He deliberately hadn't shaved or bathed in days. He was even wearing dirty, stained fatigues, like half the male population in this uncivilized town. And his sense of smell had finally dulled to his own rancid scent, making the disguise more bearable, even if the feel of accumulated dirt made his skin crawl.

Anyone looking for the old, pristine Mark Tonelli would have difficulty recognizing him. Just as no one would expect him to be hiding out in this rundown shack of a hotel in the roughest part of town.

He picked up his satellite phone and dialed another number. His contact at Susana's dig would tell him when Susana returned and he could then send in his mercenaries to retrieve her.

He'd sleep better, knowing she was safe.

Amazon Jungle

KAI OPENED HIS EYES. It was dark, but his internal timer told him he'd slept soundly for a couple hours. His chills were gone and the rocks Susana had heated, and then reheated, made it uncomfortably hot.

He was just about to push the survival blanket away, when his sluggish brain registered a heavy, uneven weight on his legs.

"Susana?" he whispered.

No answer. He knew he wasn't alone because he could hear

her breathing. He called her name again, louder and with more command.

"Kai! You're awake." Her voice, bright with relief, came from at least two feet to his right. So it wasn't her lying across his lower body.

"Susana, I think we have a non-human visitor. Is the flashlight with you?"

"Yes."

"Good. Move very slowly and turn it on," Kai told her. He tried to convey urgency through his tone, without spooking her into any sudden movements. "Keep the lens mostly covered with your hand and aim it away from you."

He heard her quick intake of breath and was afraid she was going to waste time asking questions. "Hurry, Susana."

After a bit of rustling, light warmed the darkness. Kai glanced down the length of his body.

Ah, shit.

He tried not to tense up, but his muscles were hardwired for a flight-or-fight response. The large brown snake coiled across his lower legs stirred as it felt Kai's muscles harden beneath it, but its eyes didn't open.

Okay. If it was asleep, the situation was a little less dangerous. But he couldn't just lie here, hoping the damn thing woke up in a good mood and decided to slither away.

"Kai, look at the white, donut-shaped pattern on its scales... that's a wutu pit viper. It's...uh...extremely poisonous." Somehow Susana managed to keep her tone quiet and non-threatening.

Thank God the snake had picked him to lie on rather than Susana.

Kai did his best not to move. It was likely the foil covering of the survival blanket would lessen the impact of the snake's fangs if it attacked, but he really didn't want to find out.

"Just remain still," Susana told him. "I've dealt with snakes before. I'll get rid of him."

No! He bit his tongue rather than say it out loud. He had to trust her abilities. She'd grown up at the edge of the jungle and spent much of her adult career here. Of course she'd have encountered poisonous snakes before.

But God, please don't let it bite her.

He kept his eyes on the snake and his ears trained on Susana. He heard the shush of nylon sliding over nylon, followed by the soft grinding of a zipper being undone. Susana was looking in the backpacks. He wanted to tell her to grab the Biel tool. Afraid that speaking might wake the snake, Kai remained silent.

The more he looked at the snake, the more mesmerizing he found the pattern on its scales. As if sensing Kai's regard, the snake opened its eyes. Its wide mouth yawned and a forked tongue lazily tasted the air.

Nothing threatening here, bud, Kai thought, staring into the reptilian eyes. *Go back to sleep.*

He heard a metallic click to his right. Then sensed Susana moving up beside him.

"On the count of three," she breathed. "I'm going to knock him off your legs and pin him to the ground. Be ready to pull away."

"Roger," he answered just as quietly.

"One...two...three." Susana darted forward. She hooked the claw under the snake's coils with a speed and fearlessness that stole Kai's breath.

Then she lifted the startled snake and held it suspended with its tail caught by the Biel and its head hanging down and out of immediate reach of Susana's arm.

The snake twisted and hissed in annoyance.

Kai jerked his legs away.

Susana dropped the snake and planted her left foot on its head, pinning it to the ground. The snake thrashed wildly, but Susana didn't budge. She deftly removed the Biel's claw and put it back in the bottom of the tool. Then, in a move almost too quick for Kai's fevered brain to follow, Susana brought the axe edge down and severed the snake's head from its body.

Kai gazed at the snake's death throes and the gush of blood. The darkness inside him stood up and cheered.

"Sorry about the mess," Susana said. She used the Biel to pick up the body and took it outside. From the length of time she was gone, she must have carried the remains into the jungle. Maybe even buried them.

She returned to collect the snake's head, again using only the Biel to touch it, then disappeared again. This time when she entered, she carried ashes in a trencher of leaves. Using the Biel, she scraped up the bloody soil and carried it away. Then she scattered ashes around the edges of the encampment.

Kai's vision had become super sharp. Every shadow seemed magnified. Every throw of light was elongated. He knew it was the fever starting, but he let it carry him. He was content to lie here and watch Susana. Because looking at her distracted him from the ache in his limbs. And as long as his eyes were open, he wouldn't be lost in fever dreams.

"Why ashes?" he asked. Even to his own ears, his voice sounded blurry.

"They have a strong scent that's a deterrent to snakes," Susana replied. She knelt down to lay the Biel next to her bed and he noticed her hands were shaking.

Alarmed, he tried to sit up, but found he only had enough strength to push up on one elbow. "Are you hurt?"

"What?" She shot him a startled glance. "No. Why?"

"You're trembling."

She looked away. "I'm not hurt."

"Then what?"

She shrugged and reached for her canteen. "Are you thirsty?"

He waited several beats before answering. "Yes."

She poured out a cup of water and handed it to him.

He made a big show of getting his arms tangled in the

survival blanket. She scooted closer so she could hold the cup to his lips. He sipped, then grabbed her wrist before she could move away.

"If you're not hurt, then why are you shaking?" he demanded.

She glared at him.

Oh, no, he wasn't giving in to her temper. This was too important. He wasn't going to let go until she answered him. Something was wrong, dammit, and he needed to know what so he could fix it.

"Susana," he warned.

"I was scared," she snapped. "Okay?"

In his surprise, he dropped her wrist and she scooted away.

"You're afraid of snakes? But...you handled it so calmly."

"No," she growled, her voice tinged with such impatience he sensed he was missing something. "I'm not afraid of snakes. I've killed dozens of them on my digs."

"Then what?"

"I was scared for *you*," she huffed. "Okay? I was afraid I wouldn't be fast enough and the snake would bite you. We're nowhere near a medical facility. You could have died."

He stared at her. So this was how it felt to be struck dumb. Left with a frozen brain and mouth.

She cared what happened to him? But...

"Do you want any more water?" she demanded, not looking at him.

He shook his head, still trying to wrap his mind around the fact that she'd been afraid for him.

"Okay. Sleep well." She moved over to her bed and extinguished the light.

Kai lowered himself onto his back and stared into the darkness. Susana didn't hate him. She wanted him safe.

When the fever claimed him, he was smiling.

"Jenna! Dad! No!"

The anguished cry roused Susana from a light doze. She jerked upright on her pallet and looked around, trying to figure out where she was. Early morning sun peeked through the roof of their shelter, illuminating Kai's head thrashing from side to side, his arms punching at invisible enemies.

"Blood...too much blood. Noooo! I'm sorry. So sorry." His voice cracked on a sob, then his body stilled.

I may say some things while I'm out of it. Just...ah...ignore me, okay?

But how was she supposed to ignore such obvious pain?

Susana crooned soothingly to Kai as she crept closer. But the outburst appeared to be over. She reached out and touched the tears shimmering on his face.

"Oh, Kai," she breathed. His torment touched some deep chord in her, turning her heart into a leaden weight. She had the sudden, fierce desire to fight his battles with him. To comfort and shield him.

Underneath her fingertips, his face burned. Sometime during the night he'd kicked free of the survival blanket. She reached behind her and picked up the washcloth that had been tucked into a pocket of his medicine kit.

A quick splash with water got the fabric wet enough to sooth over the heated skin on his face. His lips parted on a soft sigh and he turned his head to follow the path of the cloth. Tenderness spiraled through her veins. She smoothed her hand over his military-short hair, then realized she was stroking him like she would a cat and pulled her hand away, tucking it into her lap.

Kai moaned. Whether from loss of her touch, or pain, she didn't know. But the sound helped bring her focus back to her nursing duties.

It was too soon to give him another dose of his anti-malaria medication, but she didn't like the way his temperature kept rising. She dissolved a couple of aspirin in the filtered water, then lifted Kai's head enough to allow her to hold a cup to his lips.

He took several swallows of water before restlessly turning his head away. She straightened the wrinkles out of the survival blanket underneath him, then lowered him back down. There was one more thing she needed to do, but she found herself drying and storing the cup, trying to avoid it.

Oh, stop being a prude. You've seen plenty of naked men. Just strip the man so you can brush all of him with that cool water.

She sighed, knowing that his nudity wasn't the real issue. By removing his clothes she'd make Kai even more vulnerable and dependent on her. And Kai would hate that.

Telling herself to suck it up, her hands moved to unbutton his camp shirt. She had the shirt undone and was trying to slide it off his arms when he became agitated.

"No! I don't know where it is. Let me go!"

She ducked one flailing fist, but as she started inching his second arm out of its sleeve, his fist caught her on her temple, just above her right ear.

The force of the blow knocked her sideways. She lost her balance and toppled to the ground, then just lay there a moment while she waited for the little silver dots to stop dancing across her vision.

"Leave her alone, you bastard!" Kai's shout ended on a choked sob. "Jenna...I'm so sorry...please forgive me..."

And just as quickly as if someone pulled the plug, Kai's fit ended.

Susana cautiously sat back up. Her head throbbed where he'd hit her, but her vision was steady, so she wasn't seriously hurt.

She set about pulling off the rest of Kai's clothes, but left his boxers on. Removing them seemed too intimate. It was one thing for her to pose nude knowing that strangers would look at her image and have all sorts of reactions from envy to lust. But it would be an invasion of privacy for her to fully strip Kai when it wasn't medically necessary.

She folded his clothes and put them in a pile at the foot of her makeshift bed, then wet the washcloth and began his bath. She started with his face again, then moved on to his chest. Silt from the river had collected on his skin, and only after she'd worked the cloth over his entire body, twice, did she accept what she was seeing.

She sat back on her heels, fighting back nausea. Kai's body was covered with scars.

A series of white, aged scars crisscrossed his back, legs and feet. Newer, still pink scars overlapped in a similar pattern over some of the same skin, and also marked his chest. What she knew about torture was limited to information from novels and films, but she could only think such marks had been made by flogging.

She tasted bile and just made it outside before she threw up.

Kai had been whipped. More than once, based on the difference in age of the scars.

What was it he'd said? Something about being in a warlord's prison. In...Indonesia was it?

She bent over and was sick again.

Those weren't the only scars he had. There were also two jagged lines she thought might be knife scars, and one puckered circle she figured was from a bullet. Plus several fresh cuts and bruises courtesy of their flight from the mercenaries.

She glanced down at her own wrists, at the bruised, torn skin from where the rope had tied her. Kai had similar scars on his wrists and ankles, although his were wider and more even than hers. From manacles?

Holy cow. Who *was* this man? Why would any sane person choose a profession where torture was a very real possibility?

If Kai hadn't killed the mercenaries, and they'd recaptured her, would similar abuse have been her fate? Shame heated her cheeks. She'd been angry and afraid at the violence, when she should have gotten on her knees and thanked him.

Dammit, she didn't want to go back into the shelter. She didn't want to have to look at Kai's scars and be reminded that she had no idea of the events that had shaped this man's life.

Of the pain he'd suffered.

He didn't know her from Eve, yet he was willing to risk his life to keep her safe. Suddenly, she found herself ridiculously near tears. She didn't like the idea of Kai making any kind of sacrifice on her behalf.

Although, maybe it had nothing to do with her. Maybe he was just desperate to get the chip for himself.

Pushing that thought aside as unfair, she collected more water. Some she set into the filtering system, some she left for bathing.

She couldn't change the bandage on her shoulder by herself, so she took some aspirin, ate another quick meal of fruit and nuts, and finally forced herself back inside.

Kai shifted restlessly on his bed, his head rolling from side to side, but he remained quiet.

Susana placed her hand on his forehead. Heaven help her, he was burning up. She fumbled for the thermometer and took his temperature.

One hundred and four.

Oh. My. God.

Susana had to work hard to remind herself that a high fever was normal with malaria. There was no reason for this heart-stopping panic. Yet, it was one thing to suffer an attack of malaria herself as a child, quite another to be the caregiver.

"Okay. Calm down. He's not going to die. He's been through this before."

It was too soon to give Kai more medicine. So she decided to bathe him again.

She monitored Kai's temperature on and off for the next four hours. It rose slowly, finally reaching 105.7. His respiration and pulse increased along with his fever. When she put her hand on his chest, she could feel that his breaths were too shallow to bring him enough oxygen.

She moved her hand. Damn, it felt like his heart was trying to beat its way out of his body.

What was almost as scary, the rest of him was still. No thrashing. No wild words. Not even a spare muscle twitch, as if every cell in his body focused solely on dragging in as much air as quickly as possible.

She sat back on her heels. Now what was she supposed to do? She'd just given him another dose of aspirin water. It was time to inject him with the anti-malarial drug, but she was scared. Because what if the pinch of the needle entering his vein was too much of a shock for his system right now?

She shoved her hand into her hair, but it got stuck in the tangled mess and she angrily yanked it out. She *hated* feeling helpless. It would be so much easier if she were sick instead of Kai.

Her eyes swiveled toward the medicine kit. She had to take the chance and give Kai the injection. She'd never forgive herself if she didn't, and he continued to get worse.

Her hands trembled slightly as she removed the vial and prepared the syringe. Her mother had sometimes asked her to help take blood samples from the cattle, so she was familiar with the overall technique.

"I can do this," she muttered, trying to quiet the butterflies whirling in her stomach. "I'm not a yellow-bellied coward. If I don't help Kai, he could die." She took a deep breath. "Right. So just get on with it."

She located a vein, closed her eyes briefly and prayed for success. Then, trying to remain clinically detached instead of terrified she'd hurt Kai, she carefully slid the needle into his skin.

By the time she'd stowed the needle and vial back in their

pouch, she felt the warm glimmer of pride pushing through her nerves. She'd done it! And Kai hadn't so much as twitched.

Now she could settle in. She pulled her bedding closer to Kai and sat cross-legged on it, prepared to keep vigil until his breathing regulated.

The minutes stretched into hours. Kai's breathing remained too fast and too shallow. His breath stopped twice. Each time, Susana sprang forward ready to start CPR, but both times his breathing picked up on its own, leaving Susana sweating and weak with relief.

And struggling to moderate her own breathing.

Finally, as the sunlight peeking through the leaves lost its intensity, Kai began to sweat. Susana brushed tears off her cheeks. Sweating was malaria's final phase.

He was going to be all right.

CHAPTER ELEVEN

Tuesday, Morning
Amazon Jungle

KAI OPENED HIS EYES. Streams of daylight filtered through the leafy roof of the shelter, landing in bright patches along Susana's body as she sat cross-legged a few feet away. Her eyes were intent upon him, her eyebrows lowered in concentration.

He couldn't for the life of him read her expression.

This was the first time someone had been with him during a malaria attack and he was unprepared for the raw vulnerability of his position. Vague memories of ranting, of fevered dreams of blood, teased at the edges of his consciousness. Dammit, what secrets had he revealed?

He fought the urge to look away, to hide himself, as if by denying her now he could erase the memory of whatever he'd said during the fever.

Asking her what he'd said would only reveal his uneasiness. So he waited. Expecting to see pity, compassion, or even fear in her eyes. Instead, she wore the focused look of a scientist trying to unravel a puzzle.

But then her gaze met his and her face softened. Her eyes were filled with...tenderness?

"Welcome back," she said softly. "How are you feeling?"

"Empty."

Whoa. Where did that come from?

The myriad meanings behind the word were too complicated for him to decipher, but Susana drew her own conclusion. The corners of her mouth slid into a warm smile. "That's understandable. You were sometimes quite...energetic during your fever." She reached into his backpack.

"Let me mix some energy drink for you. Once you're rehydrated, I'll help you outside. Unless you have an urgent need?"

He shook his head. Considering how damp his boxers were, he figured he'd sweated out most of his body's water.

A faint breeze skittered across his skin and he shivered. That's when it hit him that the rest of his clothes were missing. He had no memory of stripping. Which, God, meant that Susana had undressed him while he was unconscious. And there was no way she could miss his scars.

Anger and shame twisted inside him until he wanted to run away and hide.

Stay put, act normal and keep your mouth shut. Don't give her any reason to pity you.

He looked around for his clothes and located them folded in a neat pile at the foot of Susana's bedding. He tried to reach out an arm and snag his shirt, but his whole body trembled at the effort. His hand barely rose six inches off the ground.

He did manage to pull the survival blanket over himself, but even that small motion drained him. Shit. The mercenaries were still out there and he was in no shape to fight.

Susana tore open the packet of energy powder and poured it into his canteen. She scooted close to him, filled the lid with liquid, and held it to his lips.

"I don't need you to feed me like a baby," he protested. He

started to raise his hands to take the cup from her, but she pushed them down.

"No. Save your strength for when I take you outside. If you're up to it, I think we should bathe you in the river before you put your clothes back on."

A laugh burst out of Kai, almost causing him to spit the energy drink out. Only sheer willpower kept him from wasting the precious liquid. After he'd swallowed the mouthful, he raised his eyebrows. "Are you implying that I stink?" he intoned, raising his eyebrows.

"I shouldn't be throwing stones, because I reek of river water, sweat and dirt, but...yes, Kai, you stink," she said with a grin. "You definitely need a bath."

"Ah, well. Anything to please milady." He bowed his head and was rewarded with an appreciative chuckle.

Wednesday, Morning
Somewhere over South America

RAFAEL ANDROS LEANED back against the airplane seat and pressed his eyes closed. The absence of sight didn't help his headache, but it lessened his nausea. Yet with the darkness came a jumble of images and fragments of remembered sound that he struggled to piece together into sense.

A cold, male voice, telling him to kill.

Seeing his hand jab a knife into his teammate's chest, while his mind screamed at him to stop.

Worry in his brother's voice as Niko called his name.

Rafe thought he'd phoned Niko. Told him about the mission. But he wasn't sure. It might have been a dream.

The murmurs of the other men on the team abruptly shut off.

Rafe opened his eyes as a man in a white lab coat walked

down the aisle. Everything within him went still as a rabbit trying to avoid the predatory gaze of a hungry hawk.

"It's time for the next treatment, gentlemen." Three more figures in lab coats stepped through the door from the forward compartment.

The air became so burdened with fear, Rafe almost choked on it. A little voice inside him started screaming, remembering the pain as the drugs spread fire through his veins. Then the cloud would settle over his mind, reducing everything but the doctors' demands to nothing.

His eyes darted around the small compartment, desperately seeking a way out.

"Mr. Andros, we'll start with you. Give me your arm."

No!

Rafe tightened every muscle in his arm, ordering the limb to stay where it rested on his thigh. Just once he wanted to disregard the voice.

"Your arm, Mr. Andros. Now."

Rafe watched in horror as his arm rose, offering itself to the doctor.

As the doctor prepared the syringe, Rafe felt the cold trickle of tears down his face.

Wednesday, Morning
Amazon Jungle

"We need to move out," Kai told Susana the next morning.

"Are you sure?" Susana eyed him, looking for trembling in his hands and legs. Yesterday she'd helped him down to the stream for a real bath, figuring that since the water was moving well, the chances of them picking up a water-borne parasite such as shisto were minimal.

Her mouth quirked up as she remembered how adamant Kai had been about bathing on his own. In fact, like a shy little boy, he'd sent her farther downriver to take her own bath. She'd been afraid she'd return and find him passed out in the water, but instead he'd been dressed and propped against a fallen tree trunk, dozing.

By the time she'd gotten him back to their shelter, he'd barely had the strength to keep his eyes open. This morning his skin was pale and his movements were sluggish, but his eyes shone clear and steely with determination.

"Can't we give you more time to recover?" she asked. She remembered being in bed for several days when she'd had malaria as a kid.

"I'm fine. We can't waste any more time and risk the mercenaries finding us."

"But—"

Kai didn't bother arguing with her, he just turned away and started putting items into his backpack. Rolling her eyes at his stubbornness, Susana folded up the survival blanket and stuffed it into her pack.

Kai closed the flap on his backpack and lifted it off the ground.

"Wait. Let me carry the heavier pack today," she said, reaching for Kai's bag.

He pulled it out of reach. "No. I'm okay with it." He slung the pack over his shoulders. For a moment he wobbled and she thought he might collapse, but he stuck his arms out to the side and rebalanced himself.

Susana bit her lip to keep from commenting. If the idiot wanted to wear his meager strength down by carrying a heavy pack, she couldn't stop him. All she could do was take care of him if he fell.

Yet as the day progressed, she had to admit Kai had reserves of strength she hadn't expected. He walked considerably slower than usual, but didn't fall down or even stumble. True, he had to stop and take frequent rests, and one time he gave himself another injection of the anti-malarial drug, but he managed to last far longer into the day than she'd expected.

She led them back to the edge of the main river, but they still didn't find any suitable place for crossing.

Finally, when Kai showed signs of exhaustion, she called a halt for the day. She chose a spot away from the river, so they'd be out of sight of predators heading to the water for a drink. Once again, Susana collected fruit and nuts for her meal. When she suggested Kai eat one of the nutrition bars to boost his strength, he gave her a withering look and grabbed a banana and a handful of nuts.

She didn't fight him over that. Just opened a bar, broke it in half, popped one piece in her mouth and handed the other piece to Kai. He raised his eyebrows, but obediently ate his section of the bar.

Now, though, he was digging his heels in regarding who got the hammock and mosquito net.

"You take them," Kai insisted.

"The hell I will." Susana wanted to close her eyes and count to ten, so she could get a grip on her escalating temper, but she didn't trust Kai. If she couldn't see him, he'd probably do something that would guarantee she had to sleep in the hammock with the mosquito net.

"I'll take the hammock if you'll take the net," she suggested. "You can string it between those bushes over there and sleep on the ground wrapped in the survival blanket."

"No. I don't need to be coddled. You take the net." Kai started stringing the hammock between two sturdy trees.

"Stop it!" The cup from her canteen went winging toward Kai before she could stop herself.

He spun around and stared at her.

"Stop being such a goddamn martyr, Kai. You...have... *malaria!*" She heard her volume hit concert level, but she didn't care. She had to make him listen. She couldn't go through another nursing session worrying about whether he was going to make it. Listening to his anguished cries and knowing there was nothing she could do to ease his emotional pain, but wanting to try anyway.

"I have higher resistance to malaria because I grew up in the Amazon. So you're using the goddamn mosquito net if I have to stand here and scream at you all night."

"Er—" The wary look in Kai's eyes was a familiar one. Most people got the same look when first faced with her temper. But Kai's wariness was accompanied by a calm determination that only made her madder.

"You know what? Forget the damn hammock. You're not really listening to me anyway." She stomped over and grabbed the hammock out of his hands. "I'll make us another shelter. We'll both sleep on the ground. Underneath the mosquito net. Go sit over there until I'm done." She tipped her head toward a moss-covered rock.

"Uh...sure."

"And don't talk."

Kai, wisely, just nodded and sat where she'd indicated.

Wednesday, Evening
SSU Compound, Oregon

"RAFE WAS PUT through Kaufmann's program?" Dr. Gabrielle Montague's voice verged on hysteria.

Ryker watched her pupils expand slightly. She glanced away, quickly inhaled, then let her breath out between clenched teeth. Her reaction confirmed his theory that her relationship with Rafe had been more than professional. He had no problem with that. It made his decision easier. "Yes. His brother is going after him and expects to have Rafe back soon. But it sounds like Rafe is in bad shape." He explained what Niko knew about his brother's condition.

"I'm going to need a team of medical experts to work on Rafe," Ryker said. "I want you to be part of the leadership team."

"Yes!" Her reply pounced on him and held him down, ensuring he wouldn't change his mind.

Ryker smiled. Oh, yes, Dr. Montague cared for Rafe. "I'd like your help picking a location for a lab and setting it up with the necessary equipment. I have some contacts at the CDC who are looking for unused labs we can use with complete privacy."

She nodded, her brows already drawn down in concentration.

"Then I want you to do another review of the data you brought over from Kaufmann's lab," Ryker continued. "Rafe may not have much time left."

Dr. Montague flinched. She was so easy to read, he wondered how she'd ever managed to sneak into Kaufmann's secure lab and steal his data without giving herself away. "Once Kai has retrieved Nevsky's microchip, our technical experts will decode the data and get you a full report as fast as possible. In the meantime, put together a tentative treatment plan based on counteracting the parts of Kaufmann's drug regime you can identify."

She nodded, but her mouth formed a grim line. Kaufmann had picked her for his program because he needed help mitigating the fits of lethal rage his subjects experienced. One of the aspects of Dr. Montague's research focused on lessening the rage experienced by veterans exposed to biochemical agents.

Ryker had read her research papers and knew that the biggest component of her program was time. Months, sometimes even years, were needed for success.

"I'll do my best," she said. But tears shone in her eyes.

They both knew Rafe had mere weeks before the drugs claimed his life.

Thursday, Morning
Amazon Jungle

THE NEXT MORNING, Kai searched Susana's face for lingering signs of temper. But she hummed contentedly as she helped break camp, so he figured her temper had settled down.

He turned away before Susana could see him smile. As mad as she'd been, he knew part of her anger had been a way to mask her concern. And he'd felt her hand on his forehead more than once during the night, checking for fever.

In the dark, drowsy with sleep, he'd enjoyed her attention. Although he'd never admit it to her, he'd been at the end of his reserves last night and was grateful that she'd taken such good care of him.

Today he felt considerably stronger.

"Kai?"

The worry in her voice made his head jerk up. "What?"

She stopped and pointed to a gap between the trees that gave a clear view of the river and of the bow of a military gunboat moving upriver.

"Slowly lower yourself to the ground," he instructed, keeping his voice low as he followed his own advice. Once he lay on his belly, he shrugged out of his backpack in increments, then pulled out his binoculars.

Damn. It was definitely the same gunboat that had shot at them. He recognized the scrape along its bow. Quickly calculating the distance from the boat to where he and Susana were hiding, he figured they should be safely outside of radar range.

"What are we going to do?" Susana whispered.

"Wait until it passes."

The boat traveled as close to this bank as it safely could, which meant the mercenaries didn't believe they'd crossed the river

"Once the boat is gone," he added, "We build a raft and cross the river after dark."

Susana must have heard the steel in his voice, because she didn't laugh or argue. She just groaned, and dropped her head onto her folded arms.

CHAPTER TWELVE

Susana loved thrills. She'd been whitewater rafting on Class IV rapids and enjoyed every adrenaline-filled minute. But this night ride on their homemade raft had her stomach tied up in knots and her heart in her throat. She lay on her belly, her feet almost in Kai's face, the backpacks lying flat in front of her to minimize their outline against the horizon.

Upstream, lights from the mercenaries' boat flickered faintly. Susana kept her eyes trained in that direction, praying no one would see them.

Kai had made her spread mud on her face. The moon was nearly full and he wasn't taking any chances that the mercenaries might spot them through long-range binoculars.

So far, though, their passage across the river seemed to be unnoticed. The lights remained static, and with every minute the opposite bank loomed larger before them.

They couldn't reach it soon enough. Susana's muscles were cramped from tension, and she could only imagine how exhausted Kai must be.

Because Kai, the idiot, had pulled another he-man act. The

raft they'd built was just big enough to carry her and the back-packs. He hung off the rear, acting as both rudder and engine.

This from the man who'd barely been able to lift his arm two days ago.

She was proud of herself, though. She'd kept her temper, even though she couldn't understand why Kai had to be the one using the raft as a giant kick board. Whatever happened to sitting on the raft and using an oar? Or she could be the one in the water.

But noooo. Kai had made up his mind that exposing her shoulder wound to the bacteria-laden water was more dangerous than him losing strength and drowning. Nothing she said had swayed him.

And if he did slip off the end? She wasn't in a position to help him because she faced away from him.

At least the raft was narrow enough that she was able to stick her arms in the water and assist a bit with the steering. Even so, the fast rate at which the current moved them downstream meant they'd lose maybe half a day's progress. Not to mention the extra recovery time Kai was going to need. Oh, he'd deny it, of course. But she was determined that he'd rest after they reached land. And she was prepared to suddenly fall sick, or fake a twisted ankle, if it meant Kai would set up camp earlier than usual.

The raft hit an eddy and started to turn. Susana tightened her left hand's grip on the vines Kai had fastened to the edges as safety straps, stuck her right arm in the water, and felt the raft pivot.

As her perspective changed with the turning raft, she thought she saw the mercenaries' lights move. Toward her and Kai.

No. Please. Their luck couldn't be that bad, could it? They were close to land. Just half an hour, tops, and they'd be safe. But right now, they were still too exposed, the moonlight clearly illuminating them to any probing eyes.

She looked again. Damn, the light seemed fractionally closer.

Kai had warned her not to speak, sneeze, or make any other noise, because of the way sound carried across water. So she reached back and nudged his hand with her foot, then pointed her toe upriver.

Kai's hand gripped her foot a moment later, letting her know he'd received her message. But he didn't slow the raft.

Susana lowered her eyelids until she had only a narrow band of vision, remembering what Kai had said about light reflecting off the whites of her eyes. The mercenaries' light drew closer, then receded, then drew closer again. Susana strained to hear the sound of an engine over the slap of the water against the raft. All she heard were the calls of birds and other nocturnal creatures from the jungle.

Either the mercenaries were too far away for her to hear, or their boat was drifting.

After maybe ten minutes, she recognized a pattern to the light's movement. It came toward them until it reached a clump of trees that looked like an elephant, then retreated.

Susana closed her eyes all the way as relief turned her muscles to putty. The mercenaries' boat was anchored. What she'd seen had been the current playing the boat along the length of the anchor.

After perhaps fifteen minutes, their raft nudged into a group of overhanging trees. Susana grabbed hold of a tree branch and pulled them closer to land. Just beyond the trees and to the right a clear patch of soil maybe two tent-widths across glimmered faintly in the moonlight.

The raft surged forward as Kai's feet touched bottom. He pushed, and the front of the raft slid onto the bank.

Susana knelt, heaved both backpacks up the slight incline, then scrambled off the raft. Oh, God, it felt so good to be back on land.

She grabbed one of the backpacks by its strap and dragged it farther up the embankment. Once she reached the tree line, she collapsed on her stomach. Behind her she heard splashing and a grunt of exertion. A moment later, Kai lowered himself next to her, his sodden clothes making a soft squelch as he hit the ground.

She turned her head to the side and studied him. A shaft of moonlight illuminated three quarters of his face and upper body. He lay sprawled on his back in a boneless heap, one arm thrown over his eyes, his backpack sitting sentinel behind him.

"Aren't you tired of being wet?" she whispered. The outside of her clothes had somewhat dried from the last dunk in the river, but the combination of humidity and sweat kept her perpetually damp all the way to her skin.

But Kai was soaked again from his neck down.

His only answer was a grunt that could have meant anything from yeah, to leave me alone.

"Thanks," she murmured. "You know, for getting me safely across the river."

Another grunt. Then, "Just give me a minute to catch my breath."

Within seconds, his arm dropped away from his face. His lips parted slightly and his eyes drifted closed in sleep.

Susana watched him, once again feeling a faint stirring of tenderness and protectiveness. Enjoying being the one to watch over him.

Shaking her head at her folly, she pushed to her feet. A man like Kai didn't need or want anyone's care. She was a fool to think otherwise.

Fishing around in the backpacks, she found the Biel tool and set to work dismantling and scattering the pieces of the raft.

Friday, Morning
Bank of the Branco River

KAI AWOKE to the sound of a low, contralto humming. For a moment his sleep-dappled mind thought he was a boy again, listening to his mother hum an aria from her favorite opera.

He drowsed pleasantly between sleep and wakefulness, until a fresher memory jabbed him fully awake. His mother's bloody body, her lifeless eyes staring up at him as he knelt beside her. Kai killing the men responsible, his own hands covered in blood.

He jerked into a sitting position, and found his head captured by a net.

No! He wasn't going to be a prisoner again. He punched his hands up, trying to free himself, but only succeeded in becoming more tangled. And the tighter the net enveloped him, the more panic squeezed the air from his lungs.

"Kai. Calm down. You're safe." Susana's voice finally cut through the suffocating fear. "I strung the mosquito net and survival blanket above you to protect against the sun. Stop moving and I'll set you free."

It took an embarrassing amount of willpower to force his panic back and stop fighting. Even then, tremors continued to give away his distress.

Susana, thank God, was still talking, her words speaking of comfort and safety while her hands unwrapped him.

"There we go." She peeled away the last bit of net and threw it to her left. "I'm sorry about that. You must have had some bad dream, huh?"

He could only stare at her, drinking in her familiar face, letting the warmth in her milk chocolate eyes and the tenderness in her smile banish the last of his fear.

"Hey, it's okay, Kai." Her hand reached out and touched his cheek gently, as if afraid he was going to break. "Whatever haunts you, you're safe now."

The relief at being safe, and not alone, was so great, he was afraid he was going to cry. Instead, he leaned forward and kissed her.

Holy...Christ. At the first taste of her, all the jumbled mess inside his head quieted. Regrets. Doubts. Fears.

What he'd lost. What he'd done. What he'd become.

All of it faded to nothing. Only Susana and her soft sigh of wonder mattered.

The slightly prickly feel of her chapped lips underneath his was somehow erotic. The scent of bug repellent and sweat clinging to them both was alluring rather than repulsive.

A kiss had never felt so right. Yet...

He pulled back, needing reassurance he wasn't alone in this. Susana's face mirrored the awe and befuddled desire he knew was on his own face.

A small voice in the back of his head warned him this was the wrong time and wrong place. He had no business kissing her again.

He tried to turn away. He really did. Only Susana leaned in and molded her lips to his. Her arms circled his neck, pulling him close. Then her tongue flicked out and traced the crease of his mouth, and all thoughts of stopping went up in smoke. With a low groan, he parted his lips and swept his arms around her back, fitting her tightly against him.

He tilted his head to get a better angle and the desire he'd been keeping a tight rein on slipped free. He yanked her even closer. Rolled until she lay beneath him. Then settled in to devour her.

His tongue plunged. Conquered. Took control.

God, he'd never be able to get enough of her saucy, sexy mouth.

Susana's fingers clutched at his shoulders. A whimper of need slipped from her throat to his.

He ran his hands up her back, not realizing what the lump

under his fingers meant until Susana flinched and pulled away with a low cry of pain.

Shit. He'd pressed directly on her incision. "Sorry...God. I'm sorry. Are you okay?"

She shook her head and scrambled away from him. But not before he saw the look in her eyes.

Fear.

His desire instantly shriveled up. "Susana, wait! I didn't mean to hurt you. I forgot about your incision." The thought of causing her pain again made him want to punch something.

She just shook her head. "I...no...it's...Forget it."

"No. I won't forget it. Tell me why you're afraid of me." What had he done that catapulted this courageous woman from desire to fear so quickly?

Susana opened her mouth to speak. Then closed it. Stared at the ground. Finally she said, in a low, uncharacteristically hesitant voice, "I'm not afraid of you, Kai. It's just...better if we forget all about this."

She turned away and picked up her backpack, her tension evident in the stiffness of her movements. "We...ah, should make the most of the daylight and head out."

Way to go, Paterson. You totally bungled that. What had started out perfectly, had ended in disaster. Story of his life these days. And although he wanted to push her, to demand a deeper explanation, he sensed pushing would only make her pull further away.

He rubbed his hand over the back of his neck. "Sorry. You're right. We have to keep moving." He gave a low, disbelieving laugh. "And not toward each other."

She choked back a laugh.

"Ah...sorry again," he muttered. "I'm not helping. Um...never mind. Nothing's going to improve this situation. I've walked under more strenuous conditions. Let's go."

He thought he heard another snort of suppressed laughter

from her. Okay, that was good. The situation between them was still redeemable if she was able to find humor in it.

Twigs cracked underfoot as he stood up. A glance down at the compass on his watch showed that Susana's camp was northeast. They had a lot of ground to make up today.

He pointed out the new direction to Susana and she started toward the trees. Yet, instead of following, Kai grabbed her shoulder, spun her around, and gave her another thorough kissing.

"Don't think for a minute I'm going to forget this," he told her when he finally let her up for air.

For an instant, Susana looked satisfyingly stunned, her eyelids heavy with desire. Then her eyes narrowed and her lips pressed together.

Kai ducked as her fist swung toward his head, then sent her into the jungle with a gentle shove. "Later, sweetheart. Right now I want to see you play Jane. Lead on."

As she stomped through the trees, Kai eyed the sexy sway of her ass. Whistling softly, he followed.

Friday, Morning
Airport, Boa Vista, Brazil

Niko stared at the envelope in his hand, fighting back waves of anger and despair. The printing on the outside was sloppy, like a child's, but undeniably Rafe's.

Niko was scared to open it.

Jenna took the envelope from his limp fingers.

"Niko," she said softly. "Here, I'll read it."

He hated the way she babied him. Yet the truth was, Jenna held all the strength right now. He was too afraid for his brother. Too furious at the scientists who'd done this.

Blindingly terrified about the coming confrontation.

He had to clear his throat before he could speak. "What does it say?"

She held out a piece of white, lined paper with jagged edges. It was an itinerary and a list of radio codes.

Underneath, in the same child-like printing, were two words. Stop me.

Ah, shit. Oh, God, Rafe. Please don't give in. Fight them with everything you've got, bro. I'm coming.

Niko pulled Jenna close and rested his cheek against her head, letting the familiar lemon scent of her shampoo sooth his tattered nerves. Without her, he'd have fallen apart days ago. Every time he thought of his brother, his skin twitched and his heart bled.

"Kai is like a second brother to Rafe," Jenna said. "No matter what they've done to him, there's still hope that love will stop Rafe from killing Kai. Love...it's a powerful force."

Niko let Jenna's words seep into him, but his panic wouldn't be cowed. Yes, Jenna had tried to kill Kai because she thought he'd ordered the rest of their family killed. But she'd been unable to land the killing blow because she'd realized that deep down she still loved her brother, no matter what.

While Rafe and Kai had bonded like brothers, they'd only met a few months ago. Niko didn't know if their bond was strong enough to save Kai.

"If we can't stop Rafe before he kills Kai..." Niko shook his head. "No. It would be worse if we find him..." Niko squeezed Jenna tighter. "If he's..."

Niko was afraid to say the words. Afraid that if he spoke them, somehow they'd come true.

"If Rafe is too far gone for us to save him," Jenna whispered.

"Yeah. That would be..." Niko didn't know if he was strong enough to make the choice. Kill Rafe in order to protect Kai and the Dias woman. Or capture Rafe and send him back to a lab to be studied until he died. "I love him. He stood by me always, even when I didn't deserve it. I can't fail him. Yet I don't know if I have the strength…"

Dios, please don't make me have to choose.

"We'll work it out. Somehow, together, we'll do the right thing," Jenna shushed him. "Don't worry."

The problem was, Niko was terrified of what the right thing might entail.

CHAPTER THIRTEEN

Friday, Evening
Amazon Jungle

WHILE SUSANA SCAVENGED in the jungle for food before the light went, Kai worked on improvising a more comfortable bed for her, without sacrificing her requirement that they both be under the mosquito net. He decided that if he hung the hammock low enough, he could drape the net in such a way that it reached the ground.

He'd wrap himself in the survival blanket and sleep underneath the hammock. Satisfied that Susana would accept the arrangement, Kai started digging a fire pit at the opposite end of the little clearing. He figured it was safe to start a small fire since they hadn't seen any sign that the mercenaries realized they'd crossed the river.

He was in the middle of setting rocks around the pit when Susana stepped into the clearing, her arms full of fruit and roots. She glanced at the hammock, then the fire pit, but aside from a raised eyebrow, didn't comment before heading back into the trees.

Some skewed part of him was disappointed she didn't react with another burst of temper.

He had the fire started and was feeding it twigs when Susana staggered back into camp a second time. Spotting the boa constrictor wrapped around her neck and shoulders, Kai leapt to his feet. He swore his heart stopped beating. "Susana! Oh, God, don't move."

He dashed over to his backpack, where his handgun was stored in the front pocket. Christ, could he even risk shooting the snake when it was lying on Susana?

Susana's throaty laugh stopped him in his tracks. "Kai, it's dead. This is our dinner."

His exhale of relief could have put out the fire if he'd been close enough. As the adrenaline receded, weakness swept through him. He swayed.

"Kai?"

"Dammit. Don't do that again," he said, trying for an angry snarl but managing only a feeble croak.

"Sorry."

He turned around. The wicked glint in her eye made her seem anything but sorry. Why she enjoyed scaring him he couldn't for the life of him figure out. But when she smiled at him, he felt another surge of relief as the tension that had dogged today's walk broke apart. He summoned up a smile of his own.

After a meal of anaconda, not boa as he'd thought, and fruit, they settled into a comfortable silence.

Kai watched the coals of the dying fire flare and subside. He wasn't ready to turn in for the night, but he knew they should rest up. If they pushed hard enough, they might be able to make Susana's dig tomorrow evening.

"Did you know my father?" Susana's question was soft. Wary.

Kai cursed mentally. This was the question he'd been hoping to avoid. She'd grown up without a father, so of course she wanted to know all she could about the man. But what could he say that wouldn't make her feel worse?

Kai poked the stick he was holding into one of the remaining pieces of wood in the fire, breaking it into shimmering red chunks. "Yeah, I knew your father."

"How did you meet?"

Shit. Might as well jump right in. "I have a degree in biochemistry," Kai said. "My specialty is biochemical warfare. The organization I work for, the SSU, does a lot of contract work for the government. They hired us to investigate rumors that subjects were being tortured and killed at one of the labs sponsored by the Department of Defense. Your father's lab."

Susana's soft exhale let him know she suspected that what he was about to reveal wouldn't be good.

"I was sent undercover." And when the lab was destroyed in a fire, Kai had been framed for the death of Dr. Nevsky and the theft of the microchip. Even the SSU had thought him a traitor. Add to that his suspected role in the attack against his family, and he'd spent two years on the run, desperately trying to find the microchip and clear his name. While also tracking down and killing the men who'd killed his family.

"So you're a spy?"

He gave a mock shudder. "Please, no. We prefer *intelligence agent*."

"Ah. You're a secret agent, then. Like James Bond." Her voice was tinged with laughter and he wished for stronger light so he could better read her face.

He sighed dramatically. "Not so exciting. No fast cars or fast women. Think of a bunch of middle-aged men and women wearing white lab coats and hunched over test tubes."

"Oh, poor baby." She paused and he braced himself. "What was my father working on?"

Technically, the answer to that question was classified and Susana wasn't on the need-to-know list. Right now, he didn't give a damn. The moment Nevsky had put the chip inside her, his work had become Susana's business.

"He experimented with a combination of drugs, hypnosis and gene manipulation to create humans impervious to pain, temperature and exhaustion. Needing little sleep. Men extraordinarily strong and fast, with an immune system strong enough to withstand most microbes, including some of the more common biochemical weapons, such as anthrax. Men with superior intelligence who are able to process data two or three times faster than the average human."

And who were subject to mind control. But Susana didn't need to know that her father's real passion was making a subject who could be sent out on any mission, even one that went against the subject's strongest morals, and nothing would stop him except death.

Much as nothing, not even the three-month lifespan of his subjects, had stopped Dr. Nevsky from his research. He'd continued his tests even after he'd realized his drugs were fatal.

"That sounds pretty..." Susana shrugged.

"Far out?" Kai offered.

"Yeah. Was he...successful?" Susana asked.

Memories assaulted him. Men lifting more weight than their bodies should have been able to bear without collapsing. Insane rages. Hours of torture aimed at learning at what point the subjects felt pain. Kai jabbed the end of his stick into the dirt and prayed that Rafe hadn't been captured. He couldn't bear the idea of his friend undergoing such torture.

"Depends on your definition of success," he eventually answered. "There were dangerous physical and mental side effects that made his subjects unfit for active duty." Although, right before he died, Nevsky claimed to be close to a resolution to those setbacks.

"The letter from the lawyers said my father died two years ago. Why such a lag before you came after the chip?"

"It's...a long story. Short version—everyone thought I'd stolen it and I wasn't in a position to prove otherwise. Plus, no one knew Nevsky had a daughter or that he'd used you to hide the chip."

In the heavy silence that followed, Kai could almost hear the wheels turning in Susana's mind as she processed what he'd told her. He wracked his brain, trying to figure out what she would ask next. Unfortunately, there wasn't much positive he could say about the man.

"What did he look like?"

Ah. Of course she'd want to know. But no one had thought to give him a photo to carry. They'd assumed she'd known her father.

Stupid.

"When we get you back to headquarters, I can pull up a picture for you. Until then—" He thought back two years and tried to reconstruct the man's image in his mind. "He was tall, maybe six foot two. Heavy bones. Carrying a slight paunch. Dark hair. Blue eyes." He glanced at Susana. The glow from the coals threw red-tinged shadows across her face, but he didn't really need light to remember its structure.

"You...ah...have his nose, but that seems to be about it."

She nodded. "Was he good to his staff?"

Kai wished she'd ask an easy question. He hated being the one to tell her what a bastard her father was. "No. He was rude. Demanding. A perfectionist. Egotistic. But brilliant. That's why people stayed with him." And fear. Kai was pretty sure some of the scientists in the program had stayed because of blackmail.

Susana put her face in her hands. "Great." Her voice came out muffled. "It's so nice to learn I come from such upstanding stock."

Shit. He hadn't meant to upset her. "I'm sorry. I thought you wanted to know."

She raised her head just enough to look at him. "I did. I just..." She shrugged. "I guess the little girl in me was still hoping for some good news. Like, my father gave all his profits to charity.

You know, something I could use at cocktail parties instead of just curtly telling people both my parents are dead and hoping they won't inquire further."

"So...uh...don't go to any cocktail parties."

She laughed, as he'd intended. But then she answered as if he'd been serious. "You don't understand the archaeological world. Cocktail parties, fundraising balls, or garden parties—wherever there are people potentially willing to fund an expedition, there go I."

He blinked at her. "But...your modeling...I assumed..." He'd seen her financial reports. She was way richer than he was.

"That I have money? Yes, I do. It's nicely invested and the interest keeps me living comfortably. But I don't have the kind of money to continually fund full-fledged expeditions. Even if I did, it makes no financial sense." She flashed a mischievous grin at him and something powerful pressed against his ribs from the direction of his heart. "Besides, why should I spend my money when there are plenty of people who want the prestige of funding a dig for six or eight months? My money is for retirement or an emergency."

"Very practical of you."

She gave a half bow. "Thank you."

They sat without speaking for some time, as if the revelation about her father had dried up Susana's words. Finally, she excused herself and retired to her hammock.

Some time later, Kai kicked dirt onto the coals, then rose to his feet. He wasn't sleepy so he walked the perimeter, checking for wild animals and scattering ashes to deter snakes. He wasn't completely ruling out an attack by the mercenaries, but after seeing their boat's search pattern, he was pretty sure they weren't an immediate threat.

He bent down and tightened one of the trip wires that had come loose. Susana had taken the information about her father well, considering. Although he'd seen a flash of fear in her eyes when he mentioned the chip.

Yeah, he'd be freaked out, too, if he learned he had a microchip inside him.

That was bad enough news. There was no way she needed to know that his family had been killed because of the chip.

HOURS LATER, Susana lay in her hammock and listened to Kai shift position as he sat guard nearby. She heard the faint scratch of fabric against rock and the muffled squeak of his rubber soles —had he settled onto the rock? There wasn't enough light to see, but she imagined him sitting with his knees bent in front of him, chin down as he gazed into the night.

And she wondered if he was thinking back to those kisses.

She certainly was. All day she'd attempted to distract herself by searching for signs of the city of Amerinis. The stories put Amerinis on this side of the river, but if she was right and they'd been digging in the wrong place, then anywhere along this stretch of river was a possible location for the city.

Unfortunately, she'd seen nothing to indicate former human habitation. No ruined walls. No shapes beneath the undergrowth that appeared too linear to be natural. Of course, in the jungle even items left behind a year ago would already be well hidden by vines, let alone pieces of an ancient civilization.

Still, time had a way of revealing lost items, so she remained hopeful.

For most of the day, she'd been able to keep the resonance from Kai's kisses at a low hum. But here in the dark there was nothing to do except remember. She felt her cheeks heat in memory. Dear God, she'd never experienced a kiss like that.

It had been...too unbelievably wonderful. Way too powerful. Exhilarating and frightening. She'd been completely consumed by the heat of his mouth, until time and breath had seemed inconsequential next to the almost ferocious need to taste more. To take more.

The extent of her need had shocked her. She'd never lacked for lovers. She enjoyed sex and wasn't one of those women who needed an emotional commitment before taking a man to her bed. So until today she'd thought she'd learned everything there was to know about passion.

It terrified her to realize how wrong she'd been.

As many affairs as she'd had, with all the one-night stands and hot relationships, she'd never lost control all the way to her soul. Yet Kai's kiss had burned away her common sense, her sense of self-preservation, her identity. She'd been nothing more than raw, violent need.

Thank God for the spark of pain when Kai had accidentally touched her incision. It had brought her back to her senses.

She refused to lose herself to Kai. She wanted the microchip out of her belly. She wanted the mercenaries to stop trying to kill her. Then she wanted to return to her dig and find Amerinis. Finally fulfilling her childhood dream of finding the lost city, while proving her worth as an archaeologist to all those who couldn't see past her pretty face, or who chose to believe the false accusations Elena had thrown at her.

She had no room in her life right now for the distraction of passion. Her work required all her attention. Besides, she had an iron-clad rule. While on a dig she had no personal life. She saved her impetuous, passionate outbursts for after she'd finished a project.

And that point was still weeks, even months, away.

No matter how distracting she found Kai, she wouldn't break her rule for him. So she'd just ignore this extraordinary passion and stay focused.

There'd be no more kissing.

PURE, molten terror jerked Susana awake. Some instinct kept her body still while her eyes adjusted to the dim light filtering through the mosquito net. Nothing seemed out of place to her brain. She was in the hammock. She couldn't see beyond her net, but that only meant dawn remained distant.

She didn't hear any threatening sounds, yet her nerves quivered in alarm, insisting something was very, very wrong.

Then, as she shifted position and jostled the net, she realized that the darkness was mainly due to the number of spiders and other multi-legged insects bedded down on the warm, damp strands of the mosquito net.

"Kai?" she whispered, afraid if she shouted, she'd frighten the creepy-crawlies and somehow they'd shrink to a small enough size, drop through the tiny holes in the net, and land on her skin.

As if it had already happened, her skin prickled and her stomach tried to hide up between her shoulder blades.

She'd never been particularly squeamish about bugs before. They weren't her favorite thing, but she certainly didn't run screaming for a man to come kill the icky bug for her. She knew the insects had congregated due to the humid warmth her body heat created on the net.

She just usually had her mosquito net farther away from her face when she slept without a tent. Seeing this many insects, large and small, fat and skinny, hairy and smooth, and at such close range, awakened a primal revulsion. Low-level electrical jolts of fear blasted across her skin, raising goose-bumps.

She wanted out of here and she wanted out now!

"Kai!" she repeated, louder this time, and with more than a little hysteria coloring the edges. There was no way she was going to press her bare hand against the net and knock the critters off. What if somehow she knocked one inside the net?

"Susana?"

She heard Kai's footsteps enter the clearing and her temper

erupted. He'd gone to take care of business before clearing her net of bugs? He was *so* not going to live this one down.

"What's wrong?" Kai asked.

"What the hell do you mean, what's wrong? My mosquito net is an insect playground this morning, that's what's wrong you insensitive, brain-dead hump of dung! Get them off my net!! Right...this...minute!!!" She didn't care that her tone launched into hysteria. Was she supposed to stay calm while watching tiny, segmented legs poke through the holes in her net less than a foot from her face?

She didn't think so.

"Oh." Kai had the gall to chuckle.

How *dare* he laugh when her skin crawled as if the insects touched her rather than the mosquito net. "You think this is funny?"

"Umm."

She heard the sound of feet moving over the ground, then the rustling of leaves.

"Close your eyes until I tell you to open them and don't move."

"Shit," she muttered, but did as he asked. Pressure against the net caused the hammock to cant first to the left and then to the right. She thought she heard outraged chitters from the insects as they were brushed off. "Good riddance," she muttered in Portuguese.

"Okay, all clear."

The hammock settled back to neutral and she opened her eyes. Although she told herself not to, she glanced down and saw the ground swarming with the bugs as they made tracks for the nearest dark places.

Ugh. She really hadn't needed to see that. Particularly not before breakfast.

She closed her eyes again. "Tell me when they're all gone."

"Yes, ma'am."

She didn't have to see his face to know he was giving her a slightly mocking smile, she could hear it in his voice. For a super agent, he sure was dumb about women. And she'd set him straight on that...once she was over this little bout of trembling.

"Okay, all clear."

Not taking his word for it, she opened her eyes and checked carefully to make sure that when she moved she wasn't going to have a spider or other creepy-crawly dropping on her or squishing under her feet. Once satisfied the way was clear, she peeled back the mosquito net and rolled out of the hammock.

Then she launched herself at Kai, hands pummeling every available inch of him she could reach.

"How dare you laugh! How dare you go away and leave my net covered with those...those critters! You are lower than a dung beetle! You are a sewer slug!! Did you want to scare me?"

"Hey!" He threw up his arms to guard against her flailing fists, but didn't sidestep fast enough to prevent her boot from connecting with his shin. "Ouch!" He reached for her, but she danced away.

"Did you put those bugs there because you thought it would be funny?"

"No! I swear. I didn't see them when I got up to patrol. It was still too dark. Honest. I have younger sisters..." His voice caught and the smile disappeared from his face. "A younger sister," he corrected. "I would never provoke you like that. Particularly not out here, where they'd never find my body if you retaliated."

She smacked him one more time for good measure, not entirely sure she believed him. After all, he'd laughed!

She stomped off into the bushes in the opposite direction from her hammock, keeping a sharp lookout for more multi-legged beings, muttering about the stupidity of men as she went.

She completed her toilet without company and then went in search of some fruit for breakfast. Carrying her treasures, she walked back to the clearing. Kai had his collapsible pot sitting over a fire, steam rising from boiling water. She placed the fruit next to him.

With a conciliatory smile, he held out a cup of steaming coffee. But she could still see hints of laughter on his face. She narrowed her eyes and crossed her arms over her chest.

"Are you still laughing at me, Paterson?"

"No!" He held up his free hand. "Not laughing. Honest."

She pursed her lips, then accepted the coffee peace offering with a nod and lowered herself to sit next to him.

The liquid was still too hot to drink, so she blew lightly across the surface. "Why the change from sisters to sister?"

The flash of pain across Kai's face made her want to take her question back. And yet, at the same time, it made her even more curious.

"I had two younger sisters. Jenna and Isabel." He turned away, hiding his expression as he fussed with his backpack. "Two years ago, not long after I'd been accused of killing your father and stealing the microchip, fourteen-year-old Isabel, her twin Justin, and my parents were murdered. Jenna was..." He shook his head as if he didn't want to think of what his sister had endured. "Jenna was left for dead, but she survived."

And the grief was still so fresh for him, he'd slipped and said sisters, plural. *Oh, Kai.* So that's what he'd been crying over during his fever.

Why were there no words adequate enough to express the emotions flowing through her at this moment? Sympathy. Grief for his pain. The age-old female need to comfort by offering him a hug. Guilt because he'd been investigating her father instead of protecting his family. And the uncomfortable knowledge that as Dr. Nevsky's daughter, she must be a painful reminder of what he'd lost, and why he hadn't been there to stop it.

She didn't think Kai would welcome comfort. So she settled for, "I'm sorry," knowing it wasn't enough. And still, some instinct prompted her to ask, "Is your sister okay?" What she really wanted to know, was if Kai was okay.

He shrugged. "She's doing better. She got married recently to an SSU agent." He picked up one of the bananas she'd collected and turned it over and over in his hands, staring at it as if the piece of fruit held every answer he needed. "Niko's been good for her. Yeah...she's going to be fine."

But he didn't quite sound convinced, and she knew a part of him must worry about his sister. God, what must that be like? To have someone care so deeply about you that they worried? Susana had only heard twice from her mother after she'd moved out. Both times her mother had wanted money for a new research project.

She'd never even asked how Susana was doing.

Susana tightened her hands around the warmth of the metal cup. Jenna was lucky to have Kai looking out for her.

But what about you, Kai? Who looks after you? She bit her tongue so the words wouldn't escape. She'd delved enough for today.

Kai tore open the banana. "Uh...thanks for breakfast."

She acknowledged his abrupt change of subject with a half-smile and took a sip of her coffee. "Do you think we'll reach the dig today?"

Kai glanced at the compass on his watch. "If we're lucky."

The jungle on this side of the river was thicker, making it harder to move forward. They'd only make the necessary progress if they could find another animal path to ease their trek. Or if they didn't encounter any mercenaries.

"And then what?"

"I'll use your radio to call for extraction. Then you show me the rest of your father's letter."

Although the prospect of returning to her dig made Susana's veins sing with anticipation, she knew she would soon be saying good-bye to Kai.

And that thought tugged painfully at her heart.

Susana hummed softly as she led Kai through the brush. Once upon a time, maybe the people of Amerinis had walked these woods as they traveled from the river to their homes. Or while tracking prey.

Two screeching monkeys tore through the trees to her right and Susana turned her head to watch them. Hmm. That was odd. The sun made that tree stump look like...rock.

She blinked. The image didn't change. There appeared to be a solid square of rock just off this faint animal path she was following.

Susana moved closer.

Oh. My. God.

Carved into the rock were primitive pictures in the same style as those found at her dig. Susana bit her tongue so she wouldn't squeal in excitement like a little girl. Instead, she knelt in front of the stone.

Dammit, she wanted her tools with her. Lichen and vines had compromised the surface of the rock. Feelers from the vines had burrowed deep, separating the stone into sections. She wanted to scrape the covering away so she could look at the rest of the pictures, but needed to be careful that she didn't dislodge any unstable pieces, damaging the pictures beyond repair.

Hands trembling, she pulled away as many vines as she could. When she moved around to the back, she saw a narrower segment partially buried in the soft earth.

She dug around the edges until she'd revealed a rectangle that, if set atop the larger block, would form an altar.

Susana sank back on her heels. "Oh. My. God!"

"Susana, what's wrong?"

She stared blankly up at Kai, her mouth hanging open.

"I think I've found the altar for the fabled temple at Amerinis."

CHAPTER FOURTEEN

KAI WOULD NEVER FORGET the awed elation on Susana's face when she'd announced her find, or her resignation when after an hour he'd explained that she couldn't stay and explore further. His priority was getting her safely out of the jungle and back to the SSU so the chip could be removed. Every minute they lingered gave the mercenaries another chance to find them.

While he'd marked down the coordinates, Susana had covered the altar up and notched a tree trunk to help her find the place again, then reluctantly followed him deeper into the jungle.

Now the sun sat low in the sky and Kai had to concede that Susana's dig was too far to make before dark. Between the extended stop to examine the stone of Amerinis and the denser jungle vegetation on this side of the river, they hadn't made much progress today.

Kai called a temporary halt and left Susana sitting on a downed tree while he found a thick clump of bushes to use as a toilet.

When he returned, he didn't see Susana. He searched the area again, fighting to breathe past the fingers of panic tightening inside his throat. She couldn't be gone. There'd been no sign of the mercenaries since they crossed the river. And she knew better than to return to the place she'd found the altar.

Had she wandered off, looking for more signs of her lost civilization?

He listened for her, focusing until he became acutely aware of every small sound. Birds calling to one another. The drone of insects. The rustle of leaves touched by the faint breeze.

His own labored breathing.

Then he heard a rustling from the bushes to the right of the log where he'd left her. Susana's head bobbed into view, then disappeared. He hurried over and saw that she was simply kneeling down beside the log, retying her boot.

His breath whooshed out of him, leaving him light-headed with relief.

He hated to admit it, but since the malaria attack, every time he was out of sight of Susana, he felt on the verge of losing himself. The seductive call of the jungle was louder when he was alone. An answering wildness pulsed in his veins, demanding to be released. It would be so easy to throw off the blanket of civilization. Free the savage inside him.

Finally allow himself to fully express his rage at what had been done to his family. To scream at the injustice. To grieve as he couldn't allow himself to do now. Because in civilization there were rules. Rules that bound him in guilt and responsibility.

Being near Susana calmed him and muted the lure of the jungle. This morning when he'd awoken, the first thing he'd done was search out Susana to reassure himself she hadn't left in the middle of the night. And each time they were apart today—whether it was to answer nature's call or while Susana scouted ahead—he spent the entire time fighting a low-level fear that she'd leave and never return.

Like now.

He squeezed his eyes shut. But his thoughts kept spinning out of control. Imagining what it would be like to live with no restrictions. Free from the constant need to weigh every move and word for future repercussions. Free to take what he wanted and protect what was his by any means. Never again to have to hide who and what he was, even from himself.

Shit.

His control had to hold. He wasn't a savage. He was a scientist. A man of reason. He didn't want to feel these violent impulses. He damn sure wasn't going to let them get the better of him again.

By taking the lives of the assassins he'd come too close to becoming one of the unprincipled men he hunted. He would not let his violent instincts rule him.

So fight it.

"Kai? Are you okay?" Concern sharpened Susana's voice and drew a line between her brows as she walked toward him.

"I don't need you to baby me!" His temper crackled and spit as if she'd thrown grease on the fire in his blood. His tenuous hold over his emotions slipped. His anger morphed into a potent urge to mate. To possess.

Susana's eyes widened and she licked her lips. Leaned toward him.

His hands reached out and he made a low sound of need that sounded suspiciously like a growl.

Fear flashed across Susana's face. She froze, watching him warily.

No!

He dropped his arms and stepped back, wrestling his instincts until every muscle in his body ached. A part of him wanted to let go. Wanted a violent mating. Anything to release the tension that had been building in him for days.

Yet he was terrified of hurting her. Scared that if he touched her, he wouldn't be able to let her go even if she said no. Because the instincts were all about his satisfaction, no matter the cost.

He had to get away from her.

"Uh...Kai?"

"I'm fine," he snarled. "Move out. We need to find a place to make camp." He snatched up his pack with more force than necessary and turned his back to her. He sensed her confusion and waited, muscles quivering, until he heard her push through the vegetation.

Then he closed his eyes in relief. That had been too close. He didn't know how much longer he could continue fighting his violent side. He'd been fighting for two years and he was so damn tired.

But if he didn't win, Susana would suffer.

So focus on the mission. Get her to the SSU. Turn over the microchip. He used the words to spear through the darkness in his soul, chasing the savage back into its cage.

Above all, he had to protect Susana.

Saturday, Evening
Skies over the Amazon Jungle

SEVERAL MILES from Susana Dias's archaeological dig, the hatch of a C-130 cargo plane slowly opened. A man wearing a white lab coat tapped Rafe Andros on the shoulder, then pointed to the open door.

Rafe walked over to the hatch, leaning against the strong wind. He stared into the night sky, but his attention was on the conflict in his head, not on his impending jump.

Memories of a blond man with intense golden eyes teased him. The scientists told him the man was Kai Paterson. Rafe didn't remember the name, but he knew the face.

He saw the light playing over the man's face as they shared a beer in a shadowed bar.

Friend.

No. Target. His orders were to kill this man.

Ah, God, the pain in his head nearly sent him to his knees.

The man in the white coat had given him another injection half an hour ago. Rafe could feel the drug fighting to numb his mind. Each dose took longer to work, but he didn't want the scientist to know that. Because then the man would use hypnosis and Rafe would be lost again. And when the hypnotic trance finally eased, he was terrified he'd have killed his friend.

Just like he'd killed one of his teammates.

The bright lights of the arena reflected off the sand footing, causing blinding glare. Rafe held Depaoli down. They were both bloody and bruised from their fight, but despite Depaoli's massive injuries, he continued to snarl and snap at Rafe.

Still, Rafe had a moment of clarity. Wondered why they'd been fighting. He couldn't remember. But there was no point in continuing. Despite his aggression, Depaoli was bleeding severely. He needed medical attention.

Rafe eased up.

Then a voice came over the loudspeaker. "Mr. Andros, you will kill him now. Take the knife out of its sheath at your waist and drive it into his heart.

No!

Yet Rafe's hand moved to obey the voice.

Stop. Don't do it! *Rafe tried to grab his knife hand with his other hand, but his body obeyed the voice, not his mind.*

The blade cracked through bone and muscle as it jabbed into Depaoli's chest. Blood spurted as he yanked the knife out and drove it in again.

Rafe shook his head at the memory. Depaoli had relied on Rafe, his leader, to keep him safe. Instead, Rafe had killed him.

The scientists had been triumphant, knowing they'd finally broken Rafe. Knowing that finally he was theirs to control, mind and body.

Not now, though. Not completely. Something had changed over a week ago. He'd starting having moments when his mind and body were completely his own. By pushing through the headaches that accompanied those moments, he'd extended the amount of time he was free of the mind control.

But he pretended the scientists still held all the power, hoping he'd find an opportunity to escape.

The cold air buffeted him, tearing away the memories of the golden-eyed man. As if waiting for this exact moment, the drugs took control. His sense of self disappeared under a gray fog.

Nothing mattered but the mission.

The light next to the cargo hatch turned green. Rafe stepped out into the night and tumbled toward the ground. His parachute opened behind him and he automatically went through the motions of locating and steering toward his target landing site.

Once on the ground he had to hike ten miles to the archaeologist's dig and set up an observation station. Once the woman and her companion arrived, he would radio the information to his handlers and wait for the order to kill.

Saturday, Evening
Amazon Jungle

SUSANA SHIFTED position in her hammock. Kai had turned into a scary bastard this afternoon. When he'd returned to her during that last rest stop, the pulses of angry, violent energy emanating from him had sent ripples of goose bumps up her spine. His eyes had held a wildness she'd never seen before.

Intent. Deadly. A predator waiting to pounce.

Then, for a moment his eyes had flashed with sexual heat so intense, her body had responded as if he'd stroked all her sensitive female places. The promise in his eyes had scared her with its ferocity and she'd fought the urge to run.

Some higher instinct had kicked in though, convincing her

that if she fled, it would break the fragile hold Kai had on his control. He'd chase her. Catch her. Conquer her.

Only now, alone in the darkness, could she admit she'd been secretly disappointed when Kai backed away. To have all that male intensity focused on her...the promise made her shiver with anticipation.

Instead, Kai had shut himself down with a palpable effort. Leaving her nothing to do but work her frustration out by vigorously clearing the vegetation from her path.

A tense, wary silence hung between them throughout the afternoon. When they'd finally found a place to camp, they'd fallen into their routine without speaking. He set up the hammock while she looked for food.

Now it was several hours past dark and she couldn't sleep, despite the exhaustion that made her body feel heavier than concrete.

It didn't help that she was hyper aware of Kai sitting watch in a tree at the edge of camp. She swore she could hear him breathing.

"Susana?" Kai's whisper carried across the small clearing.

"Yeah?"

"I'm...sorry...for the way I acted this afternoon."

She couldn't help but smile at the reluctance in his tone. But although she waited, he didn't offer an explanation. Well, what did she expect? Whatever demon he'd been fighting, he was a man used to keeping secrets.

"Apology accepted," she said. Even though she understood why he didn't elaborate, it still hurt. She'd believed they were becoming friends.

Half an hour later she sighed and shifted position again in the hammock. Sleep just wasn't coming. Too many images crowded her mind.

Kai tossing and turning with fever. Kai sprawled on his back after they'd crossed the river. The look he'd given her when she'd unbuttoned her shirt the other day. The heat in his eyes this afternoon.

The kiss.

Despite his surly attitude, she didn't want him way across the camp, emotionally distant and in guard-dog mode.

She wanted another explosive kiss.

Remembering the hot urgency of his lips, parts of her tingled into awareness. Oh, yes, she definitely wanted more. Forget sleep.

She rolled to her side and raised the mosquito net high enough for her to slip underneath. The chemical light stick she'd used earlier while getting ready for bed still glowed where she'd tucked it under her backpack. She picked it up and used it to guide her toward Kai.

"Susana?" Kai's soft question was followed by a muffled thump as he jumped off his perch. "What's wrong?"

"Come here and I'll show you," she replied huskily. From Kai's hesitation, she knew he recognized her invitation.

Please don't turn away. I need this. And I think you need this even more.

She was surprised by that last thought, but it felt right. Whatever emotions had been riding him this afternoon had wound Kai so tight, she feared he was on the verge of snapping.

She met his eyes. Their amber depths reflected the meager light from her chemical stick. With several days' worth of beard giving his face a fuzzy outline, he resembled a jaguar more than ever.

She wanted to stroke him. Starting with his face and moving down.

He must have seen her desire, because his eyes flared. But then he quickly took a step back.

"No," she protested. In two quick strides she closed the distance between them. She leaned forward and pressed a kiss to his chin.

His muscles jumped underneath her lips. Ah, ha! He wasn't immune.

"Don't run from me, Kai." Keeping her hands to herself so he wouldn't feel caged, Susana pressed a series of light, nibbling kisses along his jaw and across his cheeks.

The tension roiling off him was like a physical push against her skin. She ignored it and continued exploring his face with her mouth. When she took his earlobe between her teeth, he shuddered. Smiling, she reached up and flicked her tongue into his ear.

His breath shot out in a long hiss. He grabbed her and set her away from him. Stared at her with a slight frown.

Her heart sank. He didn't want her.

But then he exhaled sharply and reached for her. His hands cradled her head while his mouth plundered hers.

God, he tasted like everything sinful. Rich chocolate. Full-bodied wine. Smooth coffee.

He lifted his mouth to take a gulping breath and she trembled, she actually *quivered* damn him as she waited for his next kiss. So much for staying in control. Once again, Kai's kiss had sent her arousal status from medium to nuclear in a matter of seconds.

He shifted away from her, breaking the sensual haze.

"If we're going to continue this…" he said as his fingers closed around hers

She narrowed her eyes and dug her fingernails into his palm. "No if."

He paused and she sensed an internal struggle.

Hell no. She raised his palm to her mouth, bit lightly at the base of his thumb, then soothed the spot with a kiss. "Make love to me, Kai. Now."

He swallowed heavily. "Uh…right. But not vertical." He extracted his hands from hers, pressed a quick kiss to her lips, then tugged her across to her hammock.

Uh-oh. "Kai?"

He chuckled, and the rare display of humor warmed her. "No hammock. Promise. Well, not tonight, anyway."

She batted at him with her hand. He leaned away with another chuckle and she swore her heart melted at his playfulness.

"I know what I'm doing," he said. "Trust me."

Trust him? He had no idea how much she trusted him. So much she couldn't examine it too closely or she'd scare herself.

A minute later Kai had tugged the mosquito net lower on the hammock, so it created a deeper drape over the ground where his survival blanket bed lay.

Then, with a bow and a hand flourish, he indicated that she should precede him into the cocooned space. "Our bower awaits, Madame."

This wasn't at all the spontaneous seduction she'd intended. As she settled herself on her back on the blanket, then placed the light stick on the ground above her head, she wondered if the mood was lost for Kai.

Damn, she hoped not. Her blood still sizzled with need. "Kai," she muttered when he didn't immediately follow her. "If you don't get in here right now, I'm going to get violent."

"Just a sec."

She heard him move away. He walked around their camp, pausing every few seconds. What the heck? She was fully aroused and he was calmly setting the trip wires? Something was seriously wrong with this picture.

But then he was back, shimmying underneath the mosquito net. Since there wasn't enough room for him to have his own space, he had to position his body on top of hers.

She sighed in delight as he covered her. She separated her legs and wriggled her hips until he nestled right where she needed him to be. Ah, yes, that felt good.

"Hello," he said against her ear. "Where were we?" His tongue penetrated the sensitive canal, mimicking her earlier movement. Probing and retreating until she writhed, moaning his name softly.

She raised her hands and grabbed his ears, intending to move his mouth where she really wanted it—on hers.

"Uh-uh, sweetheart." Kai snagged her hands in his and pressed them to the blanket.

"Kai!" Her protest turned to a gasp as he moved his lips across her face.

"Payback's only fair," he murmured between kisses. "Just relax."

She arched once under his hands, testing his hold. When it didn't loosen, she softened and ceded control, letting his teasing kisses swamp her. Returning kisses to whatever part of him she could reach.

Her eyes drifted closed as her arousal built.

Then Kai was gone, the absence of his body warmth making her shiver. "Kai?" She opened her eyes.

He knelt between her legs, head pushing into the hammock above. His fiery eyes burned into her while he unbuttoned his shirt and shrugged out of it.

She licked her lips as he slowly revealed taut, sculpted muscles that would be the envy of any male model despite the scars. She reached forward, tracing the line of silky, dark blond hair bisecting his abdomen.

The muscles of his stomach leapt under her touch. So she stroked him again. Then she hooked a finger over his waistband and tugged. She wanted him closer, so she could put her mouth on him.

"Come here."

"Not yet." He pushed her hands away.

Awash in anticipation, she let her hands lie quietly at her sides.

Keeping his eyes locked with hers, Kai slowly undid the

buttons of her shirt. Like a blind man, he explored each section of exposed skin with the tips of his fingers before moving on to the next button, skipping over the fabric of her bra. When the last button was free, he pulled the shirt wide.

Then he simply stared at her. With eyes so hot and full of male appreciation that Susana gasped.

His chest heaved once. Then his hands were on her. Reaching beneath her with a curse to undo the hooks of her bra. Yanking free the buttons of the cuffs of her shirt so he could remove her arm from first one sleeve, then the other, then slip her bra away.

When she was completely bare, he groaned and lowered himself slowly to rest against her.

The weight and heat of him was just what she wanted. She arched into him, loving the friction of her taut nipples against the even tighter muscles of his chest. She could stay like this forever, it felt so right. Like finally finding a home after years of wandering.

But Kai didn't pause to savor the moment. He gently shackled her wrists with his hands and lowered his head.

KAI LET his open mouth hover just below Susana's ear, warming her skin with his breath. She squirmed and tried to move her left hand, but he kept her wrists pinned down.

"Kai," she seethed. "Get on with it!"

"Not yet." His smile pressed his lips against her skin. Too tempted, he gave in and tasted her. Lapped at her like she was the finest cream and he a starving cat.

Her taste was rich. Overwhelming. Addictive.

One taste wasn't enough. He went back for more, exploring the length of her neck, then the hollow behind her ear. The line of her jaw invited nibbles, the hollow of her throat a tiny bite. And every inch he tasted and kissed released a unique scent.

Dirt and sweat. A hint of soap and bug repellent.

Rising through it all, though, was the smell of Susana. Hot. Musky. So tantalizing, he wanted to keep on inhaling until his lungs were full of her.

"Kai, what are you doing?" Susana wriggled her shoulders, bumping her collarbone into his nose.

"Smelling you."

She stilled. "Why? We've been in the jungle for days."

He shook his head, letting his nose trail lightly across her skin, down to her armpit, where he inhaled deeply. "You smell like woman. Rich. Seductive." He slewed his eyes upward to see her expression. "I like it."

Her eyes were narrowed, regarding him with suspicion. "Really?"

He laughed and nuzzled against her. "Yeah. Your scent is more potent now. Less civilized." He inhaled and pressed his hips deeper into the juncture between her legs. "It calls to me."

He moved his nose back to the soft space behind her ear. "I want to absorb all of you into me," he whispered against her lobe. "So that if I became deaf and blind I could still tell when you walked into a room, because your scent was part of my DNA."

Susana arched her back and moaned. "Jesus, Kai, you're killing me. I want you."

"I know, sweetheart. But we have so much farther to go."

Susana wasn't sure she could survive much more. She was already on the brink of an explosive orgasm, if Kai would only stop teasing.

She was no stranger to loving. Her appetite was healthy and her looks guaranteed that she could always find a willing partner.

But Kai undid her. She'd never expected that here, in the depths of the Amazon jungle, after having no access to a bath for a week, she'd find a lover who made her feel cherished simply for being herself.

She hadn't realized how desperately she needed that. Until now.

Kai's lips found a particularly sensitive spot at the side of her breast and she writhed at the wave of pleasure.

Mmm. She felt like the first and only woman on earth. Infinitely precious and desirable.

His mouth trailed up the side of her breast. Hesitated until she felt like screaming. Then his head darted forward and, finally, finally, her flesh was in the warm haven of his mouth.

She'd always had sensitive breasts. At the third pull of his mouth, she felt the orgasm start to peak.

"Oh, no you don't," Kai murmured. "Not yet."

He let go of her hands so his fingers could explore her other breast. She tried to push him away, but he only suckled harder, pressing her nipple to the roof of his mouth.

Her throat struggled to find the words to tell him to never stop. As if reading her mind, he raised his head. In the faint green glow from the light stick, his eyes glittered.

"Now," he growled.

His fingers teased her right breast into agonizing arousal, while his mouth continued the sensual assault on the left. The pressure built to a crescendo that would not be denied.

"Kai!" She closed her eyes as the orgasm tore through her. Stars exploded behind her lids.

Then she was limp. Floating.

And clearly she'd unleashed a beast, because Kai didn't stop. He shifted his lips to her other breast. His fingers traced her waistband. Then dipped below, searching.

When he didn't find what he expected, he raised his head.

She took advantage of the moment to push him back on his knees. She unfastened the snap on her pants as she answered the question in his eyes. "Brazilian wax. I had it done last month before a formal fundraising event. I didn't want anything to mar the line of my skintight evening gown." She lowered her zipper.

Kai reached forward and helped her slide her pants and undies down her legs.

He sucked in a breath. One finger reached out and traced her bare slit.

"You're just starting to grow out," he said. His voice wavered. "I've never..." He shook his head and his lips curled in a crooked smile. "Damn. I think I like it." The smile he gave her said he more than liked it.

He started to lower his head, but she stopped him. "Not until you remove your pants, buster."

With a strained laugh, he hurried to comply. And then Mr. Always Prepared pulled a condom out of his pocket and sheathed himself.

She reached for him, desperate to feel him inside her. But once again he pinned her hands.

"I'm not finished yet," he warned her. And proceeded to savor her bare body with lips and tongue, bringing her to the brink time and again, but always knowing just when to pull back to stop her from flying.

The fire within her burned hotter with each touch of his mouth, until it was a wonder her heat didn't ignite the nearby trees.

And she cursed him for not letting her fly again. She swore first in English, then in Portuguese. Then in several languages no longer spoken. When he only laughed, she bent her head and bit him on the shoulder.

He bucked in surprise, then took her mouth in a ferocious kiss.

Yes! She tangled her tongue with his. Nipped at his lips.

His hips pressed forward, seating himself fully within her. He was so hot, and filled her so tightly, she closed her eyes on a long, low moan.

Completely lost in sensation, she didn't realize he'd stopped moving.

She opened her eyes. Shivered.

She'd never seen such an expression on a lover's face. Satisfaction hid in the background, but Kai's eyes were wide with awe and...relief.

But not physical relief. No, this was some deep-seated emotional relief that had tears shimmering in his eyes.

Dear God, was he feeling this same sense of completion? Of being home after years of wandering?

She smiled and traced her finger down his cheek to his mouth. "Hello there," she whispered. For the briefest instant, she thought she saw all the way into his soul. Into cold loneliness and grief.

But then she shifted her body to relieve the pressure on her sore shoulder, and the spell broke.

Kai sucked her finger into his mouth and began moving his body in a hard, unforgiving rhythm. Yet some of the connection remained. Even as her hands dug into his shoulders and her legs grabbed his hips, she felt like he also touched her soul.

And when the pressure was too great and she burst apart, she had absolutely no doubt that Kai would catch her. Because in this moment out of time, they were one.

CHAPTER FIFTEEN

Saturday, Night
Boa Vista, Brazil

"Have you found her yet?" Mark Tonelli demanded, his fingers tightening on the sat phone.

"No. The tracking device never reappeared and she hasn't returned to her dig yet."

Mark could hear a faint roar on the other end. "What's that?"

"Military cargo plane. Flying low." The unease in the mercenary's voice sent Mark's instincts on alert.

"What are the markings?" Was it Jamieson's men? Or just a bad coincidence that the Brazilian military was running maneuvers over that deserted section of jungle?

"Can't tell in the dark."

Mark let out a huff of annoyance. "Then how do you know it's military?"

"Was in the army for ten years, wasn't I? I know what a fucking transport plane sounds like. What it looks like silhouetted against the horizon. Been circling, like it's looking for a good place to make a drop. You expecting competition for the woman? 'Cause we're not equipped to deal with a platoon of soldiers."

Mark cursed. It was bad enough that his mercenaries were dependent on the small group of private soldiers that had fished them out of the river. He'd feel better if he knew who'd hired the soldiers and equipped them with the tracking device locator. "Have you learned any more about your rescuers?"

The man grunted. "They're part of a private army for hire, run by a former Brazilian general. Their boss claims the woman has something that will make them all very rich. And powerful."

Shit. He knew it. His contact at Susana's dig had revealed the existence of the chip. He scratched an itch underneath his detested beard. It had been a risk trusting his contact with the reason he wanted Susana, but he'd thought the price he offered would avoid just such a scenario.

"Where are you now?"

"Anchored across the river and just downstream from the dig."

"Good. As soon as it's light, have one of the soldiers contact their person inside the camp. I want you waiting for Dias when she arrives."

"We were planning to grab her when she crossed the river," the mercenary said.

"So leave your partner with the group of soldiers and tell them to keep an eye on the river. I want you in camp. Remember, the woman is not to be harmed. I don't care what the soldiers tell you. If she's hurt, you won't get your money. You can kill the man."

Mark severed the connection before the mercenary could protest further. "Soon," he whispered. He'd see Susana soon. He felt it.

And God help the mercenaries if they so much as scratched her.

Saturday, Night
Amazon Jungle

"YOUR NUDE PHOTOS don't show you bare down there," Kai said, his voice lazy and warm with amusement. Susana lay sprawled across his chest, her head tucked up under his chin. They'd draped their clothes across her back and legs as a makeshift blanket.

He hoped no one approached their camp. He wasn't sure he could move right now if his life depended on it. His muscles had turned to jelly.

Susana lifted her head enough to shoot him a mock-horrified glance. "Kai Paterson, you've been looking at my nude photos? You naughty boy."

Kai laughed and pulled her back down until her head lay over his heart. God, how long had it been since he felt this light-hearted?

"I saw the photos purely by accident," he said primly.

"Uh-huh. Right."

"Scout's honor." She poked him in the chest, and with a chuckle, he relented. "Okay, so some wise guy research tech put the photos in your SSU file. And on the off chance I ever encountered you naked from the neck down, I needed to be able to identify you. Nice birthmark by the way." She had a tiny red circle on her hipbone, just inside her panty line.

"Which you never saw until tonight because in those photos, I'm either on my belly, have a prop in front of me, or have my leg bent to hide my pubis."

And thank God for that. The knowledge that complete strangers had seen her nude pissed him off. At least there'd remained some hidden areas of her body only her lovers knew.

Dammit, that wasn't helping. He hated the idea that she'd had other lovers before him. Which was fucking ridiculous. He had no claim on her.

She was part of his mission. And when he got her back to the SSU, the doctors were going to have to cut into her to remove the damn microchip. The thought made him sick, which just proved he'd made a mistake getting this close to Susana. Nothing should come before his need to destroy the chip.

He lifted her off of him. "Get dressed. We need to sleep."

"Kai?"

He grabbed his clothes and rolled clear of the mosquito net. There was still enough light from the chemical stick to allow him to pull his pants and shirt on without fumbling. "I'm going to check the perimeter," he mumbled. He picked his flashlight off of her hammock where he'd left it, then bolted across the camp and ducked into the trees.

Where had all the oxygen gone? His lungs labored to breath and his heart beat a panicked rhythm. Because he'd done the unforgivable. He'd allowed himself to care about Susana.

Another person he could fail. Another person vulnerable to the dangers of his job, because all his promises of protection were a lie. Against a strong enough enemy, nothing he did would keep Susana safe.

Just as he'd failed to keep his parents safe. The twins. Jenna.

For the rest of his life he'd have nightmares of walking into his childhood home. Finding his parents with their throats gaping wide enough to show vertebrae, their scalped heads shiny with blood. His own hands turning red as he desperately performed CPR, even though he'd known he was too late.

He'd thought there was no way his undercover assignment could touch them.

He'd been wrong.

His work had killed them. If Susana became part of his life there'd always be the chance his work would get her killed, too.

He would *not* allow Susana to become another one of his nightmares. Once the chip was safely removed, he had to walk away. The criminals he came in contact with were ruthless. He couldn't afford to care for anyone.

But until he set her free, he would do whatever necessary to keep Susana safe. Even if it meant unleashing the savagery he'd been fighting against.

THE NEXT MORNING Susana stared into the jungle and shook her head, frantically trying to ease the need to bolt. Pressure built inside her chest. Panic spread rapidly, nearly crushing her lungs as it fought its way through her body.

Get away. Run away. The refrain became increasingly persistent. *Get away. Run away.*

She took three steps into the jungle before she stopped, fully realizing what she was doing. And why.

She was leaving Kai. Because after a night of sex, particularly fantastic sex that touched her deep inside where her heart slept, she always left. One time too many a lover had oh-so-casually asked her to get him an appointment with an agent, even though she no longer modeled. Or asked her to accompany him to an event, "Because my friends will die with envy to see you on my arm."

Sick and tired of being used by men she'd believed wanted her for herself, not what status and connections she brought them, she'd vowed never again to stay in a relationship long enough to let her emotions get involved. Because it hurt too much when she found out her lover didn't have any feelings for her at all.

Depending on her connection with a man, she might leave after one night or one month, but she always left.

Yet she couldn't leave Kai. Just the thought of never seeing him again sent a shaft of pain straight through her heart.

No, this couldn't be happening. It...

She glanced around, as if the trees and vines would suddenly spell out the truth. Tried swallowing past the lump in her throat.

It had to be just the circumstances. That was it. No matter how connected she'd felt to Kai when they'd made love, no matter how much her life depended on him, or how much she wanted to ease the hurt he carried from losing his family, she could still walk away when this was over.

Because she knew up front what he was using her for. The microchip. Once he had the damn chip, he'd be out of her life.

That knowledge would protect her heart, right?

Of course. This panicked fluttering in her chest wasn't caused by the thought of never seeing him again. This ice filling her veins wasn't because she could lose him to malaria or a bullet.

Liar.

"Susana? You ready? We need to head out."

Just the sound of his voice sent warmth spilling through her. Susana put her head in her hands.

Damn him. What had he done to her?

"They'll be worried to death about me," Susana had told Kai. And she'd believed it with all her soul. Now, lying on her stomach on a hill overlooking her dig, she fought to breathe past the lump in her throat. She'd been so sure that after she fell in the river her colleagues would look for her. That when they didn't find her body, they'd think the saboteur had her and contact the authorities. Or maybe mourn her for dead. She'd expected to find all activity at the dig halted.

But no. Activity appeared normal. Clusters of people knelt or sat around three open pits, digging, sorting or brushing off items pulled from the earth.

Just another day. Never mind Susana's disappearance.

Traitors. All their words of support and friendship had been lies. Her throat tightened and tears stung her eyes. Her colleagues didn't even care she was missing.

She swiped the back of her hand against her cheek, then wiped her damp hand against her pants. A quick sidelong glance at Kai showed him facing forward, eyes pressed to his binoculars.

Good. At least he hadn't noticed her tears.

Susana focused on the dig, and gradually her hurt over having been so easily forgotten was replaced by puzzlement. Who was running the dig? No matter how devoted her coworkers, they wouldn't continue working without guidance. And her funders had very specific criteria for leadership.

Which meant someone had replaced Susana as dig supervisor.

Down below, a woman walked out of Susana's tent. Her dark red hair, bobbed to chin length, glowed like banked fire in the late afternoon sun.

Jacie.

Suddenly Susana missed her friend's common sense. She wanted to talk this over with Jacie. Ask her what was going on.

But as Susana watched, Jacie strolled over to a shallow pit at the far right of the dig. From underneath the shade of a tree, a camera crew stepped into view. Susana's stomach cramped. "No," she breathed.

Jacie walked to the very edge of the pit, said something over her shoulder to the lighting technician, then stepped further along the rim a few feet. The sound man approached her and clipped a mike to her shirt.

With a coy smile, Jacie turned her back to the pit, nodded at the cameraman, and began to talk. At that moment, Susana's stomach drew into a knot so tight she didn't think she'd ever get it unwound.

"That sow-eared...hairy-faced...rat-whore! Jacie's taken over my television show!"

Susana didn't even realize she'd pushed to her hands and knees until Kai's hand yanked on her arm.

"Get down before they see you," he warned.

Susana fought him. "That's my assistant. Taking over my spot. Stepping into my life!"

"And if there are mercenaries waiting for us to show up, it could mean our deaths, Susana. Now get the fuck down."

She dropped to her stomach, but not before shooting a deadly glance in the direction of her former friend.

The pieces starting forming a dark picture in her mind. Jacie had sent her onto the supply boat that day. Had Jacie also pushed her into the river? What lies had she told the crew since then?

Susana pressed her forehead against the ground, well aware that Kai was looking at her with sympathy. She wished she were in the middle of nowhere where no one could hear her, instead of hidden in this clump of bushes so close to camp. She needed to throw something. The physical act of swinging her arm would help release some of this god-awful tension. Then she'd scream her anger to the skies until she felt empty, cool and ready to return to business.

Instead, she gritted her teeth and dug her fingers deep into the soil, waiting until the muscles in her fingers cramped before letting go.

It would have been better to find out one of the men on the supply boat had pushed her into the river. Animosity from strangers she could deal with, because it wasn't a betrayal.

But Jacie's actions...Susana bit her tongue to stop from screaming. This was worse than when she'd found out Elena had started the rumors about Susana selling artifacts on the black market. She'd never formed a close bond with Elena.

She'd considered Jacie her friend. She'd trusted her.

Would she never learn? She was just a means to an end for the people in her life. Her mother used her as free labor as a child, then pumped her for money once she began modeling.

People in the modeling world used her to further their careers, either by hanging onto her coattails or by trying to push her down. Elena had used her to attract the financing of a prestigious institution.

God. Why did she still keep trusting people when she knew better? Each time, she believed she'd found someone who liked her for who she was on the inside, not because she was beautiful or famous. And each time she'd had her trust betrayed and her heart broken. No one ever looked out for her interests. No one wanted to just be friends with her. Everyone had an agenda, and once that agenda was met, she no longer mattered.

Jacie's betrayal cut deep, though. Susana had worked with Jacie for years. She'd proven herself to be a true friend.

Or so Susana thought.

"Which tent is yours?" Kai asked.

She blew out a heavy breath, imagining her anger hurtling like mud across the air and hitting Jacie in the face. "The one with the green patch to the right of the door. Closest to the east edge of the dig."

"Got it."

She'd told Kai that she didn't know where in her tent the letter was. She'd tossed it aside when she heard the sound of the canopy supports collapsing.

"Supplies?"

"The brown tent on the opposite end of the dig. The kitchen tent is the bright orange one. Don't ask about the color."

"Hmm," Kai responded.

A few moments later, he nodded his head toward the deeper woods behind them, indicating his surveillance was finished. In sync, they scooted down the slight slope until they were hidden from view of the camp.

Her mouth twitched as she scrambled to her feet and followed Kai into the jungle. At least she knew up front what Kai wanted from her. The chip. Sex.

No chance of betrayal here.

RAFE LOWERED the anti-glare binoculars he'd been using to watch the man and the woman on the other side of the dig. The man was good at keeping a low profile, but Rafe was better. He knew how to wait with inhuman patience, his mind empty and his body so still the enemy never noticed him.

When the pair was out of sight, Rafe climbed out of his tree. His orders were to call his handler and report that the two had arrived, but this position was too close to the camp. He might be overheard. So he headed toward the river.

With every step, Rafe's head pounded. Something about the man's face teased at his brain. Something that had nothing to do with his mission.

Your life is ours to command. The phrase ricocheted inside his skull, knocking free bits of memory.

Chains digging into his freezing flesh...needles that set every cell of his body on fire...hallucinations of bugs and snakes crawling over every inch of him...more pain...

Rafe stumbled.

No. Weakness was not allowed. The weak were killed.

He squeezed his eyes shut. What was wrong with him? He wasn't supposed to feel pain. The men in the white coats had promised. As long as he obeyed them, the pain would stop. Only if he failed would the pain return.

He was fulfilling the mission. So why did he hurt?

CHAPTER SIXTEEN

SUSANA LOOKED ready to commit murder. She turned and started to move off, but Kai put a hand on her arm. "We'll go into camp just after twilight."

She spun to face him. "Why? What's wrong with right now?"

"First, the camera crew is filming." Christ, if anything could point out to him the hopelessness of a future with Susana, seeing the cameras was it. Being caught on film was one of the worst things that could happen to an undercover agent.

Since when did you start thinking of a future with her?

Shaking his head, he continued, "You don't want the meeting with Jacie on tape. We need to wait until all the filming equipment is packed up for the evening. Second, at twilight people will be thinking about cleaning up. Looking forward to dinner and maybe a drink. Their reflexes will be slower and their attention not as sharp. Plus, there will be deeper shadows for us to hide in."

Her eyebrows arched regally. "This isn't a war camp. I don't see why we have to sneak in. No one down there is my enemy—except for Jacie, that two-faced, traitorous, lying sack of goat turds." She pulled her arm out of his grasp.

"You're assuming Jacie's actions have nothing to do with the chip. What if you're wrong and the mercenaries are waiting in one of the tents for you to arrive?"

Her eyes widened. "But—"

"Someone put a tracking device in you while you were on site. Someone pushed you into the river. You can't assume it had nothing to do with the chip. Trust no one and your chances of surviving improve."

"That's a terrible way to live."

The pity in her voice ignited a fire of resentment in him. He tamped it down. He needed her cooperation now more than ever. He'd seen no sign of the mercenaries, but cold reason said they had to be nearby. This was the only logical destination for Susana. The nearest city was several more days by foot.

If he was tracking Susana, he'd wait in one of the tents.

He rubbed the back of his neck. His instincts screamed at him to grab Susana and run. He'd do it, except they needed a way to call for extraction and the camp's radio was their only choice. Besides, he wanted to see what her father had said in his letter. Perhaps the scientist had written instructions for decrypting and uploading his data.

Kai thought about waiting until full dark and sneaking into camp by himself, but he didn't trust Susana to stay put. Her temper was up and he was lucky to have stalled her so far. If he let her out of his sight, she'd go storming after her traitorous assistant.

"Here's the deal," he said. "If the mercenaries are down there, they'll expect us to hit the communications center first, so once we're in camp we'll instead head to your tent and retrieve your father's letter. Do you keep a first aid kit there?"

"Yeah, but just the basics. Band-Aids. Antiseptic wipes. Triple-action antibiotic. We have an infirmary tent because people are always getting cuts and bites of one sort or another."

"Good. You need some stronger antibiotic for that shoulder wound. It's not healing the way I'd like. Once I've got what we need we'll head over to the communications center. Is there a small boat or canoe?"

She nodded. "We use it for fishing. But the saboteur damaged it." She shrugged. "It's possible someone repaired the boat since I've been gone."

"After we call for extraction we'll check out the boat. A helicopter can't land, but if we take a boat onto the river, we can be airlifted."

"Kai, you're making this seem like something out of an action movie!"

"You're forgetting that someone tried to kill you because of the microchip."

Susana tossed her head, the movement flipping her braid over her shoulder. "I still can't believe the microchip is real and that it's so damn important."

"Real enough to be worth your life," Kai snapped.

As the light faded, Susana followed Kai toward her camp. Rather than enter at the front by the river, or at the rear where a trail led to the interior and a remote Yanomami village located on a small tributary several hours away, they'd circled the camp until they were as close to Susana's tent as possible.

Susana bit back a grin. They were actually going to sneak in. It was total cloak-and-dagger stuff. She loved it.

If someone noticed them slipping into camp, Susana was supposed to ignore them and continue onward.

Ha.

Kai didn't know her crew. They'd—

Hell.

Her good humor evaporated. She didn't know her crew, either. After all, she was the sap who'd thought they'd miss her.

She was so lost in thought, she almost ran into Kai when he stopped. He held up a hand, then pointed forward. Through the trees, she saw that they'd arrived at the edge between the jungle and the open clearing of the dig. Her tent sat not fifty feet away. It was unlit. The brush-strewn open space between them and the tent was covered by deep, concealing shadows.

No one was nearby. From the sounds of laughter and conversation coming out of the kitchen tent, dinner was in full swing.

A wave of nostalgia tightened the back of her throat. She missed having dinner with her crew. The teasing and banter. The heated arguments and occasional bursts of song. She was a social animal at heart, never more content than when she was in the middle of an enthusiastic crowd.

Yet she couldn't help feel a tiny twinge of resentment. A mere week after her disappearance and everyone was laughing. Had they even bothered to search for her?

She felt her anger rising and pursed her lips, fighting it back. This was not the time to lose control.

Kai put his hand on her shoulder.

"Let's go," he breathed in her ear. He started to draw away, but a sudden impulse had her grabbing on to his biceps and halting him.

"Wait," she demanded just as quietly. His hair was too short to give her a good handhold, so she pulled his ears to bring his head lower.

She brushed her lips across his in a quick kiss, then released him. "For luck."

Then she gestured for him to proceed.

Shaking his head, Kai edged forward, moving out from the trees in a low crouch. She followed, unable to keep the James Bond theme from running through her head. Kissing him had restored her equilibrium and she felt wonderfully energized.

It was all she could do not to laugh as they slipped unnoticed underneath the back wall of her tent. They'd made it!

Shooting a grin at Kai, even though she knew he couldn't see her in the darkness, she stayed on her hands and knees and crawled over to her workstation. This was where she'd opened the letter. She used the light from a chemical stick tucked into her shirt to briefly illuminate the tent floor.

There!

The crumpled up pages of the letter shone eerily in the neon green light. She snatched them up and shoved them in the pocket of her backpack. "Got it," she murmured.

Kai, in his ever-present paranoia, had insisted they keep their packs with them. In response to her exasperated, "Why?" he'd answered, "Because I spent two years on the run. It's critical to be prepared to evacuate on a second's notice."

Too stunned at the idea that he'd been hunted for two years, she'd given in.

Now she resettled her pack across her shoulders and stood up. Across the tent, Kai had opened the trunk she used as a catch-all while on site. His flashlight, muted by a bandana over the glass, was strapped to his wrist. She saw him pick up her supply of cookies and nutrition bars, then search through her meager first-aid kit.

Leaving Kai to his pillaging, Susana walked over to her clothing trunk. Ah...fresh socks...undies...she couldn't wait to take a shower then put on an entirely new set of clothes. The vision was so luxurious, she almost purred out loud. Being clean was one of life's simplest pleasures.

But cleanliness would have to wait until they'd been extracted. Kai refused to let her linger in camp once they'd accomplished their mission.

From beside her, Kai whispered it was time to go. She jumped and only barely managed to swallow a squeak of surprise.

She hurriedly added a few more items of clothing to her pack, added the document-carrying case that held her passport, her permit for digging here in the jungle, and all her spare cash, then zipped the waterproof lining of the pack closed.

When she settled the straps of the pack across her shoulders, she groaned at the increase in weight. Not a huge difference, but her shoulders were already sore from the constant pressure and her wound throbbed.

Nodding to indicate she was ready, she followed Kai out the front of the tent. They weren't sneaking like before, but still stuck to the shadows.

Susana wanted to confront Jacie next, but Kai insisted it was more important that they call his boss, because it would take time to mobilize a helicopter.

She'd expected to see some people around camp as they walked through, but the place was empty. She tilted her head, listening for sounds of movement inside any of the tents. Nothing.

That was...odd. There'd never been a meal where every crew member was present. There were always a couple of stragglers who decided to work an extra few minutes and missed the start of the meal, or, like her, got so absorbed in their work they forgot to eat.

Even the conversation from the mess tent had stopped.

She wasn't supposed to talk, so the only way to signal Kai something was wrong was to stop and hope he noticed her. He'd warned her not to touch him unexpectedly because his instincts would react as if she were a threat before his brain could recognize her.

She waited until they were next to another tent, deep in shadow, before she halted.

Sure enough, Kai took only two more steps before he realized she wasn't behind him. He backtracked, a question in his eyes.

She gestured at the camp. Frowned. Made a walking movement with her fingers, then shook her head. Put her hands over her ears, then took her hands away and shrugged in question.

Kai surveyed the camp. He nodded and made a shushing gesture.

Good. He understood.

This time as they moved toward the communications tent, they were definitely sneaking. The entire journey took perhaps three minutes, and in that entire time she didn't see a single person. In fact, the only lit-up tent was the too quiet mess tent.

No camp was ever that light-efficient. The infirmary, for one, usually kept a light on. And a couple of the less sociable workers liked to eat fast and return quickly to their tents, or would skip the meal altogether.

Something was wrong.

Sunday, Evening
Boa Vista, Brazil

MARK TONELLI PUT his satellite phone back in his pocket and continued down the street toward the busy restaurant. A smile tried to break across his face, but he held it back. It wouldn't do to draw attention to himself by grinning like a fool.

His man at the dig had just reported that Susana and a male companion had been spotted at the outskirts of the dig. The couple would be under control within the hour. But the mercenaries now wanted ten thousand additional dollars for Susana Dias.

Not a chance in hell.

He'd ordered them to grab Susana, disable the private soldiers, and steal their boat. Then head for Boa Vista. If they failed him, he'd pass along their location to a certain military court. Seems his mercenaries had never officially left the army and were considered AWOL.

He hoped the threat was strong enough, because there was little else he could do to make certain they brought Susana to him.

He would delay telling Jamieson that he'd found Susana as

long as possible, giving him time to get to know her first. Then he'd broach the subject of the chip and getting it removed.

Mark paused outside the restaurant door. His stomach rumbled, but he turned away. He needed a secure location to meet Susana. Before he ate, he'd just take another tour of town. There were one or two possibilities he wanted to reassess.

He felt strong enough to lift buildings. Susana was coming.

Sunday, Evening
Amazon Jungle

KAI'S INSTINCTS told him their entry into Susana's camp had been too easy. The mercenaries had to be nearby, waiting. Yet he didn't have the feeling of being watched. He'd seen no trip wires or other early-warning devices around the perimeter of the camp or Susana's tent.

Still, the lack of people around camp bothered him. It seemed too big a coincidence that everyone just happened to be in the mess tent when he and Susana arrived.

Susana's silent warning made him more certain they were walking into a trap. But he wouldn't retreat. He had to reach the radio and call Ryker for transport. And until he knew what danger hid in the camp, he didn't dare let Susana out of his sight, not even to send her back to the safety of the jungle.

He stepped carefully around a tent that stank of incense. A few yards beyond that, the communications tent loomed like a giant beetle, the radio antennae piercing the night sky. He led Susana around back, searching for guards.

There were none.

Which meant there had to be someone waiting inside. The communications tent was the natural destination for him and Susana.

He signaled her to wait.

Ten minutes later he hadn't heard any sounds from the tent's interior. If there was a guard inside, he hadn't so much as exhaled loudly.

Kai slowly lifted the canvas and shone his shielded flashlight around the interior. He saw no human-shaped shadows or obvious alarm systems. He nodded to Susana and ducked inside.

Susana pointed out the radio. The display screen was dark.

He strode toward it, wondering if the mercenaries had disabled the device. But a flip of a switch had the machine humming to life. Lights across the front glowed and static echoed from its speaker as it warmed up.

Kai turned the dial to an emergency channel and began transmitting a coded message giving their location and requesting a pickup. If Ryker or anyone else at the SSU was monitoring radio waves down here, they'd understand.

Then light speared into the tent and a shrill female voice shouted, "Put your hands up, I have a gun!"

CHAPTER SEVENTEEN

THE LIGHT briefly illuminated Kai's face before moving away, but didn't reach deep enough into the corners to reveal Susana.

The light abruptly disappeared. A male voice, speaking in heavily accented English, berated, "Woman, what are you doing? This is for us to handle. Go back to the dining hall with the others!"

The sounds of a struggle ended with a muffled thump.

Kai motioned for Susana to slip out the back of the tent. She shook her head and took a step forward just as two men with AK-47's entered. Susana bumped into the lead man. He swung the butt of his weapon up and sideways in a quick jab that connected with the underside of her jaw.

Kai heard her teeth snap together, then she toppled backward with a low cry of pain. He tried to catch her, but the second man jabbed the muzzle of his weapon into Kai's stomach.

Amateur.

Kai grabbed the barrel of the gun and pulled. Before the mercenary had time to let go, Kai slammed his hand up under the man's chin. A second blow to his temple, and the man blacked out.

Kai glanced across the tent. The other man had forced Susana to her knees. He knelt behind her, knife at her throat.

The world shrank to the blade and Susana's fragile skin. Visions of his scalped family pushed the limits of his sanity.

"I don't need the woman alive," the man said, his voice sounding far away. "Or in one piece. All I need is the abdomen so I can grab the damn chip. So don't step any closer or I'll start cutting."

Focus, Paterson. Or you're going to lose Susana.

Kai snapped back to the present. He studied the man with the knife. Definitely the cooler of the two men. His eyes were calm and his voice remained steady. From the almost new condition of the man's uniform, Kai figured he was one of the private soldiers from the gunboat. The unconscious man, with his faded, frayed fatigues was probably one of the mercenaries who'd kidnapped Susana.

"Get facedown on the ground," the soldier ordered. "Hands clasped at the back of your neck."

Keeping his eyes half-lidded, watching for an opportunity to strike, Kai slowly lowered himself to his knees. He'd left the radio's microphone in the "on" position. Assuming its sensitivity was strong enough, all conversation was being broadcast.

"Hurry," the man snarled.

Kai had no intention of hurrying. The man intended to kill Susana either way.

Kai would die before he let that happen.

"Do you want her to bleed?" The soldier prodded the sensitive area under Susana's chin with his knife, forcing her to tip her head back or be cut.

Even across the tent, Kai could feel Susana's anger rising. The blow to her chin might have dazed her, but the look she shot him was heavy with impatience. He couldn't see her hands because they were behind her, but he saw the telltale signs of shoulder muscles bunching.

Shit. She was going to try something. If this guy was good enough, fast enough, Susana was going to get hurt.

A woman stumbled through the tent door. "What's going on?" she demanded. She had red hair and wore flimsy expedition clothes that were all look and no function, but would look good on camera.

It was the assistant. Jacie.

The soldier holding Susana turned his head toward the door, startled by Jacie's appearance. "I thought Paco had dragged you back to the mess tent," he growled. "Get out of here, woman. This is no longer your concern."

His grip on the knife loosened.

Susana leaned back, forcing the man's torso to take her weight. Then her elbows jerked. The man screamed high-pitched like a girl, dropping the knife as his hands went between his knees.

Susana rolled toward the door, knocking into Jacie's legs and toppling the woman to the ground. Jacie's alarmed shriek was answered by Susana's furious snarl.

Leaving the two women to fight it out, Kai knelt beside the knife man. He was no threat now. He lay on his back, hands covering his family jewels, writhing in pain.

"Who hired you?" Kai demanded.

The man shook his head.

Kai stood, raised his foot and pressed it lightly over the man's crotch. The man's face paled.

"I swear, I don't know who hired us." But his eyes cut over to where the women were fighting.

Ah, shit. Jacie. This was going to devastate Susana.

"What was your mission?" he asked.

"To retrieve the woman, dead or alive. Or just her abdomen if she died and body parts got separated."

The image of Susana bloody and missing limbs condensed Kai's fury into a cold, deadly intent. "Where were you supposed to take her?"

"Belém. A warehouse."

After a few more questions, Kai determined the soldier had nothing more useful to say, so he knocked him out. The women were still kicking and biting and screaming at one another.

"Traitor...bitch..."

Kai shook his head, mouth quirking up at one corner. Susana had apparently lost her ability for creative curses.

He hopped out of the way as they rolled by. Then he saw where they were headed and jumped forward, trying to get a hand on one of the women and stop their momentum.

Too late. They slammed into the table holding the radio. Someone's leg tangled in the wires and a moment later, both battery and radio crashed to the floor.

The radio went dark.

Shit. He hoped Ryker had received his message.

Keeping one eye on the cat fight, he stripped the mercenaries of their weapons and radios, then tied the men using some spare cable he found in a corner.

By the time he was done, Susana sat on Jacie's lower back. The woman's face pressed into the floor and Susana held Jacie's arms high above her back.

Ouch. He knew from experience how painful that position was. He rolled his still tender shoulder. If Susana wasn't careful, she'd dislocate Jacie's shoulder. Although, given the furious expression on Susana's face, she probably wouldn't care.

Susana tossed her hair back. Blood trickled from the corner of her mouth, and her left eye was already swelling. Nail scratches ran down her cheeks like tribal marks.

She looked wild and fierce. A surge of lust roared through Kai with such power, his knees almost buckled. He sucked in a breath of air. *Not now, dammit!* They weren't safe yet.

"Kai, do you have something I can tie her with?"

Another deep breath, and he managed to get himself under

control. "Yeah." He passed her some cabling. But after he helped Susana tie Jacie's wrists and ankles, he couldn't stop himself. He kissed her.

It was a harder kiss than the one Susana had given him earlier, but not nearly as strong or as deep as he wanted. Still, the flare of heat in her eyes and the way her hands jerked, as if she'd started to reach for him then stopped herself, was gratifying.

"Later," he breathed in her ear. "Right now you have a traitor to question."

She licked her lips and he groaned. He started to lower his mouth for just one more taste, but she moved away, focused already on Jacie.

He bit back his disappointment. Susana took Jacie's right arm and he took her left and together they pulled the woman to her feet and dragged her over to the lone chair in the tent.

Susana's eyes widened as she spotted the trussed-up mercenaries, both still unconscious.

Kai glanced over at Mr. Family Jewels and noticed that there was now a red stain on his crotch. "Jesus Christ, what did you do to the guy, Susana?"

The smile she shot him was pure feminine evil. She walked over to where she'd been held captive and picked something up from the ground.

"I stuck this into his groin."

He closed the distance between them. Shit. No wonder the guy was bleeding. On her palm lay a long, thin, needle-sharp pick. "Ouch." He picked it up and saw blood on it. "What do you normally use it for?"

"Getting dirt out of tiny crevices. It was sitting on my trunk and I thought it would make a good weapon, so I brought it with me."

He nodded. "Good thinking. Just remind me not to piss you off again."

She grinned. Then she turned to Jacie and her good humor evaporated.

Jacie stared defiantly up at Susana, her dark green eyes glittering with insane fury. Kai took a step back, giving Susana the field, but staying close enough to offer his support if necessary.

"I saw you being filmed earlier," Susana said. Her tone was flat, completely unlike her usually warm, passionate voice.

"How long have you been planning to step into my shoes?" Kai heard the underlying note of pain in Susana's voice and wished he could take this hurt away from her. "Were you the one behind the sabotage? The tracking device? Did you push me off the boat?"

Jacie tossed her head and shot Kai a coy glance out of the corner of her eyes. "Of course."

TRYING NOT to show how much she was reeling emotionally, Susana searched Jacie's eyes for some sign of the generous friend she'd loved like a sister. She found only cold ambition and madness.

How had she been so blind?

"You intended for me to die?" The anger from their fight simmered at the edges of Susana's consciousness, barely held back by the need to understand why.

"Of course." Jacie's sly, satisfied smile sent a chill slithering down Susana's spine.

There wasn't a trace of remorse anywhere in Jacie's eyes or expression. The hairs at the back of Susana's neck stood on end and she was suddenly very glad she had Kai at her back.

This Jacie was capable of things Susana didn't want to think about.

"Why?" Susana asked.

"Oh, you mean besides the fact that I've been waiting years for you to get out of my way? Money, of course. My contact offered me a huge payoff if I made sure he got the microchip first. But how much more satisfying to make you run scared back to civilization." Jacie sat up straighter in the chair and tried to bring her arms in front of her, but the cables binding her wrists restricted her movement. She frowned, stuck her lip out in a pout, and glanced at Kai as if she thought he'd feel sorry for her and release her.

The woman's lack of fear wasn't normal. Nor was the way she jiggled her chest, trying to get Kai's attention.

From behind her, Susana heard Kai smother a laugh behind a cough.

"It was my decision to hire the private soldiers to kill you," Jacie said. She rocked her head side to side, preening. "The general is one of my lovers. I knew he had enough contacts that we could take the microchip for ourselves and sell it to the highest bidder."

"And the tracking device?"

"Oooh, very cloak-and-dagger wasn't it?" Jacie purred. "I'm surprised you found it. My lover gave it to me. I shot it into you using a blowgun the first day you were here."

As much as Susana wanted to turn away from the hatred burning in Jacie's eyes, she wouldn't show the woman any weakness. "What story did you tell the rest of the crew to explain my disappearance?"

Jacie's pitying smile made Susana want to throttle her.

"I told them the network had decided to replace you as the show's host in favor of me." Jacie sighed dramatically. "Poor Susana, hiding a diagnosis of clinical depression for years. When you got the news about being replaced, you committed the sabotage, determined not to let me ruin your career. But when I caught you, you committed suicide by jumping into the river." Jacie had the gall to bat her eyelashes. "And oh, how convenient. The fishing boat had been sabotaged. By the time the boat was repaired and a search party was ready to go, you were already in the hands of the mercenaries."

Susana clamped her molars on her tongue to stop herself from asking why no one had questioned Jacie's tale. Why no one seemed to have mourned her. She was afraid she wouldn't like the answer.

"I even forged a letter from the head of the network supporting my claim that you had been replaced, so when the television crew arrived, they never questioned why I was in charge. Because of the production deadline, they didn't hesitate when I insisted we continue filming the very next day." She tossed her head so her hair flipped back over her right shoulder. "The rest of the crew never even missed you. Not a single sad eye among them," Jacie smirked.

"And because I'm such a better host, the viewers will never miss you." The malice in Jacie's eyes speared through Susana, chilling every cell it hit. Susana instinctively took a step back. "Finally, I'm getting the fame I deserve."

"Excuse me?"

Jacie's lip curled up. "No one looks at the rest of us poor archaeologists and offers us television contracts. They only want Susana. Beautiful Susana. Smart Susana. The golden girl of the archaeological world. Not even charges of black marketeering stuck to you, and Elena made an excellent witness."

Spots danced before Susana's eyes as her rage roared back. "You were behind Elena's charges?" She'd spent five hellish months being questioned by the police and by Interpol, being trashed by the press, because of Jacie? Jacie, who at the time had given Susana a shoulder to cry on?

"Of course it was me. Elena wasn't smart enough to think up the idea, even though she resented you as much as I do." Jacie laughed. "At least she hurt your feelings, didn't she? Remember all those tears?"

"You traitorous, lying, conniving, whore-bitch!" Susana lunged toward Jacie, fingers aiming for the woman's eyes. But Kai wrapped his arm around her shoulders from behind, trapping her arms to her sides and pulling her to a stop.

"Easy," Kai murmured. "We need her conscious to answer the rest of our questions."

Susana shot a murderous glare at the smirking Jacie. She so wanted to fight again, but Kai was right.

She sucked a deep breath into her lungs and exhaled slowly. Four more breaths, and enough tension had left her that she relaxed her fists one finger at a time.

"That's it, sweetheart. You've already done enough damage to her. She's going to be hurting for days," Kai said.

Yeah, he was right. Jacie's normally perfect appearance was ruined. Deep red scratches marred the normally flawless skin on her face. Her lips were swollen and bloody. The skin around both eyes was bruised.

Susana's lips quirked into a satisfied smile. Jacie would freak once she looked in a mirror and saw the hunk of hair missing from just above her left temple. And the bloody rips in her expensive clothes.

"Who told you about the microchip?" Kai demanded.

Well, that just made her feel small. She'd been so focused on Jacie's intent to kill her, she'd forgotten that there was a bigger picture.

"Mmm...now there's a man of culture. My other lover. Tall. Brown, curly hair. Looks straight out of *GQ*. You danced with him at the fundraiser last month, but it was me he took to bed."

Kai glanced at Susana. "Ring any bells?"

Susana shook her head. She'd danced with a lot of men that night. "Did he give you a name? A reason?"

"Oh, he called himself Antonio, but I doubt that was his real name." Jacie's smile turned sexual. "He claimed the microchip inside of you belongs to the American government, and that you stole it. He claimed he needed to get the chip back because it contains data critical to national security." She rolled her eyes. "So very patriotic of him. But I knew that if he wanted the data so badly, there had to be other people who would pay even higher for it."

"You've lost everything, Jacie," Susana sneered. "The potential money. The fame. You'll never—"

"Tomás, are you there?" a male voice squawked from one of the two-way pagers Kai had removed from the mercenaries. "A black military helicopter is heading your way very fast. Get out of there now, brother. They just tried to sink us with an explosive charge."

"Shit. Grab your pack," Kai ordered. The urgency in his voice propelled Susana across the tent to where she'd dropped her backpack.

Kai pulled his knife and took two steps toward Jacie. Susana felt a juvenile thrill as the other woman finally showed terror.

But Kai only sliced the cables at Jacie's ankles, then the ones at her wrists.

"Run!"

"What? Why?" Jacie sputtered.

Kai cut the mercenaries free next. Then, knife still in hand, he scooped up his pack, grabbed Susana by the arm, and bolted for the door.

"What's wrong?" Susana gasped, trying to keep up with Kai.

"Helicopter's almost on us. Can't you hear it?"

Um, no, she couldn't. Not over the sound of their pounding feet. After several yards he finally let go of her arm and she found a pace that allowed her to stay by his side.

"Head straight into the jungle," Kai said. "Keep going no matter what happens."

She did not like the sound of that. "What if they're friends?" she gasped.

"There hasn't been enough time for our side to mobilize."

They were next to the mess tent now. Without slowing down, Kai shouted, "The camp is under attack. Run for the trees!"

Susana joined his cry, thinking her crew might respond better to a familiar voice. She was afraid to risk her balance by glancing back over her shoulder, so she sent up a little prayer that her colleagues would obey.

As they passed the shower tent, she finally heard a deep thrumming that had all the hairs on her body leaping to atavistic attention. The helicopter!

She lengthened her stride. The jungle seemed no closer, while the helicopter drew nearer until the noise from the rotors pressed against her back like an invisible wall.

Just a few more feet. She put every bit of effort into breaching the distance between her and the trees, then gave in to fear and leapt the last foot.

Yet even within the shelter of the jungle, she still felt hunted. Caught up in the urgent need to get away, she panicked at the slow pace forced on them by the increased darkness. She turned and looked back at camp, hoping she'd see her crew evacuating.

But there wasn't a person in sight, not even Jacie or the mercenaries.

No!

Susana started back toward camp.

"Stop," Kai ordered. "Susana, there's nothing you can do about your crew now. We have to keep moving if we're going to stay alive."

As if to prove Kai right, the sound of the helicopter became an engulfing roar. Then two headlights rose over the tree line, following the road into camp from the river.

The desire to save the people she'd considered her family warred with her need to stay alive. She took a step away from Kai.

The roar of the helicopter was punctured by the rat-a-tat-tat of gunfire.

Someone screamed.

Her crew. "No!"

"Susana, we have to move!" Beside her, Kai switched on a flashlight.

Susana kept her eyes on camp, praying for someone to leave. Finally, she saw Jacie race out from between two tents. The helicopter swept in behind her, and like a slow-motion scene in a movie, Jacie's body arched back, then fell to the ground.

The helicopter zoomed on, heading straight for Susana.

She turned and sprinted after Kai.

SHIT. Kai hadn't expected the helicopter to be a military gunship.

He heard the impact of bullets tracing a path in front of the helicopter. The bird was close enough now that the rotor wash blew leaves off the surrounding trees and molded their clothing to their bodies.

Bullets slapped into the trees behind him.

He glanced back and felt a surge of relief to find Susana at his heels. But the helicopter was almost to the edge of the jungle. Dammit, if it didn't turn away soon, they were dead. A few more yards and those bullets would find them.

Or the helicopter would crash into the trees, creating a fireball that would burn them alive.

Come on, come on, pull up, dammit.

He grabbed Susana, ready to throw her on the ground and protect her with his body, when the helicopter veered up and to the left.

Thank you, God.

But shit, whoever was piloting that thing was crazy. The camp barely had enough cleared space to allow the helicopter to swoop in, shoot, then pull up before hitting the trees.

The pilot had waited until the last possible minute to retreat, but Kai suspected the helicopter would be back.

He led Susana up a slight embankment into even deeper tree

cover. The narrow beam from his flashlight proved a meager guide in the thick darkness, but using any light at all put them in danger. Remove the tape covering the lens would give the helicopter a larger beacon to follow.

They'd only run a hundred yards or so, when someone back at camp started screaming. The helicopter zoomed overhead, accompanied by a loud whoosh.

Kai threw Susana on the ground and dove on top of her just as a flash of fiery light illuminated the woods. After a minute, he spared a look behind him.

Shit. A wall of fire surged toward them.

Kai leapt to his feet, dragging Susana with him. He grabbed her hand and ran full out, not caring where they went, as long as they outran the flames.

The smoky air was sticky with the scent of burning resin, and underneath that the sickly chemical smell of an accelerant. Heat expanded out from the burning trees, pushing at their backs as if someone had opened an oven door behind them.

What the fuck were the idiots doing? The chip wouldn't do them any good if it melted.

Susana pulled his hand and turned right. Kai didn't know what she'd seen, but he trusted her jungle knowledge a hell of a lot more than his own. A few feet later the ground dipped. They skidded down the sandy slope and splashed into a shallow stream.

Susana turned left. The pull of the calf-deep water hampered their progress, but at least the air here was less smoky.

Without the accelerant to fuel it, the fire behind them slowed, having to work harder to burn the water-dense vegetation. The glow from the flames seemed farther away now, leaving them barely enough light to see by.

When the air finally cooled around them, Kai pulled back on Susana's arm, slowing her to a stop.

"What?" she asked.

"Hold on a sec." He listened. If the helicopter was still out there, maybe scanning the jungle with infrared, staying within the above-body-temperature air closer to the fire would hide their heat signal.

Angry birds squawked their alarm and animals roared in fear, but he didn't hear the thrumming of helicopter blades.

"Okay. Keep going."

She nodded and continued wading upriver. But after a few minutes her steps began to drag.

Dammit, they both needed to rest, yet the farther away from her camp they moved, the better their chance of survival.

Susana tripped and went down to her knees, Kai set her back on her feet and conceded they had to stop soon. He removed her backpack and slung it across his chest. The fact that she didn't protest proved her level of exhaustion.

They'd moved far enough from the fire to need the flashlight. The pale light shimmered across Susana's face, illuminating the blank, slack look of a person in shock.

His anger flared back to life, coupled with a fierce protectiveness. He wanted to pull her into his arms and lend her his strength. Instead, he hooked her fingers into the rear pocket of his backpack, then continued wading upstream.

With each step he took, the need for retribution burned through his veins. He wanted to turn around and confront their enemies. To kill as Susana's friends had been killed. His muscles trembled with the need to act. A bellow of rage made it up to his throat before he managed to contain it.

No. He was not one of Nevsky's monsters. He believed in law and justice.

He dug the fingernails of his right hand into his palm. His left hand tightened around the flashlight as he reached deep inside himself and dragged sanity out from its hiding place. Used it to bludgeon his savage instincts back into their cage.

He had to stay in control. Be calm.

Susana needed him.

Slowly, his anger faded. But the fight to master his temper left him as drained as an attack of malaria.

CHAPTER EIGHTEEN

Rafe lay on his back and blinked up at the hellish shadows dancing across the jungle canopy. Where was he?

Reddish light. Smoke. The crackle and pop of living things exploding. His mind struggled to make sense of his surroundings. To remember...

Fire. Helicopter.

Right. He'd been moving around the perimeter of the camp, intending to intercept his targets, the man and the woman, when the helicopter attacked. The targets dashed into the jungle. He'd followed for several minutes, the light from the fire making his job easy. But the helicopter had returned, firing into the jungle. Something had slammed into his shoulder. He'd tripped. Fallen. And...then what? He must have blacked out, because he couldn't remember.

What was he supposed to do next? Wait for orders? Or go after the targets?

Sweet Jesus, he couldn't remember past the pain in his head.

He tried to sit up, but the pain throttled him into oblivion.

"Stop," Kai whispered.

He'd heard a sound behind them. Like...

There. A wheezing, *human* cough.

Someone was following them. Ten minutes ago, rapids had forced them to leave the river, entering this clearing dappled by faint spots of moonlight.

Kai reached out for Susana's hand, but met empty air. He swung his flashlight up and back.

Shock body-slammed him.

Susana stood three yards behind him. A man's arm encircled her throat, his forearm shoving her chin up. His other hand held a pistol to her temple.

Kai recognized the more intelligent soldier from the communications tent, and cursed himself for being careless. His M-4 was strapped to the top of his backpack. He hadn't expected pursuit, not by foot.

He'd assumed everyone died in the fire.

What a friggin' amateurish mistake.

The man snarled a demand in Portuguese. Kai didn't bother trying to translate. His focus was on Susana's terrified eyes as she clawed at the man's hands, trying to break his grip.

Trying to breathe.

The man tightened his grip, cutting off Susana's air. She sagged against him.

Rage erupted within Kai. He pushed a button on his flashlight, triggering a laser pointer. With a flick of his wrist, the light shone directly in the mercenary's eyes.

The man cried out and turned his head away, letting his arm fall to his side.

Susana dropped to her knees, then onto her stomach. Kai could hear her gulping for air. And suddenly he was very glad he didn't have his weapon in hand.

The mercenary took several stumbling, circular steps. His

hands rubbed at his eyes, as if the pressure could bring his vision back.

Kai lifted Susana up and set her on her feet. "Can you run?"

She nodded.

"Good." He planted a quick, hard kiss on her mouth. "Go!" He pushed her in the direction they'd been heading. "I'll catch up with you later. Don't stop."

The mercenary used the sound of Kai's voice as a beacon and charged.

Kai met him head on.

Even blinded, the mercenary was a strong, fierce opponent. He fought dirty.

Good. Because Kai wanted to fight. Wanted to feel his hand strike bone. Wanted to hear the man grunt in pain when Kai slammed a knee into his kidney.

God, he felt so alive, so powerful, he barely noticed the pain from his opponent's punches.

Two years ago, he wouldn't have been able to hold his own in the fight, despite self-defense training. His assignments had been in labs, where all fighting was verbal. But after Nevsky's lab burned down, he'd been hunted by the government's top agents. To avoid detection, Kai had hidden in the roughest places on earth. He'd quickly learned how to defend himself, and win, against men who fought to kill.

He dodged an elbow aimed at his throat. Channeled all his fear and rage through his nerves and muscles. He took a blow to the face that slammed his head against the ground. The mercenary's hands went around his neck.

Kai let his body go slack, pretending to lose consciousness.

The mercenary eased his grip. Kai brought his hands up inside the man's arms and swept outward, breaking the man's hold. Then he grabbed the man's neck.

The man snatched at Kai's arms. Tipped his body sideways so they rolled.

Kai grappled for a secure hold. Feinted.

The man fell for it, and Kai pinned him on his stomach.

Kai straddled the mercenary. His knife was at the man's throat, although he didn't remember pulling it.

"Where's your friend?" Kai demanded.

"Ran...back...to river..."

"Why did you come after us?"

"Woman...dead...worth money..."

"Wrong answer, asshole." Kai's knife jerked, slitting the man's throat.

"Kai! Kai stop. What are you doing?"

Kai growled. His knife hand whipped around, slashing toward the intruder.

Susana's scream cut through the murderous haze filling his head. She jumped back just fast enough to avoid being cut.

Kai was trapped by the fear in her eyes.

Trapped, and humiliated. She was his to protect. Yet he'd almost cut her.

The savage inside him tucked its tail between its legs and slunk back into its cage.

His fingers opened. The knife dropped to the jungle floor. "Jesus. I'm sorry. Are you okay?"

Kai reached for her, but she shook her head and stepped away. Her gaze flicked between him and the mercenary.

Even in the stark shadows cast by the beam of the flashlight, he knew she could see the man's blood streaming out of the wound. "Susana, I—"

"Can we move out? Or...do you...want to bury the body?"

Dammit, her voice was thin and shaky. She'd already seen Jacie's death tonight. She didn't need to be reminded of the violence he was capable of.

He wanted to pull her into his arms and tell her everything was going to be okay. He'd never hurt her. But why would she believe him?

He picked up his knife, cleaned it on the back of the man's shirt, then re-sheathed it. "We'll leave the body," he said as he stood up. "If his partner is out there, we need to keep moving, not waste time on a burial."

Keeping her eyes averted, Susana nodded.

He retrieved his flashlight and started to walk past her into the jungle. Helpless, frustrated anger tightened his throat and squeezed like a fist around his heart. When he was beside her, he paused. "This is who I am, Susana," he said in a low, furious voice he barely recognized. "A killer. This knife isn't for show. I kill to protect and I kill to avenge." The words came out in a rush, forced by a sudden need to expose all his darkness. To just get it over with. Susana would push him away, but that was okay. She lived in the spotlight. He lived in the shadows.

They had no future together.

"The men who murdered my family?" he growled. "I hunted them down, slit their throats and scalped them. Just like they did to my parents and the twins."

He risked looking over at her and saw her eyes on him, wide with shock and denial. Her lack of acceptance only pissed him off further. "I will never hurt you, but if anyone threatens you I will kill again. Count on it."

He didn't wait for reply. Just stalked into the jungle.

THEY NEEDED TO MAKE CAMP. Kai pushed forward through the shallow stream, Susana trudging like a drone behind him, so exhausted she didn't even lift her feet out of the water. He wanted to tell her it was more work to push forward through the water that way than to raise her feet, but he was afraid to speak. He didn't want to give her a reason to focus on him and remember what he'd done.

What he wanted was a safe place for her to crash.

He halted, listening for sounds of pursuit. Still nothing. The dead man had probably told the truth, then. His buddy had run the other way. Which meant it was safe to make camp.

At the next break in the trees, Kai led them out of the river and up a shallow bank. When the trees finally thinned out around a small clearing, he stopped. They were far enough from the water not to be bothered by animals out for their nightly drink.

"Let me set up the hammock," Kai said.

"No. I can help." Without meeting his eyes, Susana picked up the hammock and walked over to a tree.

Her fear kicked him in the solar plexus.

Dammit, he wasn't dangerous to her. He just...

Stop.

You're both exhausted. Tomorrow you can make her understand.

Yeah, but understand what? That he'd killed without making a conscious decision? How could he expect her not to be afraid when he wasn't in control of himself?

Shit.

He jerked the trip-wire system out of his backpack and strung it around the perimeter of the clearing. When he was finished, he turned toward Susana, expecting her to already be asleep.

But the flashlight showed her standing in front of the tree, the hammock dangling from her hand. And, dammit, she was shuddering.

He reached her side in two seconds.

"Susana? What's wrong?"

She turned to him, her face crumpled in grief.

"Ah, sweetheart."

He held out his arms. With a low keening cry, she rushed into his embrace, burrowing against him like she wanted to climb inside. Which was right where he wanted her. Tucked behind his heart so no one could ever hurt her again.

"They're all dead," she sobbed. "Because of me."

He closed his arms more tightly around her and rested his

cheek against her forehead. "Shh. Don't think about it. I've got you." Her whole body bucked on a sob so violent, she almost threw off his hug. He shifted his body, entwining his leg with hers and snugging her more securely to his body with an arm at her shoulders and hip.

She tightened her arms around his back and pressed closer.

Damn, but she felt perfect against him.

Mine.

For once Kai agreed with his primitive instincts. Susana was his to protect.

Just like that, all the dark, powerful emotions he'd thought satisfied when he killed the mercenary, reappeared. He burned to make Susana's enemies bleed for scaring her. For making her feel a guilt she'd carry the rest of her life. And for allowing her to see him at his worst.

He nearly howled in frustration.

It wasn't safe to leave her and hunt down the men responsible. Which meant her enemies would continue to live.

For now.

Susana couldn't sleep.

Maybe half an hour ago, Kai had tucked her into her hammock like a child, then settled the mosquito net above her. Despite feeling physically and emotionally drained, she'd been staring into the dark ever since, shivering with fear and fighting back panic.

Night under the shield of the canopy was completely devoid of light. The darkness pressed heavily on her, making it difficult to breathe.

And it was too quiet.

Usually, forests had myriad night sounds. But tonight the critters were silent, perhaps scared away by the fire. Without the comforting harmony of chirping insects and rustling leaves, she felt isolated. Terrified of what waited beyond the boundaries of her hammock.

Up to now, she'd never considered herself afraid of the dark.

And what did that mean, anyway? If you'd asked her yesterday, she would have said being afraid of the dark really meant someone was afraid of the bad things that can happen in the dark. Such as being attacked.

But now she understood. The truth was that the darkness—this utter lack of light that denied her the ability to know where she was in relation to her surroundings—was something to fear in and of itself. Because with the darkness came the certainty of her own lack of power.

Robbed of the comfort of seeing, she remembered the look of triumph on Kai's face as he'd knelt over the dead mercenary. The way the blood had...

No.

Her mind shifted away from that image, but immediately pictured Jacie as she fell, shot by the helicopter. Imagined she could see the faces of her crew as they died, flesh burning, voices screaming. Swore she could sense men creeping through the trees, trying to find her. Waiting for a chance to kill her.

She pressed her fists to the rims of her eye sockets. *Stop it!*

If anyone threatens you I will kill again. Count on it. Kai would protect her. But what if something happened to him? How did she even know he was still out there, guarding her?

The only way to fight the fear was to use light. And to break the silence with talk.

But only two light sticks remained and Kai's flashlight was losing power. He'd also ordered her not to speak until morning, unless it was an emergency. He didn't want anyone locating their position.

Riding the edge of hysteria, she wondered if he'd consider her potential loss of sanity an emergency.

Ashamed at her weakness, she bit her lip until she tasted

blood. *C'mon girl, you're stronger than that.* She could keep silent. Ignore her desperate need for Kai to say something. Say *anything.* Heck, she'd be satisfied if he simply recited the alphabet. She just needed a reminder she wasn't alone.

She shifted position again. Her eye caught movement off to her left and she jerked upright, banging her head on the mosquito net. A hard male hand against her lips stopped her from crying out.

Oh, God, they'd found her!

"Shh, sweetheart, it's only me." Kai's voice was a barely audible thrum against her ear.

Everything within her relaxed. She nodded and he moved his hand away.

"Can't sleep?"

"No." She tried to be as quiet as he was, but to her ears, her whisper sounded like a shout.

"Here." The hammock tipped slightly as he raised the mosquito net. She heard a soft crack, then he passed her a glowing light stick.

"Keep your hand shaded around this. Or better yet, hide it under your shirt so you only see a faint glow."

"But...that leaves only one."

"We'll be extracted soon. We'll be fine." The mosquito net settled back into place and she sensed Kai moving away.

She bit her lip to keep from crying out in disappointment.

What did you expect? That he'd hold you?

She opened her shirt and tucked the light inside. Yeah, fool that she was, she wanted his arms around her again.

She didn't cry often, but when she did, it always left her feeling alone and vulnerable. Having Kai's body pressed against hers during her earlier crying fit had staved off the loneliness. She'd felt safe. Cherished.

The protectiveness of his embrace had buried her fear. Had broken through the shock of seeing Kai slit that man's throat.

But apparently, his earlier show of comfort had been a one-shot deal. Holding her had probably been damage control. A way to make sure she didn't have a noisy meltdown and draw the attention of the mercenaries.

She knew better than to believe that if a person offered you comfort, your emotions were safe with them. Jacie had given her many a reassuring hug over the years, but all along, she'd been plotting to destroy Susana.

Now she was dead.

My fault. Tears burned down her cheeks and pooled in the corners of her lips. If only her father had never put the damn microchip inside her. If only they hadn't returned to her camp. If only...

Depressed by the direction of her thoughts, Susana concentrated on blanking her mind and focusing only on the light. After a long while her mind calmed and her fear receded.

Well, a little bit, anyway. She was still aware of the darkness crouching just outside the reach of the light, waiting for its chance to pounce.

Get a grip, girl.

This sudden fear of the dark was ridiculous. She should be grateful to it for hiding her from the men in the helicopter.

That's it. Think positive.

She tried to picture holding a massive party after the chip was removed. There'd be a live dance band belting out pulsing Latin rhythms. Streamers and balloons and bright, cheerful clusters of flowers would decorate the room.

All her friends...

The vision popped. Too many people she cared about would be missing.

Including Kai.

THE FIERY LIGHT had diminished to a warm glow when Rafe next regained consciousness. This time he managed to sit up. When the world didn't tilt or whirl, he worked his way to his feet.

The mission.

He had to complete the mission. Not remembering exactly what the mission was, he nonetheless checked to make sure his weapons were still in place.

Check.

But he couldn't locate his night vision goggles. The fire's glow made it too bright to use them now, but he'd need them when he walked deeper into the jungle.

Dammit, what was he supposed to do?

He glanced around him and finally spotted the goggles hanging from a bush to his right. As he reached for the strap of the goggles, a long-forgotten voice cracked the shell holding his memory.

Get the lead out, Andros! Rangers don't sit around on their butts. Grab your gear and move out.

"Yes, sir, Sergeant Miller, sir!" Rafe snapped to attention, only to realize his sergeant wasn't there. He wasn't back in the jungle of Costa Rica with his former Ranger team.

A different voice echoed through the darkness in his brain. *Forget who you were.*

An older man wearing a white lab coat tightened the chains holding Rafe to the wall of his cell. Rafe flinched, trying to escape the pain that invaded every muscle and speared through his brain.

Obedience is the only reality. Stop remembering, do as we order, and the pain will stop.

Rafe put his hands to his head. God, his brain felt like it was tearing apart.

He didn't know who he was. What he was supposed to be doing. He...

His phone vibrated in his pocket. He opened it and listened. Each word brought a higher level of calm. "Understood," he said.

For several minutes after he ended the call, he stared blindly into the night.

He knew his mission again. Find the woman. Kill her escort. Kill anyone else who got in the way.

Bring the woman out alive...or dead.

Some closed-off part of his brain struggled to tell him something. There was a reason he shouldn't move forward. There was...

Rafe shook his head.

No. Complete the mission. Then there'd be no more pain.

Rafe took a step. Then another.

Within four steps, the thrill of the hunt overtook him and he ran.

CHAPTER NINETEEN

Sunday, Night
Amazon Jungle

KAI STOOD next to Susana's hammock, watching her nose scrunch up and her lips purse as she slept. The light stick added an other-worldly radiance to her face that highlighted the many cuts and bruises on her skin.

She'd never seemed more precious to him.

Her hand moved restlessly along the edge of the hammock, batting at the mosquito net.

It was hot under the protective covering. The tiny holes didn't allow much air to circulate.

Knowing he shouldn't, he knelt down beside her and slipped his hand underneath the net. He captured her fingers in his own and was surprised at the strength with which she grabbed on.

And how the contact settled her down.

One thing he'd learned from nights spent awake, guarding her until he was forced to take a few hours' rest, was that in sleep, as awake, Susana was rarely still. Sometimes only her lips moved, but moments of complete immobility indicated something was deeply wrong with her.

Odd, how quickly he'd come to treasure her idiosyncrasies.

He sighed. She was part of his mission. He wasn't supposed to like her. He certainly wasn't supposed to be haunted by how it had felt to lie naked with her. Or to be so desperate to have her again that the only thing stopping him from waking her was respect for her exhaustion.

That...and the fact that he'd viciously killed a man in front of her. When she woke up, she'd be afraid of him again.

Yet a little voice demanded that he ignore her condition and take her anyway. Kai turned away, sickened by the constant struggle to control the violence within him. Knowing that until he figured out a way to rid himself of this savagery, he had no business getting involved with Susana.

Sunday, Night
Boa Vista, Brazil

"TELL ME AGAIN WHAT HAPPENED," Mark Tonelli demanded. He couldn't believe the story the mercenary told him. It made no sense. Yet the man had no reason to lie.

"Like I said before, we followed your orders and split up. One team went into the woman's camp. The rest of us stayed onboard the gunboat." The man paused. So far, what he'd said matched his previous words. This next part was the unbelievable part. If the man was lying, this was where the description would change.

"But then a fucking helicopter gunship swooped in. It dropped an explosive charge next to us that nearly sank our boat, then continued on toward the dig. A couple of minutes later, flames shot up from the jungle."

Mark hated the sweat pooling in the creases of his palms almost as much as he hated the fear that prickled through him, making his skin itch. Was Susana dead? That beautiful, vibrant woman burned to death? The chip incinerated?

Dammit, the attack made no sense. Mark paced back and forth in his hotel room, feeling trapped. He needed to know if Susana had survived. He needed to make certain this situation didn't backfire on him.

"The man, the one with the woman, he told everyone to run when he heard our warning on the radio. My brother ran back to the river," the mercenary continued. "He thinks the woman and the man escaped into the jungle. That's the direction they were running."

Susana was alive! Mark stopped his pacing, quivering in anticipation. "Go on."

"That's it. The helicopter made another pass, fired into the jungle, then took off. The helicopter shot your contact, the assistant, as she tried to escape. The rest of the crew were tied up in the mess tent and burned to death."

Mark didn't care about the crew. Or Jacie. This was partly her fault for bringing in the private soldiers and trying to double-cross him. He should have known her hatred of Susana was too fanatical to make her a trustworthy partner.

But if there was a chance Susana had survived…

He shook his head and told himself not to get his hopes up. It was possible Susana was dead. But if Paterson had helped her escape, then where would they go?

He asked the mercenary that.

"Depends. They fled inland, so eventually they'll come to the highway. But that'll take them a couple of days at least. I'd circle back to the Branco River."

Okay, he could work with this.

He still had one contact within the SSU. If Paterson had radioed for help, his contact might be able to tell him the coordinates for their extraction.

"Where are you now?" Mark asked.

"Still on the river near her camp."

"I want you to head upriver, toward Boa Vista. I'm going to find out where the woman is. If I'm right, you'll be on a course to intercept."

Sunday, Night
Amazon Jungle

PEOPLE WERE DYING. Burning to death in front of her eyes. Crying for Susana to save them. Blaming her.

A man fell at her feet, his body charred and his throat slit. His eyes were open, revealing distinctive amber irises.

Kai!

Susana awoke with a scream dying on her lips.

For an instant she panicked, not knowing where she was. She sat up abruptly, her head bumping into and stretching the mosquito net. The hammock tipped to the left and she started to fall.

Something tugged on the wayward hammock, righting it.

"Easy, sweetheart. You're okay."

Kai. Alive.

She closed her eyes against a wave of relief so strong it scared her. She wanted to fling herself into his arms. Feel his warmth against her, just to reassure herself he was real. The impulse was so strong, she hugged herself to keep from reaching for him.

"Susana?"

"I..." Her voice came out husky and broken. "Just give me a minute. Nightmare."

"Okay. As soon as you're ready, we need to move out."

She opened her eyes. It was barely light enough to see Kai standing beside her, but his jaguar's eyes seemed to glow. She shivered.

"I'm going to keep you safe," he said.

She wondered what he'd seen in her face to offer that promise. They both knew it was impossible to keep. If the helicopter came back and shot into the trees in the right spot, neither of them would survive.

Still, she gave him the words he needed. "I know. I trust you." And despite, or maybe because, of the way he'd killed the mercenary, she realized it was true. Kai had killed to protect her. Twice.

His violence scared her. No doubt about it. Violence wasn't something she was used to. Yet she trusted him to keep her alive.

Some emotion passed briefly across his eyes. Satisfaction? She had the unsettling feeling something important had just happened between them. She only wished she knew what.

She climbed out of her hammock.

Five minutes later, Kai held out her backpack and helped settle it on her back. His eyes held a silent apology as he handed her a nutrition bar.

Then he checked his watch and pointed out their new direction. As she took the lead, she munched on her breakfast. It was odd. She knew Kai's main interest in her was the microchip. Yet he managed to make her feel she mattered to him on a personal level.

Technically, he didn't need her alive to retrieve the chip. His care of her, the gentle way he'd held her while she cried, and his willingness to put his own life at risk to keep her alive, assured her he would never hurt her.

There you go again. Hoping that someone will love you.

Whoa. Love?

No way. She did not want Kai to love her.

See her as a person, not just a microchip carrier? Yes. Give her another round of mind-blowing sex. Absolutely. Develop an emotional attachment to her? No. Uh-uh. No way.

Yet last night, when he'd held her, she'd felt safe. Cherished.

Think of something else.

Unfortunately, what came to mind was the image of Jacie's

green eyes, smug with satisfaction as she described how she'd betrayed Susana. She swallowed past a bitter lump of betrayal.

Jacie had wanted Susana dead. Because of ambition. And Susana hadn't suspected. She'd been doing everything possible to help Jacie's career.

No, amend that. She'd been doing everything to support the career Jacie *claimed* to want. A false tale, meant to lure Susana into a false sense of security.

Susana felt the ragged remains of her confidence fluttering inside her. Once again she'd misjudged someone and been cut by betrayal.

Her confidence had been torn before. By her mother. By Elena, who had lied to her, robbed her, and tried to destroy her reputation.

But after the hurt from each incident had faded, she'd regained confidence in herself and found someone new to trust, convinced this time the person would be worthy. That she'd chosen smarter. That this time she'd found someone to love and trust her as unconditionally as she did them.

Susana sighed and hitched the straps of her pack higher on her shoulders.

No matter how deep Jacie's betrayal, she hadn't deserved to pay with her life. Lose her job? Definitely. Spend some time in jail. Absolutely.

But bullets in the back? Too harsh a punishment.

Susana shivered and prayed the helicopter wouldn't come back.

Monday, Morning
Amazon Jungle

"JESUS H. CHRIST!" Niko stared at the scorched wasteland that had once been Susana Dias's archaeological dig.

Beside him, Jenna coughed.

"This is insane." Charred bits of tent pole poked through piles of ash. A piece of partially melted hiking boot sole lay atop a glaring white shinbone. The back of a skull sat at an angle on a jumble of bones.

Heat rose from the ashes. The scent of death and smoke dissipated as a breeze carried the jungle's rich perfume across the site. Underneath it all Niko caught the distinctive odor of accelerant.

Murder.

Had there been any warning? Was there any chance people had run to safety? Or was Kai dead?

He and Jenna had come in from the northwest. The area they'd walked through had been mostly untouched until just a few yards from camp. The fire seemed to have been stopped from spreading in that direction by a small creek.

The jungle to the east and south had burned. He couldn't tell from here how far the devastation spread, but they'd seen no signs of survivors.

He pulled out his sat phone and dialed Ryker. Jenna started snapping photos with her phone's camera.

"Kai's alive," Ryker informed him immediately. "The satellite still shows the signal from his tracking chip. And Rafe's chip is transmitting again."

Niko squeezed his eyes shut in relief, then relayed the good news to Jenna. Joy lit up her face and she made a victory sign.

"Rafe's not far behind Kai," Ryker continued. "I'm downloading their last recorded positions to your phone." It was precisely for situations like this that Ryker had asked all his agents to submit to having tracking devices implanted under their skin, and Niko could only thank God for it.

Niko told Ryker about the fire.

"Ah," his boss said. "That explains it. The satellite picked up an intense heat signal from that sector last night."

Ryker paused, and Niko could imagine him pacing his office,

calculating risks and possibilities. "Watch your six, Niko. Whoever ordered this attack won't want any witnesses. And I think it's safe to say they've decided to kill Dias and take the chip from her corpse."

That's the way Niko figured it, too. "I estimate we'll catch up with Kai within thirty-six hours."

"As soon as you've found them, signal Gonzales for the pick-up," Ryker said. "Don't try to reach the extraction point. If the helicopter has to hover over the trees and lower a sling to you, we'll do it. I want you all out of there as soon as possible."

"Will do." Niko ended the call and opened up the phone application that monitored the tracking devices.

Both Rafe and Kai were heading northeast.

Bro, when I find you, please tell me you had nothing to do with this destruction. Niko swallowed back nausea at the thought. Took a deep breath. Looked at his wife.

She glanced up from photographing a pile of charred bones. Her skin was pale, her mouth drawn in a tight line. She looked as sickened by this level of random destruction as he felt.

"Ready to move out?" she asked.

He wondered if, like him, she wanted to run away from here. If it even occurred to her Rafe could have done this.

God, I hope not.

But as Niko skirted the destruction, looking for Rafe's trail into the jungle, he couldn't help but think that only someone not thinking straight would wreak such annihilation.

Someone, say, like his brother, who'd been given drugs known to destroy reason and compassion. Drugs that resulted in highly aggressive behavior.

Monday, Midday
Washington, D.C.

"You told me this latest team was stable enough to send on a mission. And what happened?" Jamieson didn't wait for Dr. Kaufmann to answer. "The men stole a helicopter and fire-bombed Dias's dig, killing everyone! Do you have any idea what a disaster this is?" Jamieson felt wetness on his lip and reached up with a finger.

Spittle. He'd been reduced to a slavering maniac. He scrubbed his mouth with his handkerchief. But the action did nothing to quell the cold snake of panic wending its way through his gut.

Dr. Kaufmann's failure could very well spell the end of Kerberos.

"I believed the issues with aggression and judgment had been sufficiently dealt with," Dr. Kaufmann replied. "The entire team shouldn't have become so violent. And the men should have been incapable of thinking up such a plot and carrying it out. Their handlers should have possessed sufficient control to stop such an action. Once the team has returned, we'll take blood samples and see where we went wrong."

Jamieson didn't bother explaining that he'd authorized a cleanup crew to fly down to Brazil and eliminate Kaufmann's men before they could tell anyone else what they'd done. And his team would do whatever was necessary to alter the site of the fire to make it look like an accident. Maybe disguise the fire as a propane explosion. Or an airplane crash.

Anything to hide what really happened.

Jesus Christ. They'd killed over two dozen innocent people! If word of this got out, it would cause an international incident.

At the very least, there was going to be an investigation. Which might eventually tie the men involved back to Kaufmann. Jamieson knew that, if pressured, the self-important scientist wouldn't keep his mouth shut about who funded his project.

The chip had to be retrieved now, while the cleanup was going on. Before anyone started nosing around.

"The situation is actually quite fascinating," Kaufmann continued. "I thought we'd sufficiently wiped out all memories of the men's prior lives. But obviously one of them recognized that the helicopter was an old military model, complete with weapons. A prior mission's order must have interfered with our programming, causing one or more of the men to convince the others that stealing the helicopter and using it to kill Susana Dias fell within the parameters of their current mission."

The scientist hummed thoughtfully. "We've clearly underestimated the strength of our mind control protocol. After we gave them their mission commands, the subjects should not have been able to improvise. Particularly not regarding the use of deadly force. More tests will need to be run."

Jamieson twisted his handkerchief into a noose. "Forget your damn research. We're facing a real risk of exposure. Susana Dias is the host of a popular television show on the Adventure Channel," he explained with what he considered commendable patience. "The film crew was on site. Even if the Brazilian government doesn't investigate, the network executives are bound to go to our government and demand an accounting of what happened. Are you beginning to see the size of the problem you've created? This isn't something we can easily brush under the carpet.

"Plus, Susana Dias is still alive and running free in the jungle somewhere. Tonelli hasn't checked in, so we can't count on him bringing us the microchip. And your men are so unstable, they're likely to destroy both Dias and the chip. That's if they catch her before Paterson takes her back to the SSU!"

But that wasn't even the worst of it. The imbecile on the other end of the telephone didn't understand the fine line Jamieson walked in order to keep his position of power.

He stared at a print of the Mona Lisa hanging to the left of his desk, barely aware he was gripping the phone receiver so hard, his knuckles had turned the color of his preferred vanilla ice cream. He'd always thought that Mona Lisa was a woman who possessed many secrets and knew how to leverage those secrets. That she smiled because she'd recently completed a successful power play. Right now, he wished he had so subtle an ally.

Dr. Kaufmann didn't understand the meaning of the words nuance and subtlety. Genius hadn't given the scientist the ability to understand that sometimes the obvious move was the wrong move for many hidden, yet critical reasons.

"Tell me again why you sent Rafael Andros after Dias," Jamieson demanded.

"We need to test the power of our imprinting with this latest batch of drugs. Andros proved to be a very hard subject to get under control initially. He's made satisfactory progress since then, but only a real-world test can prove whether this formula is worth continuing."

The pride in Dr. Kaufmann's voice annoyed Jamieson. The scientist clearly had no clue they were on the brink of being exposed. Arrested. Tried for murder. Not just for the attack on Dias's dig. But for the deaths of Andros's teammates and all the unmourned former soldiers and law enforcement agents who had entered Kaufmann's lab and been buried anonymously.

If Andros broke free of his conditioning and returned to the SSU, he could expose Kaufmann's program. Andros knew names. He could recognize faces.

Jamieson's temple began to throb and he rubbed the spot with his fingers.

"Paterson was once a close friend to Andros," Dr. Kaufmann continued. "We want to determine if outside of the lab Andros will obey our order to kill anyone who gets in his way, even a friend. If anyone can pick up Dias's trail, Andros can."

From her position slightly above his desk, the Mona Lisa appeared to mock Jamieson. He turned away from the smile that suddenly seemed smug, rather than sly.

Over the years he'd worked with dozens of fools. None of

them had outlasted him. This oblivious scientist would not be his downfall.

"What you failed to take into account in your excruciatingly poor planning, is that Rafe Andros has a brother, Niko," Jamieson said. "Niko is also an SSU agent. And he's married to Kai Paterson's sister. So Paterson is family to Rafe Andros. Do you really think he'll be able to kill Paterson?"

"Perfect." Kaufmann sounded excited. Delighted.

Blind, crazy fool. This was a disaster.

"It's the ultimate test of our imprinting," Kaufmann continued. "Better than we expected."

"Get your head out of the lab and think of the big picture." Jamieson pushed to his feet. "What if the Brazilian authorities catch Andros and question him? Or Paterson turns the tables and captures him? Are you sure Andros's programming is strong enough to prevent him from telling everything he knows about the lab?"

Heavy silence on the other end of the line indicated that Kaufmann had finally comprehended the extent of the danger.

"Do you finally understand what you've done?" Jamieson demanded.

"The risk of detection by the authorities is statistically small—"

Fucking scientists. Jamieson disconnected the call.

Kaufmann was fast becoming a liability.

CHAPTER TWENTY

Monday, Mid-morning
Amazon Jungle

"IF YOU ASK me one more time if I'm okay, I'm going to throttle you!" Susana snarled. "I'm not made of glass, Kai. I'm fine."

Kai watched Susana stomp behind a rock to take care of personal needs, her hands waving as she muttered to herself. He couldn't stop a smile. He liked her mouthy anger much better than her silent grief.

Hell, he liked her, period. She was smart and strong and, despite this show of temper, she was holding up remarkably well.

He rubbed the back of his neck. Hopefully, Susana had more reserves left, because the hardest part was ahead of them. Rescue by the SSU was a distant hope. The odds were slim that anyone had heard his message last night. So he and Susana were on their own.

A helicopter had flown over a couple hours ago, quartering the area to the west. The canopy directly overhead was thick enough to conceal them, and the warmth of the air should make infrared unreliable.

Still, the helicopter's pass-over was a sign that someone believed there were survivors of last night's attack. Kai suspected there'd already been a team on the ground watching for him and Susana. How else would they know they'd run deeper into the jungle rather than toward the river?

So he had to assume there were men on foot following them. A simple thing to do, since he and Susana had crashed through the damn jungle, carelessly breaking branches and crushing vegetation underfoot. Leaving behind a trail that screamed, "Find us!"

"Kai."

He glanced up, alerted by Susana's tone that something had changed. Her anger was gone. The trepidation on her face had him reaching for his knife. "What's wrong?"

She held up several crumpled sheets of paper. "I found these in my pocket. I'd forgotten all about them."

"What?" Then realization hit like a boxer's glove. "Your father's letter."

"Yeah."

He glanced around. Listened hard for any sounds indicating the helicopter's return or that men waited in the bushes to ambush them.

Nothing.

Still, his instincts insisted that they keep moving.

At the same time, he needed to know what her father had said. "If I lead, can you read and walk at the same time?"

She nodded. "Just go slow."

Slow was better than stopped. "Okay."

"Dear Daughter," she began as he headed into the trees. A trace of anger struggled to overthrow her carefully neutral monotone.

Kai commended her control.

"...My name is Dr. Mikhail Nevsky and I am your father. Perhaps your mother has mentioned me to you. Or perhaps bitterness has kept her silent. Whichever the case, it does not matter. Without me, you would not have life. That creates a bond of obligation and rights between us. I had need of a safe place to store my research notes, and your appendectomy was the perfect opportunity. Who would think to look for my microchip inside a human being? Let alone inside a daughter no one knows I have. These notes are the sum of my life's work. Work that, once finalized, will make the world a more easily controlled place."

Kai couldn't stop a snort of disbelief.

Susana cleared her throat, then continued, "But there are men and governments who wish my notes for their own. So I hid the microchip in your abdomen, with a transmitter that allows it to update whenever I make significant changes."

Susana cursed vehemently in Portuguese. "Since you have received this letter, I am no longer alive to carry out my important research. However, I have a colleague in Moscow, Dr. Pieter Ivanov, who is conducting similar research. You must go to Moscow and let Dr. Ivanov remove the microchip so that he can continue my work."

Now it was Kai's turn to swear. The last thing they needed was more of these damned inhuman labs destroying people's lives.

"But perhaps you are wondering why you should obey the order of the father you've never met? Particularly if your mother has shared her opinion of me. To make certain of your obedience, I have set a self-destruct on the glass vial surrounding the microchip. Inside the vial is a dose of deadly poison."

Kai halted and spun to face Susana. He had to hold out his hands to stop her from walking into him. "Wait. Read that part again."

She did.

"Son of a bitch." Sweet Jesus, she'd fallen on her belly more than once. What if the vial had burst?

He could picture it all too well. Susana on the ground, writhing in excruciating pain as her muscles contracted and her internal organs failed. Bleeding from her mouth. Eyes wide and terrified in death. Betrayed by the man who should have given her unconditional love.

Kai rubbed his arms. When did the temperature drop to arctic levels?

"Kai?"

He could barely move his lips. "Go on."

Giving him a puzzled look, she continued. "By holding the paper of this letter, you have allowed tiny microbes to enter your system. They will interact with the outer coating of the vial, eroding it. You now have sixteen days to get to Moscow and Dr. Ivanov before the microbes dissolve the vial, releasing the poison into your system." Her voice trembled to a halt and her gaze jumped from the page to Kai. Her pupils dilated with alarm.

Kai barely resisted the need to pull her into his arms. "Go on, sweetheart. We need to know what else your father planned."

She cleared her throat twice and resumed reading. "Should you decide to have someone else remove the vial, know that it is booby-trapped. Only Dr. Ivanov has the instructions to safely remove the vial. Improperly handled, the vial will self-destruct, releasing the poison. You will die and the microchip will dissolve."

Susana's hand spasmed on the paper. She licked her lips. "Kai. Is it possible? About...the poison? And the microbes?"

Seeing her fear gave him the strength to lock away his own terror. She needed him to be strong. To be calm. "Yeah. He had scientists working with him on all sorts of chemical and biological substances, poisons included." Her father had even used low doses of poison to break down his subject's minds and bodies before giving them a treatment.

"*Mãe de Deus*. Kai, I touched the letter when it arrived. That means..." Her lips moved as she counted. "I've only got five more days." Her voice climbed the rickety scale into hysteria. "Kai, if we don't find transport, it will take us nearly that amount of time to reach Boa Vista!"

"Then we'd better move it." He hesitated, then nodded at the letter. "Is that all?"

She glanced down. "Yeah, pretty much. He gives the address and contact information for the guy in Moscow. There's even a code word I'm supposed to use." She rolled her eyes. "Very James Bond."

He wanted to kiss her for trying to find some humor in the situation. But they needed to keep moving. He started walking.

No.

To hell with it. He needed to touch her. To feel her vitality.

He turned back. Clamped his hands on her shoulders and yanked her against his body as his mouth captured hers.

Susana wrapped her hands around his head and pulled him closer with a whimper of need. She bit his lip, and he damn near came right then.

The sound of the helicopter returning broke through the sexual fog. He pushed Susana away. "Helicopter," he gasped.

Looking down into her befuddled eyes, he almost didn't care if they moved on. But the rational side of his brain kicked in, reminding him that the helicopter could start shooting at any moment.

He dropped his hands away from her shoulders. Gave her one last brush of his lips. Then took her hand and urged her deeper into the jungle.

"Niko," Jenna called. "Take a look at this." She held up a pair of night vision goggles. "I found them hanging from that tree."

Niko's throat shrunk two sizes, making speech impossible. They had to be Rafe's. A sign that his brother had enough control to leave a trail any decent tracker could follow.

But only Niko and Jenna would understand the importance of this find.

He glanced down at the tracker in his hands that showed the positions of Rafe and Kai. "I don't know if not being able to see at night will slow him down enough," he said. His voice came out harsh. Gravelly as a chain-smoker. "He's almost caught up with them."

Jenna hung the strap of the goggles around her neck. "Then we'd better move fast." She brushed his cheek with her lips.

She started to walk past him, but Niko grabbed her hand and brought it to his mouth. "God, I'd be lost without you, Jenna. I love you so damn much."

Her eyes glimmered with tears. "I love you, too." She pulled her hand free and stepped into him, hugging him fiercely.

His arms swept around her and he held her tightly. Then he let go and nudged her away. "Thanks." He kissed her forehead. "Let's go get my brother."

As they walked into the jungle, he put the tracker in his pocket and intertwined the fingers of his free hand with Jenna's.

He hadn't taken more than five steps when the earth shook and the sound of an explosion rent the air. Niko dropped to the ground, pulling Jenna with him.

They crossed their hands behind their necks, waiting for fallout.

One minute passed, then another. The jungle was devoid of animal calls. But there also wasn't any sound of men, bullets, or falling debris.

"What was that?" Jenna asked. She pushed to her feet and brushed herself off.

Niko stood up and stared back in the direction they'd come.

Destroying an archaeological dig and killing nearly two dozen people was enough to start an international incident. If he'd been responsible...

"Best guess?" he replied. "Dynamite. Maybe a plane crash.

Something explosive at the archaeological site to make the fire look like an accident."

"But won't the accelerant show in soil tests or something?"

"Why would investigators bother if such an obvious reason is presented to them?"

Jenna stared at him, her eyes wide, her mouth slightly open. Then she snapped her teeth together. "If they're going to such lengths to hide what happened, then Ryker was right."

Niko nodded. "Whoever is responsible is eliminating all witnesses. We're all in danger." He checked his tracking device again, then headed into the brush at a fast jog.

Her father's words reverberated in Susana's skull like shards of pottery being shaken in a sorting tray. Poison. Inside her.

Unable to think past what her father had revealed, she let Kai lead her through the tangle of vegetation.

What if they didn't make it out of the Amazon in time? What if the vial self-destructed, releasing the poison into her system? They only had five more days and they hadn't even reached the Branco River yet.

Moscow seemed an eternity away.

She could die. And the chip, so critical to Kai, might be destroyed.

The trees pressed in on her like walls of a prison, cutting off both air and hope. God, if she was going to die, she didn't want this frantic rush through the jungle to be her last experience. There were so many places she hadn't been. So many adventures yet to try.

Amerinis to find. *Deus*, she was so close to fulfilling her childhood dream of finding the lost city. She couldn't bear to consider that someone else would carry on her work after she died.

Get a grip.

She forced herself to take a deep breath. Okay, enough with

the negatives. She refused to buy the worst case scenario. Her crew had died because of the chip. Susana would not let their deaths be for nothing. She would survive. The chip would be safely removed and given over to the proper authorities.

Kai halted without warning and she plowed into his back. His right arm shot out to steady her. "Hold up a minute. There's a snake crossing our path."

Susana murmured assent, but she wasn't really paying attention to what he was saying. Being in contact with Kai's body brought all her tangled thoughts and dark fears into focus. No matter what happened in the future, right now she had Kai.

She let her head rest on his shoulder, enjoying the feel of his strength underneath her cheek. Wanting to wrap herself around him and never let go.

"C'mon, it's gone."

Susana blinked twice, then realized that Kai was tugging on her arm.

"You all right?" he asked.

She nodded. "Let's go."

As she followed the back that had become so dear to her, Susana vowed that tonight she wasn't going to sleep alone. She'd always been one to seize the moment. Today that meant showing Kai with her body how much he meant to her.

NIKO FOLLOWED the signal from Rafe's tracking device through the jungle. Jenna was a comforting presence at his side. With each step he took, the tranquilizer gun strapped to his thigh bounced slightly. He knew it weighed no more than any other gun he'd carried, yet it seemed far heavier. Tranquilizing Rafe would be better than killing him, but the thought of shooting his brother like a rabid dog made him break out in a cold sweat.

It shouldn't be this hard. Years of undercover work had hardened him. Taught him to lock away all emotion, allowing him to do whatever unsavory action was required to stay alive.

He knew better than to linger on regret. And yet...this was Rafe. His little brother. Every one of Niko's protective instincts rebelled at the thought of hurting Rafe.

The locator beeped and Niko glanced down. The dot that represented Rafe had disappeared. Niko walked several paces in each direction until the signal was back.

This time they turned east.

Under normal circumstances, a tranq wouldn't pose a mortal threat. But given the unknown drug cocktail sliding through Rafe's veins, no one could predict how the SSU's sedative would react. The sedative might increase Rafe's aggression when he awoke. It might send him into a coma. Or it could kill him.

The deeper truth was that Niko feared the tranquilizer gun because...hell, it made this nightmare all too real. Put Rafe in the category of a feral beast.

What would he do if his brother didn't recognize him? And if Rafe attacked him...Niko shivered and rubbed his biceps. Then he reached for Jenna's hand.

Her sympathetic smile gave him strength. She'd almost killed Kai a few months ago. But she hadn't.

Niko could only pray that both Kai and Rafe survived the coming confrontation.

RAFE STARED at the trail leading around a particularly dense grouping of trees. No matter how many times he tried to move in another direction, he always found himself back on this trail, with no memory of how he'd gotten here.

He growled and swiped at a vine that straggled down from a tree. When the vine bounced back, slapping him in the forehead, his rage erupted. He grabbed the vine and yanked it free of its tree. Then he attacked it with his machete until there was nothing left but scraps.

An angry bellow reverberated through the forest. The ever-diminishing sane part of Rafe recognized the sound as his, and was afraid. These violent outbursts were becoming more frequent.

But before sanity could voice a warning, Rafe was swept away by an urgent need to run. Because his prey was near.

And only with the successful completion of his mission would he find peace.

Yet although he ran for hours, he didn't overtake his prey. His steroid and gene enhanced body wasn't tired, but night had fallen.

The scientists had failed to give him the ability to see in the dark. He groped for his night vision goggles. Realized they were gone and released another angry bellow.

He circled, needing something to hit. To destroy. Pulled out a bush. Then another. Tore leaves and branches off of trees.

Finally, his anger cooled and a bit of reason returned. He would have to make camp here. Wait until daylight to continue his hunt.

But tomorrow...Tomorrow he'd corner his prey and tear their throats out.

CHAPTER TWENTY-ONE

Kai was losing it. If he didn't get his hands and mouth on Susana soon, he'd slip into the realm of the certifiably insane.

All day she'd been throwing him looks promising heaven tonight. But he'd been good. He'd kept walking instead of doing what he'd wanted, which was to whirl around, grab her and make love to her until they both collapsed.

Half an hour ago, he'd found a place to camp in an empty space hugging the base of a large tree. As he and Susana settled into their routine of setting up her hammock and his ground bed, then preparing a meal, he should have been relaxing. Even though it was only nearing seven o'clock it was already dark here under the canopy. He should be starting to wind down so he could catch up on much-needed sleep.

Instead, he was hyper-aware of every move Susana made. Always focused on her no matter which direction she walked.

He almost laughed. Yeah, there was definitely a part of him that was steel-hard. The urge to get between her legs again had driven away all other appetites.

He choked down his half of an energy bar, but he might as

well have been eating dirt for all the attention he paid it. His focus was all on Susana's lips as she ate her meager meal.

He imagined her taking him into her mouth and nearly ignited with lust.

Shit. He wanted her, but not like an animal. He crumpled the energy bar's empty wrapper and shoved it into his backpack. "I'm going to make a perimeter check," he threw out as he beat a retreat. No matter that he'd just set up the alarm system ten minutes ago. If he didn't get away from Susana now, he was going to push her onto her back and be inside her before she could say hello.

He walked around the small circumference of their camp, but he couldn't focus on security. All his thoughts were on Susana. He had to do this right. She deserved another gentle seduction. This could be their last time together until...

Hell. Maybe ever. Things would happen fast once they reached Boa Vista. He'd find a phone, put in another call to Ryker, and they'd be on the first plane to Moscow. Once the vial was removed, he'd never see her again.

He paced around the jungle, his flashlight bobbing like his thoughts, until he felt a measure of calm.

When he returned to camp he expected to find Susana in her hammock. Instead, she sat on a fallen tree trunk with the survival blanket wrapped around her.

"Susana, what's wrong? Are you sick?" He hurried toward her. Dammit, she'd seemed fine all day. Was the wound in her shoulder festering, lighting her up with fever?

He was a yard away when she stood up and released the survival blanket. It drifted to the ground.

Dear God in heaven. She was naked. Looking at him with such heat, his wire-thin control snapped.

He took two steps toward her and then she was in his arms, meeting his starving lips with her own, surging against his body as if she intended to become part of it. Light from his flashlight arched through the darkness as it fell out of his hands.

He was too busy trying to touch every part of her bare skin to care. His palms came to rest on her butt. She made a purr of satisfaction and he lifted her against him.

"Want...your...clothes off...now!" Susana tugged at his shirt.

He lay her down on the fallen survival blanket, stripped, then covered her body with his own. He groaned. Her softness felt like coming home.

His tongue plundered her mouth. She nipped at his lip, drawing blood and startling a growl out of his throat.

His hands skimmed desperately across her body, trying to touch as much of her as possible. She urged him on with low moans and gasped suggestions until she was writhing underneath him.

But he wasn't satisfied. He wanted full possession of her.

Unwilling to release her mouth, Kai levered his lower body into position. One violent thrust was all it took to sheath himself in her heat. Her legs locked around his hips and her arms encircled his lower back, trapping him right where he wanted to be. Where he needed to be.

But Jesus, this was moving too fast. He had to slow this down.

He pulled out, ignoring Susana protests. But he should have known she wouldn't roll over and let him take charge. She leaned up and bit the side of his neck. The sharp pain snapped the chains holding down his primitive instincts. He cried out and his vision dimmed as her teeth pierced his skin. God, he'd never before considered pain a turn-on, but he didn't want her teeth to ever let go.

His hips surged forward. "More," he growled.

A cry tore out of her throat, yanking her teeth away. Her body nearly threw him off as a powerful orgasm ripped through her, arching her back off the ground.

His heart pounded like a stake driver as he pumped into her. One stroke. Two.

"Susana!" Kai came with such violence his sight dimmed. Then peace filled him and he collapsed on top of her.

When he could breathe again, he shifted position and pulled Susana against him. He put his lips to her throat and nuzzled. Licked. The taste of her was the final comfort he needed.

Just before he dozed off he had the thought that if their enemies didn't already know where they were, he'd just given them a really loud beacon.

Monday, Night
Over the Branco River

"SATELLITE PICTURES SHOW FIVE HEAT SIGNALS," the captain of Jamieson's cleanup crew told his team. The men sat in the back of a transport helicopter, heading down the Branco River. Last night, they'd located the crew of Kaufmann's men that had fire-bombed the archeological dig. The men had been too drunk to put up much of a fight and had been captured quickly. Their extraordinary strength and speed had been dulled by alcohol, which acted as a sedative when combined with the drugs already in their systems. The scientists in charge knew the dangers of drinking yet had failed to stop the men. Instead, the scientists had been holed up in their rooms, making them even easier to kill.

This afternoon, one of his men had flown a small plane loaded with barrels of gasoline back to the dig. The cargo hold had contained the bodies of the five crew members and three scientists. Once over the dig, the pilot had parachuted out, leaving the plane to crash.

The resulting crater and fire would obliterate any evidence of the firebombing. Once the site cooled down, he and his men would return and gather any skulls and bones that weren't destroyed in the fire, making certain nothing could tie the explosion back to the United States.

But for now, they had a different mission.

He held up a color photo of the jungle taken from thousands of miles above the earth. "Kai Paterson and Susana Dias are believed to be the dots farthest to the north. Rafe Andros is the lone signal slightly southeast of them. Intelligence suggests that Niko and Jenna Andros are the two dots following Rafe Andros."

He pulled out a photograph of Susana Dias. "It doesn't matter how we kill Paterson and the others. But this woman has to be intact." He flashed a smile that would freeze the balls of less ruthless men. "Well, mostly intact. All we really need is her torso. But it will be a lot less messy to transport her if we keep her in one piece."

The men laughed.

"Why not keep her alive, then?" a man to his left asked. "We can have some fun with her on the trip back."

The captain felt a thrill of sexual anticipation. "Right. Take her alive and you'll each get a turn with her." An orange light went on over the side door, warning them that the door would soon open.

"Prepare to move out."

With grunts of approval, his men checked the straps of their packs and positioned themselves along the rope that would soon lower them into the jungle.

Monday, Night
Amazon Jungle

THANKS TO THEIR NIGHT-VISION GOGGLES, Niko and Jenna were able to continue moving for several hours after dark, although at somewhat reduced speed. By the time Niko called a halt, he estimated they were only a couple hours behind Rafe, and maybe another hour or two behind Kai and Susana Dias.

"Niko?" Jenna called. "The trees are too close together here. We can't string the hammocks up."

He pointed into the trees. "We're not sleeping at ground level. Jump up and catch that branch. Then continue climbing until I tell you to stop."

One of the things he loved best about Jenna was her willingness to follow his directions, no matter how crazy she thought his ideas. Such trust continually humbled him.

As she grabbed the branch and wriggled her way onto it he admired her strong, dancer's body. And wondered how she'd feel about making love in a hammock, dozens of feet above the jungle floor.

Deus.

Susana's head lay on Kai's chest, just above his heart. His heartbeat was deep and solid now, not the frantic call-to-arms of a few minutes ago. His even breathing let her know he slept.

She checked his forehead for fever, but he felt normal.

What had just happened between them had been beyond normal. Beyond wonderful.

Wild. Overpowering.

Perfect.

If you'd asked her this morning if she held anything back during sex with her previous lovers, she'd have said no. She loved sex and had always thrown herself fully into her relationships. She'd never been afraid to push the envelope.

But the biggest surprise tonight hadn't been Kai's ferocity, it had been her response.

She'd never bitten a man before.

Used her nails, sure. Used her teeth to nip without breaking the skin, yep. She'd never felt the urge to draw blood once, let alone twice. But tonight she'd sunk her teeth into his neck until the salty, metallic taste of blood hit her tongue, sending her into a back-bowing orgasm.

Who knew she had aspirations of being a vampire?

She smiled. It wasn't the blood that had turned her on. What had done it for her was Kai's trust. He'd allowed her access to his throat, leaving himself vulnerable to her, then begging her for more.

Just thinking about it, her nipples hardened. God, she wanted that again. Only this time she wanted to be on top. Wanted to use her teeth on different places.

Wanted to mark him as hers. To possess him.

Because their time was running out. Even if she made it to Moscow in time and this Dr. Ivanov removed the chip safely, her association with Kai would be over.

He lived in the shadows. She lived in the spotlight. And no compromise would get around one glaring fact.

She hadn't told Kai everything in her father's letter.

When he found out, he wouldn't want to see her again.

But until then, she didn't want to waste a single second. So she let her hand trail down his body and let her heart ignore the ache heading toward her at sonic speed.

Two hours later, Kai sat on the low branch of a tree, watching Susana as she slept in her hammock.

Her dark hair, loosened from her braid by his fingers, flowed across her shoulder, onto her breast. Those hot cocoa eyes that usually sparkled with energy were closed, showcasing long, thick lashes.

Her hands crossed over the soft mound of her belly. God, he loved the feminine grace of her hands. Sensual despite their grime and numerous cuts.

Her long, perfect legs were crossed at the ankles. His pulse quickened as he remembered having those legs locked around his hips as he moved inside her.

Jesus, but she fit him perfectly. And her aggression had been arousing as hell.

His blood began to burn. Dammit, he'd promised himself he wasn't going to touch her again. They'd already made love three times.

Yet he still wanted her.

Forget it. She needed sleep and he needed distance. Because as soon as the chip was removed, he had to say good-bye.

The hell I do, his primitive side snarled. *She's mine.*

Kai flinched. For a moment he allowed himself to hope there was a way to keep Susana in his life. But there wasn't. Not now.

The fact that he'd killed without remorse upset her. Made her wary. But violence was integral to his job. Kai still struggled with the satisfaction he felt when he permanently rid the world of a bad guy. How could he expect Susana to feel differently?

He dropped down from his perch to prowl the perimeter.

But the cold truth was that even if he managed to get his violent tendencies under control, his work was dangerous. Being associated with him put people at risk. The next time his cover got blown, it could be Susana lying dead in a pool of blood.

He shook his head as a wave of panic flooded him. No. He wouldn't allow it.

Which meant he shouldn't touch her again. The smart move would be to piss her off so badly, she'd never want to talk to him again. But that could wait until the chip had been removed. He wanted these last few precious hours to stockpile her smiles and kisses.

Thinking about the chip, his fingers curled into his palms. What if he took her to Moscow and this Dr. Ivanov wasn't where he was supposed to be? What if he was dead?

Until they reached civilization, he had no way of giving the SSU the man's name so they could locate him before Susana boarded a plane to Moscow. Why take her all that way if the man had died?

Yet without knowing what poison the vial contained, Kai didn't dare try to circumvent the booby-trap. He wouldn't even know what antidotes to have ready.

Knowing Nevsky, the poison could be of his own making with no antidote.

Kai leaned his head back against the trunk of the tree. *Face it, you know that's not the alternative to taking her to Moscow.*

Yeah, he did. But he couldn't do it. Couldn't send Susana into the hands of a doctor at the SSU with instructions to cut out as much of the flesh surrounding the vial as possible to keep the vial stable.

Such an operation could have serious repercussions for Susana, depending on just where the vial was embedded. And on how many layers of booby-traps her father had set.

He rolled his skull back and forth against the rough bark at the back of his head. The only acceptable outcome of this mission was for Susana to get to Dr. Ivanov and have the chip removed safely.

So Moscow it was.

Five days and counting.

Susana awoke alone. She shivered, partly because of the loss of Kai's body heat. But more because he'd left her alone. Not a good sign.

And with him gone, the darkness pressed down on her, reminding her that if they didn't get out of here soon, she would die.

"Kai?"

From across the camp she heard a faint rustling of leaves. "Here."

She closed her eyes at his voice. *Safety.*

But he didn't move any closer and she couldn't bear being alone. "Could you please come over here and sit near me?"

She sensed his hesitation and her relief dried up. He was distancing himself from her.

No, dammit. How could he do this to her after what they'd just shared? "Please, Kai. You don't have to touch me. I just...need to know you're near." Her voice broke and she cursed silently. This wasn't at all how she'd expected the rest of the night to go. They'd made love twice more after that initial frenzy, but she still ached to have him inside her.

He made no sound crossing the clearing, but when he spoke again, his voice was right next to her. The hammock tilted as his hand reached for hers. "What's wrong, sweetheart?"

Her fingers latched onto him. Nothing had ever felt so good as his calloused, dry skin.

The words that tumbled out of her weren't the teasing, seductive words she'd planned. "I'm scared."

Kai squeezed her hand.

"I don't want to die," she whispered.

With a gentle tug, Kai tipped her out of the hammock and into his arms. "I'm not going to let you die." His words were fierce, but his hands as they lay her back on the survival blanket under the hammock were gentle. He stripped away her clothing with near reverence and moved over her.

She welcomed him into her body with a long sigh of completion.

"No one is going to hurt you." The words were low, almost indistinguishable, as if his throat was full of rocks and the words had snaked their way through the blockage.

She found his face in the darkness, traced his features from memory. "Thank you," she told him. Even though she knew it was a promise he wouldn't be able to keep, she loved the fact that he wanted to protect her.

She brought his mouth to hers for a kiss that held both promise and loss. Joy and sorrow.

Kai kissed her back, building her pleasure slowly. Breaking her heart. Because she suspected this was the last time they'd be together like this.

After their sighs of completion faded, she asked, "Please don't leave me alone tonight. Just hold me."

Kai's answer was to tuck her close against his side and wrap his arms around her.

Surrounded by his strength, she slept.

CHAPTER TWENTY-TWO

Tuesday, Mid-morning
Amazon Jungle

PAIN SPLIT Rafe's head in two. He put his hands to his forehead, surprised to find his skull intact. But at least, for the moment and for the first time in hours, his mind was fully his own.

Christ, he couldn't take much more of this. He had to leave Niko another sign. And pray that his brother found him quickly.

He inhaled deeply. Cursed when breathing only increased the pain. His vision wavered. The moment of clarity, of being in control, faded.

The animal came back. The part that was controlled by the men in the white coats. Men who had programmed him to hunt and kill.

He glanced around him.

There. Leaves trampled.

He stepped out, anticipation of the kill driving away the remnants of his sanity.

"Stop," Kai ordered. "Quiet."

Susana froze, her left foot hovering inches above the jungle floor. Dear God, that look was back on Kai's face. Cold. Concentrated.

Lethal.

His head was cocked to the side, listening.

She didn't hear anything unusual, but he obviously did. In one fluid movement he straightened, grabbed her arm and shoved her in the direction of a large tree. "Up there. Hurry!"

His urgency sent a shiver of alarm down her spine and she didn't question him. She leapt toward the lowest branch several feet above her head. But sweat made her hands slick so her palms merely slipped down the bark. Damn it. She wiped her palms on her pants, then bent her knees and jumped again.

This time, her grip held. But the weight of her backpack almost pulled her down. She tightened her fingers and pulled with every muscle in her arms and shoulder. For a terrifying second she sank, but then she rose the few precious inches closer to the branch, so that when she swung her legs up, they wrapped around the branch.

She quickly shimmied around so she was sitting on the thick branch.

"Take this!"

Kai held up his backpack. It was so much heavier than hers, it almost dragged her off the branch. But she gritted her teeth, braced her body, and heaved it to a spot next to her.

"Lift both packs into that notch to your right."

As she pushed and heaved to get the backpacks hidden, she cursed softly, so that whatever threat Kai had heard wouldn't overhear her.

"That's good enough," Kai said. She could still see the top of one of the packs, but snatched her hand back from trying to push it farther into the leaves when Kai said, "Forget that. Climb! Get as high as you can. Now."

"What about—?"

"Just do it, Susana!" His voice cracked, sharp as lightning splitting a tree. "No matter what happens, stay out of sight and stay silent. If I go down, you have to get to Boa Vista on your own. Use the compass on this." He tossed her his watch. "Move!"

His harsh, impatient tone shocked her into obeying. She scrambled further up the tree until the thick leaves almost completely obscured her view of Kai.

Who wasn't moving to climb the tree.

Of course. Had she really been so foolish as to expect him to follow her?

What he thought he could do in a fight against the type of men who'd burned her camp, she didn't know. Dammit, she should have knocked him out and dragged him into the bushes instead of letting him send her scurrying up this tree.

She lay down on the branch she'd been sitting on, trying to get a better view. There was one group of leaves in the way, but she wasn't inching all the way out there to rip them off and risk the branch breaking under her. She wouldn't do Kai any good if she fell on him.

Down on the ground, Kai moved into the bushes. Susana shifted a little further out on the branch, so she could still see him. The branch groaned, warning her that she was pushing her luck and it wouldn't be able to hold her weight if she moved much farther.

Kai settled into a hunter's crouch, his automatic weapon raised, just as Susana finally heard heavy footsteps approaching from the direction they'd just come. She bit her lip and prayed that Kai wouldn't be hurt.

KAI HELD his breath and listened intently for several heartbeats. It didn't sound like a group heading toward him. Not enough sound variation. More like one man, two max if the second one walked in sync with the first.

He'd chosen this clump of bushes to hide behind because it was in shadow, while the thin beams of light poking through the canopy acted like stage spotlights to highlight the place where he and Susana had come through the trees.

He raised his weapon, his finger on the trigger. A man-shaped shadow coalesced in the trees. Stepped forward into the light.

Kai's brain recognized the man prowling forward in time to stop his finger from tightening on the trigger. My God, what the hell was he doing here?

The man's nose was slightly up, his head moving side to side as if sniffing the air. He held his M-4 at waist level as he moved silently through the underbrush.

"Rafe!" Kai called. "Buddy, don't shoot. It's Kai."

Kai ducked and rolled anyway, just in case his friend was wound too tightly to recognize his voice and understand his words.

The roll saved his life. A round of fire from the M-4 shredded his former hiding place.

Kai came to rest behind a fallen tree. He snuck a glance around the side and saw Rafe slowly quartering the area, trying to get a bead on him. "Rafe, come on man, don't shoot. It's Kai Paterson."

Rafe fired again.

Shit. He almost hadn't rolled away fast enough. What the hell was Rafe thinking?

Kai had his back pressed against a tree several yards away from Susana's hiding place. He took a deep breath and let it out slowly. Set his weapon on the ground where he could retrieve it later.

He waited until he heard Rafe's footsteps draw near, then dove out of hiding and rolled past Rafe.

Kai stopped his roll several feet away, turned, and knelt facing Rafe's back, his hands up. "Don't shoot, Rafe. I'm unarmed."

Rafe pivoted, weapon up. For one tense moment, Kai stared down the muzzle of the M-4.

Something dark flared in Rafe's eyes.

Shit. He'd made a mistake coming into the open. Rafe should have recognized him by now. Instead, his friend was a hairsbreadth away from killing him.

"Rafe, buddy, I know it's been over two months since we last shared a beer. But come on, you remember me. Kai Paterson. We went through physical therapy together. The SSU medical team called us the dynamic duo because of our fast recovery rate and the number of nurses we had hanging around." Damn, he might as well be talking to himself. Rafe continued to scowl at him.

He tried another tack. "My sister Jenna is married to your brother Niko."

Okay, Niko's name brought a slight softening of Rafe's expression. But it vanished almost immediately, replaced by a feral curl of Rafe's lip.

Ah, damn he did not want to die here. But if Rafe was a dog, he'd be whining to attack right now. He had the same intense, I'm-going-to-rip-your-throat-out look in his eyes.

The same look Kai had seen in the eyes of Dr. Nevsky's subjects.

Shit, shit, *shit*. Rafe had disappeared leading a team into Kaufmann's lab, and Kaufmann had been using some of Nevsky's formulas. If Rafe was on some superhuman drug combination, then Kai had no chance of winning against him hand-to-hand. And no matter how fast he retrieved his weapon and fired, Rafe would get a few rounds off.

And if Kai died, who'd protect Susana?

"So, Rafe, are you going to lower the weapon? Because Jenna will be pissed if you shoot me." Kai felt sick at the idea of having to shoot Rafe. "And you know if Jenna's angry, Niko will be mad, too."

"Jen...na...Ni...ko..." Rafe's voice was thick, his words doled out with a drunk's care. He shook his head as if trying to clear a fog. By inches, the muzzle of his weapon tilted toward the ground.

But there was still no recognition in his eyes as he looked at Kai.

"Rafe, I'm gonna stand up now. No threat, just friends, okay?" He didn't wait for Rafe to answer. As he pushed to his feet, he palmed the knife he kept up his sleeve.

The butt of Rafe's weapon came up so fast, Kai didn't have time to duck. It caught him square under the chin. His knees buckled and he folded to the ground. Before he hit, the rifle butt slammed into his stomach, then his kidneys.

Kai gasped. Tiny silver dots pulsed behind his lids, but he held on to consciousness as if it was the winning mega-million lottery ticket.

"Where's the woman?" Rafe's voice was a deep growl, nothing like his usual teasing tone.

Kai shook his head and rolled, narrowly avoiding Rafe's boot before it connected with his ribs. He grabbed Rafe's ankle and yanked. Rafe landed on his back and Kai lunged for the M-4. They fought for it, tumbling across the ground.

Kai finally wound up on top, straddling Rafe, pressing the length of the M-4 against his friend's windpipe.

"Rafe, what the fuck is going on?"

Rafe let out a sound like an enraged bear. With inhuman strength, he flipped them over so he was on top.

Rafe's fingers closed around Kai's throat and squeezed.

A FERAL HOWL ECHOED through the jungle.

"What was that?" Jenna asked. But part of her knew. Dear God, no. Don't let them be too late.

"Rafe," Niko answered. He sprinted in the direction of the howl.

Jenna followed, pushing herself hard so she wouldn't lose track of her husband. Rafe must have found Kai and the Dias woman. As she ran her brain kept cadence with a plea. *Don't let them die. Don't let them die.*

She couldn't bear to lose Kai after she'd just found him again. Or to lose Rafe.

Up ahead, Niko burst into a small clearing.

"Rafe, no! Let him go!"

Panting, Jenna arrived in time to see Rafe kneeling over Kai's prone body. His hands encircled Kai's throat and he pounded Kai's head on the ground, growling at him, "Woman, woman, where woman?"

From the way the muscles in Rafe's fingers stood out, he had such a tight grip on her brother's throat that Kai couldn't answer even if he wanted to.

Niko dove across the clearing. He collided with Rafe, knocking his brother off of Kai. The two of them careened across the ground in a deadly tangle of arms and legs.

Jenna rushed over to Kai.

He was conscious, but his eyes were slightly unfocused. "Kai? It's Jenna. Can you hear me?"

"Jenna, no! Get out of here," Niko shouted.

She glanced up.

Rafe's boot slammed into Niko's head and her husband went skidding across the mulch. "Niko!" She started to crawl over to him, when she heard Rafe approaching.

For one terrifying instant her eyes met his. The world froze and she shrank back. Dear God. There was nothing remotely human about him.

Rafe smacked her aside as if she were nothing more than an

annoying pest, his focus entirely on Kai.

Hell no, he wasn't going to hurt her brother again. As Jenna fell, she swept her legs out, then hooked her foot around Rafe's shin and let momentum pull him down. He roared and lashed out with a large fist.

Jenna narrowly avoided it.

"Rafe!" Niko's voice was a bit wobbly. He was up on his knees, the tranquilizer gun in his hand. "Stop!"

Rafe didn't so much as flick an eye toward his brother. He lunged for Kai again.

Jenna heard a slight whoosh as the tranquilizer dart was released. It hit Rafe in the side of his neck.

He ignored it. He reached Kai and flipped her brother onto his stomach, pulling Kai's arms behind him. "Where woman?"

There was another whoosh and a second dart hit Rafe between the shoulder blades. He still didn't drop.

Jenna threw herself on his legs and pulled.

SHIT.

"Jenna, get out of the way!" Niko shouted. She'd managed to pull Rafe off of Kai, but in the process, she'd ruined his aim.

Dammit, two darts down and his brother was still moving. Unstoppable as a monster out of a sci-fi movie. And there were only two darts left.

Niko's vision doubled for a moment. He sucked in a breath and shook his head, waiting for it to clear.

Across the clearing Kai slowly crawled away from Rafe. Rafe shook his leg, trying to dislodge Jenna, but she clung with the tenacity of a starving hawk to a field mouse. So Rafe used his upper body to drag himself toward Kai.

Jenna's brother was slower than a tortoise. Dammit, Rafe was going to catch him.

Niko moved closer. His next shot hit Rafe in the upper arm.

This time Rafe turned his head. He looked down at the feathered end of the dart, then up at Niko, his face contorted with rage.

Rafe snarled.

Holy Mother of God. There was nothing of his little brother in Rafe's expression. This was an animal.

Jenna's hand reached up and took hold of the back of Rafe's shirt, her body weight pulling his head back. Rafe bellowed and fell, crushing Jenna under his back.

But Rafe's neck was exposed.

"Jesus, I'm sorry bro." Niko sent his last dart into the base of Rafe's throat.

Rafe let loose a roar of pain. He broke free of Jenna and charged Niko.

Fuck, even with the darts in him Rafe's speed was unbelievable. Niko dove out of the way seconds before Rafe landed beside him. His hand scrambled for the pistol at his belt.

Before his hand undid the safety, Rafe was on top of him. Niko was more muscular and that usually gave him an edge in their fights, but Rafe's new strength was beyond normal. Within seconds, Niko found himself in the same position Kai had been in, flat on his back with Rafe's hands around his neck.

"Rafe, no," Niko said in Greek, hoping the language of their father would penetrate Rafe's brain. "I'm Niko. Your brother. Remember?"

Rafe's hands tightened.

"Don't do this," Niko gasped. His hand fumbled for the knife on Rafe's belt. "*Mamá* will be so sad..." His fingers found the hilt. Spots obscured his vision, but he fought them. He couldn't pass out yet. He undid the snap on the knife sheath and slid the weapon free. But he could feel his strength slipping away.

Hell no. He wasn't going to pass out. Not going to leave Jenna to face this monster.

God help him, he'd kill Rafe first.

"Ni...ko?" A faint flash of recognition crossed Rafe's eyes.

"Yeah, little bro, Niko." His voice was so raspy, it was barely recognizable. Please, let him get through to Rafe anyway. "I'm here, Rafe. You're safe now."

"Save...me." Horror widened Rafe's eyes. Then he dropped, heavy as an anvil, across Niko, the tranquilizer finally taking over.

Niko let the knife slip out of his grasp. He put his arms around Rafe in a hug.

He tried to swallow, but his throat muscles had locked up. He coughed, but it didn't help. Finally he managed to push words out, even though he knew his brother couldn't hear him. "Don't worry Rafe, I've got you. You're safe now."

Niko blinked back tears. Sometimes he still thought of Rafe as the kid with the runny nose who had followed his big brother around with adoration in his eyes. But that sweet kid who'd always been asking "why" was gone, lost to time.

Niko pushed Rafe off of him, then rolled to his hands and feet. "You're going to be whole again," Niko promised. "No matter what it takes. But until then," Niko pulled a pair of reinforced flex cuffs out of his pants pocket. "I'm sorry, bro, but this is necessary."

Niko cuffed Rafe's hands and feet. He removed the darts from his brother's skin, then pulled out a special net from his backpack and wrapped his brother in it from neck to feet.

He sat back on his heels and surveyed his brother.

Shit. His chest hurt. Niko put a hand up to his sternum, certain he'd find a hole there. But the flesh was intact.

It was just his heart that felt hollow. Because, Christ, Rafe looked dead.

Niko reached out and felt for his brother's pulse. It was strong and steady under his fingers. "I'm sorry, bro. It had to be done." Niko smoothed back Rafe's hair. Unconscious, his brother's youthful good looks had reclaimed the face that moments before had been distorted by animal fury.

But Niko saw lines of strain and recent scars that testified to horrors endured since Rafe had left on his last assignment. Niko pushed to his feet, slow as an arthritic eighty-year-old. Struggling to breathe through the weight of too many emotions, he walked over to Jenna and Kai.

"How is he?" Niko asked his wife.

"Getting there, thanks," Kai croaked. "Rafe okay?"

"Subdued, anyway," Niko said.

"What...was that all about?" Kai asked. He put his elbow underneath him and with Jenna's help, managed to sit up.

Niko glanced across the clearing. "He was captured by Kaufmann's group. They gave him their version of Nevsky's drugs."

"Oh, man. Shit. I'm sorry."

Niko shrugged. "That's why we need the damn chip. To help us reverse what's been done."

He heard the faint sound of something hard hitting the ground behind him. Niko dove for Jenna, covering her with his body.

And the world exploded in sound and noxious smoke.

CHAPTER TWENTY-THREE

Susana had just started to climb down the tree, thinking it was safe, when an explosion almost knocked her off her perch. She wrapped her arms and legs around the trunk of the tree, closed her eyes, and waited for a second explosion.

Instead, there was silence. And a faintly sweet, chemical smell that made her throat and eyes burn. Susana snatched at the collar of her shirt and pulled it over her nose and mouth, then pressed on the edges so no contaminated air could seep in.

She risked a peek down. Smoke hovered over the bodies of Kai and his friends.

No! Kai couldn't be dead. He couldn't.

She leaned so far forward, scanning the ground for life, she forgot to keep a firm grip on the tree. She slipped. Her stomach leapt into her throat as she fell a foot before she caught herself on another branch. Taking a deep breath, she tried to steady her heart. But she needed to reach Kai, so she lowered her foot and felt around for a strong branch below her. Then froze as a group of men burst into the clearing. They carried automatic weapons and wore camouflage uniforms. Gas masks covered their faces.

The first four men who arrived took up positions around the

edge of the small clearing. The final two men walked from Kai to his friends, turning the unconscious figures over and prodding them with the butts of their guns.

Kai groaned.

Susana bit her lip so her cry of relief wouldn't escape and give her away.

When the mercenaries reached the woman, one of the men bent down and snapped old-fashioned metal handcuffs around her wrists. Then he removed the bandana from around his neck and gagged her. He slung her over his shoulder and nodded to his companions. As quickly as they'd arrived, they disappeared back into the jungle, heading toward Boa Vista.

The last man turned and threw something into the center of the clearing. Then he bolted after his comrades. Seconds later, the clearing burst into flames.

"No!"

Susana scrambled down the tree. She kicked the backpacks free from their hiding place, then jumped the last ten feet.

She yanked the survival blanket out of Kai's backpack and slapped it against the nearest flames. When they were low enough, she tossed the entire silver square on the fire, then jumped on it to eradicate the flames.

But the fire just shot out the other side, moving closer to Kai and the other man.

"Kai! Wake up, damn you."

She was rewarded by coughing.

"Susana? Wha—? Oh, fuck." Kai's scratchy voice was the most beautiful thing she'd ever heard.

"Niko, wake up, man." Kai was sitting up now, trying to wake his friend.

Susana returned her attention to the flames. The fire underneath the blanket was smothered, the blanket melted in several spots. The rest of the fire burned dangerously close to Kai and Niko.

Susana pulled the mosquito net out of the backpack. It was fire retardant, wasn't it?

"Where's Jenna?" Kai asked.

"The mercenaries took her," Susana said.

Kai and his friend were on their feet now and headed toward her. "Forget fighting the fire," Kai told her. "Move." He grabbed his backpack and pulled her to her feet.

Her hand snagged the strap of her pack as Kai hustled her into the cool relief of the trees. A moment later Niko followed with the man he'd tied up slung across his shoulder.

Susana glanced behind them with an odd sense of déjà-vu, watching the flames devour a tree. But Kai didn't let her linger. He yanked on her arm and once again she ran behind him through the jungle.

Five minutes later they stopped. Both men turned to her. Niko let the unconscious man slide off his shoulder and gently set him on the ground.

"Tell me what happened to my sister," Kai demanded.

"My wife," Niko said, shooting Kai a look that claimed equal possession.

Oh, God. The woman was Kai's sister? The one he'd cried out for during his fever?

"After the gas knocked you out, a group of soldiers arrived," Susana said. "They put handcuffs on the woman, gagged her and carried her off. They headed this way. I don't think they have more than a ten-minute lead on us."

Kai and Niko exchanged a long glance. Both men wore grim expressions. But it was the almost frantic fear in Kai's eyes that squeezed a tear out of her heart.

Niko swallowed heavily. Clenched and unclenched his fists. Rubbed his biceps as he stared at the jungle where the soldiers had disappeared. Finally, he turned away. He glanced down at the bound man, then sighed and looked at Kai.

"You go after her," he told Kai. "I've got to get Rafe out of here. If he sees you again when he wakes up, he'll probably have a fit."

Kai nodded toward Rafe. "His behavior..." Kai shook his head. "You're sure he was given some of Nevsky's drugs?"

"Yeah. Modified by Kaufmann. They also put him through mind-control sessions." Niko's voice cracked and he looked away. "We need the goddamn data on the chip to create an antidote. But God, if anything happens to Jenna..."

Kai squeezed Niko's shoulder. "I know. I'll get her back. I promise."

"Take my pack," Niko said. "It's got a backup radio and rations for four days."

"Right." Kai's eyes briefly met Susana's before bouncing away. But not before she saw something that looked like regret.

Kai took Niko's backpack, added a few items from his own pack, then slipped his arms through the shoulder straps. He drew a deep breath and Susana knew what Kai was going to tell her. And suddenly she couldn't bear for him to say good-bye.

"Niko, this is Susana Dias," Kai said. "Susana, meet Niko Andros, my brother-in-law."

Niko nodded hello and somehow Susana managed a polite, "Pleased to meet you." Although what she really wanted to do was scream at Kai not to leave her.

"That's his brother Rafe on the ground." Kai's mouth firmed into a grim line. "Niko will get you out of here safely." Kai unscrewed the top of his canteen and took a long drink.

"Niko, Susana has four days left to get to Moscow or she'll die and the chip will be destroyed. Susana, show him the letter. The SSU will take care of you from here."

Even though she'd been expecting it, Kai's words hit her with the force of a tsunami. The world tilted and for a moment she thought she was going to fall.

This was the last time she'd ever see him. She shivered, feeling a bleakness that she hadn't experienced since she turned eight and her mother shipped her off to boarding school.

Well, to hell with him. Her anger simmered up and saved her from humiliating herself with tears. "Here, you'll need this." She removed Kai's watch from her wrist and held it out to him.

Kai didn't even meet her eyes as he took the watch, the coward. As if the past several days of shared body heat and shared confidences had never happened.

"Good luck," she snarled before turning away.

As much as she wanted to, she wasn't going to yell at him in front of Niko. And she didn't want Kai to see her face. Because then he'd realize she was in love with him.

What a hell of a time to realize how she felt.

"Glacier-hearted piranha spawn," she muttered under her breath. She was done loving people who didn't love her back. If it killed her, she'd keep her pride.

She'd taken two steps when Kai growled, "Fuck it" and spun her around.

His mouth slammed down on hers in a bruising kiss that had her arms clasping him around the neck and her body up on her tiptoes, trying to get closer to him.

When he pulled back, she whimpered and tried to bring his lips back to hers.

He gave her a fast kiss, then removed her arms from his neck. "Stay safe," he ordered. "You can trust Niko." Another quick kiss. "I'll see you in Boa Vista."

Then he disappeared into the jungle.

Niko fussed over his brother, but she saw the corner of his mouth lift in a smile. She didn't care. Kai had promised to meet her, and she was going to hold him to that promise.

She wasn't done with him yet.

A radio squawked behind her and she heard Niko requesting a new pickup location. When he was finished, he told her, "Our boss, Ryker, is sending a helicopter for us. They were already on the way to search for Kai. Once they locate an opening in the canopy big enough, we'll meet them and they'll lower ropes to pull us up. Until then, we'll hang out here."

Susana nodded.

"When you're ready," Niko said, "how about you show me that letter?"

SUSANA FOLLOWED Niko through the jungle toward the extraction point. She wanted to apologize to him, but what words could possibly be strong enough to take away her guilt? It had finally dawned on her that his wife—Kai's sister—had been abducted because the mercenaries thought Jenna was Susana.

She wished the mercenaries had taken her, instead. That way Kai and the others could return safely to Boa Vista.

She slapped at a mosquito on her arm. No, given the way Kai had kissed her, she knew he'd have followed if she'd been taken instead of his sister. Because that kiss proved Kai cared. The knowledge fanned the warm glow surrounding her heart and she smiled.

Up ahead, Niko shifted his brother to his other shoulder and Susana's good mood fizzled.

"What's wrong with Rafe?" Susana asked. She'd never seen a man so crazed. Or heard such animal noises from a human throat.

"He was given a variation of the drugs your father created."

She stumbled.

Oh, God, no. "I don't understand. I thought my father's work was destroyed in a fire. Aren't the only remaining notes on the microchip?"

"Dr. Kaufmann, one of your father's assistants, stole samples of your father's drugs then left and set up his own lab."

Niko maneuvered through a particularly dense patch of vegetation, his hand keeping branches and vines away from his brother's vulnerable head. "Whoever is given the drugs and put through the conditioning program," Niko continued, "comes out physically strong and obedient to his handlers, but violent and mentally unstable. If the subjects don't commit suicide, their internal organs fail and they die within three months."

"And—my father knew about these side effects?" God, why hadn't Kai told her this?

"Yeah. Sorry."

Her mother had been right. Her father was evil. She bit her lip, trying to keep back words of anger and pity. "Is there an antidote?"

Niko's stride faltered. "Not that we know of. We don't even know exactly what drugs they gave Rafe. We have notes from Kaufmann's lab, but most of his drugs came from Nevsky, so we need the data on the microchip. With the formula in hand, our scientists should be able to reverse the drugs. I'm not giving up until Rafe is back to normal."

Niko's love and determination made Susana feel as if a piece of glass had lodged in her throat. What it was like to have someone love you so much they'd fly thousands of miles to rescue you?

She looked at Rafe's head flopping against Niko's back. Did Rafe even have the time it would take to develop and test an antidote? He'd been nearly insane with rage. What if he deteriorated further? How were they going to keep him under control while the scientists worked on a solution?

"What happened to the subjects of my father's experiments?"

"You really should talk to Kai about this. He's the one who went undercover at your father's lab."

"Yes, I know. But you're here now." And Kai had apparently left a lot of details out of his explanation.

"As far as we can tell, all of the men from your father's program are dead. But we think several men from Kaufmann's lab are loose in the community. If we can find an antidote, we can save them, too."

Oh, great. Like she needed more pressure. Now it wasn't just her life at stake if she failed to reach Dr. Ivanov in Moscow in time to have the chip removed. Rafe and any surviving subjects of the lab also depended on her.

"You...uh...don't show any symptoms of your father's work," Niko said. "Do you know anything more about what he did to you?"

"No." She wanted to scream at Niko for reminding her of the final paragraph in the letter. The part she'd withheld from Kai. The words explaining that her father had experimented on her as an infant before her mother took her away. Her father also promised that she'd find details in the journals he'd sent to Ivanov in Moscow.

A few simple words on a piece of paper and her world had altered.

Was she even normal? Were her bursts of temper caused by an earlier version of the same drugs that had sent Rafe into an animal-like frenzy? Is that why she'd reacted so ferociously to Jacie's betrayal?

Susana was terrified of what she'd learn.

She took a deep breath. At the same time he'd requested a pick-up, Niko had sent an encrypted text message to the SSU requesting that they locate and detain Dr. Ivanov and prepare for her arrival.

Niko assured her they'd get to Moscow in time.

God, she'd never been so afraid. As much as she wanted the chip removed, even though she swore she could feel it burning in her belly, part of her wanted to stay here in the jungle.

And she'd give anything to have Kai's arms around her.

THE MEN who'd taken Jenna hadn't made any effort to hide their trail. As Kai followed, he fought against a nearly overwhelming sense that he'd doomed Susana by not staying with her.

Which was bullshit. Niko would get her safely out of the jungle. They'd all meet up in Boa Vista, then Kai would escort her to Moscow.

No, the real problem was that none of them knew what awaited Susana in Moscow. Would the SSU be able to find Dr. Ivanov in time? Would the man have the tools to safely extract the chip? Could he be trusted not to break the vial while extracting the chip?

Cold sweat trickled down Kai's spine.

His mind told him to focus on getting Jenna back. But his heart wanted him to return and protect Susana.

Up ahead a boat motor kicked over.

Shit.

Kai sprinted toward the sound. By the time he reached the river, the boat had already pulled too far away from land for him to jump. He caught a brief glimpse of Jenna as her captor dumped her onto the bottom of the boat. Someone had put a sack over her head and wrapped her in netting.

He glared after the boat. It was a rubber, inflatable boat. The type that could be dropped from a helicopter. A boat that would ferry the men just far enough to be picked up.

He slowed his breathing to better listen. Yes, that was the sound of a helicopter downriver.

The boat disappeared around a bend. Kai ran after it. Jenna was going to be airlifted away and he had no idea where to start looking for—

An explosion tossed Kai to his knees.

What the hell? He glanced up in the direction the boat had taken and saw a cloud of smoke.

"Jenna!"

Tuesday, Afternoon
Boa Vista, Brazil

"WE GOT THE GIRL," the mercenary told Mark Tonelli next time he radioed in. "A group of soldiers had her on a boat."

Mark cursed. Jamieson's men. Had to be.

"When a helicopter arrived to pick them up, we blew it out of the sky. While the soldiers on the boat were distracted by the explosion, we opened fire. They're all dead."

"Good. And the girl?" God, Mark couldn't wait to see Susana again. His eagerness was pathetic, yet he couldn't stop his blood from racing with excitement. He didn't want her scared when she first met him, so he'd rented this small bungalow where they could get to know each other without strangers upsetting her. Once she felt comfortable with him, he'd fly her back to the States. To a surgeon Mark trusted to remove the microchip and keep his mouth shut.

A man with no connection to Jamieson. Mark would take the chip and use it to bargain with Jamieson to give him the name of his father's killer.

"The girl's tied up in the cabin."

The mercenary's words jolted Mark out of his reverie. "You haven't hurt her, have you?"

"No, man. 'Course not."

Damn. He wanted to order the man to untie Susana. Yet he couldn't take the chance of her escaping again.

"Call me when you're close to arriving and I'll meet you at the dock."

Amazon Jungle

KAI SAT on a rock at the edge of the river, staring at the wreckage of the helicopter. Bodies floated among the debris.

Jenna, thank God, was not among the dead. He'd arrived in time to see a familiar gunboat nosing away from the overturned inflatable. One of the mercenaries who'd kidnapped Susana had carried Jenna's wrapped figure into the cabin.

Kai then used Niko's extra satellite phone to call for extraction, and to notify the SSU of Jenna's abduction. They promised to track the boat.

Waiting for his ride, Kai had nothing to do but think. He scrubbed his hands over his face, trying to wipe away memories and quiet his brain.

He didn't want to remember how, after the attack that had killed their parents, he'd found Jenna in the backyard and believed her dead. He refused to consider that Jenna might die now. Wouldn't think about what new scars she might accumulate before he rescued her from the mercenaries.

Instead, he replayed Susana's last words. *"Good luck."* Her voice had trembled with fury and she'd muttered a curse under her breath.

Yeah, he'd intended to leave her so mad she'd never want to see him again. But when he'd seen the hurt underneath her anger, he'd wanted to wipe her pain away. So he'd kissed her and promised he'd see her in Boa Vista.

God, he missed her already.

He put his head in his hands, pressed his palms against his eyes, and fought to blank his mind.

A low thrum announced the presence of a helicopter upriver. His satellite phone beeped twice, letting him know the approaching bird was friendly. Kai walked out onto the long spit of sand that jutted into the river.

It was still several minutes before the helicopter appeared. A long rope hung from its belly like an umbilical cord. Kai grabbed hold as the rope whipped past. He swung through the air, rising quickly above the river as the helicopter continued its journey.

A man dressed in jungle fatigues pulled Kai on board, then slid the door closed, cutting off the roar of the wind.

Kai sat up. His eyes landed on a familiar group at the back of the cargo bay—Niko, Rafe and Susana. Rafe was still wrapped up and out cold. Niko sat with his knees up and his back against the wall next to his brother, eyelids at half-mast as he kept watch. Susana lay on her back on the other side of Niko, her eyes closed and a bandage wrapped around her head.

Kai's heart stopped. For a moment he was so filled with terror, he couldn't see. Couldn't hear. Then his body sprang into motion. He flung off his backpack and knelt next to Susana. "What the hell happened?"

"Wind tossed her against the strut as she was being pulled up," Niko answered. "She's unconscious, but the gash on her forehead isn't deep enough to need stitches."

Kai checked her pulse, her pupils and the cut underneath the bandage. Niko was right. She'd have a hell of a headache once she woke, and the cut would hurt, but she'd been lucky it wasn't deeper.

He lay down beside her and pulled her into his arms. And finally acknowledged the truth.

There was no way he could let her go. He just cared too damn much.

CHAPTER TWENTY-FOUR

Tuesday, Evening
Boa Vista, Brazil

MARK TONELLI WAITED IMPATIENTLY on the dock as the boat carrying Susana positioned itself for boarding. It was after dark and this section of the waterfront had emptied out when the warehouses shut down. Leaving no witnesses to the approaching boat.

Still, as the engine cut off and the men looped the thick rope around the post, Mark decided he'd have to postpone checking on Susana. The hairs at the back of his neck tingled. He wasn't going to risk some petty thug making off with his lady.

He called the head mercenary's sat phone. "Wait for me to bring my car up," Mark ordered. "Do you have something you can put her in or wrap her with so it's not obvious you're carrying a body?"

Mark took the mercenary's annoyed grunt as a yes. "Good. Wait for me to call you back."

Five minutes later, Mark backed his car up to the gangplank. One of the men met him at the bottom.

"We want the money first."

Mark shrugged and pulled a wad of cash out of his pocket. The man grabbed it, flipped through it suspiciously, then tucked it into the inside pocket of his lightweight jacket. He raised his arm. Two mercenaries emerged from the cabin carrying Susana, who was wrapped in a rolled fishing net. They tossed her in the car's trunk without a word, turned, and headed up the gangplank.

Mark pulled out his silenced automatic and shot them in the back, watching as their bodies tumbled into the river. It took another minute to walk up to the pilot's station and kill that man as well. After dumping the pilot's body in the river, Mark unwound the rope holding the boat to the pier. No one in this part of town would care about a couple extra bodies, and with any luck the tide would carry the boat out to sea.

He couldn't leave them alive and risk Jamieson finding out that he had Susana. He'd tell his boss eventually, but first he would spend some quality time with his lady.

Mark got back into his car and drove toward his bungalow with barely leashed excitement. Susana was finally here. He couldn't wait to see her beautiful brown eyes looking at him with gratitude as he provided her with a bath, then new clothes, and finally, a hot meal.

His foot pressed a little too hard on the accelerator and the car jerked forward. He forced himself to back off. It wouldn't do to draw attention to himself. Not now, when he was so close to realizing his goal.

KAI PARKED his car down the quiet street from a small, tidy bungalow that glowed faintly pink in the moonlight. His prey had just pulled into the driveway leading around back.

It had been ridiculously simple to follow the GPS signal from Jenna's phone to the dock. He'd watched the men load her into the car's trunk. Watched as Tonelli shot them. The dock had appeared deserted, but Kai hadn't wanted to take the chance that Tonelli had men hidden, guarding his back, so Kai opted to follow the man, rather than attack him.

Mark Tonelli. That arrogant asshole was everywhere these days, wasn't he? He'd interfered with Niko and Jenna's mission several months ago and left Rafe to bleed to death on an airport tarmac in Mexico.

Now this.

He'd never liked Tonelli. They'd worked a couple of assignments together back when Kai had been with the CIA. Tonelli held an arrogant belief that only certain high-profile cases were worthy of his superior skills, so his work was sloppy on any assignments that failed to meet his standards.

And Kai had always suspected Tonelli dipped into the other side of the legal river now and then for profit or thrill.

Kai disabled his car's overhead light, then stepped into the humid night air. The SSU didn't have enough available agents to send backup for Kai and crew two flights—one to take Susana to Russia and another to ferry Niko and Rafe back to headquarters. But that was okay with Kai. He was used to working alone. Keeping to the shadows, he moved down the street. Tonelli had driven around to the back of the bungalow.

Air soughed in and out of Kai's lungs in choppy discord. His muscles tightened, preparing for battle as he released the hold he'd kept on his temper. His sister had been trussed up and tossed about like a friggin' carpet. Tonelli was nowhere near as vicious as Jaime Alvarez, the deceased crime lord who'd captured Jenna a few months ago, leaving Jenna with a faint knife scar on her cheek, but Kai didn't care. He couldn't feel generous toward any asshole who touched his baby sister.

He lengthened his stride, shredding the distance between him and the bungalow.

Up to now, Kai had figured the mercenaries that kidnapped

Jenna had mistaken her for Susana. But he hadn't known Tonelli was involved.

Now he had to wonder if something else was going on. If maybe his sister was being used as a tool in some larger game. Or maybe Tonelli was just out for revenge. He'd hated Jenna ever since he'd been paired with her on a joint SSU/CIA mission to Moscow to lure Kai out of hiding.

Kai paused at the house next to Tonelli's. He scanned the area for guards.

Saw no one. He shook his head. Sucker.

As he moved across the lawn toward the bungalow, he heard Tonelli yelling. "Where's Susana?"

Kai grinned. Okay, so Jenna hadn't been the target. Man, he wished he could see Tonelli's face now he knew he'd kidnapped the wrong woman.

Tonelli's yelling cut off on a yelp of pain.

Kai ran toward the front door. He'd just reached the lawn when a slight figure stumbled out the door onto the short concrete porch.

"Jenna!"

At his shout, she turned her head. The movement caused her to lose her balance and she started to topple toward the lawn.

Kai dove, catching her before she hit the ground. "Hey, baby sis. You okay?"

She grunted behind her gag.

"Just a sec." He set her back on her feet and swiftly cut off the bandana.

She spit the cotton out. "I'm fine," she croaked. "Go get that bastard Tonelli before he escapes."

Just then a car rounded the house, nearly mowing them down as it swerved onto the street.

Tonelli.

"Don't worry," Kai said. "We'll get him eventually. He's no immediate threat. Let's get you out of here."

MARK TONELLI GLANCED in the rearview mirror, watching as a familiar shape of a man put his arm around the woman. Who wasn't Susana Dias.

No, just his luck it was Jenna Paterson. He'd hoped to never see her again. She still had the same spooky amber eyes that seemed to peer right through him. Eyes that matched her damn brother's. Her hair had grown out since he'd last seen her, but instead of dying the white strands a normal color, she'd gone with a camouflage pattern.

Who wanted green and brown hair? Why hadn't she put on a hat to hide her distinctive hair like a normal woman?

Well, let her brother take care of her now. Mark was going to find Susana.

He indulged himself and let the speedometer creep up. What the hell, he didn't have a trussed-up female in his trunk now and it felt good to take out his temper on the road. Barbaric as ever, Jenna had driven her feet into his groin the moment she woke up. The throbbing pain still lingered.

Typical violent SSU agent. His lip curled. He didn't think much of their recruitment policies. A bunch of savages, every one.

His cell phone beeped, indicating an incoming text. Mark divided his attention between the screen and the road. When he was done reading, he laughed.

At least one of those SSU savages was useful, though. His mole had just sent a text explaining Susana's true location.

An hour later, Mark was still in a generous mood as he pulled alongside a private airplane. His instructions had been to go inside and seat himself in the front section. Although Mark was anxious to see Susana for himself, he agreed it was better to get airborne before revealing his presence, just in case Paterson had warned Susana about him.

Susana couldn't run from him if they were a mile up.

Niko set Rafe down on one of the couches in the SSU's private airplane, thankful the tranquilizers were still working to keep Rafe unconscious.

The door to the cockpit opened and the pilot stuck his head out. "Y'all strapped in okay? We're cleared for takeoff."

"Almost," Niko replied. He sat down, but then his hands stilled over his seatbelt. "Jim, I thought you were flying Susana Dias to Moscow." Enrique Gonzales, another SSU agent, had met the helicopter and taken Susana to a different plane.

"Change of plans. Gonzales said they weren't flying out today. He told your pilot to turn back and assigned me to fly you to the States."

"Shit." Susana only had four more days to get to Moscow. What the hell was Gonzales thinking?

Niko whipped out his phone. He dialed Gonzales, but got no answer. The call bounced straight to voicemail. He swore.

"Hey Andros?" Jim called from the cockpit.

"Yeah?"

"Another private plane just took off from the other side of the hangar. We were supposed to be the only ones cleared for takeoff tonight."

Shit. Niko started to dial Ryker, then his phone rang. "Andros."

"Hey, lover. You still on the ground? Because Kai and I could use a ride."

Despite the tension crawling up his spine, Niko smiled. Jenna's voice did that to him every time. He loved the river-smooth tones of her voice. "You okay, *querida*?"

When she assured him she was fine, he said, "We're about to take off, but I'll have Jim wait for you. What's your ETA?"

"I don't know. Ask Kai. Love you."

He didn't have time to reciprocate the sentiment before Kai was on the line. Niko didn't know Boa Vista, but it was small. He estimated Kai and Jenna to be about ten minutes away. "So Kai, you heard from Susana? Or maybe Gonzales?"

"No. Why?"

"'Cause Gonzales told Jim that Susana's departure was being delayed until tomorrow, leaving Jim to ferry us back to the States. But a private plane just took off and I have a bad feeling that Susana was aboard. I just tried calling Gonzales but it went right to voicemail."

"Shit." Niko heard Jenna's voice asking what was wrong and Kai's brief explanation.

"Tonelli's work," Kai told Niko. "Has to be. Jenna confirmed that he'd wanted Susana, not her. But the bastard escaped. How much do you want to bet Gonzales is working with him? Fucking hell. That sonofabitch has Susana."

The note of desperation in Kai's tone made Niko's eyebrows rise. He hadn't missed his friend's wording. He was worried about Susana, not the chip.

Niko grinned. Oh, man, this was going to get interesting. Cool-headed Kai was in l-o-v-e. As that steamy good-bye kiss had shown.

Perfect. But first...

"I told Gonzales about the self-destruct deadline," Niko said. "How the chip will be destroyed if it triggers. Whatever he and Tonelli are up to, they have to take her to Moscow in order to get the chip."

From Kai's end of the line Niko heard a car engine revving, then Kai's outraged voice. "Who taught you how to hot-wire a car?"

Niko couldn't hear his wife's response, but he grinned again. After two years alone and on the run, Kai hadn't yet accepted that his formerly sunny, innocent little sister was now a force to be reckoned with. She'd completed the SSU's operator training course in the top ten percent of her class. And while Niko would never hold her back, he'd been relieved when she decided to pursue a degree in wildlife rehabilitation instead of joining the SSU full-time.

He'd discovered that husbands had as many protective feelings as big brothers.

"Damn," Kai said. "It seems my sister has found us transport. We're on our way. You'll call Ryker and warn him about Tonelli and Gonzales?"

"Yeah," Niko said. "I also need to get further instructions for Rafe."

"He doing okay?"

Niko let out a harsh laugh. "Being tranq'd is probably the most peace he's had since we lost him."

"I'm sorry, man. Hey!" Kai's voice moved away from the mouthpiece. "Jesus, Jenna watch where you're going. You nearly blindsided that truck...Yeah? Well I'm the one in the passenger seat and I'm telling you, you came within millimeters of peeling this side of the car open and spilling me onto the street."

Niko heard a long-suffering sigh from Kai. "Listen, Niko. I gotta go. Your damn wife is trying to kill me again."

"Yeah, yeah, I'm cryin' for ya. See you in five." Niko disconnected the call. Jenna and Kai had come a long way if Kai could joke about her killing him. Five months ago, in Jaime Alvarez's dungeon, Jenna had raised her knife with every intention of killing her brother. At the last second she'd discovered that her love for Kai trumped her hate. Kai had been conscious enough to see her strike and to feel the knife as it passed his cheek with millimeters to spare. Jenna had been terrified nothing would repair the divide between her and her brother after that. But their love was too strong to let even attempted murder separate them.

"Jim," Niko called. "Tell the tower we're holding for ten. We're going to be taking on two more passengers." As Niko dialed his boss, he made a private bet Ryker would redirect them to Moscow.

Susana sat alone in the rear section of the posh Gulfstream 550 as it took off. As luxurious as the interior of the plane was, with cream puff leather seats and mahogany paneling, she'd flown in more expensive planes during her modeling days. It seemed odd, though, that the SSU would spend money on such luxury items as a fully stocked bar and a wall-covering plasma television.

Shouldn't they spend their money on weapons? Or body armor? Something that related to their dangerous work. If she were Kai, she'd complain.

The door to the forward compartment slid open so quietly, she wouldn't have noticed if she hadn't been facing it. SSU agent Enrique Gonzales walked through, followed by a man with short, perfectly-styled curly dark hair. She had the feeling she'd seen the man somewhere, but wasn't sure where or when.

"Susana, I'd like you to meet my colleague, Mark Tonelli," Gonzales said. "He's fluent in Russian and very familiar with Moscow. He'll be in charge of getting you to Dr. Ivanov."

"I am delighted to meet you again." Tonelli took Susana's outstretched hand, raised it to his lips, and placed a kiss on her knuckles.

Every hair on Susana's body tried to jump off of her skin at the contact. Only years of keeping her expression neutral during photo shoots allowed her to hide her revulsion.

It wasn't just that the touch of his mouth felt too intimate, too soon after her separation from Kai. It was the way he lingered over the kiss, taking it beyond courtesy into presumption.

She could have forgiven him that. After all, she was a beautiful woman. He wasn't the first man to behave so brashly. But when at last he allowed her to reclaim her hand and his eyes met hers, she recognized the feverish glint of possession.

"I'm sorry, do I know you?" she asked, putting a bit of haughty reserve into her tone to hide her discomfort. Surely if they'd met she would have remembered the vibes he gave off.

Tonelli smiled with little boy charm, revealing a dimple in his left cheek. She'd bet her entire investment account he practiced that smile in a mirror.

"I had the honor of dancing with you at the Archaeological Society fundraiser last month," he informed her. His shoulders rose slightly, as if to apologize for assuming she'd remember him.

But Susana was no novice to the game. "I'm terribly sorry," she replied. She curled her lips just enough to make him believe she was sincere. "Those events have so many handsome, charming men. I simply can't keep them straight." She let her mouth tilt up even more and sure enough, he jumped in to reassure her.

"It was only one dance and we were never properly introduced. I'm not surprised you don't remember me." Then all light left his face, as if he were suddenly standing underneath a storm cloud.

"Your father has put you in unforgivable danger, Susana. I promise I will keep you safe."

The tinge of anger in his voice confirmed what her body had already figured out. This man was dangerously obsessed with her.

"Thank you." She smiled and reached out to place her hand lightly on his arm. She lifted her shoulders and tilted her body forward while looking at him in false gratitude. "I just know I can trust you."

Hah. She'd felt safer tumbling through the Amazon River while being shot at by the mercenaries. God, she wished Kai were here.

For the next few minutes she exchanged small talk with Tonelli, asking him innocuous questions about Moscow that allowed him to show off. After each question his chest puffed out a little more, until she was tempted to find a needle and see if she could pop him.

Gonzales hung around, but contributed little to the conversation. He puzzled her. If it had been just her and Tonelli, she would have been convinced she'd fallen into enemy hands. Whoever the enemy might be.

But Niko had passed her off to Gonzales with a relieved smile. She trusted Niko, if for no other reason than because he was so gentle with his brother's unconscious body. More importantly, Kai trusted Niko. So if Niko thought Gonzales was okay, then Tonelli was also.

Her instincts had to be off.

Still, she was relieved when Gonzales told her to feel free to use the onboard shower, then accompanied Tonelli back into the other cabin. Once the cabin door closed, she searched for a way to lock it.

Nothing.

And since all the furniture was bolted down, she couldn't even create a trip zone with chairs to warn her of an uninvited entrance. But, hallelujah, there was a lock on the inside of the bathroom door. She took a long, hot shower, reveling as days' worth of grime slipped down the drain.

If only her fear would disappear so easily.

Dammit, she wanted Kai here. Wanted to soap him up and have wild shower sex, then have him hold her and reassure her everything was going to be fine.

She turned the water off with a snap of her wrist. *Stop whining. Kai has every right to rescue his sister.*

And she was a strong, intelligent woman. She could protect herself.

All she had to do was stay on her guard until they reached this Dr. Ivanov. How hard could that be?

CHAPTER TWENTY-FIVE

Tuesday, Night
Washington, D.C.

JAMIESON STARED AROUND HIS OFFICE, fighting back the panicked urge to pack everything and run. He reminded himself that only the weak ran. Besides, the best way to appear innocent was to stay put in times of greatest danger.

Events were at critical mass, though.

Dr. Kaufmann had called earlier, a tinge of suspicion in his voice when he reported the team he'd sent after the chip had disappeared. Jamieson had made appropriate sounds of sympathy, but both men had known the truth. That Kaufmann's men had been eliminated on Jamieson's orders.

What Jamieson hadn't told Kaufmann was that his cleanup squad had also disappeared. His men were professionals. Only another well-organized military team would have been able to take them down.

Someone was onto him. This was a warning.

Jamieson wished he knew who was after him, so he could plan a counter attack. Ryker didn't have the guts. Maybe—

His phone rang.

He glared at it and considered ignoring the interruption. But he had to keep up appearances.

"Jamieson."

"This is Mark Tonelli, sir. I have Susana Dias."

What flooded through his body might have been relief, but Jamieson preferred to think of it as satisfaction. "It's about time," he snapped. "This is where I want you to bring her—"

"We're on our way to Moscow."

"What?"

"Dr. Nevsky booby-trapped the microchip. Only his colleague, a Dr. Ivanov, can deactivate the trap and prevent the chip from being destroyed upon removal."

Jamieson's lips moved in silent curses. Russia was too far away. Anything could happen to the chip between there and his hands. He—

"I have contacts who are searching for the scientist, but the SSU is also on the man's trail. Gonzales's cover is blown, so I thought perhaps you might want to deal with that side of the problem."

Jamieson's fingers tightened around the receiver. How dare the man presume to give him an order. Tonelli was nobody. He was...

...currently in possession of the woman and therefore the chip. It wouldn't do to antagonize him just yet. Jamieson briefly closed his eyes. "Of course," he said. "I'll put a team at your disposal." He'd have to eliminate Gonzales now that the man could no longer provide Tonelli with inside information on the SSU. He couldn't afford to have Gonzales change his mind and decide to work with the SSU to stop Jamieson.

"Thank you, sir."

After a few more minutes discussing logistics, Jamieson ended the call. Then he set about creating a roadblock for the SSU.

Tuesday, Night
On a Plane Heading to Moscow

SUSANA GLANCED out the airplane window. The plane lowered out of the clouds and for the first time in hours, she saw the ground. Unfortunately, the earth was getting closer, not farther away. If she could, she'd turn the plane around. Never land in Russia.

But she didn't have a choice. If everything her father had written was true, then her life depended on following through with this crazy journey.

Susana dug her fingernails into the already deep crescents in her palms and pushed her head against the seat back. She was scared.

No. Scared was too weak a word.

Try terrified.

There was no dancing around the truth. Her survival depended on this unknown Dr. Ivanov. In a few short hours, she could be dead at his hands. Most likely *would* be dead. After all, she had no value to Ivanov after he removed the chip. If he was anything like her father, he wouldn't care about her life.

The optimism that had led her through most of her life was gone. Evaporated in the jungle heat the moment Kai left her. Because once the chip was removed, she had no value to any of the men involved. She trusted Kai to keep her alive, but not these strangers. Not even Gonzales, who she suspected wasn't the man Niko thought.

She rolled her head back and forth on the head rest. The past several days were like something out of an adventure movie. Unbelievable. Fantastical. Deadly.

Welcome to her new life. Where no one was as they seemed and everyone wanted something from her.

Once upon a time, she'd have laughed at the absurdity of it all. But she had the cuts and bruises to prove that this crazy turn of events really was her life spinning wildly out of control.

And somehow, as illogical as it was, despite everything he'd done, with Kai by her side she felt safe. Around him, a tightly wound spring deep inside her, one she'd never known existed, turned into a limp noodle. It was more than a little disconcerting to realize he'd become as vital to her peace of mind as a child's security blanket.

Snap out of it, girl. Since Kai's not here, you'll have to take care of yourself.

Same old, same old. She'd been taking care of herself all her life. Her mother hadn't wanted to be bothered with her daughter, first letting her run wild in the jungle with the other children, then when she was old enough, shipping her off to boarding school. If she needed or wanted something—food, clothing, a trip to a museum—she got it on her own.

And now she suspected why. Because of her father. He hadn't been the savior she longed for. Just the opposite.

She bit her lip.

God, her stomach was doing tumbling routines. She desperately wanted Kai beside her. Just to be able to hold his hand and know that for once in her life, she wasn't alone.

But fat lot of good that did her, when he was thousands of miles away in Brazil, while she was only half an hour away from landing in Moscow.

Tuesday, Night
Boa Vista, Brazil

"What's your ETD?" Ryker demanded.

Kai waited for the plane's engine to turn over before answering. "We were lucky. Jim carries spares of all critical engine components. He had the plane operational in two hours." Someone, probably Gonzales, had sabotaged the plane. Jim had discovered the ruined engine parts during his pre-flight check. "We should be wheels-up in five."

But that still meant Kai was dangerously behind Tonelli and Susana. Even a delay of one minute could mean Susana's life.

"Good," Ryker said. "I have men searching for Dr. Ivanov. A team should be on the ground when you arrive. They're also on the lookout for Gonzales and Tonelli."

"According to Niko, Boa Vista airport personnel reported seeing Gonzales and Susana board a Gulfstream 550," Kai said. "About half an hour before that, a man entered the plane. His description matches Tonelli." Kai watched the tarmac pass underneath as the plane finally taxied toward the runway.

He knew he was lucky to have transport. When Niko had called to update Ryker, it was decided to have Jim fly Kai to Moscow. Niko, Jenna and Rafe would board a diverted military plane set to arrive in four hours. The plane was ferrying troops back from a special operations training mission, giving Niko additional muscle should Rafe wake up.

Kai rubbed the back of his neck. An invisible metronome in his head ticked faster with each breath he took. The rhythm urged him to run. To catch up with Susana now.

If Tonelli or Gonzales hurt Susana, Kai was going to kill them.

"There's another thing," Ryker said. Something in the slow, heavy way he pronounced each word had Kai sitting forward in his seat.

"My men say Tonelli attended a fundraiser a month ago and danced with Susana. If he's after the chip, that would have been a prime opportunity to snatch her."

"Unless the extraction fell through." Sweat prickled along Kai's forehead, his heart racing along with the metronome. Jesus, if Tonelli had tried a month ago to remove the chip from Susana, the booby-trap around the vial would have been triggered, killing her.

Dammit, he'd almost lost her before he'd found her. The one

woman he needed more than he'd ever imagined needing a woman. And even though he still didn't have his violent side under control, during that good-bye kiss he'd decided he wasn't giving Susana up. Not without a fight.

And if she's dead?

Jagged shards of denial tore at Kai's heart. His hands clenched so tightly around the armrests, pain shot from his wrists all the way to his shoulders.

No. He wouldn't accept that.

But Christ, just the thought that Gonzales and Tonelli were with her now drove him nuts.

Kai closed his eyes and willed his muscles to relax. God, he was really losing it. Never before had a woman raised such primitive possessiveness. He'd never understood men who went into jealous rages.

Now he did. If Susana was hurt, he'd exact vengeance in the most violent way possible.

He needed to keep her safe. Needed to put his life up as a shield for hers. And more than anything else, Kai needed the peace he felt in Susana's arms. She kept his rage and savagery at bay.

It took several minutes for him to calm down, and when he did, he realized he'd totally lost any sense of the conversation.

"Sorry," he said to Ryker. "Could you repeat that?"

"You know both Tonelli and Susana. Is it possible they're working together?"

"No." Kai's denial was swift and firm.

"Think about it," Ryker insisted. "They meet at the fundraiser. She takes him home. We know she's had numerous one-night affairs. Why not a sex-based alliance with Tonelli?"

"Fuck. That." His rage blasted the internal metronome into pieces, boiling his blood. Susana's face as she orgasmed flashed in Technicolor across the movie screen of his mind. No other man would see that expression from here on. She was his, dammit.

And Ryker could show a little respect. "Susana likes sex, so she must have slept with Tonelli? Not only screwed him, but let him guide her in some criminal plot? That's bullshit. She wouldn't work with Tonelli. She wouldn't sleep with him." There was no way. Susana wouldn't be fooled by Tonelli's urbane veneer. *And she couldn't possibly go from his bed to mine so smoothly that she makes me believe in things I'd never thought possible.*

Like love.

Kai's heart jerked in his chest, then a feeling of peace settled over him. Yeah, he loved her. But this wasn't the time to lose focus. So he forced his thoughts back to Ryker's question.

"According to Susana, she left the fundraiser early and headed out of Belém soon after. Tonelli had no time to contact her."

"Unless they'd met before the event and were only solidifying their plans," Ryker said.

"Not buying it. She's honest."

"Okay." Ryker's voice held a tinge of amusement. "I expected you'd react that way, but I had to make sure. If we bring her out alive, I want to know whose side she's on."

Kai wanted to protest Ryker's statement. It shouldn't be if they got Susana out alive, but when. Yet...even if Susana was surrounded by every available SSU agent while in Moscow, the vial might break during removal, no matter how carefully Dr. Ivanov handled it. Or Susana's father could have been lying about the timetable and she'd die of poisoning before she even reached Moscow.

Ah, fuck. This totally wasn't helping. If he wasn't careful, he'd be a furious wreck by the time they landed in Moscow.

Unacceptable. Susana needed him at his best.

Tuesday, Night
Remote Airfield
Georgia, United States

A THUNDEROUS CRY of outrage echoed against the walls of the metal hangar. Ten feet away, three burly men in U.S. army fatigues struggled to lock Rafe in a straightjacket. He fought them with all the brutality of an animal, the sounds coming out of his mouth more suited to ape than human.

Niko stood behind Jenna, his arms draped over her shoulders, gripping her hands tight enough to cut off her blood supply. He barely noticed. Just as he ignored the pain from ribs cracked by Rafe's feet and elbows.

His brother had finally woken up while the soldiers were carrying him off the plane.

Rafe had erupted in rage. He'd twisted hard enough to unbalance the soldier holding his feet. The man tripped on a crack in the asphalt and went down, losing his grip so that Rafe's feet hit the tarmac.

Niko and the soldier at Rafe's head had tightened their holds, but Rafe fought back, breaking the soldier's kneecap and cracking Niko's ribs. The other soldiers had pulled Rafe away before serious damage was done, but now they struggled to contain Rafe.

Niko watched the fight, his teeth clenched and his body stiff. Each twist of Rafe's body, every inhuman cry, sent poisoned barbs into Niko's soul, eclipsing his physical pain. If not for the reassuring, restraining presence of Jenna, Niko wouldn't be able to stop himself from rushing over and pulling the soldiers away from Rafe.

The big brother in Niko couldn't bear the anguish in Rafe's voice.

"Easy," Jenna whispered again. "This is necessary. We have to contain him so he doesn't hurt anyone else." She pushed back against him, bringing her body closer to Niko's in comfort. And as a reminder that to get to Rafe, he'd have to go through her.

Niko rested his chin on the top of her head. "I know." He wrapped his arms tighter across Jenna's middle. "But, Jesus Christ, it's hard to just stand here." He refused to acknowledge the possibility that even once the chip was recovered and the data evaluated, no cure might be found.

He would not accept that Rafe would stay in this animal state until he died.

Rafe tried to bite one of the soldiers.

"Rafe, no!" Niko called out.

At the sound of his brother's voice, Rafe swiveled his head. Wild, furious eyes met Niko's. Fury changed to resentment. Then puzzlement. Finally, like a gentle wave moving up the shore after a storm, recognition filled Rafe's eyes.

For a moment, Niko looked deep into the cage of Rafe's mind, seeing his brother as he'd once known him. A man whose eyes now pleaded with Niko for help. For mercy.

Niko took an involuntary step forward, but Jenna used her body to stop him.

"I'm going to save you, Rafe," Niko called. "I promise." He didn't know if his brother heard or understood. The fleeting moment of recognition vanished and Rafe snarled at Niko.

But the momentary lull in Rafe's resistance had given the soldiers enough time to force his arms into a straight jacket. He bellowed in outrage and tried once again to use his teeth, but the soldiers stayed out of biting range.

While they fought to shove a gag in Rafe's mouth, another soldier hurried out from the office, holding a syringe. "I've got it!"

No one had expected Rafe to wake up this soon, not after receiving multiple doses of the tranquilizer from Niko's darts. So there hadn't been more sedative on hand.

"It's a stronger formula," the soldier told Niko. "But Ryker says this should safely knock him out."

Niko nodded. He watched, teeth clenched, as the man knelt beside Rafe. The other soldiers managed to pin Rafe's head down, exposing his neck. When the needle jabbed into Rafe's vein, Niko flinched.

Rafe's eyes flew to Niko's. *You betrayed me*, they accused.

"Forgive me," Niko said.

But only rage remained in his brother's eyes. Niko kept his gaze locked with Rafe's until the tranquilizer took effect and Rafe's lids slammed down.

The soldiers finished securing Rafe, then hoisted him up and moved toward the truck that would take him to the temporary SSU research facility.

Niko released Jenna and turned away. He was shaking.

"Niko?"

He shook his head and made his way slowly toward the office and the tiny washroom. "I...need to be alone for a few minutes," he called over his shoulder. He didn't have to glance behind him to know that Jenna's expression would be a mix of hurt and sympathy.

He couldn't be with her right now. He'd just condemned his brother to being locked in a padded, secured room, studied by scientists as they tried to find a way to reverse what had been done. Treated like a dangerous lab rat.

He pushed open the washroom door, the groan of rusty hinges setting fire to his exposed nerves. He hammered the door with his fist and it slammed closed. Then he stood in the middle of the floor, trembling. Fighting back waves of fury and helplessness, until finally all that remained was an empty, aching core.

An old, cloudy mirror hung over the small porcelain sink. Niko braced his hands on the edges of the basin and looked at his reflection.

He saw the same face he'd always seen, only depressingly haggard. Beaten down as he'd never looked even while deep undercover and surrounded by sadistic murderers. His mind knew Rafe had to be contained, but his heart insisted he'd failed his brother. As the oldest, Niko was supposed to protect his younger siblings.

He closed his eyes and let his forehead rest against the cool surface of the mirror.

Someone knocked at the door.

"Niko?" Jenna called. "Are you all right?"

No. He wouldn't be all right until his brother was back to normal. But at least with Jenna's support, Niko wouldn't follow his brother into insanity.

"Give me another minute," he answered.

He pushed away from the washbasin. Ran the taps and splashed cold water on his face. Then opened the door and let the woman he loved hold him and offer the comfort of not being alone.

CHAPTER TWENTY-SIX

Thursday, Midday
Dr. Ivanov's Compound, Russia

MARK TONELLI EXCUSED himself and left Susana with Gonzales in Dr. Ivanov's waiting room. Their arrival in Moscow and the short helicopter ride out to this former Czarist estate had gone smoothly, thanks to Jamieson. Even now, a team of soldiers waited in the woods to make certain Mark and the chip left the compound safely.

Mark pushed open a door that led into a long, thinly carpeted hallway and followed the directions he'd been given over the phone. Just before the door swung closed behind him he caught sight of Susana's smile as she responded to something Gonzales said.

An unseemly surge of jealousy washed over Mark. Once the feeling passed, he reminded himself that Gonzales meant nothing to Susana. It was Mark she'd flirted with during the flight, not Gonzales. As soon as she healed from the surgery, Mark would have her in bed.

Everything was going as planned. Jealousy wasn't just base, it was unnecessary.

As he walked down the hallway, Mark reflected that Susana wasn't nearly as intelligent as her file suggested. She'd talked gaily of travel and her days as a model, but had shrugged off all attempts to discuss her work. "I've been through such an ordeal," she'd told him. "Please let's talk about something fun."

Being near Susana's beauty was intoxicating. As if she replaced all the stale, foul air in his lungs with perfume. Who cared if she lacked intelligence?

Standing next to her he felt invincible. Virile. He'd barely been able to keep himself from pushing her into the intimacy he craved. But he knew the gentlemanly thing to do was give her space, and he prided himself on his civility.

Mark turned the corner and counted doorways. Three doors down he stopped and pressed a buzzer set next to a shiny tan door.

The door opened to reveal a striking man in his early sixties. Tall, broad, bearing an uncanny resemblance to Sean Connery, but with a full head of graying black hair and a neatly trimmed goatee, he was the antithesis of every mad scientist stereotype. He belonged on the pages of *Town and Country*, advertising quality Scotch.

Mark hated him on sight.

"Mark Tonelli?" the man asked in Russian.

"Yes," Mark replied in the same language.

"Welcome. I am Dr. Pieter Ivanov. The woman is in our waiting room?"

Mark nodded.

"Good. Come in." The scientist waved Mark into a tidy office. Bookshelves filled with medical journals lined two walls. A third wall held a light board for viewing x-ray films, and several anatomical charts.

Ivanov pushed a button on the intercom on his desk. "Alexei, escort Susana Dias to the preparation room and start the pre-surgery routine. Give her Dr. Nevsky's journals to read while she's waiting. Notify me when all is ready."

"Yes, doctor."

"Since you are here," Ivanov told Mark, "and we have some time before the woman is ready for surgery, please allow me to give you a tour of our facility. I have been waiting years for the woman to be found. We are deeply indebted to you."

Something about the statement seemed off to Mark, but he merely nodded and followed the doctor from the room. At first, the tour consisted of nothing extraordinary. Examination and surgery rooms. Offices.

But then Dr. Ivanov led him to an area reminiscent of a special exhibit hall at a zoo. Each enclosure was perhaps twelve feet by twelve feet, the front wall three-quarters glass. The first room housed a man with the slender, muscular build of a gymnast. He wore an olive green unitard and was barefoot. As Mark watched, the man ran up onto the back of a couch, then leapt toward a trapeze hanging from the ceiling.

His hands caught the bar easily and he swung himself up and onto the seat.

Mark gasped. No ordinary man would have been able to make that leap. The distance had to be twenty feet nearly straight up.

"Ah, I see you are impressed. After Dr. Nevsky left for America, I dropped my research on intelligence and immunity, instead focusing on strength and agility. We continued to share notes, however, and he eventually incorporated some of my data into his program."

Mark watched in growing horror as the man dropped off the trapeze. He landed in a crouch, then suddenly grimaced and grabbed his hair with both hands. His mouth opened on a scream. The next second he bent forward and slammed his forehead into the floor. Then did it again. And again, until a man in a white lab coat rushed in.

Ivanov shook his head. "You see here one of the weaknesses of our program. Subjects don't remain sane for long. I understand that before his death Nevsky discovered some chemicals that extended the useful life of his subjects. Here, we only get three to four weeks before cognition is lost. Once the subjects are immune to directions, they cease to be of use."

"What happens then?"

"It depends on the level of physical ability. For subjects that lose the ability to walk, we inject their bodies with new commercial drugs, testing for side effects." Dr. Ivanov pointed to the room, where the man in the lab coat was escorting the gymnast through a door on the opposite wall. "But if they are ambulatory, we use them as targets for subjects in the initial stages of treatment."

"Targets?" Mark asked slowly.

"Of course. At the core, we are a military program. Our subjects must be programmed to perpetuate violence on humans. What better targets than those subjects we no longer can use in the field?" Dr. Ivanov led Mark over to the door. It opened into a small observation area.

Ivanov pushed a button on the wall to his left and a shutter rose, revealing a plate glass window. On the other side of the window, a man used a baseball bat as a club against another man. A woman in a white lab coat stood in the corner. The man with the bat hesitated, stopping himself from landing the next blow. He glanced over at the woman and Mark could see the anguish in the man's eyes.

The woman's lips formed words Mark couldn't hear through the glass, but from her excited hand gestures and the way she bounced eagerly on her toes, he guessed she was urging the man to continue hitting his opponent.

Although any more blows would be redundant. The second

man was on the floor, blood pouring from his mouth and nose in a way that indicated internal bleeding. He was already dead.

Mark glanced at Dr. Ivanov. The scientist watched his subject raise the bat and slam it against the fallen man's head. Ivanov's eyes glittered with mad approval. "Excellent," he murmured. "Very good."

Mark turned away. He'd never admit to being squeamish, but the sight of all that blood was too much for him. And the senseless violence left a dull, metallic taste in his mouth.

He was supposed to trust Susana to this man?

Dr. Ivanov glanced over at Mark and chuckled. "I do apologize. Sometimes I forget that not everyone enjoys the sight of blood. But this man, he represents a huge breakthrough. That is his beloved younger brother he just killed. He resisted our commands for days, but we finally found the right combination of drugs and pain to overcome his resistance."

Mark choked back a protest. Now he understood why the man had looked so tormented before he'd inflicted the final blows. He'd known he was killing his brother, but been unable to stop. Mark's uneasiness strengthened. Having someone take away his free will would be his worst nightmare.

Yet if he understood Ivanov, Nevsky had also been working on mind control. And Jamieson wanted Nevsky's chip so he could create a super soldier.

Something Gonzales said to him on the flight came back to him. The man claimed that Rafe Andros had been captured and turned into a furious, mind-controlled beast by a program that had originated with Dr. Nevsky. As much as Mark disliked the Andros brothers personally, he respected them as operators. Rafe hadn't deserved to end up like one of the men here in Ivanov's lab.

No man deserved that.

Mark's mouth dried up. What were the odds that the U.S. government had more than one super soldier program? Not good. Besides, Mark didn't believe in coincidences. Which meant Jamieson was involved with the program that captured Rafe.

God, what had he gotten himself involved with? Breaking the law to protect his country was one thing. Changing a man's humanity by turning him into an animalistic mind-slave was abhorrent.

"Come, let us return to my office." Dr. Ivanov's voice still rang with pride as he ushered Mark through an exit that led into the office corridor.

Mark made certain he didn't look back as he left the exhibit hall.

"I am excited to begin work on Nevsky's daughter," Ivanov commented. "She is the first embryo he genetically altered. Although the private investigators he hired claimed she showed no signs of extraordinary intelligence or immunity, I look forward to testing her myself."

Every cell in Mark's body froze. Susana's father had done *what*?

Dr. Ivanov nodded. "I see that you are shocked. Dr. Nevsky eventually gave up embryonic manipulation, because he never achieved the results he wanted. His daughter is the only such subject to survive, perhaps because he'd given her such low doses of the drugs. He injected her mother with chemicals intended to change the genetic makeup of the fetus. Then, once the child was born, he worked on further gene manipulations. He was furious when her mother stole the girl away before she was even three months old."

Mark couldn't breathe. "What—" He cleared his throat and tried again. "What was her father's goal?"

"The same as he was working on when he died. A strengthened immune system, extraordinary intelligence, limitless endurance. Unfortunately, as I mentioned, he never did achieve success with embryonic manipulation." Dr. Ivanov scratched his chin, his gaze focused on some point behind the wall. "Nevsky later married, but the woman died in childbirth due to side effects of the drugs he'd used on her. He never tried again." Ivanov shook his head. "Well, it is a pity he won't be here to see his first experiment finally studied."

"Stop. What do you mean?" Ivanov had made a similar allusion before.

"The woman, of course. Once I extract the chip, she will become part of our research program. She is the only fetus that survived. I need to see how she differs from normal humans. How her body responds to our treatments." He strode down the corridor, arms waving. "She could be the answer we have been looking for. Just as crucial as the data on the chip." He turned toward Mark, face aglow with possibilities. "With the data we learn from her, perhaps our treatments will take without destroying the host. We could finally create the perfect human!"

Mark stopped, immobilized by the words. Something shifted inside him.

It felt remarkably like his long-lost conscience.

Susana was going to be used as a test subject? She would end up like those men back there? Locked in a cage? Her vitality stolen until she was a mindless killing machine?

Not if Mark could help it.

Thursday, Midday
Moscow, Russia

KAI WAS ABOUT to step out of the plane onto the portable steps, when three black town cars came racing across the tarmac.

Shit. He had a feeling these weren't reinforcements from the SSU. He shifted back inside, out of sight, but it was too late to move the stairs away and they couldn't close the door with the stairs in position.

The cars fanned out nose first, then screeched to a synchronized halt, forming a perfect half-circle around the base of the stairs. A moment later the doors on the sedans opened, cutting off all exits.

Trapped.

Kai glanced over his shoulder. Jim stood just a few feet away. His hands dangled at his sides, making him seem relaxed...if you didn't notice the Glock nestled in his left palm. "Your call," he said.

"We cooperate. But first, see if you can get hold of Ryker."

Jim nodded and pulled out his satellite phone.

Kai checked outside. Four shooters with AK-74 rifles had taken up positions within the formation of cars. Two men in dark suits strode toward the plane.

"Kai Paterson!" the heavyset man in front called, his Russian accent barely noticeable. "You and your pilot are under arrest for smuggling. Please exit the plane with your hands above your head."

Smuggling. Ri-ight. If he were stupid enough to let the men into the plane, he was certain they'd "find" a packet or two of hastily planted contraband.

Both sides knew the charges wouldn't stick. They were just a delaying tactic. Kai raised one brow as he met Jim's gaze.

The pilot nodded. "Ryker's on it," he said quietly.

As the Russians reached the stairs, Kai stepped out to meet them. He crossed his hands on top of his head and felt his stomach pitch as if he was about to skydive without a parachute.

Please let me reach Susana in time.

Thursday, Midday
Dr. Ivanov's Compound, Russia

SUSANA'S HAND shook with such violence, the next page of her father's journal slipped out from between her clumsy fingers.

Almost an hour ago a male nurse had brought her to this tiny examination room, ordered her to change into the gown, handed her the journals, then disappeared.

Deus. She'd thought she'd understood the type of man her father had been, and what he might have done to her.

She'd been wrong. A combination of scientific logbooks and diaries, the four journals detailed his experiments into creating perfect humans. Through a combination of gene manipulation and drugs, he'd originally strived for advancements in four areas. Intelligence. Strength. Speed. Immunity.

He'd given her mother drugs while she was pregnant, hoping to influence Susana's development. Put the chemicals into her mother's food and drink, given her "vitamins" and even injections, all in the name of good prenatal care. Her mother hadn't known the truth.

Then, after her birth, her father had extracted samples of Susana's DNA, added to them, and introduced the improved strands back into her body. Her mother had found him sticking a needle into three-month-old Susana, realized what was going on, and fled in horror.

A tear dropped onto the page and Susana dabbed at it with the edge of her hospital gown.

Her mother's dying words came back to her. "What he did to you...so wrong...unnatural."

Susana had always assumed her mother meant her father had molested her when she'd been too young to remember. It explained the hatred her mother had for the man she refused to even name, no matter how many times Susana asked, desperate to have some piece of her daddy to hold in her heart.

Susana tried to swallow, but something hard and painful seemed lodged in her throat. Now she understood why her mother had always looked at her with a combination of admiration and revulsion. Why Susana could count on her fingers the number of times her mother had hugged her.

Susana put her hand to her mouth, willing herself not to be sick.

The door swung open. Her hands jerked in surprise, knocking the journals to the floor.

"Hello, Susana, I am Dr. Ivanov." It was a man's voice, speaking heavily accented English.

She jumped down from the examination table and faced the door, her shoulders tight with wariness. Her gaze bounced from the tense features of Mark Tonelli, to Dr. Ivanov, an older gentleman with the sophisticated appearance of the head of a Fortune 500 company.

His eyes roved over her with such cold calculation, she shivered. Dammit, she wished she had more covering her than this flimsy cotton gown. He was a colleague of her father's, mentioned often in the latter part of the journals. She didn't trust him.

Not that she trusted Mark either.

"Excellent," she thought she heard Dr. Ivanov mutter. "A prime specimen."

Ignoring the goose bumps on her arms, Susana held out her hand. "Thank you for seeing us, Dr. Ivanov."

"The pleasure is entirely mine." Dr. Ivanov bowed over her hand.

His touch was even worse than Mark's. She had the fleeting thought that if she didn't remove her hand promptly, her skin would freeze.

"If you're ready, I need to give you the antidote. After that, I'll run an x-ray to see exactly where the implant resides," Ivanov said.

"You know how to disable the booby-trap?"

His smile was all wolf-meets-Little-Red-Riding-Hood. "But of course. I created the mechanism. Your father borrowed the technique from me. And I created the poison. Once you've been given the antidote, you'll be safe in case the vial breaks prematurely during surgery."

She knew his words were meant to reassure her. But they didn't. After reading the journals, all she wanted was to get far away from here. To find a place where nobody had heard of the chip.

God, what if she was like the other subjects, with a predetermined self-termination date? So what if she'd lived longer than any of the other subjects, maybe her time was rapidly approaching. She could start losing her mind any day now.

Snap out of it!

She cleared her throat. "Will you personally be performing the surgery?" she asked. *Mãe de Deus*, she did not want this man cutting into her. He looked at her like she was a specimen under a microscope. One he couldn't wait to dissect.

"Most definitely. I could not entrust the daughter of my dearest colleague to another."

A woman poked her head into the room. "We're ready, doctor."

"Thank you." Dr. Ivanov took Susana's arm. "If you'll excuse us," he told Mark. "I need to get my patient started on the x-ray. You will wait here."

"No. Perhaps I didn't make myself clear earlier. My government considers the chip a matter of national security. I will stay with Susana during the operation. Afterward, you will hand the chip directly over to me."

"That is not possible, I am afraid." Dr. Ivanov opened the door. "Captain."

Two uniformed men stepped into the room. They positioned themselves on either side of Mark and grabbed his arms. Susana glanced uneasily between Mark and Dr. Ivanov.

"Am I being held prisoner?" Mark demanded, looking down his aristocratic nose at the doctor with icy anger.

Dr. Ivanov bowed his head slightly. "Just until the surgery is complete. You must understand, the data on the chip is crucial to my program. Almost as crucial as the lady herself. I cannot allow your government to interfere."

"Wait a second!" Susana protested. "What program? What are you talking about?" But she had a sinking feeling she knew.

Ivanov ignored her. He put his hand on her shoulder and nudged her toward the door. "Come, time grows short."

"But—!" She glanced back at Mark. He seemed resigned to his fate, yet there was some hint of apology in his eyes. Damn him, she didn't want his apology. She wanted him to do something and get them out of this mess.

"You need have no fear, dear girl," Ivanov said. "As long as Mr. Tonelli does nothing, he will not be harmed. The guards will merely make certain he stays out of my way." With that, Ivanov dug his fingers deeper into her shoulder and propelled her out of the room. They were immediately joined by two more uniformed men.

For an instant, Susana thought about fighting free. But the clock on the chip's self-destruct was ticking down and she didn't want to die from the poison.

Still, she preferred not to be herded like cattle.

She shrugged her shoulder and dislodged his hand. "After you, doctor," she said.

She followed him down the corridor on bare feet, her thin hospital gown gaping open in the back and affording their escort a view of her bare skin they didn't deserve.

It seemed unreal that these might be the last minutes of her life.

Deus, why hadn't she told Kai she loved him?

Thursday, Afternoon
Moscow, Russia

Knowing every move he made in this holding cell inside a Moscow police station was being observed, Kai forced himself to stay still. But inside, he was pacing. Barely holding onto his control. He was moments away from trying to tear down the walls with his bare hands so he could find Susana.

Kai didn't know if the CIA had decided that they wanted the microchip and had arranged for his arrest, or if one of Tonelli's private contacts had been responsible. He'd let Ryker sort that out.

All that really mattered was how soon Kai would be free. Tonelli and Susana were probably already at Ivanov's lab, which meant Tonelli was dangerously close to getting the chip.

And Susana's value to everyone but Kai was running out.

Kai started to raise his wrist to check the time on his watch, but stopped himself. He had to stay cool. Act like he had nothing better to do than stay here all day. He had to bore his captors to tears by giving them nothing interesting to watch, all the while praying Ryker came through with one of his famous miracles.

Thursday, Afternoon
Dr. Ivanov's Compound, Russia

Mark's guards patted him down, took his two-way radio, satellite phone, and gun, then left the room and took up positions in the hallway on either side of the door. Mark made sure the door didn't shut completely behind them, allowing him a narrow view of the corridor. That was all he needed to see which direction Ivanov took Susana.

Satisfied he knew where to go when he got out of here, he let the door shut fully.

All right. So he'd been a fool. The leader of Jamieson's team of soldiers had told him to bring guards, but Mark had been so certain he'd be able to talk Ivanov into turning over the chip he'd refused to let them accompany him. And he'd never suspected the doctor would want to keep Susana.

He paced around the small exam room.

He was willing to make a deal with Ivanov. The scientist could download a copy of the data from the chip onto his computer. Then Mark would take the chip back to Jamieson.

Yet, as Mark's legs ate up the tiny distance between door, wall, and exam table, an unfamiliar weight pressed on his lungs, nearly suffocating him.

All his dreams of revenge were within reach. All he had to do was give Jamieson the microchip and he'd receive the name of his father's murderer.

Only…he wasn't certain he wanted Jamieson to have the chip.

Because now he understood what was at stake. This wasn't simply a case of using drugs to enhance performance, making more successful soldiers.

Ivanov created monsters.

Memories of the men and women he'd seen in Dr. Ivanov's exhibit hall wouldn't leave him alone. Worse, he kept imagining Susana as one of those subjects. He pictured her locked in an observation room, her sanity gone as a man beat her to death.

Mark knew that Jamieson had some sort of experimental program going on as part of Kerberos. Could he really turn the microchip over to Jamieson if it meant Americans would suffer similar fates to Ivanov's subjects?

What if Jamieson demanded Mark turn over not just the chip, but Susana as well, before he gave up the name Mark needed?

The suffocating feeling intensified, until he was forced to stop pacing and sit down. If he didn't call Jamieson's soldiers for help getting out of here, he wouldn't be able to save Susana or the chip. But if he did call the men, how could he both protect Susana and prevent Jamieson from getting the chip?

Could he live with himself if he turned his back on learning the name of his father's true murderer? Mark quickly sorted through various scenarios, but he couldn't see any way to reconcile the different paths before him.

He should be furious that a woman he barely knew had such power over him. But thinking of Susana only made him feel warm. And anxious to see her again, despite Ivanov's hints that her father had tinkered with her genetic code.

Given time, he knew they would become close. But they wouldn't get that time unless he made the right choice.

Mark stared across the room, not seeing any of the furniture, or even the color of the walls. He concentrated on examining the consequences of what he was about to do. Slow as a man ordering his own execution, he removed his shoes and put together the emergency sat phone he always carried.

Then he took a deep breath, and dialed.

CHAPTER TWENTY-SEVEN

"Before we take the x-ray, we need to get a blood sample," Dr. Ivanov told Susana. He pushed her gently into a chair.

"I'm sorry, I don't understand." He'd just made her drink something so horrible-tasting, she still felt her stomach doing unhappy loop-de-loops.

"Given your unique genetic makeup, we have to make certain our anesthesia and blood supplies are compatible with your body." Dr. Ivanov tied a piece of rubber tubing around her arm, then inserted the needle into her vein.

The vial slowly filled with her blood. Blood that was the same normal color as everyone else's. Only it wasn't normal.

Dr. Ivanov pulled the needle out of her arm and placed her fingers on a small gauze pad on top of the puncture. "It's a pity your mother stole you away before he could continue his experiments."

The doctor patted her on the head. "Don't worry. We'll run tests on you as soon as the chip has been extracted. Your father's work will be continued."

That was the last thing she wanted. But if Dr. Ivanov intended to run further experiments on her, then he needed her alive after surgery. As long as she was alive, she could find a way out of here.

He passed her blood off to an assistant, then led her into the x-ray chamber. Before she knew it, she'd completed the x-ray and was lying on an examination table, covered only by her thin gown while a sedative dripped through an IV into her body.

She was so cold. Clearly another ice age was starting inside her.

Oh, God. Her father had experimented on her.

That's why her mother had gotten worried, frightened looks when Susana told stories of her successes. That's why her mother had hesitated to hug her. Why she'd been sent away to school and never been encouraged to get close to her mother.

Because her mother considered Susana a freak.

She took a deep breath and pushed away the hurt. That was the past. She had to concentrate on surviving this operation, then escaping.

And then she'd find Kai and just hold him until her trembling stopped.

Thursday, Afternoon
Moscow, Russia

FROM TWENTY-THREE STORIES above the ground, Kai stared out the window of the small conference room at the grey Moscow landscape, thinking over the bizarre conversation he'd just had with Mark Tonelli. If the man could be trusted...

Kai put his thumbnail underneath the top of his flip phone, but before he could open it, the device beeped to indicate an incoming call.

"Paterson," he answered.

"You out?" Ryker demanded.

"Yeah," Kai said. "Thanks. Jim's on his way back to the plane."

Ryker had indeed pulled off another miracle. Not only were Kai and Jim free, but Kai had a team of Russian security agents at his disposal. A helicopter was due to arrive any minute to take them to the large country estate that served as Ivanov's compound.

"What'd you do? Threaten a nuclear strike?" He had no doubt Ryker could pull even that off if necessary.

His boss snorted softly. "Nothing so dramatic. First I played the 'kidnapped American woman turns into international incident card.' That grabbed their attention, but not enough to ensure full cooperation."

Kai saw the helicopter appear over the horizon and mentally willed it to move faster. Susana's time was running out.

"As soon as I mentioned Ivanov's name," Ryker continued, "and promised them access to all his research files, they couldn't help me fast enough. The FSB has been after the data for years, but the military refused to share."

Kai smiled and shook his head, even though his boss couldn't see him. Inter-agency rivalry at its best. Gotta love it. And trust Ryker to not only know about it, but find a way to use it to their advantage.

Ryker went silent and Kai jerked his attention away from the approaching helicopter. "What's wrong?"

"The men I assigned to watch Ivanov's lab haven't reported in. You have to consider them compromised. Probably captured," Ryker said.

God. Just like Rafe's team when they went after Kaufmann's lab. "By lab security? Or the military?"

"Probably the military, since they're Ivanov's sponsor. Assume they're watching and protecting the lab. How close are you?"

Kai checked with the FSB agent sitting at the table behind him. "Forty minutes, tops."

"Right. I'm working on getting another team on the ground. Don't trust your new comrades."

"Who me?" Trusting too much was not one of Kai's weaknesses. "By the way, I just got a call from our trouble-making friend." He didn't want to use Tonelli's name in case the men in the room knew Tonelli from his previous assignments in Russia.

Ryker's breath hissed out. "What did he want?"

"To cooperate. He's inside the lab, with Susana." And Kai hadn't been able to stop a threat from shooting out of his mouth. He'd promised vicious retribution if Susana was hurt in any way.

"He confirmed that Dr. Ivanov has a lab running similar experiments to what Dr. Nevsky had—genetic enhancement, some mind control—with similar deterioration of the subjects. Our friend claims Ivanov intends to add Susana as a research subject as soon as he's extracted the chip." Kai wanted to scream in denial at the image of Susana as a snarling, snapping beast like Rafe.

"He'll get Susana and the chip away from Dr. Ivanov, but he wants our help escaping. He says there are soldiers outside the compound. Some of them are Russian military, others are American, sent by his boss." That kind of influence outside of the United States was impressive.

"Christ. Ivanov's compound is a busy place. What do you think of Tonelli's offer?" Ryker sounded as skeptical as Kai had originally been.

"I think he's serious. There was something in his voice when he talked about Susana." Something that had sent Kai's instincts into a jealous frenzy. "I think he's infatuated with her."

The long silence that followed might have indicated Ryker couldn't picture Tonelli caring enough about a woman that he'd jeopardize a mission, or because Ryker was running possibilities. Finally, he asked, "Did Tonelli say anything about the situation inside?"

"Yeah. Two guards, minimum, are with the good doctor and Susana. Two more are guarding the door of the waiting room where our friend is cooling his heels, keeping him prisoner until after the operation. Susana is already being prepped for surgery."

Kai hated that he was going to be too late to stand by Susana's side.

Hated to think of her alone and terrified. And shit, he had to face it. He was scared for her as well. Some stranger was going to touch a knife to her skin and Kai had no way to ensure that Ivanov treated Susana carefully.

He clenched his fists to keep himself from snarling in frustration and forced himself to bury the fear that Susana could be dead before he arrived.

What was taking the damn helicopter so long?

Thursday, Afternoon
Dr. Ivanov's Compound, Russia

MARK PULLED OPEN THE DOOR. "I want to see Dr. Ivanov. Now," he told the guards in Russian. "I want to make a deal."

"That is not possible."

The hell it wasn't. Mark stepped into the corridor, forcing the guards to either move with him or get run over.

At least, that was the plan.

They didn't budge. Which left Mark no choice but full body contact in order to force his way out of the room. He rammed his shoulder into the man on his right, knocking the man enough off balance that he took a small step back.

The other guard grabbed Mark's arm. "You must go back inside. The doctor will see you when he is finished."

"No."

Mark twisted free, spun to his left and lashed out with the heel of his hand. He connected with the man's temple hard enough to drop him.

The man on Mark's right swung a fist. Mark dodged, then moved into the man. He tangled his leg in between the other man's, pulled the man's back flush against his chest, then used the bend of his elbow like a nutcracker against the man's throat until he lost consciousness.

Mark dragged the men inside the waiting room. His work at the CIA had been more about relationships and information manipulation than physical danger. But after three years on the streets of Moscow as a kid, he'd made a vow to never lose his fighting edge. So he'd kept those skills honed, even if these days he rarely needed them outside of the dojo.

This fight had barely raised his heart rate.

Mark fastened the guards' flex cuffs around their wrists, then stripped them of their weapons and communication devices. He pocketed one of the handguns and piled the rest of the equipment on the floor behind the exam table.

Pulling out his handkerchief, he dusted off his hands and left the room. There were at least two security cameras in the hall, so reinforcements would soon be on the way. He glanced in the direction Dr. Ivanov had taken Susana, but ran toward the outside door instead.

Yes, he'd promised Paterson he'd retrieve Susana and the chip. He still intended to. But this facility was extensive. Searching it by himself would take too long. Better to enlist the help of the military team outside. With luck, Paterson would arrive by the time they found Susana and he'd get both Mark and Susana out of here.

After that, well, he'd fight Paterson over the chip. Mark didn't quite know how he was going to best the man, but unlike Paterson, Mark had desperation on his side. The chip was his only bargaining tool. He wanted it all. Susana safe. The name of his father's murderer. And if Jamieson was truly running a program similar to Ivanov's, then he'd shut that program down.

Mark's control of the chip was the only way he could guarantee he wasn't going to be killed by Jamieson's assassins before he had a chance to bargain with his boss.

And if Jamieson refused to give up the name, then Mark's

next stop was going to be the SSU. He bet Ryker would deal for the chip.

One thing was clear, though. He wanted Susana safe and with him when this was over.

As he pressed open the exterior door and checked for danger, he wondered if he'd been wrong about reinforcements arriving for the two downed guards. He didn't see any additional security guards. Were the dots in the corners not security cameras after all but flaws in the décor? Or dummy cameras?

He strolled outside, acting for all the world as if there was nothing unusual about him leaving the building unescorted. But his scalp tingled, so he knew someone was watching him.

He continued down the driveway, taking large steps so that he covered a lot of ground without appearing to run away.

Three steps from the entrance, a bullet nicked his arm. He lunged for the gate. Yanked.

Locked.

The gate rose six feet in the air and ended in sharp metal spikes. At the bottom, it cleared the ground by mere inches. No way to go over or under.

The metal surface facing him was smooth and reflective as glass. No handholds to help a man escape.

He dropped and rolled as a second bullet ricocheted off the gate.

A shout of warning in Russian came from the other side of the fence. "Clear the gate, sir!"

Finally, his military backup.

A moment later the gate blew open. Mark dashed through the smoke left by the explosive charge. With the soldiers providing covering fire, he made it to the safety of the woods.

SUSANA STARED AT THE CEILING, puzzled as to why the long fluorescent lights were fading in and out. Actually, her entire surroundings seemed to pulse.

Where was she? And where was Kai?

The sudden ache to have his arms around her cut through the fuzziness in her brain. Tears focused her blurry vision.

The ceiling above her was standard acoustical tile, the walls a hopeless dull gray. She was lying on some sort of table...

Her heart lurched, then nosedived into the churning vat of acid that was her stomach. That's right, she was at Dr. Ivanov's lab. But...

She closed her eyes and searched her mental files. Remembered blood filling a vial.

Blood...her father...genetic tampering.

Dammit!

Her eyes flew open. No needle or tubing in her arm. Good.

Susana tried to sit up, but rose only a scant few inches before leather straps at her ankles and wrists forced her back down onto the table. She pulled and twisted, but the straps didn't give.

Her stomach did a quick sideways roll and tried to hide somewhere under her right breast.

Wasn't one of her father's goals to create increased physical strength? What was the point of being genetically altered if she couldn't break free of these straps?

Putting every ounce of strength into her left arm, she jerked against the strap.

The strap didn't so much as stretch a millimeter.

Susana closed her eyes and tried to be brave. Tried not to humiliate herself by gibbering in terror. But she couldn't think of one legitimate reason for her to be restrained. And too many scenarios that ended in death.

Thursday, Afternoon
Approaching Dr. Ivanov's Compound, Russia

KAI CLOSED HIS CELL PHONE. This day just kept getting worse.

The helicopter that had picked him up in Moscow had landed ten miles away from Ivanov's compound. Kai now sat in an ubiquitous black town car about half a mile from the entrance.

He turned to the FSB agent sitting next to him. "Change of plans," Kai said. "It's not safe to approach the lab from the front drive. We'll have to walk in."

The man nodded and pulled out his two-way radio to relay the information to the cars following them.

Kai let his head fall back against the seat. Tonelli had just called again. He'd fled the compound, leaving Susana alone with Dr. Ivanov. Kai beat his fists against his thighs. He wanted to kill Tonelli for leaving her. The man's excuse had been that the compound was too big for him to find Susana on his own. Tonelli claimed he was about to reenter the building with a military team and find her.

Right. Like a firefight between Ivanov's security team and Tonelli's group was going to keep Susana safe. What if Ivanov panicked and killed Susana when the fighting started?

Or what if the fight moved into the depths of the compound and Susana was killed by a stray bullet or grenade?

He rubbed his temples, but it did nothing to relieve his fear.

Kai hadn't told Tonelli he had the FSB with him. He didn't trust the military to stay focused on finding Susana if they knew their rivals were on the way.

He'd asked Tonelli to hold off storming the compound until he arrived, but the man had ignored him. Once again, Kai had heard something possessive in Tonelli's tone when he talked about Susana.

If it helped save her, good. But once she was safe, the bastard better leave her alone. She was *Kai's*.

CHAPTER TWENTY-EIGHT

Thursday, Afternoon
Dr. Ivanov's Compound, Russia

WHAT THE HELL HAD HAPPENED? Several minutes ago Susana had heard alarmed shouts and pounding footsteps in the corridor. She'd braced herself for visitors, but the people in the corridor passed her by.

She gave another yank against the leather restraints fastened to her wrists and ankles. Was it her imagination, or were they slightly looser than the last time? She relaxed her muscles, then tightened against the restraints and pulled so hard her arm muscles burned.

There! She definitely felt more room around her right wrist. She wriggled and twisted and scraped the skin raw, but her hand slipped free.

Yes! Tears filled her eyes. She blinked them quickly away. She didn't have time to waste with crying. Her fingers moved to the left restraint and found the buckle. A moment later, it fell open.

She sat up so quickly, the room wavered in front of her. Squeezing her eyes shut, she allowed herself two long, deep breaths to regain her equilibrium before she went to work on her ankle restraints.

Once the leather straps hung loosely down the legs of the exam table, Susana put her feet on the floor. She lowered her weight carefully. Certain her legs weren't going to turn rubbery and give out on her, she made a beeline for the door.

Of course, it was locked. She slapped her hand against the wood, then narrowed her eyes and studied the door plate. Hmmm.

She returned to the table. The leather restraints passed through metal loops, but weren't themselves attached to the table. She slid one of the straps out of its loop, then brought it over to the door and used the flat edge of the tongue as a makeshift screwdriver to remove the door plate. Once she'd exposed the interior of the lock, it was easy to disengage it.

The door popped open. Susana bit back a whoop of triumph. She peeked outside. The short corridor was empty.

She looked left, then right, but neither direction sparked a sense of familiarity. So she closed the door behind her and ran left.

She'd almost reached the end when she heard voices rapidly approaching from around the corner. Despite her leaden legs, she put on a burst of speed and ducked into a supply closet seconds before a man and a woman wearing white lab coats rushed by.

A tiny, rational part of Susana's brain pointed out the low probability that she'd be allowed to leave the facility. Besides, wasn't she supposed to get the chip removed before it self-destructed? And, you know, *killed* her?

The rest of her wasn't listening. Instinct told her to run.

So she cracked open the door and peeked back into the corri-dor. The scientists had nearly reached the door to her room. She held her breath, crossed her fingers and hoped they wouldn't check on her.

They didn't even glance at her door. The man tugged on the woman's arm, and they broke into a jog. Moments later, they vanished down a side corridor.

Susana let out a gusty sigh and stepped into the hallway. She still had no idea where the exit was, but since left had worked for her so far, she cautiously made her way to the end of the corridor and turned left.

Damn, Susana thought several eternal minutes later. *I'm lost.*

No matter which way she looked, she saw the same white corridor walls stretching into the distance. No windows to show her which direction she needed to move. No identifying artwork or scuff marks on the walls, and the few signs she'd seen were in Russian. One of the few languages she couldn't read.

And while it was lucky for her that the corridors were mainly deserted, it was creepy, too. She'd only had to hide twice more. Both times, the people passing by had seemed frantic.

Something was wrong. This was a huge compound. There should be people moving about. These rooms should be occupied.

Yet each time she'd ducked into a room to avoid being noticed, the rooms she'd chosen had been both unlocked and empty.

Maybe she was in a new wing of the compound. One not used much.

She bit the inside of her cheek. What if she was heading deeper into the compound? Toward the place where all the people had been running? Any moment she could walk around a corner and run into the entire staff.

Don't think like that. Just keep moving.

She shivered. At the next intersection, she turned left again. When she'd made it a third of the way down the corridor a small group of people appeared at the opposite end.

Someone cried out. She didn't have to understand Russian to know she'd been spotted.

Susana ran back the way she'd come. She'd nearly reached the corner when something sharp pricked between her shoulder blades.

Two more steps and she stumbled into unconsciousness.

KAI WATCHED Ivanov's compound from a small ridge. Through the borrowed binoculars, Kai saw Tonelli's assault team skirmishing with Ivanov's security force along the front wall and in the gap formed by the destroyed front gate. Tonelli, the coward, stood behind a tree, waiting for his team to overpower the security men.

Kai swept his glasses toward the training ground at the rear of the compound. Camouflage netting strung overhead guarded against aerial spies, but not from someone in Kai's location.

A large exercise area sat behind walls with maximum security level fortifications. In the center, six men ran through an obstacle course.

Kai frowned. No, they weren't running. They were lumbering through it with a distinct lack of coordination. One soldier ran into the large wooden A-frame instead of climbing it. He shook his head, backed up, then ran into it again.

Three men with bullhorns dashed out from the shadow of the main building, shouting and waving their arms. Within moments, the soldiers had abandoned the obstacle course and had lined up, although their crooked attempt at formation more closely resembled the effort of a ragged group of second-graders than an elite military team.

One of the men with the bullhorns pointed toward the front of the building. The men broke ranks and dashed to join the fight against Tonelli's men. The man who'd run into the A-frame stopped, looked around in confusion, then moved slowly back toward the obstacle course.

A man with a clipboard stepped in front of the wayward

soldier. He pointed in the direction the other men had gone. The lost soldier shoved clipboard man hard enough that he fell.

The other two men with bullhorns jumped on the soldier. Clipboard man scrambled to his feet and joined them. The soldier fought like an angry bear and Kai thought for sure he'd break free.

Then a man wearing a lab coat approached. The disobedient soldier immediately tried to run, but was blocked by two of his opponents.

Lab coat jabbed a syringe into the man and he collapsed as if someone had cut the nerves controlling his limbs. The men fastened an odd restraint system on him, then carried him inside.

Kai lowered the binoculars. Rubbed his eyes and tried to pretend that he wasn't freaked out. God, the man's fighting behavior reminded him of Rafe.

Dammit, they had to get the chip back. It was the only way to reverse what had been done to his friend.

But even as Kai worried about Rafe, he nodded in the direction of the empty training ground, indicating to his FSB companions that the back was their entry point. Let Tonelli's team battle it out with Ivanov's men.

Kai was going after Susana.

KAI ACCOMPANIED his FSB team through the halls of Ivanov's compound. As they moved deeper into the building, the white, sterile walls started to close in on Kai, as oppressive as jungle heat. And each room they cleared without finding Susana caused his fear to rise.

His companions flung open another door. Three men and a woman jumped to their feet and spun around in alarm to face the intruders. Notebooks and voice recorders dropped unheeded to the floor. White lab coats indicated these were staff members.

On the other side of an observation window a naked man in

chains strained to reach a single banana placed millimeters too far away. His body was covered with electrodes. Kai turned his head, fighting back pity, revulsion, and fury. His hands clenched into fists. He knew the frustration and desperation of being chained and tortured. But having your pain recorded as part of some sick experiment?

That was enough to break a man. No wonder Rafe was so wild, if he'd been treated like this.

One group of soldiers took control of the scientists while their teammates opened the door to the other room, but Kai didn't stick around to watch them free the chained man. With every room they exposed, his need to find Susana grew more urgent.

The next two rooms were empty. Kai called Tonelli and learned that the battle at the front still raged, so the other man wasn't even inside the facility yet.

Kai smiled. Tonelli had gone silent when Kai explained his location. No doubt the man would soon figure out how to join them.

This corridor ended at a hub of five intersecting hallways with an abandoned nurse's station in the center. Several monitors showed different views of the surrounding hallways.

Kai threw a brief glance at the monitors as he passed, then did a double take. He stopped so suddenly, the agent behind him trod on his heels. Kai motioned for the man to go around him, then leaned forward to get a better view.

One of the monitors showed three lab-coated people pushing a gurney. He caught a glimpse of a woman's long, dark hair, and a bare arm dangling toward the floor.

Susana!

Was she alive? Was he too late and the chip had already been removed? His chest spasmed and he struggled to breathe around the chunk of his heart that lodged in his throat.

He grabbed the sleeve of the closest FSB agent and pointed

urgently to the picture on the monitor. "That's the woman I'm looking for," he said in Russian.

The man studied the screen, which showed two intersecting corridors, then looked at an evacuation map stuck to a faded cork board. With the tip of his finger, he traced a route from their location. "The woman is roughly there."

He moved his finger along a different route. "This is our target. The main offices." From down the hall, one of his comrades called for him to hurry up.

The man glanced at Kai. "You're on your own. Good luck." Then he took off at a run.

Kai ripped the map off the cork board and headed toward Susana.

MARK DREW BACK behind the safety of a tree as some of Ivanov's men fired toward his location. The nearest soldiers returned fire and advanced, but not quickly enough for Mark.

That bastard Paterson was already inside. Given the size of the building, Paterson's odds of finding Susana without help were slim. However, it did mean Mark needed to get inside and find one of Ivanov's staff to lead him to Susana. He had to reach her before Paterson.

Finally, the leader of the assault team gave the all-clear. Mark wasted no time hurrying up to the front door and past the soldiers methodically clearing the building room by room. He beat the team through the door into the lab section, startling the wide-eyed guard on the other side. Mark shot him.

Moving deeper into the building along the corridors he'd taken with Ivanov, Mark soon came across a conference room where a group of scientists and administrative staff huddled, whispering fearfully and shooting nervous glances at the door to the hallway.

He spun them a story about Susana being his wife and how,

since he'd been alone in the waiting room for so long, he was worried. Could someone please tell him where to find his wife? A young female lab assistant with sable hair contained in a tight bun shyly raised her hand and said she could take him to the most likely location Ivanov would use for the surgery.

Mark eagerly followed the woman farther into the building through eerily silent halls. None of the noises from the assault team's movements carried this far, a testament to excellent sound-proofing.

The woman's heels clicked rapidly on the tile as she scurried along. Tonelli lengthened his stride to keep up with her, but stopped himself from breaking into a run. He didn't want to make the woman suspicious.

"There," the woman said, pointing toward a half-open door at the end of the corridor. "That's the preparation room. You don't need anything else?"

Tonelli shook his head, all his attention on the door.

"Then...I will return to my friends, yes?"

"Yes, thank you," he murmured.

He reached the door and stepped inside.

Empty.

Before disappointment had a chance to settle in, he heard voices on the other side of the door leading into the next room.

He put his hand on the door and cautiously opened it.

KAI SPRINTED DOWN THE HALL, driven by the urgent sense that time had run out. His fear and anger fed on each other, increasing his need to hurry. If Susana was dead, he didn't know how he'd...how he'd...

Hell. He loved her so much he couldn't even think straight.

Push the fear aside. Focus.

After a quick glance at the map, he turned right at the next corner. Yes. This was the corridor where he'd seen the gurney via the monitor.

Kai forced himself into a walk. He gently opened each door he encountered. If he burst into a room and Ivanov was in the middle of surgery, he might scare the man into making an accidental cut on Susana. And her skin was so smooth, so fragile. It would tear quickly under a finely-honed scalpel.

Just as it had yielded easily under his own knife when he'd removed the tracking device.

Kai closed his eyes and willed away the image of her blood on his hands before it triggered darker memories. Tried to convince himself that when he found Susana, she would be alive.

The next door opened onto the anteroom of an operating room. On the other side of the observation window, a man in hospital scrubs lifted a scalpel from a shiny array on a portable tray.

Ivanov.

Susana lay on the table. All Kai could see was her face and her bare legs, but it was enough to weaken his knees with relief.

Kai hurried forward. The doctor appeared to be alone. No nurses. No anesthesiologist. God, was the man about to operate while Susana was awake?

As he pushed open the door to the operating room, a man stepped out from the shadowy corner.

Mark Tonelli had beat him to the scene.

CHAPTER TWENTY-NINE

Kai wanted to rip Dr. Ivanov away from Susana. But fear bound him in iron shackles, keeping him immobile two feet away from the operating table, barely daring to breathe.

Dr. Ivanov shot Kai an annoyed, dismissive glance. "Do not come any closer or the woman dies," he warned, before lowering a scalpel to Susana's skin. At the moment of incision, Kai sank his teeth into his tongue, stifling a bellow of protest.

As blood flowed out of the cut, Kai took one lurching step forward. A growl rolled out of his mouth as he waited for Ivanov to finish. The second the chip left Susana's body, Kai would snatch her away from the scientist.

"Don't move."

At Tonelli's command, Kai looked up. The man's gun was pointed at Kai's chest, but Tonelli's eyes kept straying to Susana.

Kai dismissed him with a glance, and returned his attention to what was important. Watching Ivanov. Protecting Susana. If anything went wrong with the procedure, Dr. Ivanov wouldn't make it out of the room alive.

Kai would see to it.

Ivanov's tweezers began to rise out of the cut in Susana. Kai stepped closer.

Ivanov's hand stilled. He picked up another set of tweezers with his other hand and carefully probed the incision. Searching for the booby-trap.

Kai waited for Ivanov to disarm the trap, breath suspended. Memories of his time with Susana flashing before his eyes.

Her laugh. Her curses. The way she smelled.

Her taste.

The look on her face as he'd walked away, leaving her with Niko.

Ivanov's hand twisted sharply. He yanked and the tweezers pulled out a thin wire attached to a pea-sized box.

He tossed them onto the floor. The box exploded with the force of a miniature firecracker.

Next Ivanov removed a blood-smeared glass vial about the size of Kai's thumb from his knuckle to nail. Ivanov dropped the vial onto the surgical tray.

Finally, after two years, the chip was within reach.

Kai didn't give a damn. Fresh bruises in the shape of fingers purpled Susana's arms and calves. Blood seeped out from under the straps restraining her, indicating she'd struggled. Been afraid.

Kai couldn't control the surge of fury that tore through him. Demanding he act. Ivanov had hurt Susana. So he needed to be hurt.

Every muscle straining, Kai forced himself to wait while Ivanov sewed closed Susana's incision and swabbed away the blood from the short line of sutures across her belly. When Ivanov pulled down her gown and stepped away from the operating table, Kai struck.

"You don't know what you're doing," Dr. Ivanov gasped.

"Yes, I do." Kai had the scientist pinned against the wall. His hand pressed a scalpel to the scientist's throat. Although he didn't remember grabbing the scalpel, he was itching to use it.

The scientist reached up and tried to pry Kai's fingers away. Kai pressed harder with the scalpel blade and was rewarded by a few drops of blood.

"Only I can decode the data on the microchip," Ivanov gasped. "It was meant for me. Nevsky always said his successes were mine to share."

Keeping the scalpel at Ivanov's neck, Kai shuffled close to the tray where the chip sat. With his free hand, he grabbed the vial and stuck it in his pants pocket.

"If you must take the data," Ivanov continued, his words coming fast with desperation, "at least leave the woman. She is unique. Her genetic code was altered by her father. Studying her DNA will make up for losing the rest of the data."

Kai's whole body stilled. "Explain."

"Ah..."

Kai lightened up slightly on the pressure. "Talk."

"Dr. Nevsky injected her mother several times with substances meant to enhance the fetus's genetic code. Strength. Intelligence. Endurance. Extraordinary immune system."

Christ.

"If I am to succeed in making a super human I must study her to see which alterations took." Ivanov's hand groped Kai's pocket, searching for the chip.

Kai shifted so his forearm pressed under Ivanov's chin, then lifted so the shorter man's feet barely touched the floor. "You will—"

Tonelli slammed into Kai from the side. As Kai fell, he felt the scalpel in his hand scrape along the skin on Ivanov's neck before his arm swung free. Then he lost his grip on the scalpel and it went flying across the room.

He landed on his left side, with Ivanov and Tonelli both piled on top of him. Ivanov's hands clawed at Kai's pockets. Tonelli grabbed Kai's right arm and pulled it behind his back.

Kai's still-healing shoulder muscles screamed. Fuck. A few more inches and all his hours of physical therapy would go down the drain. He rolled onto his back, pinning Tonelli's hand beneath him. Then Kai lashed out with his feet, knocking Tonelli into the corner of the operating table.

Tonelli crumpled and lay motionless.

Kai heard a crack, then something sharp jabbed into his left wrist. Damn, that burned. Kai glanced down. The empty vial stuck out of his skin.

Shit. Ivanov had taken the vial, broken it open, and shoved the remainder into his hand. Injecting him with the poison. Kai yanked the glass out and flung it across the room.

Ivanov stood up, his face triumphant. Between his thumb and index fingers he held the microchip. "I have prevailed. You have half an hour before the poison kills you." He glanced at Tonelli's inert body. "Leave now and take Mr. Tonelli with you. I will see that you are given the antidote once you are outside these walls."

Kai raised his hands overhead in surrender position and slowly stood up. The poison burned through his veins like acid, making his mouth water and his stomach churn, but he wasn't leaving here without Susana and the chip.

The room shook from an explosion farther down the hall.

Ivanov turned his head slightly.

Tonelli launched off the ground, tackling the scientist.

The chip dropped to the floor as Ivanov and Tonelli staggered across the room. Kai scooped up the chip, popped it in his mouth, and swallowed.

Ivanov broke free of Tonelli. He lunged toward Susana.

Kai saw the scalpel in Ivanov's hand. Saw him aiming at Susana's throat, and with a roar, Kai charged. He grabbed Ivanov's wrist, spun the man away from Susana, and twisted, reveling in the crack of breaking bone.

Kai caught the scalpel as it fell from Ivanov's hand. He pulled Ivanov flush against him, yanked the scientist's head back, and put the scalpel to the man's throat.

Susana cried out.

Keeping his grip on Ivanov, Kai met her eyes. Her expression was clouded with pain and fear. "Don't...kill...him..." she rasped.

No. He needed to do this. It was just. Vengeance for what Ivanov had done to Susana. And what the scientist had done to all the men and women he'd used as test subjects.

But as Kai held Susana's eyes, he saw something else. Saw her belief in him. Belief that strengthened into something he'd never expected.

"Love...you..." Her eyes backed up her words with a gentle force his savage side couldn't fight. Kai sighed as some of the intense rage bled away.

He pressed his thumb against Dr. Ivanov's carotid artery until the man blacked out, then let the man fall to the ground.

"Thank...you..." Susana's eyes closed.

Heart in his throat, Kai stepped over Ivanov's body to reach Susana. He pressed his fingers against her throat, desperate to find a pulse.

His relief at finding the faint beat sent him to his knees. He let his forehead rest against the cool metal operating table.

A sound behind him had him whipping around, scalpel held in attack pose.

Two Tonellis knelt over Dr. Ivanov, tying him up with surgical tubing.

Kai blinked and the double image shimmered into one man. Shit. He'd been so focused on Susana, he'd forgotten about the poison. Kai glanced down at his hand. The skin around the wound was red and puffy.

Tonelli stopped and held his palms out in front of him. "Truce. I'm no threat to Susana."

When Kai didn't answer, Tonelli shrugged. He lowered his hands and finished securing Ivanov. "What did you do with the chip?"

"Swallowed it," Kai rasped.

"Ah." Tonelli stood up and stepped away from Ivanov. "That complicates matters."

The burning in Kai's veins spread. Intensified until it felt like he'd swallowed the sun. Sweat ran down his back and he swayed with dizziness.

Dammit, all Tonelli had to do was let him die, then ship his body off to have the chip removed.

Then what would happen to Susana?

Kai's legs buckled and he hit the ground on his knees. The scalpel fell from his hand.

"Promise me...she won't be hurt."

Tonelli's eyebrows lifted slightly. "I promise."

Kai gasped as the poison surged into his heart. The last thing he saw was the floor rising up to meet him.

MARK STARED at the unconscious bodies of Ivanov and Paterson. Should he wake up the scientist and demand the antidote so he could save Paterson? Or just let the bastard die and have Jamieson remove the chip from his corpse?

Susana whimpered. Her eyes opened and immediately found Paterson. "No!" she struggled to sit up, but she was strapped to the table.

Her eyes met Mark's. "Is he...dead?"

She was still the most beautiful woman he'd ever seen. They would have made a perfect couple. Except that her eyes were frantic with worry for Paterson. He could practically feel her willing the SSU agent to move. Damn her, why couldn't she look at him in that way? Like he was her only hope.

Her love.

He could lie and tell her Paterson was dead. Then take her away and start a new life together.

But he didn't want secondhand affection.

"No. He's just unconscious. He's been poisoned." Mark moved to the table and began unfastening her restraints.

"Please...help him." Tears streamed down her cheeks.

Mark released the last strap. She tried to roll off the table, but he put his hands on her shoulders. "Stay here. I'll wake Dr. Ivanov and find out where the antidote is."

The gratitude in her eyes warmed him. He reached out and smoothed her hair back from her forehead. She flinched and he dropped his hand.

He turned away, angry at the hurt he felt at her reaction.

"Hurts," she murmured.

He glanced back. Her eyes were closed. She was unconscious again.

Good. Because he didn't want her seeing how he persuaded Dr. Ivanov to talk.

Ivanov succumbed quickly to Mark's painful persuasion and wasn't long before Mark had the antidote in hand. Unfortunately, the scientist hadn't survived.

Mark jabbed the needle into Paterson's neck and pressed the plunger. He didn't know how long it would take for Paterson to recover. He'd forgotten to ask Ivanov that.

The room shook under another explosion.

He had to make a decision quickly. Should he pick up Paterson and try to escape with the man's unconscious body?

Too risky. The last thing he wanted was to be seen as behaving suspiciously and be shot by an overzealous soldier.

He could call the head of his assault team, ask for a rescue, and explain that Paterson had to come with them. But that would involve explaining that Paterson had swallowed the chip. And he didn't trust that the man in charge wouldn't have orders from Jamieson to shoot Mark and take Paterson straight to Jamieson.

Mark sighed. He walked over to Paterson and pulled the two-way radio off the man's belt. The safest option was to trust the SSU.

CHAPTER THIRTY

Thursday, Morning
Temporary SSU Research Facility
Georgia, United States

NIKO LET Jenna lead him toward the tall iron gates that surrounded the grounds of the old Victorian mansion. The elegant gables and wide front porch were more suited for a bed and breakfast, but the electrified fence was all about security.

Niko didn't want to know what secrets the CDC had been protecting on the property before they closed it down. The only things that mattered were that this was Rafe's new home, and Niko was being kicked out.

He stopped and glanced over his shoulder. He hated leaving Rafe to the mercy of the SSU's scientists. In order to cure him, they'd treat Rafe like a lab rat. Yeah, Niko knew his brother needed help, but Jesus, it killed him to return Rafe to a situation that would remind his brother of his time as Kaufmann's prisoner. Niko wanted to be there to support Rafe, let him know he wasn't alone.

But since Rafe continued to fly into a murderous rage every

time he saw Niko, the psychiatrist had banned Niko's visits. "We suspect Rafe's been brainwashed to kill anyone from his previous life," the man had told Niko. "In order to break that conditioning, we need him calm. Besides, his recovery is going to be difficult. He's barely functioning at the intellectual level of a two-year-old. Do you really think your brother would want you as a witness to his weakness? Let him have his privacy. We'll call you when it's safe to return."

Niko had nearly shoved the psychiatrist against the wall and dared the man to stop him from seeing Rafe. Logically, he got the message. But in his heart?

Hell, no. This was his baby brother. He'd done a piss poor job of protecting Rafe so far. He needed to help his brother through this. But in the end, Jenna had convinced him to give the psychiatrist a chance.

As he neared the gate to the property, Niko stared back at the house. He knew how it felt to look in the mirror and hate the man he saw staring back. He'd wanted to hide from his family when he'd come out from his first undercover assignment, knowing that the violence he'd done to keep his cover had taken him so close to the line between good and evil that some days he hadn't known which side he stood on. But Rafe hadn't let him hide. He'd been there, hovering just out of sight sometimes, but always letting Niko know of his support.

Niko wanted to return the favor.

Fuck. Leaving felt too much like abandonment. Maybe he should just march back inside and tell the doctors to go to hell.

"How's your eye?" Jenna asked.

Niko shrugged. He'd gone in to say good-bye and Rafe had thrown another fit, snapping his restraints and attacking Niko. The discomfort from his black eye and other bruises would soon disappear. Not so the memory of his brother's face.

Jesus, he'd seen men in drugged rages before, but he'd never seen anything like Rafe's wild, single-minded destruction. For the first time, he wondered if Rafe was too far gone for help. "What if...they can't cure him?"

Jenna put her arms around him. "They—"

"Mr. Andros!"

A woman in a white lab coat ran toward them across the grass. Her dark blonde bob swung sharply against her chin. She looked vaguely familiar.

She stopped in front of him. "Mr. Andros, I'm glad I caught you."

"Has something happened to Rafe?" Niko demanded. Shit. He knew it. He should never have left Rafe alone.

"What? Oh...no. Your brother is still unconscious from the sedative they shot him with. The doctor is examining him. That's not why I came." Her eyes bounced away and she tugged down the sleeves of her coat. "I'm Dr. Gabrielle Montague. The—"

"You're the one who worked at Kaufmann's lab."

She nodded. "I'm so sorry. I'm the one who gave your brother the layout of Kaufmann's lab for his return mission. I never thought...I never would have..." Her fingers twisted and un-twisted her left jacket cuff.

Her eyes sought his, pleading for forgiveness. Hell, there was nothing to forgive. She'd done the right thing, giving the SSU the information to launch a second assault on the lab. "It's not your fault. Rafe knew there was danger. It's part of his job."

Christ, that sounded lame. But it was true. Rafe hadn't known he'd end up as a test subject, but without a doubt he would have led the attack even if he'd been forewarned. "The other subjects deserved to be rescued from Kaufmann's torture. That's why he went back. Rafe couldn't turn his back on those men."

Dr. Montague turned her head away, but not before Niko saw the tears welling in her eyes.

"I...your brother is a very special man. We...uh...grew close... before he..."

Jenna reached out and gave the woman a one-armed hug.

The gesture seemed to give Dr. Montague strength. She straightened her spine and looked Niko squarely in the eye. "I'm heading the team who will be treating him. I promise you this. I will not stop until he's whole again."

"Thank you."

"And…I know it must seem wrong that you're not allowed to be here. I'm not sure I agree with the philosophy, but that's not my call. I just wanted to let you know that he won't be alone. The agent who is retrieving the chip, Kai Paterson, he's your brother's friend, right?"

Niko nodded.

"He'll be my co-leader when he returns. And…I think…I hope…Rafe will recognize me, too." The last part was said so quietly, Niko knew she hadn't really meant for him to hear it.

She plunged her hand into her coat pocket and pulled out a business card. "Here's my cell phone number. Call me any time you have questions or just want an update."

Knowing he had someone to keep him updated on Rafe eased Niko's need to storm to his brother's rescue. Between Kai and Dr. Montague, Rafe was in capable, compassionate hands. "Thanks. Promise me you'll call if there's any change at all." He dug around in his own pockets, but he couldn't find any business cards. Dammit, when he'd left home to chase after Rafe he hadn't planned on networking.

"Here," Jenna said. "This has both our cell phone numbers on it."

Thank God for his organized wife.

Dr. Montague grabbed onto the card. "I swear, I'll keep you updated." She glanced at her watch. "I need to get back. Good-bye"

Niko watched her go. He remembered Rafe's good spirits after his team had brought Dr. Montague to the SSU. At the time, he'd suspected Rafe of having an affair with the pretty doctor. Now he was certain. "What do you think?"

"I think Rafe made another conquest," Jenna said with a smile. "She's in love with him. She'll fight harder for him than anyone else on the team except Kai."

"Yeah." And it went a long way toward easing his pain at having to leave his brother behind.

Thursday, Afternoon
Moscow, Russia

"YOU'RE WANTED in connection to the firebombing of Susana Dias's archaeological dig in Brazil, and the death of SSU agent Enrique Gonzales," Ryker told Mark across a secure phone connection. "Turn yourself in to me," he continued. "Give me the name of the man behind Kaufmann's lab and I'll work to clear you of all charges."

So Jamieson had cast him in the role of scapegoat, had he? Mark let his outrage simmer. He didn't like being used. And he hadn't intended for Jamieson to kill Gonzales, only to put him somewhere safe from the SSU. The man had provided a great deal of useful information to Mark over the years and helped undermine the SSU's status in the private special operations community. He'd deserved better than having his throat cut and being dumped in a rough Moscow neighborhood.

"No," he told Ryker. Mark stepped up to the window of the suite's master bedroom, aware that the SSU agents in the other room blocked his escape. Ryker's men had arrived at Ivanov's compound just as the Russian security agents who'd accompanied Paterson had finished securing the place. One group of Ryker's men had grabbed Susana and Paterson and rushed off to a medical center, while another group brought Mark to this hotel while the team decided what to do with him.

"It's not safe—" Ryker started.

"I know. But if word gets out that I'm with the SSU, my boss will cover his trail. You'll never get him." On the streets down below, Muscovites went about their business, unaware that Mark was about to make the most important decision of his life.

He opened his palm and stared down at the tiny microchip. He'd taken it out of one of the machines in Ivanov's lab while he'd waited for help to arrive. It looked enough like Nevsky's chip to fool Jamieson.

He hoped.

"I have a decoy chip," he told Ryker. "My boss doesn't know Paterson swallowed the real chip. He'll talk to me."

"So?"

Mark closed his fingers over the chip. "You need more than just my word. Even if I tell you his name, it will take time for you to find evidence against him. I can get it for you." He needed to do this.

He'd known when he'd joined Jamieson's department, In-House Projects, that IHP and its military arm, Kerberos, pushed the envelope of legality. He had no problem with that. Most of the rules pertaining to the intelligence community were put in place by frightened politicians who rode the latest liberal wave in order to avoid being defeated at the polls. As a result, the existing laws favored the criminals, despite repeated assurances to the contrary.

Mark had looked forward to working for a group that didn't have to adhere to those laws. He'd spent his whole life bending the rules, even breaking them when it suited him and when no one could take action against him.

Molding the world to suit his needs.

He'd turned his head from some pretty nasty scenarios over the years. Been involved in a couple of situations that turned his stomach in order to get closer to the men who'd murdered his father. Made certain that the murderers died in as painful a way as possible.

He'd vowed to do anything Jamieson wanted to get the name

of the man who'd ordered his father's death, so he could complete the vengeance he'd promised as his father lay dying.

But the shock of what he'd seen at Ivanov's lab still reverberated through him. Violence he understood, even approved of under the right conditions. At the core, however, he considered himself a civilized, erudite man. Human in the best sense of the word.

No matter what morally questionable acts he'd committed in his life, the people Mark dealt with always retained their biological integrity at the end.

He wouldn't have called any of Ivanov's subjects human.

He closed his eyes to fight back the rage and fear. He'd do whatever he needed to get deeply into Kerberos. Not just for the name of his father's murderer, but because he'd discovered he still had a conscience left. A conscience that wouldn't let him look the other way while men were turned into monsters against their will.

Thank God he'd always been paranoid. He had copies of tapes and correspondence with Jamieson tucked away in an untraceable Swiss bank vault. As soon as he was out of here, he'd send another set to his lawyer, to be released to the SSU in the case of his death.

"Let me go," Mark said. "I have contacts here who will help me free a couple of Ivanov's scientists from jail. I'll take them back to my boss with the fake chip. With those kind of prizes in hand, he'll let me deeper into his organization. I'll be able to find proof to tie him to what happened to Andros."

"If that's what you want, then good luck," Ryker said. "I'll tell my men to leave you alone. Call me personally if you need help."

"Thank you."

Mark walked into the other room and handed the phone back to one of the agents. As he turned back to the bedroom, he shoved his trembling hands into his pants pockets.

He'd never been so scared. Or so excited.

He closed the bedroom door behind him. This was it. The ultimate game of deception. Was he good enough to fool Jamieson? To keep hidden the fact that he wanted more than just the name? That his conscience had been resurrected? He flicked a glance at his reflection in the mirror over the bureau. Cool brown eyes stared back at him from an expressionless face developed at a very young age.

Oh, yes, he was more than a match for Jamieson.

In fact, he was looking forward to it.

Sunday, Afternoon
United States Military Hospital, Germany

KAI'S EYELIDS FLUTTERED. The beeping of the life support monitors changed tone. Susana leaned forward and put her hand on his arm. Kai licked his lips and groaned.

"Kai? Love, it's Susana. Can you hear me?" She traced her fingertip down his cheek. Kai had been in a coma for three agonizing days.

On the other side of the bed, Kai's sister Jenna squeezed his hand. "Hey Kai, you awake? It's Jenna."

Along with Susana, Kai's sister spent most of the day by his side. Yet Susana had studiously avoided talking to the woman, her usual outgoing nature crushed under a press of guilt. Because of Susana, Jenna had been kidnapped. Because of Susana, Kai fought for his life. Because of Susana's father, Rafe had been turned into a raging beast.

Susana had never felt so defeated by guilt before, yet the one time she'd tried to apologize, Jenna had brushed her off. "It's not your fault," Jenna had said. "Stop blaming yourself. We don't."

Easier said than done, particularly when jealousy also started eating away at Susana's confidence. The love Jenna had for her brother shone so brightly, and Susana knew how deeply Kai returned that love. Susana had never experienced unconditional love. Watching Jenna speak softly to Kai now, then brush his hair back off his face, Susana's throat tightened up.

She wanted that kind of loving relationship with Kai with a ferocity that made her chest ache. Oh, she knew Kai liked her. And he definitely lusted after her. But she'd give anything to have Kai love her.

Right now, she'd settle for having his arms around her, but who knew how he'd respond to her once he woke up. Maybe what they'd shared had only been born of proximity and adrenaline.

Kai's eyelids cracked open and Susana's heart jumped into her throat. The corners of his mouth twitched slightly upward. "Jen... na..." He coughed. "Sus...san...na..." He sighed deeply, then closed his eyes again. But the tone of the monitor stayed upbeat.

Susana took that as a good omen. She brushed a kiss across his lips, then stood. She didn't want Jenna to see the emotion on her face, so she walked over to the window.

Deus, he'd scared her.

When she'd regained consciousness after blacking out in Ivanov's surgery room, she'd panicked, thinking she was still at the compound and terrified that Kai was dead. She'd stumbled out of bed and into the corridor, then fought wildly when nurses arrived to restrain her.

Finally, a man named Ryker had approached her and explained that she was safe. That she was in a U.S. military hospital in Germany. When she'd asked about Kai, he'd told her that even though Mark Tonelli had successfully administered the antidote, the poison from the microchip's vial had sent Kai's body into near shutdown.

Susana had wanted to sit vigil by Kai's side, but the staff refused, saying hospital rules forbade persistent visitors for patients in Kai's condition. Since the worst of Susana's injuries was a surgical incision smaller than her appendectomy scar, she'd been officially discharged and had no legitimate reason to stay in the hospital beyond visiting hours. But Ryker had spoken with the staff and found Susana a visitor's bedroom down the hall, then arranged for her to spend as much time as she wanted at his bedside.

In the background, Susana heard Jenna talking to one of the nurses. Susana listened long enough to understand that the antidote had finally neutralized the poison and the nurse expected him to recover quickly. Tests also showed that Kai's system had finished excreting the toxin and that his body had passed the microchip yesterday.

Now that Kai had opened his eyes, Susana felt their time together running out. According to Ryker, once Kai recovered he would head to a secure location to work with the SSU team trying to reverse the damage done to his friend Rafe.

So the SSU had her father's data, and Kai had a new mission. Susana stared blankly out the window at the evening sky, trying to ignore the hollow ache of once again being on the outside. Maybe it would be better if she left before Kai woke up. Save them both from an awkward reunion scene. Because no matter how much she loved Kai, they lived in different worlds. While she respected Kai and the other SSU agents who fought daily against the hidden dangers in this world, could she handle knowing Kai's life was constantly at risk?

Call her a coward, but she wanted nothing more than to flee back to the security of her old life. She still wanted to explore that altar she'd found with Kai, to see if it indicated the true location of Amerinis. But most of all, with the memory of her dead crew mates sitting like a rock on her breastbone, she needed to pay her respects to their families.

Ryker had fed a story to the media about how Susana had been kidnapped by slavers, so she hadn't been present when the fire destroyed her dig. Close enough, but Susana hated not being able to tell the entire truth. Particularly when it came to those who'd lost loved ones because they'd been working for her.

She shook her head. Not that anyone would believe her if she did explain all.

If the Adventure Channel didn't drop her contract because of the deaths, Susana intended to funnel her salary into a memorial fund to provide assistance to the families. A poor substitute for the lives that had been stolen, but the best she could do.

Susana heard Jenna leave, saying something about letting Niko know Kai had opened his eyes. Now that they were alone, Susana walked slowly over to the bed. For a long time she simply stared down at Kai's beloved face, watching the even rise and fall of his chest. He was going to be okay. She was sure of that now.

So it was time to leave. She loved him so much, but she couldn't put her life on hold for him, not when she saw no future for them. Besides, how would he react once he learned that her father had experimented on her? She couldn't even face the possibilities without wanting to scream.

Just go.

Lips trembling, she pressed another kiss to Kai's mouth, then, brushing tears from her eyes, she hurried from the room.

"What's wrong? Is Kai worse?" Ryker strode toward her, concern on his face.

"No," she said. "He opened his eyes and spoke for a moment. Jenna's gone to get Niko."

Ryker raised his eyebrows, but didn't ask the question hanging between them.

She answered it anyway. "I'm leaving."

His eyes flicked to the door. "Ah. Does Kai know?"

"No. He didn't come fully awake."

Ryker's eyes bored into her. Weighing everything she wasn't saying. And probably guessing far too accurately the thoughts in her head.

But all he said was, "Well...Is there anything you need?"

"Yes." Before she could return to her life, she had to know exactly what effect her father's tampering had had on her development.

What about her was natural? Her looks? Probably not. Her intelligence? Unlikely. Her strong immune system?

If Ivanov was right, everything that defined her was a result of the tampering her father had done to her DNA.

Deus, she wished she could scrub her blood, her muscles... every molecule of her being until her father's influence was gone.

She looked Ryker straight in the eye and said, "This is what I want..."

CHAPTER THIRTY-ONE

Monday, Morning
CIA Headquarters
Langley, Virginia

"Drop the charges against me," Mark Tonelli said over the phone. "If you want Nevsky's chip."

Jamieson's eyebrows rose in surprise. The bastard hadn't lost any of his arrogance, despite the trouble he was in. "That's a rather bold statement," he replied. "For a man the authorities in three countries are searching for."

"We both know I had nothing to do with the firebombing," Tonelli said. "You told me to get Nevsky's chip and then you'd let me into Kerberos. I did as you asked. Are you a man of your word?"

Hmm. Tonelli was proving to be more of a challenge to deal with than expected. Jamieson eyed the small, bronze horse head on his desk and allowed his lips to curl in an appreciative smile. He'd always enjoyed a challenge. And if Tonelli proved to be lying, well, Jamieson knew how to take care of difficult men.

But if there was a chance he told the truth... "How do I know you really have the microchip?"

"You don't," came Tonelli's surprising response. "All I have is Ivanov's dying word that this is the right chip."

Meaning that if they made a deal, Jamieson could end up with a fake and Tonelli none the worse for it. Completely unacceptable. "I find, after consideration, that the chip is not good enough for entrance into Kerberos. I require more. On the off chance Ivanov was mistaken."

"Of course," Tonelli countered smoothly. "Would sending over a couple of Ivanov's scientists, and a stack of notes from his lab suffice as additional incentive?"

Jamieson thought about Kaufmann and his whining. "Should you be able to provide what you promise, then yes, I think I can safely say you'd be welcomed into Kerberos."

"Good. Expect the notes and the microchip within a few days and the scientists within a week. I'll be in touch."

Jamieson stared at the phone. Tonelli had the nerve to hang up on him? He really wished he could arrange for the man's death. But until he had the chip, his hands were tied.

He ran his finger over the horse head. Yes, for now he'd be content to watch Tonelli squirm to get back into his good graces. But the man's obsession with finding the man who'd ordered the hit on his father would eventually become a problem.

He looked forward to revealing that name to Tonelli, and watching the man's reaction.

The phone rang. Jamieson sighed as he recognized Kaufmann's number. "Hello."

"Where's my data?" Kaufmann demanded.

Jamieson closed his eyes and counted to ten. When that failed to cool his temper, he did it again. Only on the third set was he able to force words out of his mouth that were even vaguely civilized.

"I don't have it yet," Jamieson said. It galled him that the scientist assumed he held the power, not Jamieson. If he didn't need Kaufmann so much, he'd arrange for a quiet disposal. But Kaufmann was even more essential than Jamieson had realized. He'd sent out feelers to test the loyalty of the lab staff. Each one indicated the program would fall apart without Kaufmann. Not just because of high staff loyalty, but because Kaufmann, like Nevsky, had compartmentalized the program to such an extent that none of his scientists even realized what the full program entailed.

For once, Jamieson wished the scientist was a little less paranoid. He wanted the arrogant scientist gone. Preferably, he wanted to lay the blame for the destruction of the archaeological site in Brazil at Kaufmann's feet.

"How do you expect me to continue without Nevsky's data?" Kaufmann's voice was intolerably close to chiding. "Are you willing to extend the deadline?"

"No." Jamieson clenched and unclenched his fist until his fingers ached. "The deadline stands. I'm working on getting you a scientist or two from the Russian lab. The program run by Dr. Ivanov was more advanced than yours, although not quite as advanced as Nevsky's. With Ivanov's help you should still be able to meet the President's deadline for providing him with a team of enhanced soldiers." Assuming Tonelli wasn't lying.

The man had sounded as ambitious and arrogant as always, though. Perhaps Tonelli's loyalty had never really strayed. Time would tell. In the meantime, Jamieson had to deal with Kaufmann's incessant complaints.

The scientist should be excited about the promise of new scientists. But was he? Of course not.

"And the chip?" Kaufmann demanded.

"I expect to have it shortly." Jamieson's finger tapped against his desk. The date for the planned attack to avenge the death of the President's son was fast approaching. Jamieson needed

Kaufmann's program trouble-free by then. He'd have to make certain Ivanov's scientists were rushed straight to the lab.

Kaufmann remained silent, but Jamieson could sense him gearing up for another round of criticism. So he chose to strike first.

"Your team failed in its mission, Dr. Kaufmann. Kai Paterson survived the attack by Rafe Andros. Both Andros and Paterson are back with the SSU. If Andros remembers—"

The scientist laughed. It was a sound completely without warmth. "Andros won't remember a thing. There's no way the SSU will be able to reverse his conditioning. His mind equates disobedience to our commands with agony. They'll never get information out of him. His body will self-destruct first. You have no worries from that quarter."

"Even if your missing Dr. Montague is helping the SSU engineer a reversal?"

Kaufmann sucked in air so sharply, Jamieson jerked the phone away from his ear.

"You're sure she's with the SSU?" Kaufmann demanded.

"Yes." Tonelli had given him the information as another good-will gesture. "Is she a threat?"

For the first time in their conversation, the scientist sounded unsure of himself. "Possibly. It depends on what information she took with her when she ran."

"You're saying that she has the capability to create a solution to the conditioning?"

"Possibly, yes."

"You should have found and eliminated her when you first realized she was missing. Now she's had weeks to start on a reversal."

"Are you saying you can't handle the problem?" Kaufmann suggested with a hint of malice. "Should I send in my own team to take care of her?"

The scientist really was too arrogant for his own good. "None of your teams has succeeded in doing anything but create mass destruction and draw unwanted attention." After Kaufmann's team of enhanced soldiers had firebombed the dig, Jamieson's cleanup crew had successfully eliminated the men. But then Jamieson's cleanup crew had been eliminated by a group of mercenaries with lucky aim. Mercenaries hired by Tonelli, who'd had to do some remarkable groveling when confronted with that news. Thank God Kaufmann didn't know about the incident. The man's arrogance would be even more insufferable. "Your team certainly isn't capable of going against the SSU," Jamieson snapped. "I'll handle it."

"No. Wait." Kaufmann said. "Bring Dr. Montague to me instead. In the absence of Nevsky's chip, she's the best hope I have of strengthening the formula."

"Do you really think that's wise? She ran from you. What makes you think you can coerce her into helping you?"

Kaufmann's reply was a chilling, inhuman sound, reminding Jamieson that whatever else he disliked about the scientist, the man had no morals.

"Trust me," Kaufmann said. "If our experts were able to break Rafe Andros, they'll be able to force Dr. Montague to cooperate."

Jamieson tapped his pen against his blotter. "Very well. I'll arrange for Dr. Montague to be returned to you."

"Good."

Jamieson stared at the Mona Lisa print to the left of his desk and allowed a similar smile to form on his own lips. "I'm sending over a team to secure your facility. You will be in complete lockdown until the program is successful and we are confident there's no longer a threat from the SSU." Internal affairs had been tipped off that the men who'd stolen the helicopter had ties to the CIA. Worse, someone had suggested that Jamieson knew the truth, forcing him to waste valuable time covering up Kaufmann's mistake. He had to ensure that Kaufmann finished his work without any more interruptions.

The silence that followed was so thick Jamieson wondered if he'd finally provoked the scientist into rebellion. But Kaufmann once again surprised him. "That is acceptable. We can't afford to divert our own resources from the hunt for the remaining renegades."

Jamieson closed his eyes. It was true, then. He'd thought all the escaped subjects, except for Rafe Andros and one other man, had been either returned to the compound or accounted for as dead. "How many men are you missing? And why the hell didn't you mention it before?"

"We have it under control. The men were found by the authorities and put in a mental health facility. They all should be entering Level 5 and deteriorating so fast the doctors won't know what to make of them. Still, we will send in a team to make certain no data on the men survives their deaths."

Jamieson had thought nothing more could go wrong. He really ought to have learned differently by now. "Are your men prepared to destroy all paperwork involved? To eliminate anyone who came in contact with the subjects?"

"Yes." The word was spoken with the heavy emphasis a frustrated parent gives a wayward child and Jamieson bristled. "Once the subjects have been secured," Kaufmann continued, "the team has instructions to burn the facility and its inhabitants to the ground."

Jamieson shook his head. It wasn't that simple. If one person who'd interacted with the subjects escaped the fire, or wasn't there at the time the fire was set, the authorities might receive another call about abnormal human behavior. It was the last thing the program needed. He made a note to send a cleanup crew to guarantee the job was done to his satisfaction.

Jamieson glanced out his window. "Make sure that this time you fulfill your obligations," Jamieson warned. Then he hung up the phone.

He tapped his fingers against the heavy cotton paper of his

blotter. He needed that damn microchip. He was also going to have to find a way to eliminate Andros and destroy the SSU in the process. Jamieson couldn't afford any leaks regarding Kaufmann's work. Not now, so close to the anniversary demonstration. Nothing could interfere with the President's plans.

The President had been promised a uniquely vicious, absolutely loyal private army to carry out the attacks he demanded. Jamieson had been confident Kerberos would exceed the President's demands. But now he wondered if Kaufmann's men would remain mentally stable long enough to carry out their mission.

Or if the CIA or DOD would find the program and shut it down before the team deployed.

He heard a tearing sound and glanced down. His fingernails had scratched deep grooves into the otherwise pristine blotter.

Fucking scientists. Why couldn't they live up to their promises? If Kaufmann failed him, Jamieson would make certain the man was torn apart by his own subjects. While Jamieson watched.

CHAPTER THIRTY-TWO

Five Weeks Later
Monday, Evening
Georgia

A MAN with short blond hair and the golden eyes of a jaguar stepped into Rafe's room deep inside the SSU's recovery center, Gabby by his side. Emotion flooded Rafe and he trembled, remembering voices telling him to kill this man. Feeling the other man's throat under his hands. But not in the lab. Someplace green. And hot.

"Jungle," Rafe said, pulling the word from his deepest memories. "Kai."

There were other images, too. Not of violence, but of happy times. Kai laughing. Kai grunting with exertion as he bench pressed while Rafe spotted him. Kai tipping a bottle of beer to his lips while Rafe slugged down Ouzo.

Kaufmann's scientists had ordered him to kill this man, but he was no enemy. Now that the voices in his head were mostly silent, Rafe remembered what this man was to him. Friend. "Sorry," he said, wishing he could fully express himself in words. Hating that his communication skills remained blocked.

Kai nodded. His eyes were suspiciously bright as he cleared his throat. "Apology accepted." He stepped further into the room.

Gabby moved back, easing toward the door, but Kai's hand reached out and stopped her.

"It's good to see you again, Rafe."

Rafe barely heard Kai's words. The sight of those masculine fingers encircling Gabby's wrist sent him into a rage.

He grabbed Gabby's arm and yanked her away from Kai, then shoved her behind him. He took an aggressive step toward Kai and shoved the man back hard enough to make him stumble.

"No touch Gab-by," Rafe warned the other man, his voice little more than a growl. "Gab-by mine."

Kai held up his hands palms out and backed up a step. "Hey, there's no threat from me, Rafe. I've got a girl of my own." Then his face twisted in realization. "Ah, shit. That's right. You don't know."

Kai's words should have eased Rafe, but the primitive part of him still insisted that he keep Gabby sheltered from the other man's gaze. He shuffled to the side, blocking Gabby from moving around him.

"Rafe, Kai's no threat," Gabby pleaded. Her hand came to rest gently between his shoulder blades. "Come on. Get out of my way. Kai's a friend. And a colleague. We're both in charge of your recovery team. Kai's not my lover."

"Rafe, remember Susana Dias? Dr. Nevsky's daughter?" Kai asked. "You were sent to kill her and retrieve the microchip."

Rafe nodded slowly. He remembered fire. Shadows in the jungle. Following Kai and a woman.

Kai ran a hand over his hair. "I'm uh..." He sighed and looked down. "I'm uh, kinda..."

"Coward," Gabby taunted over Rafe's shoulder.

Kai raised his head and threw Gabby a glare. "I'm in love with Susana. Okay?"

Rafe sensed that this confession was out of character for Kai. But it made Rafe feel more comfortable. "Good," he said. He looked around the room. "Here?" He didn't mean here in this room, but here in the building.

Kai's expression tightened. "No."

"He's too much of a coward to go after her," Gabby muttered, stepping around Rafe and crossing her arms over her chest.

Rafe looked from Gabby to Kai and back again. He didn't understand. Why would Kai want to be away from his woman? Rafe pulled Gabby closer, so her back was against his chest. He crossed his arms over her stomach and pressed his cheek along the side of her head.

She stiffened, then relaxed against him.

"Gab-by go. Rafe go, too." God, she felt so good in his arms. Made him feel strong in a good way. Protective rather than destructive. "Why Kai no go Su-sa-na?"

Kai raised his eyebrows. His eyes went from Rafe's arms circling Gabby to Rafe's face. He blew out a breath and gave a wry smile. "Why indeed?" Then he added under his breath. "Although she's more likely to kick my ass than welcome me back."

"Fight," Rafe said strongly. "Fight for woman's love." He squeezed Gabby and pressed a kiss below her ear. Gabby was his strength. His center. His calm. Without her, he'd have lost his mind long ago. "Worth everything."

"Yeah," Kai said softly. "You got that right."

KAI LET himself into his room. For a moment he stared blindly around the small space, feeling like a different man than when he'd headed down to the labs this morning.

His first meeting face-to-face with Rafe had gone smoother

than expected. Rafe might not be able to communicate yet at an adult level, but his rages were finally under control. For the first time, Kai felt they were close to having the old Rafe back.

Maybe tonight he'd be able to sleep without nightmares waking him up. Nightmares of Rafe rampaging through the jungle, killing everyone Kai loved. Dreams where Kai stalked Rafe, then was forced to kill his friend.

Kai rubbed the back of his neck. One thing these weeks working with Rafe had given him was acceptance of his violent instincts.

Compared to Rafe, his instincts were quite tame.

He walked over to the bookshelf in the corner. On the top shelf sat Dr. Nevsky's journals, covers worn from the countless times Kai had flipped through them. He'd tried to understand the mind of the man who had created the program that had nearly destroyed Rafe. Nevsky's absolute belief in his purpose and his complete lack of morals had made for chilling reading. How much worse had it been for Susana, knowing Nevsky was her father? Knowing he'd experimented on her? God, Kai wished he'd been with Susana when she read them. And he damned Ivanov for giving the journals to her in the fist place.

He fingered the binding of one of the journals. He'd tried calling Susana to see how she was doing, but she'd refused all his calls. He'd sent letters she never answered. Would it have killed her to let him know she was okay? The only reason he knew she was alive and well was the recent broadcast on the Adventure Channel, highlighting her recent discovery.

That altar Susana had found on their way back to her camp had indeed been part of the lost city of Amerinis. The archaeological world was abuzz with the find.

Kai was damn happy for Susana. She'd achieved her dream. Only...beneath her brilliant smile, he thought he saw a hint of sadness. Of vulnerability.

Or maybe that was just wishful thinking. Hoping she missed

him as much as he missed her. Without her, life was dull. He needed her.

Needed her laughter. Her passion for life.

Seeing the affection just now between Rafe and Gabby had caused an ache to form around Kai's heart. He wanted a future with Susana. Wanted to be able to wrap his arms around her and feel her body pressed against his.

Hell, he was completely in love with her. And terrified that the real reason she'd left was because, despite what she'd said back in Ivanov's lab, she didn't really love him.

Why else would she have left without saying good-bye?

"Fight for woman's love," Rafe had told him. "Worth everything."

Yeah, buddy, you got that right.

It was time for Kai to go get his woman.

Tuesday, Morning
Montana

NIKO SLOWLY SET down the phone. The soft click of the receiver hitting the cradle echoed in the silence of his cathedral-ceilinged living room. A kernel of hope struggled to unfurl deep inside him.

God, he so wanted to believe that this time Rafe really was improving.

At night he dreamed of stalking the halls of the SSU labs, coercing the scientists into working harder. But he knew that Kai, Gabby and the rest of their team were doing their best. Their problem was that Kaufmann had only used some of Nevsky's complex and unconventional drugs. And Gabby had only copied a few of Kaufmann's formulas to disk before she ran.

Every time the team thought they'd managed to counteract all the drugs working in Rafe's system, they'd been thwarted by an unknown compound blocking their progress and had to start again.

On top of that, Rafe had been psychologically and physically tortured to the point that he felt physical pain whenever asked about his captors.

Although Ryker had forbidden the team from discussing their work, Gabby had stayed true to her promise and called every week with an update. She'd just phoned, saying she thought Rafe was finally on the road to recovery.

She warned Niko not to come rushing to the compound yet, because the progress might not last. Although Rafe still wasn't allowed to have outside visitors, she'd told Niko that Kai had just met with Rafe and the meeting had gone well.

Niko spun away from the phone, hope stubbornly refusing to stay cowed. Dammit, he wished Jenna was here. He needed...

Jenna's golden retriever, Monroe, leapt up from his place in front of the empty fireplace and ran to the door, barking excitedly. Niko's three dogs chased after him, adding their voices to the din until Niko could barely hear the sound of an approaching vehicle.

Niko yanked the front door open as Jenna's hybrid SUV pulled into the drive. He bounded down the steps. As soon as his wife was out of the car, he pulled her into a fierce hug.

"What's wrong? Is it Rafe?" Jenna demanded even as she returned his hug.

"Gabby thinks this is it. They've seen some improvement in cognition and his rages are subsiding."

"Oh, thank heavens." Jenna squeezed him again and ran her hands soothingly over his back.

Niko pressed his cheek against her hair. He wanted to say something, but his throat was too tight for words. Fine tremors shook his body.

"I've been so afraid," Jenna murmured. "For you and for him." She held him for several long moments until his trembling stopped and the tears that had threatened to unman him retreated.

Finally he set her away from him and pressed his lips to hers.

"When do we leave?" she asked.

He smiled, loving the way she understood him so well. "As soon as we can find transport. The SSU doesn't want us there—"

Jenna snorted. "Tough. Let them try to keep us away."

Niko laughed. He picked her up around the waist and swung her around. The dogs barked happily and danced around their legs. "God, I love you."

She smiled down at him. "Let's leave right now."

Wednesday, Evening
Georgia

THE LAST PERSON Kai expected to see on his way out of the research facility Wednesday night was Jenna. But she stood waiting for him at the bottom of the steps.

"Jenna!" Kai engulfed his sister in a hug. "What are you doing here? I thought you and Niko were in Montana." After Niko had been banned from seeing Rafe, Jenna had convinced her husband that some quiet time at their Montana cabin was in order. But Niko could only tolerate a few days of peace and had quickly convinced Ryker to send him out on missions.

Jenna gave a rueful smile. "We were. Then Gabby called and told us you'd made a breakthrough with Rafe." She held her hands out and shrugged. "I know we're not supposed to be here, but Kai, it's been killing Niko to be so far away. How would you like it if I needed help and Ryker told you to stay away?"

Kai shook his head. "I'd hate it." She was all the family he had left.

"So, how's he doing?"

"Walk with me and I'll tell you." He filled her in on Rafe's progress. "Seeing Rafe so savage has been rough. Until recently he was angry all the time." Kai looked down at his sister. "I felt the same after seeing what happened to mom, dad and the twins. And you."

Jenna glanced at him in surprise. No wonder. Although he'd helped his sister work through her emotions, he'd never talked about his own reaction to the murders.

He cleared his throat. "I...uh...felt guilty for putting them in danger. And I was scared that even if I'd known about the threat from Alvarez ahead of time, I would still have gone undercover because Nevsky had to be stopped."

Jenna's eyes were soft with sympathy, but he expected that would soon change.

"I was angry at the injustice of it all. Sickened by the brutality of the attack. I kind of lost it." He looked away, unable to bear seeing her eyes change from sympathy to revulsion. "I...ah... tracked down the assassins and killed them. Slit their throats and scalped them."

"I know."

He whipped his head around. "What?!"

"Ryker told me how the men died. I always suspected it was you. Who else would kill them that way? Thank you."

He stared at her like a fool. Unable to accept that she wasn't rejecting him. Unable to believe the love shining from her eyes. "You're not...repulsed? Scared of me?"

Jenna hugged him. The warm weight of her against his chest soothed the open wounds in his heart.

"Kai, when I tried to kill you in Alvarez's dungeon, my knife missed because I was hit with the truth. I loved you, even though I thought you'd ordered the attack on our family. I love you even though you scalped and killed those men. No matter what you do, I will always love you." She pulled back and smiled up at him. "At heart you're an honorable man. A good man."

"But—"

"Uh-uh. No buts. If I hadn't been so focused on finding and killing you, I'd have gone after the assassins myself," Jenna admitted. Her eyes held the dark knowledge of a seasoned combat veteran. It twisted his heart all up in knots. He didn't like seeing his little Jen-shine so hardened.

Yet he could see the truth in her eyes. She would have killed in the same way.

He laughed, but it came out self-mocking. "Well, killing the assassins that way shook me up."

Jenna nodded. "It changed the way you think about yourself, didn't it?"

He realized she would know all about having your self-image shattered. Of learning you were capable of a darkness you'd never before imagined. God, but that hurt.

"Yeah," he said. He put his arm around her shoulders. "We're a pair, aren't we?"

Jenna turned her face into his shoulder. "Don't ever think I don't love you, Kai. Don't ever think you don't deserve love. From me...or from someone like Susana."

Ah...shit. He felt his eyes warm with tears. He'd forgotten what it was like to be loved and accepted for himself, faults and all. He squeezed her. "Thanks, Jenna. I love you too. Just as you are."

From the way she suddenly relaxed against him, he knew she'd been worried he might not like this new Jenna. That even with Niko's love and acceptance, she still needed her big brother's love.

"Don't worry, Jen-shine," he reassured her. "I'm leaving tomorrow to find Susana. I'm already packed."

Jenna laughed.

CHAPTER THIRTY-THREE

Thursday, Night
Rio de Janeiro, Brazil

Susana let her partner lead her onto the crowded dance floor, struggling to feel the same joy as the rest of her newly hired crew. They'd just finished setting up an excavation site around the spot where she'd found the altar. The initial survey suggested that this time she'd found the true heart of Amerinis, bringing her dream close to fulfillment.

Plus, the Adventure Channel hadn't cancelled her show. Instead, they'd run a tribute show on her deceased crew members, earning record ratings. To her great surprise, she'd actually had to turn people away from joining her replacement team. Footage of Susana and her new crew setting up the relocated site would air later this week. For once, there was no doubt about the excavation continuing. In fact, there was a bidding war going on among several top museums as to who would get the honor of having their name associated with the second phase.

Tonight's party was her crew's way of celebrating their last day before the hard on-site work began. As Susana and her dance partner passed the cameraman dancing with a busty blonde, the cameraman gave her a victory sign. Susana responded with one of the artificially bright smiles she'd perfected during her modeling days.

She knew she should be elated. This was everything she'd dreamed of. Professional success and respect that washed away the lingering suspicion from Elena's charges of black marketeering. A significant enough find that even her worst critics couldn't continue to paint her as just a pretty face with no brains.

More importantly, she'd been vindicated. Amerinis existed. And from the evidence they'd already uncovered, it had indeed been a society run by warrior women, just as the legends claimed.

But Susana didn't feel like celebrating. Instead, she wanted to go back to her apartment and crawl into bed. Every night on site she'd tossed and turned, unable to sleep. Afraid of what might be lurking in the dark, even though she knew the mercenaries were no longer chasing her.

Unable to shake the fear that something would happen to her crew, she'd ended up walking the perimeter of the dig every night, freaking out the guards on duty who thought she didn't trust them. But she couldn't help it. The safety of her team was her responsibility. She needed to be aware of any threat.

Her last crew had died because of her. She wasn't going to let it happen again.

To remind her of the consequences if she lost her vigilance, she'd insisted on seeing the ruins of her former dig.

Big mistake.

Ryker's men had told her the stench wasn't so bad since they'd removed the bodies, but she'd still vomited at the smell. Or maybe she'd been sick because seeing the charred remains of her tent made it all too clear how close she'd come to dying.

And how many of her friends hadn't survived.

Her partner stopped on a vacant patch of dance floor and swung her around to face him. For a moment she stood frozen. Trapped in the past. Caught by sadness and regret.

Desperately wishing the man putting his hands on her waist was Kai, not the pilot who'd ferried her crew out of the jungle.

But then the music started, driving away her sorrow. Within minutes, the pulsing bass of the music took over her soul. She became the music, letting the sensuous rhythms move her body. Living only in the moment.

Here under the hot, shifting lights, your dance partner was your great love. The one you desired most. Or the one who'd hurt you and needed to be teased and punished.

Susana explored all those emotions with her body, so that a casual observer would think her in love with her partner. But in truth, her heart and mind remained untouched.

She turned her back, raised her arms, and shimmied. Her partner grabbed her around the waist from behind and pulled her flush against him.

As one, they moved sinuously up and down, pressed together from shoulders to hips. Her partner's hand skimmed from her side up to her cheek, trying to turn her face toward his. Since for this dance she was playing a lover who'd been emotionally hurt and didn't want to commit, she jerked her head away.

Her gaze skimmed the crowd as she leaned away from her partner. Then she stumbled as she found a pair of familiar amber eyes. Her breath stopped. The music and her partner ceased to exist.

Kai's remote expression turned molten as he caught sight of her. He stalked toward her, his jaguar's eyes focused on her with such intensity, she couldn't look away. She sucked in a deep breath as her heart started shimmying in her chest.

The crowd parted before Kai, people wisely taking one look at his fierce expression and getting out of his way. Susana took a small step forward, only dimly aware of her partner's protest as his hands fell away. As she moved toward Kai, she searched his face for some clue as to why he was here.

Deus, he looked exhausted. The corners of his mouth drooped as if even holding a straight line was too much for his lips. Troughs under his cheekbones gave his face an even more angular look.

His eyes, though, were on fire. And, merciful heavens, when he reached her, she could feel the emotions pouring off him in a heated wave that pulsed against her sweaty skin.

She had time only to gasp before he held out his hand.

"Dance with me." His voice was a husky command that tightened every lonely place on her body.

Helpless to deny him, she moved into his arms and almost forgot how to dance, she was so overwhelmed by the relief of touching him again.

"I've missed you so much," he murmured against her ear, echoing what she felt in her heart. "Why did you leave me?"

She pulled back. He wanted to talk? Here? On a noisy, crowded dance floor?

"Answer me, sweetheart."

Couples danced around them, occasionally telling them to get the hell out of the way.

She grabbed his hand and tugged. "Let's find someplace quiet to talk."

He shook his head and pulled her back into his arms. "No. I want to do this here. Tell me why you left. Was it because of the men I've killed?"

Her temper flared. Fine. If he wanted to fight in the middle of the freaking dance floor, so be it. She pulled his head down so she wouldn't have to shout. "No. You haven't killed anyone who didn't deserve it. I left because I have a life of my own. Responsibilities and dreams. Besides," her breath caught, "thanks to my cockroach-eating father, I'm a genetic freak."

She was still waiting for the results from the extensive

number of tests she'd undergone with Ryker's help. "Who knows what side effects might show up as I age?"

Kai turned his head and ran his tongue along the rim of her ear before answering. "You're no more a freak than I am. I love you just the way you are."

"Kai, I—"

"We can work out the differences in our lifestyles, Susana. That's no obstacle. As for the other?" His finger traced a delicate path from her eyebrow to her chin. "You're not going to turn into Rafe, Susana. Your father's drugs would have manifested that behavior long before now. Whatever he did to you is of no consequence. He didn't make you the warm, giving, temperamental woman I love. He didn't shape your soul."

Dammit, she actually trembled. Could she believe him? Did she dare?

The man must have read her mind, because he smiled tenderly and began to move to the music. He wasn't practiced, but each swivel of his hips melted a piece of the ice around her heart, until she gave herself up to the dance. Let herself fall into a rhythm of love and lust. For Kai. Only Kai.

"*Mãe de Deus*, how I love you," she murmured.

When the dance was over, Kai bent her over his arm and kissed her. Marking her in front of the entire club and earning the applause and catcalls of everyone around them.

Susana clutched Kai to her. There was no way she was letting him get away this time.

This time it was for life.

Kai knew it, too. She saw it in his eyes when he raised his head from the kiss. And then her man surprised her. He set her upright and got down on one knee, heedless of the dozens of people watching. There, before her crew and the rest of the club's patrons, he asked her the question she'd never thought she'd hear.

"Susana Dias, love of my life, soul of my body, keeper of my heart. Will you marry me?"

Her heart swelled and tears blurred her vision. "Yes." What else could she say? "Yes, I'll marry you. Just try and stop me."

EPILOGUE

Five Days Later
Tuesday, Afternoon
Washington, D.C.

Susana sat next to Kai in Ryker's office, her heart beating triple-time as she waited for the results of the physical and genetic workup done on her before she'd left the hospital.

"Ready?" Ryker asked.

She nodded and he handed her the manila envelope with the results. Susana glanced over to her left. Kai gave her a warm, supportive smile. It was hard to believe, but he honestly didn't care what the data showed. He loved her. He accepted her. She had his full support. Kai's only concern was whether the information would upset her.

It was a novel sensation. She wasn't used to facing life's challenges as part of a team.

Despite Kai's insistence that it didn't matter, she needed to know whether she truly was a freak. For one thing, it would affect her decision to have children.

And, okay, a small part of her was still afraid Kai would leave her if it turned out she was markedly different.

Susana mentally shook her head. She had to stop borrowing trouble.

Taking a deep breath, she pushed her thumb under the edge of the large manila envelope. Kai's hand gently squeezed her shoulder. Absorbing his strength like sunlight, she flipped up the envelope's flap and spilled the contents into her waiting palm.

She skimmed over the medical terminology to the conclusions.

Heart and lungs—highly efficient and healthy.

Blood and muscles. The same.

Immune system—very strong.

Genes—several genes known to enhance intelligence and stamina were turned on, but a few were not.

Overall conclusion—she was in exceptional health. Slightly off the charts, but not enough to scream of tampering. Athletes using performance enhancing drugs scored higher than her in several categories.

Susana's muscled softened in relief. If not for Kai's hand anchoring her in place, she thought she might slide off her chair onto the floor.

"Susana?" Kai asked.

She realized that both Kai and Ryker waited for her to give them the news. She took a deep breath. Her ribs expanded almost creakily.

Her lips tried out a smile. But that wasn't good enough. She grinned and put her hand over Kai's. "You were right. Whatever my father did to me had negligible effect, if any. All the tests show that I'm slightly better than average, but not so exceptional that doctors will clamor to study me."

Kai pulled her to her feet so quickly the world spun. She flung her arms around him, threw back her head and laughed.

Kai grabbed her head, held her still, and kissed her.

It wasn't until they broke for air, gasping and grinning, that Susana remembered Ryker. She glanced over at his desk, but the man was gone.

"I'm not a freak," she crowed.

Kai lifted her up and spun her around. As he lowered her back to the floor, she whispered, "Do you have an office here?"

"No, but there's an empty office anyone can use as needed. Why?"

"Because I want you. Here. Now."

Kai's eyes flared. He grabbed her hand and pulled her out of the office, down the hall, and around the corner to another office. Susana entered first. While Kai closed the door and slid the lock home, Susana shed her shirt and pants. Leaning back against the edge of the desk, she gave Kai her sultriest smile. "Lose the clothes, Kai."

"As you wish." Kai prowled toward her as his fingers worked at the buttons of his shirt. By the time he reached her, his clothes lay scattered behind him on the carpet.

Susana finished wriggling out of her panties, sat on the edge of the desk and pulled Kai into her arms. Her mouth devoured him, while her body squirmed, trying to get as close as possible.

"Kai," she protested when he refused to lower them to the desk surface. "Dammit, I'm ready." She guided his hand between her legs, so he could feel how wet she was.

"Not yet," he murmured.

Some day she was going to tell him how much his refusal to go fast annoyed her. But... "God, yes!" She writhed as his fingers pushed inside her, hitting just the right spot. The lecture on his lack of speed could wait. "Do that again," she demanded.

Kai didn't answer. He was too busy using his fingers and tongue to send her into a screaming orgasm.

"I hope...these walls...are sound...proof," she gasped minutes later.

Kai looked at her and his lips curled in a wicked grin. "You better believe it. Because I'm not done with you yet."

Two hours and some four orgasms later, Susana lay curled on top of Kai on the floor of his hotel room. She barely remembered their hasty dash out of the SSU building after that first frenzied lovemaking. Now she stared across the carpet at the legs of the armchair in the corner. Her bones had liquefied at least an hour ago, and she figured Kai was going to have to scrape her off of him when he was ready to get up.

She grinned, then traced a circle around his nipple. "I hope your reputation won't suffer because your colleagues suspect that we had sex in the spare office."

Kai chuckled, his hands stroking over her back. "Hell, no. I'll be the envy of every man there." A moment later his hands stilled and he gently lifted her head. The expression in his eyes was so earnest, she knew what was coming.

"I'm happy for you that the results came back the way they did. But it wouldn't have changed my love for you. You know that, right?"

She nodded through the tears brimming in her eyes.

"Good. You're perfect just the way you are."

"I love you so much," she said with a watery smile.

"You better," Kai said. He pressed a quick kiss to her mouth. "Because I don't plan on ever letting you go."

RYKER SMILED as he logged on to his computer. It was good to see Kai with Susana. After two hellish years, the man deserved to be happy. And Ryker liked and respected Susana.

With Gonzales dead, and confirmed as the mole within the SSU, Ryker no longer had to split his attention. He could focus on the situation with Rafe. He double-clicked the icon to open the latest report from Rafe's medical team.

Despite the new drugs he'd been given, Rafe still didn't

remember the location where he'd been moved after Kaufmann abandoned his first lab. Ryker wished he had the time to let Rafe remember on his own, but the latest intelligence he'd received indicated that Kaufmann's team would be participating in an upcoming attack that would have dire consequences for the United States. The SSU had to find the lab and shut it down before the team could be deployed.

Which meant Rafe's memory block had to be resolved. How to safely do this was the problem. The lab's location was one of the few remaining triggers that set off Rafe's rage. While Ryker had confidence that Kai and Dr. Montague would eventually free Rafe's memories, they didn't have time to spare.

Although it went against his protective instincts when it came to his people, Ryker typed out an order for the team to use the most aggressive treatment, regardless of the threat to Rafe. The lives of thousands of people depended on him regaining his memory.

Ryker just hoped that breaking Rafe's mental block wouldn't destroy the man's newly regained sanity.

DEAR READER

Thank you for spending time with Kai and Susana. I hope you enjoyed reading *Betrayal* as much as I enjoyed writing it!

Betrayal was heavily influenced by the movies *Raiders of the Lost Ark* and *Romancing the Stone*. In fact, I listened to the soundtrack for *Raiders* while writing some of the action scenes.

Susana's creative cursing is due partly to my attempt to come up with non-offensive swear words or phrases I could use when my nieces were young. I still use some of those curses today, even though my nieces are teenagers now.

Finally, if you enjoyed reading *Betrayal*, please consider recommending it to family, friends, and anyone else you think might be interested in Kai and Susana's adventures. Leaving a review on the retail store where you purchased it or on Goodreads will also help other readers discover *Betrayal*.

Thank you for your support!

If you'd like to know what happens to Rafe, pick up *Retribution*, the third book in the series.

Happy reading!

Vanessa

ACKNOWLEDGMENTS

Once again I'd like to thank my critique partner Virna DePaul, my editor Valerie Susan Hayward, and my proofreader Angela Pike. Thanks also to Frauke Spanuth of Croco Designs for creating another awesome cover.

ABOUT THE AUTHOR

Photo by Gigi Pandian

I confess. I spend way too much time thinking up ways to torture my characters. As a worst-case scenario thinker, I channel my persistently dark what-if questions into writing romantic thrillers that combine intense emotion with action-packed plots.

I'm best known for The Surgical Strike Unit series about a privately run special operations group. My new series, WAR, is set in West Africa, where I lived for a time.

When I'm not writing, listening to music, or playing puzzle games on my mobile device, I help writers learn Scrivener and take long hikes in the nearby hills.

JOIN THE KIERDEVILS

Receive snippets-of-life stories, writing updates, sneak peeks, and other exclusive content such as *The SSU/WAR Bonus Pack* when you join the KierDevils newsletter.

www.vanessakier.com/kierdevils